D1608238

Glasśigh of Ganymede Trilogy
Book 1:

Light of Ganymede

by
Peter Greene

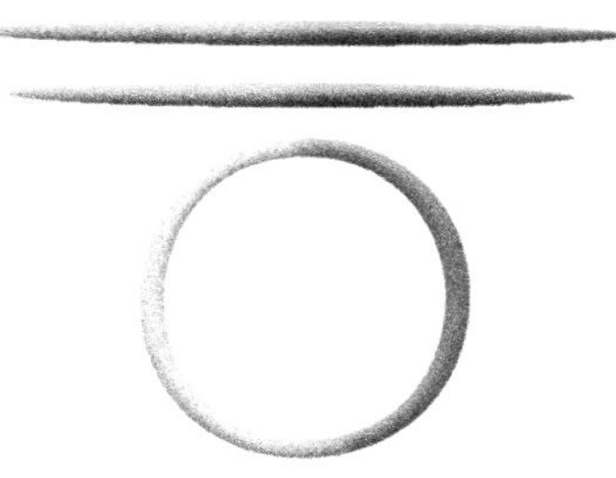

Award-winning books by Peter Greene

The Adventures of Jonathan Moore books have won:

The Clive Cussler Adventure Writer's Grand Master Award
The Independent Author Network's Book of the Year for Action/Adventure
The Chanticleer Book Reviews' Goethe Historical Fiction Award and Best YA Fiction Series Award

Book 1: Warship Poseidon

Book 2: Castle of Fire

Book 3: Paladin's War

All available in paperback, eBook and audio books (narrated by award-winning actor and writer Chris Humphreys)

The Glasśigh of Ganymede Trilogy
Book 1: Light of Ganymede

Cover by Sven Gillhoolie

Sven Gillhoolie
15418 N Castillo Drive
Fountain Hills, Arizona, USA 85268

ISBN-9798653644825

To purchase and learn more about books by Peter Greene, please visit:

www.lightofganymede.com or www.glassighofganymede.com or www.svengillhoolie.com

Chapters

Map of Tar Asséllo

600 earth miles long

Sindian Province
Falls of Caymana
Asséllo's Spire
Falls of Krymenos
Field 73
Asséllo's Well
New Asséllo Front Base
Treagor
Jaydi's Arch
Oso-Gúrith Province
Éhpiloh
Sea of Geeves
Ultos Base
Palace City
Etain City
Gláysien Province
Western Territory
Central Territory
Óhzásó Sea
Yamillian Province
Yamillian Fields
Girth Sea
Thermal Desert
Bortus Bay
Falls of Kyte
Targan Base
Eastern Territory

50 miles

map by Sven Gillhoolie

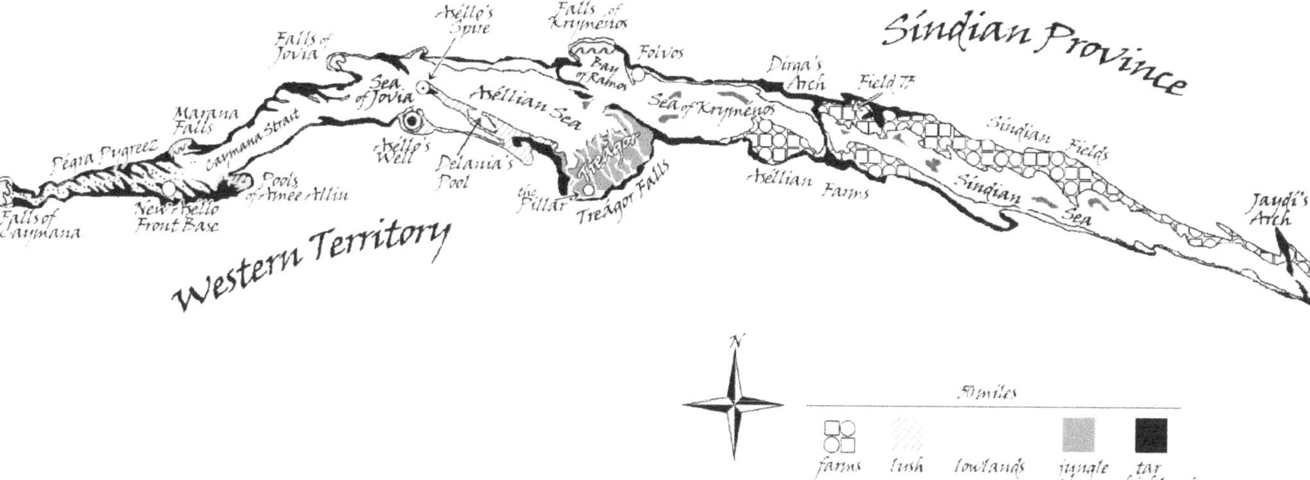
Tar Asello
(west)
Falls of Jovia
Asello's Spire
Falls of Krymenos
Folvos
Bay of Ramos
Dirga's Arch
Field 73
Sindian Province
Sea of Jovia
Asellian Sea
Sea of Krymenos
Marana Falls
Caymana Strait
Pegra Pygreez
Asello's Well
Delania's Pool
Treagor
Sindian Fields
Pools of Amee Allin
Asellian Farms
Sindian Sea
the Pillar
Treagor Falls
Falls of Caymana
New Asello Front Base
Jaydi's Arch
Western Territory
N
50 miles
farms
lush
lowlands
jungle & bogs
tar highlands

Tar Asèllo
(central)

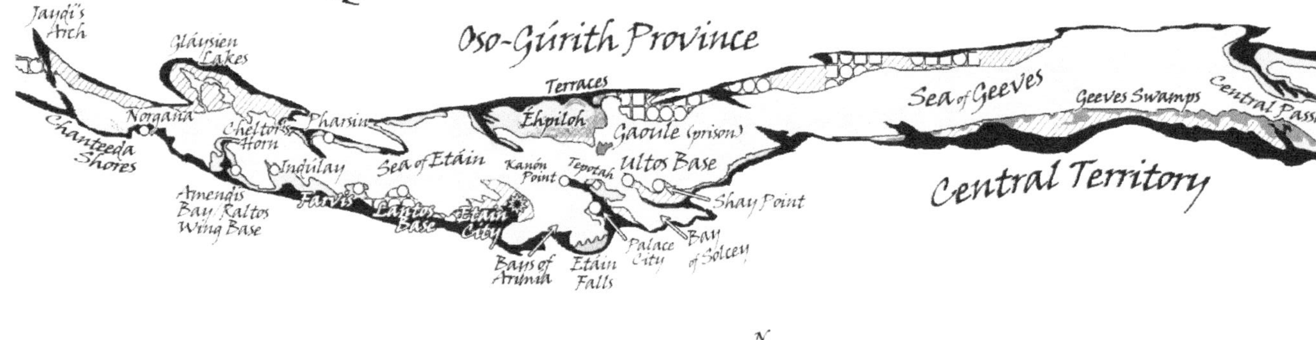
Gláysien Province
Oso-Gúrith Province
Central Territory
Jaydi's Arch
Gláysien Lakes
Chanteeda Shores
Norgaña
Pharsin
Indúlay
Sea of Etáin
Terraces
Éhpiloh
Gaoule (prison)
Kanón Point
Tepotah
Ultos Base
Shay Point
Amendis Bay Raltos Wing Base
Bays of Arumia
Etáin Falls
Palace City
Bay of Solcey
Sea of Geeves
Geeves Swamps
Central Passage

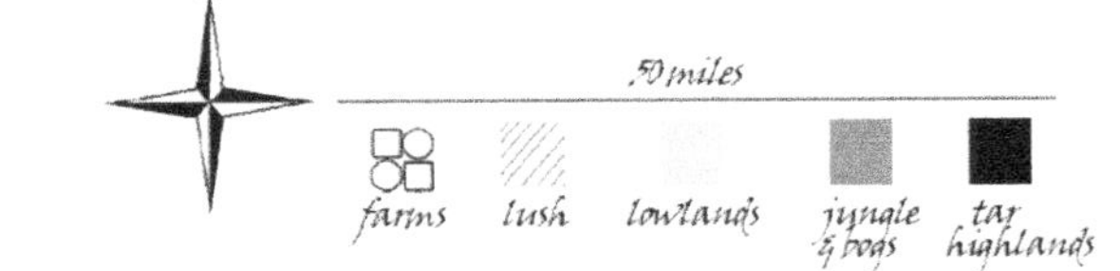
N
50 miles
farms
lush
lowlands
jungle & bogs
tar highlands

Tar Asello
(east)

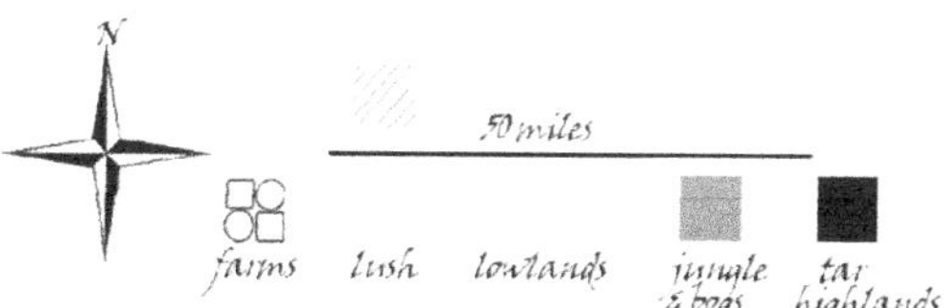

Yamillian Province

Kreedge's Inlet

Falls of Kyte

Bortus

Targan Base

Thermal Desert

Degas Point

Yamillian Falls

Yamillian Fields

Óhzásó Sea

Girth Sea

Girth Sea

Eastern Territory

Central Territory

N

50 miles

farms

lush

lowlands

jungle & bogs

tar highlands

The Glasśigh of Ganymede Trilogy
Book 1:

Light of Ganymede

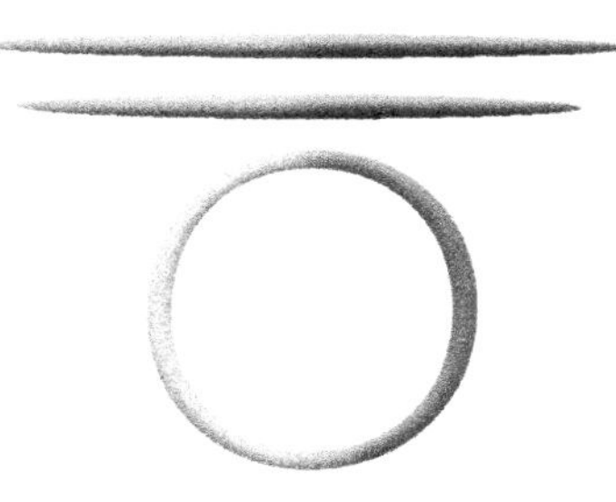

1
Coeur d'Alene, Idaho
December 13, 1956

Everything was going to change for Gladys—her home, her past, her future, even her time—but mostly her purpose. Though it all could be prevented and well enough left alone, her uncle believed that it was his obligation to bring about this change.

As he walked along the stone footpath beneath the evergreens, he could already hear the notes of a piano drifting through the night's cold winter air, breathing the opening of something familiar: "Ave Maria," Shubert's masterpiece. This meant the high school's evening Christmas concert had already begun, and he was late.

Quickening the pace, he realized he would miss this place, especially the snow and the sound it made as it fell through the cold air to glance off the fine needles of pine trees before settling onto the ground. He often walked at dusk in the winter when no other human echoes were heard. Any remaining sound was absorbed into nothingness by the existing white blanket, leaving only the gentle sigh of the falling crystals.

Rounding the final bend in the path, he saw the high school ahead, lit by the few lampposts of Coeur d'Alene, their faint golden glow making muted circles on the snow. Some light escaped the several high, narrow windows of the school, promising comfort and warmth within. After opening the door, he entered the vestibule and removed his hat. The warmth of the room rushed to him, caressing his face.

A voice had joined the piano, drifting through the double doors that led to the gymnasium. He was immediately startled by its beauty.

Could it be her? he asked himself. No, it couldn't be.

He opened the left door to the gymnasium ever-so-slowly, then silently moved to a position where he could stand in the rear and look toward the stage. As his eyes fully adjusted to the darkness, he could make out the setting. The entire town of Coeur d'Alene was present: people packed the aisles. They sat shoulder-to-shoulder in bleachers and folding chairs arranged tightly together on the gym floor. A stage made of low wooden risers was set on the far side of the room. A platform held the choir, though they were barely lit, mostly hidden in the shadows.

The soloist, however, was clearly visible. She stood center-stage wearing a while gown and, bathed in a soft light, the fabric appeared to glow. A cascade of flowing hair made of black ringlets tumbled behind her, falling to well below her waist. She simply held her hands together, waiting. About to begin again, she opened her eyes, those deep green eyes, and stared straight ahead, looking slightly above the audience.

Oh dear! her uncle thought as he looked upon this seventeen-year-old girl, a child he had known since her birth. It *is* Gladys! His heart sank at the realization.

Two months ago, while traveling in Africa, he received a letter from her parents, summoning him home to Coeur d'Alene. The letter explained that the high school choir teacher had discovered that Gladys had a gift for singing, and soon everyone in town knew of the shy, mostly friendless girl with the voice of an angel. Now she was being requested to sing at parties, churches, and all school functions. A college in California had just offered her a full scholarship, and, as per previous agreement, her parents left any life-changing decision to him, her uncle. So here he was.

In the gymnasium's front row sat her parents, surrounded by neighbors and strangers, all listening quietly and intently. The entire room realized that they were witnessing something special: a performer far beyond her years in ability, with a voice that reached out to them and into their hearts. As Gladys continued, even her typically stoic parents began to shed tears.

The piece continued, and all held their breath. Gladys sailed through the aria with absolute perfection, not warbling in vibrato but gliding clearly, like a beautiful sailboat upon quiet waters: smooth and calm, yet powerful and purposeful.

Her uncle was also affected by the purity and grace of the performance. In fact, he was affected more than anyone else in the auditorium. And though he was proud of her ability, he felt mostly concerned. Where did this talent come from? he wondered.

Too soon, the performance ended, bringing a bitter relief to those who had not taken a breath in over three minutes. What followed was complete silence, then the slight thump as the pianist's foot released the sustain pedal.

Gladys blinked and then lowered her eyes to the audience. No one was moving. A few soft sobs came, apparently from some of the women in the audience. Then, building slowly: applause. It grew until the room filled with the roar of admiration and approval.

Gladys flashed an embarrassed smile.

Her uncle shook his head before donning his hat, then walked out into the night. Dear! She indeed possessed an amazing talent, but where she was headed, this talent would only present problems. Her world, literally, was going to change, be turned upside down! And how would she react? After some thought, he concluded that she would be all right with it.

2
Eleven Years Earlier
Ganymede

Tar 79th, Áhthan year 1022 (March 1st, Earth year 1938)

Ganymede was ugly. The dark ice-moon of Jupiter, as seen from space, resembled a ghostly face: pale green-gray skin with dark purple scars from ancient impact craters and tectonic splintering left schisms in the frozen surface. Some of these rifts were hundreds of miles long, crisscrossing the moon as if it were a victim of a celestial knifing.

Under a thin atmosphere that clung to the surface were several layers of dense matter. The first was cratered and splintered ice, up to fifty miles thick. Directly beneath was a mineral-rich crust, roughly ten miles thick and born of early volcanic activity. The third deepest layer held ancient condensed ice riding atop a planet-wide subterranean ocean. Below that sea were additional layers of ice, then a mantle surrounding the molten iron core, still cooling from the moon's violent birth.

Ganymede was also beautiful. If conditions were right, passersby could witness intense and shimmering blue auroras shooting a thousand miles into space from both the north and south magnetic poles. Water from the moon's subterranean ocean, heated by its core, burst upward by way of vents, passed various layers of ice and crust, blasting liquid a quarter-mile into the sky. The rocketing water quickly froze into gigantic white and green-tinted ice towers that formed a sprawling forest covering hundreds of thousands of square miles.

However, the true wonder of this world was hidden deep within.

In the great canyons that had been formed on the moon's surface, life took hold. Several canyons were up to five miles deep and seventy miles wide and stretched to over eight hundred miles long. They were each a geothermally heated ecosystem, complete with seas, lowlands, small mountain ranges, and sprawling jungles. Unlike the surface of Ganymede, the atmosphere within the canyons was rich with oxygen, nitrogen and hydrogen, and moisture from thermally heated oceans that created dense clouds. These elements were held inside each canyon by a swirling blue *fálouse*, the topmost atmospheric layer.

Each fálouse extended outward past its canyon's edge for several miles in all directions, over the surface of the moon. Here, moisture met with subzero temperatures and fell as snow. Vast glacier fields were formed and eventually crept back toward the great canyons' edges where, again, they encountered heat. The ice sheets melted and water charged over the rim, creating countless waterfalls that traveled five miles, rushing to the canyon floor. Some falls crashed directly into the seas, sending clouds of mist that rose a thousand feet. Lakes and rivers formed in the low-lying areas.

Life-giving elements were trapped in the continuous cycle of each canyon's biosphere. Lifeforms flourished in the lowlands, the air, the sea, and even clinging to the steep stone walls. In countless and varied species, a bioluminescent effect occurred on a massive scale. The result was a persistent greenish-blue glow, which cast everything inside the canyons with a steady, unwavering twilight. The seawater's violent churning caused by the enormous waterfalls initiated bioluminescence of the abundant marine life, lighting the mist and water with what looked like a billion sparkling blue and green stars. Only when distant sun rays or the glow of the ever-present gas giant Jupiter found its way through the fálouse did the blue-green aura change. Gold and white beams pierced through high clouds to reflect off the seas and sheer walls of ice, creating countless speckles of brilliant, glimmering light.

One humanoid species successfully advanced, and over the eons, formed great civilizations that populated every major canyon on Ganymede.

Áhtha, they called their world, and the canyons they called *tars*.

Each of the five great tars held its own nation. The two most advanced, *Tar Asésllo* and *Tar Éstargon,* worked closely together, developing technology. Eventually, they built spacecraft that orbited and studied the gas giant Jupiter, even landing on several neighboring moons. They ventured further, rocketing to see the rings of Saturn and its hundred satellites.

But in the early days of the Áhthan year 1021, the discovery of radio signals from within the solar system created a frenzy of scientific activity and great excitement. Life existed elsewhere!

After listening to broadcasts and gazing through newly developed high-powered telescopes, they learned a great deal about the distant world. Once video signals were discovered, they had seen images of the beings there. They were quite similar, except for 'hair' and the number of digits on hands and feet. Áhthan's were almost a head taller, but otherwise, both were basically the same size. Though Áhthan civilization was a thousand years older than their newly discovered neighbors, they realized the two societies were alike in many ways, including technological advancement—except in the area of space travel. Here, the Áhthans had progressed years beyond those living on the third planet from the Sun.

The lure of exploration was strong, and though cautious, the Áhthans decided to visit the planet that the beings residing there called *Earth*.

▲▲▲

In the Eastern Province of the enormous canyon of Tar Aséllo, Bortus Bay sat next to the turbulent gray water of the Girth Strait. Dark waves pounded the shoreline made of a hundred reddish-brown weathered boulders, each nearing one hundred feet in width. Some piled upon others while many rested halfway submerged in the water, creating islands of solid rock. Few land animals made the bay home. Plants were scarce on land and in the water, meaning sea life, abundant throughout the tar, ignored the waters of Bortus Bay.

Two miles east of the bay sat Targan Base. Surrounding the facility on three sides were steep walls of stone and ice, reaching the blue, misty fálouse. The Base was a simple series of buildings constructed in the towering style that mimicked the natural stone pillars that appeared throughout Tar Aséllo and on the moon's surface. Targan was initially a military base built during the last of the wars with the nearby nation of *Tar Fórtus*. With that conflict over, the base was modernized technologically through a partnership between Tar Aséllo and its western neighbor, Tar Éstargon. In just two-thirds of an Áhthan year, Targan transformed into a center for space exploration.

The Targan Base Command Center contained a viewing lounge on the twenty-first floor. It looked out over the base, giving an expansive view of the launch pad, launch control tower, and the rocket ship *Explorer Eleven*. The ship would be home to three Áhthan astronauts: two from Tar Éstargon and one from Tar Aséllo.

Explorer was neither sleek nor bulky. It was over two hundred feet long and, at its widest, sixty feet. Shining polished silver-blue metal covered most of the craft.

The topmost quarter of the craft contained the crew section. Two delta fins on each side jutted outward, each holding hoverjet units that allowed the vessel to retain its position above the ground. They were for atmospheric maneuvering only.

Inside the crew section in the forward-most area was the command deck. Three seats were situated forward-center. Here, each doubled as a cryogenic sleep chamber. A mostly screen-based control board sat immediately in front of the seats, and above was a bubble-like viewshield that ran the width of the craft and along the sides, even offering a view to the rear.

Behind the command deck was the lounge, a good-sized area used for some work but mainly as an eating, hygienic, exercise, and conferencing space. Behind the lounge was a firewall, then the atmospheric and sub-space engines, to be used when approaching Earth and maneuvering through its thick atmosphere.

The remaining three-quarters of the ship was made entirely of the main propulsion engines, driven by both nuclear and rechargeable compressed hydrogen fuel cells. Seven circular adjustable engine nozzles were positioned at the rearmost portion of the section and were used for lift-off and reaching escape velocity. The incredible speed generated would propel the craft through the depths of space to Earth. This section would be detached and set in orbit when not needed, then eventually re-attached for the return trip.

Today, on the 79th day of the Áhthan month of *Tara*, in the year 1022, *Explorer Eleven* was to begin its almost four-year journey to Earth, traveling four hundred million miles. Arrival was scheduled for the Earth date of January 6th, 1942. The three-person crew was to make first contact with the intelligent beings there and learn and share information. In late 1956, they would leave Earth to begin their four-year journey home. The entire trip would span just under twenty-two Earth years.

One figure was the center of attention, at least for today: Minister Commander Eno Ćlaviath. He was tall and thin, arms gangly, and large expressive eyes ready to engage with anyone on any subject. Eno's 'hair'—actually a full head of thick, feather-like strands referred to as a *mane*—was cut short. As with all Áhthans, manes changed color in whole or in part to reflect their mood. This was mostly an involuntary condition and could be embarrassing at times. But Eno was rarely embarrassed. His smile was infectious, his wit famous, his knowledge vast, his demeanor welcoming. As a science minister, he was often seen on various media outlets explaining 'how things work' in the physical world. A geologist, a physicist, a physician, and a sociologist, among other talents and skills, Eno was the perfect choice to command this historic mission.

"A momentous day for Aséllians, my dear Eno," said Pronómio Tok, the current *Yahyéth,* the governor of Tar Asépllo's North-Central province named *Oso-Gúrith*. Upon seeing Eno, he stood and motioned for him to join his small party at a window-side table overlooking the launch site.

Pronómio was in his prime, a robust man square of face and imposing to many as he stood almost a half a head taller and outweighed virtually everyone. He had a mane of jet-black that curved backward and fell just below his shoulders. One of his best-celebrated talents was not his political will or acute sense of planning, but his ability to make each person he spoke with feel as if they were the most important person in the world. He was gracious, polite, engaging, and most famously, devious. He had risen quickly through the levels of Tar Aséllo's government. His tough talk and zero-tolerance policy for uprisings led by the *Zakéema Front* resulted in his promotion to Yahyéth of the troublesome Oso-Gúrith Province.

Many of the poverty-stricken people in Oso-Gúrith's largest city, *Éhpiloh*, secretly supported the Zakéema. Soon the Front matured into a well-disciplined rank of dedicated soldiers, carrying out rare but effective attacks on the established government and the Aséllian citizenry.

Eno Ćlaviath gladly approached Pronómio, and they touched foreheads lightly, as was the Áhthan custom between close friends.

"Please, please sit down for a moment if you can spare one," insisted Pronómio. "I know it is a busy day for you. Join us? For a moment?"

"Of course," said Eno.

Seated with Pronómio was Gákoh Kalífus, the Security Minister of Oso-Gúrith. He had a short and spikey dark gray mane. Eno knew him as a quiet and serious man who had been associated with Pronómio since school days, both coming from families entrenched in the upper echelon of the *Kor̋eefa* class. Pronómio had brought Kalífus to his team as Province Security Minister. Under their collective control, the crackdowns on the Front's suspected supporters were effective and, at times, brutal. Soon the Zakéema were all but gone from Éhpiloh. The popularity of Tok and Kalífus skyrocketed.

"The excitement, dear Eno!" said Pronómio Tok. "You will soon travel to meet beings from another planet!"

"Yes," agreed Eno. "Since the day we intercepted the radio-wave signals from Earth, I had hoped that we would visit them."

"Are you prepared, Eno?" asked Pronómio with deep concern. "The ship is functioning properly?"

"Yes," replied Eno. "This is the eleventh vessel of its kind to reach the stars—we are quite confident in its capabilities and condition. It will be a long journey and, as I believe, a safe and successful one."

"You, my friend, have circled the planet Ofeétis!" Pronómio stated with a sigh and a smile, "and have photographed Gayída and its rings up close! If you are confident, then that is good enough for me."

"I wish you good fortune," added Kalífus. "And be wary of the

Earthlings. Though their 'war to end all wars' is over, they are a violent race. Some transmissions suggest there are still minor conflicts. Maybe I should go with you, yes?"

"If there is a security issue," joked Eno, "I will send for you immediately!"

The four years it would take to voyage to Earth would make that ridiculous, of course. They all laughed, hair flashing a tinge red for a moment.

"I am happy to see the Ef Keería of Tar Éstargon here!" exclaimed Eno. "His two scientists are exceptional, a joy with which to work. The three of us make an excellent crew, I must say. It is a pity this may be our last joint venture with them."

Pronómio nodded his head in agreement. "The renegotiation of trade agreements between our two nations is deteriorating quickly. The Éstargonians insist that we abolish our class structure and adopt one that mimics theirs! What has that got to do with trade?"

"They believe, offered Eno, "that their society is more fair and just, superior in a way—"

"Oh, I have been to Tar Éstargon," interrupted Pronómio, "and I have seen their system of government. It is not the jewel they claim it is! It is unruly, overcrowded, and progress is slow. Many citizens do not know their place. We will not abolish our way of life, our class structure! Tar Asélło is our nation, our tar."

"As you say, it is our nation," stated Eno. "The class structure is the most important cog in the great wheel that is Tar Asélło."

"I am not sure the Tażath agrees," said Pronómio, gesturing to another table. There sat the *Tażath*, Tar Asélło's elected leader, Hátha

ters and governors, all in their

many, Feh was not as popular

ber of ministers and Kośeefa

Feh of being too soft on the

say," said Kalífus.

though, as you know, I try to

said. "But Tażath Feh is

nians. It will upset the entire

g upset, his mane changing to

self, then took a breath. "It is

ed, "but there will be a vote of

a close vote, I calculate."

cement?" asked Eno.

Pronómio only smiled, somewhat evilly, his mane now returning to black but with a few red streaks now appearing.

"You?" asked Eno, surprised. "Really? Well, well, well! There is no better choice for our leader! I will have my assistant draft a proclamation and send it to the Board of Ministers before I leave!"

"I thank you," said Pronómio. "Unfortunately, I need a few more supporters. I have heard that your brother and his wife will vote to retain Hátha Feh and her policies."

Eno knew that his brother Tye Ćlaviath, the Minister of Law, and his wife, Dypónia Asёllo, the Minister of Tar Relations, held radical positions regarding the long-established social caste system. They had worked with the Éstargonians to bring about change in Tar Asёllo. With the revered and historical last names of Asёllo and Ćlaviath, they had considerable influence.

"Tye and Dypónia still hold the same beliefs as always, I am sorry to say," answered Eno, disappointedly.

"They have influenced the Taźath," said Kalífus. "And I am sure she will soon give in to the Éstargonian demands. Can you imagine? Uneducated *Graćenta*? The lowest class? Voting? The result would be an emboldened Zakéema Front!"

"My brother, Tye Ćlaviath," countered Eno, holding up a hand to calm the discussion, "does not advocate for the violent Zakéema."

"Yes, yes, but he does support the Graćenta, and he agrees with the Taźath, at least partly—" Pronómio realized he was getting upset again. Taking a breath, he calmed himself. His smile returned. "I only wish your brother agreed with me on this."

"I know him well, Pronómio," replied Eno. "His heart is in the right place, and I would speak to him, again, however…"

"Yes! Yes!" interrupted Pronómio, promptly returning to the bright and pleasant friend. "You have a rocket to catch, and we will not see you for almost two years! That is what? Twenty-four Earth years?"

"Very close!" Eno stood. "Twenty-three point seven, give or take a few days!"

Pronómio stood and embraced Eno with the customary head-to-head touch and wished him good fortune and a safe return.

"Your crew awaits, Commander Eno Ćlaviath," said Pronómio, his voice cracking slightly.

Eno took leave of his friends and left the building.

On the way to the rocket in a comfortable but small base transport, Eno contacted his assistant and had him draft and deliver his letter of support for his friend, Pronómio Tok. Once at the Launch Control Tower, he took the lift to the top, staring at the rocket the entire time.

The lift stopped, and Eno exited into the Control Room, a one thousand square-foot center of technology and activity. Metal-walled workstations for the technicians, computer screens, monitoring equipment, and personnel filled the room. The only thing out of place was the couple holding the child.

"A final word with you, Eno?" asked Tye Ćlaviath.

"Of course, brother."

Eno followed Tye and his wife, Dypónia, to a large view window that overlooked the rocket.

"I want you to know that we will miss you," said Tye, his brown mane dulling to a muted gold. "Almost two years will pass before you return. That is a long time for my younger brother to be gone. And who will play the game of Bowilberweeks with me, eh?"

"And the *Glasśigh* will be almost old enough for marriage when you return!" said Dypónia, referring to her baby daughter in the pod. "It will not be the same without you, helping her to grow and learn."

"Your wedding brought together the two most storied families of Áhtha!" Eno said. "And now the progeny of both the Aséllo and Ćlaviath families, this Glasśigh, is the joy for all."

Tye frowned as he looked to the child. "She is popular. The posters, books, media broadcasts! The requests for information about every facet of her life—it can be quite ridiculous."

"Such is the life of the famous," replied Eno.

Though there were no more clan kings or queens in Tar Aséllo, Tye Ćlaviath and Sypónia Aséllo were the closest things to royalty that existed in the tar, and their daughter was the closest thing to a princess—even though there was no such word in the Áhthan tongue. She was simply referred to and understood as *the Glasśigh*.

Dypónia smiled at her sleeping daughter. "She belongs to history now and to all in Tar Aséllo, but she is still *my* Glasśigh."

"I will surely miss her!" Eno said as he peeked under the veil that covered the pod. As if on cue, the Glasśigh stirred from her slumber and opened her eyes, each looking like a precious and rare flower, emerald green with sparkling flashes of deep yellow and gold.

"Ah!" cried Eno softly, "she looked at me! A parting gift!"

"Then return to us, my brother," said Tye.

"We will miss you," added Dypónia.

They touched foreheads. Reluctantly, Eno turned and made his way to the bridge door. He activated his Arm Band Communicator, an *ABC*. These hi-tech wrist bands were combination audio and holographic video devices used for communication and displaying data from various systems, such as news broadcasts, entertainment, and research in government-supplied archives. They were also used for 'face-to-face' communication between citizens. They were perfect for the *Explorer* program as well. Eno preferred his Personal Display Tablet, his PDT. It was simple, had a larger yet more private display, was more tactile, and, if configured correctly, unconnected from the tar-wide network. But for this mission's communications, he would tolerate the ABC.

"Mosca and DaJees, this is Commander Eno. I am done with the pleasantries and am on my way," he said. "What is our status?"

"This is DaJees," came her easy-going, professional voice. "I have completed the final diagnostic of the Voice-Activated Command Interface. *VACÍ* is now in control of *Explorer Eleven*. Mosca and I are seated at the command deck."

"Launch Control has transferred command of the ship to us," said Mosca, his tone a bit more anxious. "We only await your voice activation to start the launch."

"Excellent, and I apologize," Eno offered. He pressed a button on the panel of the doorway to the bridge. The door hissed open, and Eno turned to give one last wave goodbye to his brother, Dypónia, and the Glasśigh.

An alarm sounded.

"Security alert!" broadcasted a computerized voice. "Unauthorized access to the launch area has been determined."

Tye and Dypónia nervously looked to Eno.

"Someone probably opened a locked door by accident," he called out to all. "Stay calm. Nothing to worry about, I am sure."

The small group of workers wanted to believe him.

Eno stepped out to the bridge to look downward. There, in the west corner of the launch pad, he saw figures in ragged black clothes running swiftly toward the base. Zakéema! Today? Now? He thought. Those rebels, in their dirty rags! It most certainly was something to worry about!

Eno watched as the Zakéema split into two groups: one heading straight for the Base Command Center, the second group, more than a dozen, was sprinting toward the Control Tower and *Explorer Eleven.*

Small projectile weapons opened fire on the first group of Zakéema as they ran toward the Command Center. Base security had been increased by a few dozen members of the Aséllo Military Force, the AMF. Surely they outnumbered these terrorists! thought Eno.

However, looking to the area below the Launch Tower, Eno saw that the group of intruders rushing to the rocket remained unchecked.

"DaJees! Mosca!" Eno called into his armband. "This is a serious threat. We are being attacked by Zakéema terrorists. Stand by."

"Eno, what is your status? Where are they?" asked Mosca.

Eno looked over the side of the bridge railing again. Two hundred feet below, he saw the invaders reach the tower.

"They are at the door to the tower!" Eno replied into his ABC. "Targan Base Command, do you hear me? We are under attack at the tower!"

"We hear you, Commander. Stand—"

The reply was cut off.

Eno could see multiple streaks of heavy arms fire striking the windows and doors of the Command Center, coming from the Zakéema. AMF troops from within continued returning fire.

Tye stepped onto the bridge. Peering over the railing, he saw the havoc below. "Eno! What is this?"

Eno pushed his brother back inside and closed the bridge door. "Listen to me!" Eno called out so all could hear. "Zakéema are here. The Command Center is under attack. Rebels are at the base of the tower. But do not fear! We are safe here."

"Safe?" cried Dypónia as she held the pod that cradled her daughter.

"They cannot reach us," Eno explained. "The tower lift is locked down automatically during an emergency. Only a technician can operate it with a passcode!"

Within seconds, they heard the lift motor whining as it came up to speed. A gauge above the door showed that the car was ascending. Eno ran to the lift control panel and entered a series of digits. A red light glowed around the mechanism. A video image from the lift camera came to life on a small screen adjacent to the door. It showed several Zakéema, in the lift car, with hand-carried weapons and two large crates. They opened one as the lift rose.

Eno entered a security code into the door panel.

"I have locked the door," exclaimed Eno as he ran back to the bridge. "They will not be able to get in!"

Tye grabbed him by the arm and pulled him aside.

"Brother, if they have heavy arms like what they are using on the Command Center, then what will stop them from destroying the tower in the same manner?"

"If they were going to destroy the tower, why come up the lift?" Eno replied. "But to be safe—listen! Everyone! Get behind the metal workstation panels or larger pieces of equipment! Spread out! Stay low to the floor."

"Have you no weapons?" asked Tye.

"We have two guards with small arms. But that will not hold them if they find a way in."

"Then there must be a way out!" his brother yelled.

"Unless we want to go for a ride on that rocket, no, there is no way out. But the lift doors are thick metal and reinforced with—"

The lift stopped.

Nothing happened.

The door was not opening.

All was still. The only noise was the crackling of Eno's armband and the voices of Mosca and DaJees asking for an update on the situation.

"We can hold out here until help arrives," said Eno quietly.

An ear-piercing hiss came from the lift. Soon it turned into a high-pitched whine.

Eno rushed to the display screen by the door. He could clearly see the Zakéema inside unloading something from one of the crates, though he couldn't make out the device. Within moments, the lift door began to glow in a perfect circle as the torch rotated at high speed, digging a hole in the metal, sending sparks flying through the area.

"They have a torch drill!" exclaimed Eno.

"How did they get that?" Tye asked.

"It appears," observed Eno, "that the Zakéema have a bit more resources than we thought."

Eno realized that they were coming inside. Did the Zakéema intend to destroy the rocket? Kill the crews? The technicians that were here? He suddenly felt sick to his stomach. How could this be happening? Targan Base was the most protected area of Tar Aséllo, besides the Palace of the Taźath.

"If they are Zakéema," his brother stated, "I can possibly reason with them."

"I don't think that would help," argued Eno.

"Yes, it might," countered Tye. "They know that I have been a proponent of the Graćenta, those that support them."

The ring on the door grew brighter.

"Harming me would damage their position," Tye continued. "They couldn't negotiate effectively if they—"

"Negotiate?" Eno laughed nervously. "If they wanted to negotiate—Tye! Who comes to a negotiation with heavy weapons? No, brother, stay hidden. Guards! Take up defensive positions at the door!"

The torch drill stopped.

The metal circle cut by the drill was kicked out from inside the lift, hitting the floor with a *CRANG!*

A smoke canister was tossed into the tower control room, expelling its contents into the air. Visibility dropped to almost zero. Eno and Tye joined the others in hiding.

A Zakéema soldier, in his greasy rags and mask, stormed inside and rolled to the floor. The tower guards saw him through the smoke and fired, missing him. The intruder spun around as another of his kind entered the room, firing his weapon. Eno and Tye watched from behind a panel as the first guard caught a bullet to the head. Another shot fired, and the second guard fell.

More Zakéema entered the room cautiously. There were at least ten of them with weapons level with the floor.

Eno could see Dypónia next to him, less than a few feet away, holding the pod with the Glasśigh inside. She was cowering, shaking, and then covered the child with her body as she wedged herself against the bridge door. Eno turned to Tye, but he was gone.

"I have contacts here!" yelled a Zakéema in a gruff voice.

"Do your duty!" called another Zakéema. "For the rebellion!"

The gruff-voiced Zakéema replied affirmatively then fired his weapon. Screams rose and filled the large room.

"More here, sir!" came another voice, followed by pulsegun fire.

"Cease fire!" yelled a voice. It was Tye. "Stop this massacre! I am Tye Ćlaviath! Speak to me!"

A short but muscular Zakéema approached Tye.

Eno stood and looked in horror. What was his brother thinking? A last effort? To buy time? Or did he really think he could reason with these traitors?

"You are Tye Ćlaviath?" asked the Zakéema.

"Yes, please, let us discuss—"

The Zakéema raised his weapon and fired.

Tye fell.

Eno shuddered in disbelief, falling to his knees in shock.

How could this happen? What purpose did this serve? To flex their muscle? The Zakéema Front was vastly outnumbered; they could never win against the forces of the Taźath. Were they insane?

Eno looked at the fallen body of his brother, then up to the killer. Their eyes met. The Zakéema fired as he ran closer, missing Eno by inches.

"Dypónia! We must go! To *Explorer*! Come!"

Eno pulled her along as she held her child in the pod, running, ducking behind panels and equipment as pulse shots missed them by inches. Once they reached the bridge door, Eno slammed his hand down on the access panel, and the door opened. The firing from the Zakéema intensified as they exited, the gun noise drowning out all other sounds. Eno paused at the outer door control panel and attempted to lock the exit. The hail of gunfire was intense, projectile and pulse rounds slamming into the walls and door frame. Unable to close the door behind him, he sped across the bridge with Dypónia and the child.

The infant began to cry as she was jostled about. Looking over his shoulder, Eno could see that the Zakéema had reached the open door. They were kneeling, taking up positions to fire across the fifty yards of the bridge leading to the rocket. Shortly, he could see the flashes from their pulse guns whizzing past.

Ahead, he saw hope: the door to *Explorer* was opening! Mosca and DaJees were now visible, standing in the opening and waving them onward to the safety of the ship.

Projectiles and pulsegun beams continued to race across the divide.

"Hurry!" called Mosca.

"I have the bridge controls in hand!" shouted DaJees.

"Start bridge separation! Start it now!" Eno yelled.

With a violent jerk, the bridge shuddered and began to move away from the rocket.

The pulsegun firing continued. Eno looked to *Explorer*. The gap between the bridge and the ship was only a few feet at the most, an easy leap for them.

We might just make it! he thought.

"Run! Faster!" cried Mosca as he held out his hand. DaJees ran to his side, extending her arms, at times ducking the rounds that were hitting nearby.

Several pulsegun beams raced across the gap from the control room toward *Explorer*. Eno watched as DaJees and Mosca were hit multiple times. Their bodies went limp, then dropped forward off the ship's ledge, falling through the gap.

Suddenly, Dypónia let go of Eno's hand. She fell to the metal grating of the bridge—a stain of blood forming around her midsection. The pod carrying the Glasśigh had also fallen. It tumbled toward the metal grating of the bridge. Eno leaped toward the pod as it bounced between the rungs of the railing. He dove, extending his arm, and grabbed the pod by the handle an instant before it fell.

"Eno!" the dying mother called.

"Dypónia!"

"Take her!" she cried with her last breath, "take my Glasśigh!"

A round from a pulse weapon struck Dypónia where she lay. She was gone.

Zakéema were now running across the bridge.

Eno turned toward the rocket, rushing with the child as fast as he could. The gap between the ship and the bridge had grown to over six feet. With the pod in his hands, he leaped. Landing hard on the thin metal ledge surrounding the door to *Explorer*, Eno fell inside, unceremoniously dragging the pod across the deck. A hail of pulse and projectile rounds struck the door to the craft. One bullet made it inside the ship, piercing Eno's arm just below the shoulder, spinning him around and knocking him to the floor. Wincing in pain, he reached up, and with his uninjured arm, slammed his hand on the access panel by the entry. The door whirred on its hinges and closed tightly with a soft thump of the vacuum-seal mechanism.

Eno breathed a sigh of relief and spoke a command.

"Vací! Engage force field!"

"Force field engagement underway," came her even, unemotional reply.

Within a few seconds, the blue glow of the force field surrounded *Explorer*. The shielding was strong enough to repel most of the dangers from micro meteors and other space debris. As the Zakéema continued firing, it was soon apparent that their weapons could not penetrate the ship's protected hull.

Now in the safety of the ship, Eno gripped his wound. It was bleeding steadily, blood dripping down his arm.

The child wailed incessantly. Eno took her from the pod and quickly placed her in the center seat in front of the control deck, adjusting the safety harness meant for a much larger occupant. She would be safe in the chamber if the Zakéema made it into the ship, for a little while at least.

"Vací! Activate seat two's cryo-chamber and adjust for an Áhthan infant of one hundred days!"

"There are no crew members of that age or physiological classification," she said.

"I know! Execute! Now!" Eno yelled. "Sedate her and darken the glass completely. Lock the chamber!"

After a moment, Vací responded:

"Chair two chamber set for Áhthan infant of one hundred days. Executing order to lock."

From above the command seats, a heavy steel and glass cryo-lid descended over the Glasśigh, and locked into place, creating an air-tight chamber. The glass darkened, hopefully hiding its contents. A click signaled that the lock was in place.

Holding his wound, Eno ran to the door's viewport and looked across to the bridge, now over fifty feet away. Four soldiers strained to remove something large and metallic from a rolling cart. It soon became apparent: they had a portable multi-fiber optic laser cannon. Eno had read about this weapon: once loaded with a power cartridge, it would produce almost 500 kilowatts of destructive power in a single beam. Piercing the hull of a ship would be easy, he knew. Would *Explorer*'s advanced force field stop the blast? He wasn't sure, and his head was too foggy to complete that type of calculation. And how did they acquire a laser cannon? Eno wondered. It was experimental!

Suddenly, he swooned. The blood loss from his injury was beginning to affect him. If the bleeding wasn't stopped, he would soon lose consciousness and undoubtedly die. Eno ran to the cabin aid station, punched open the wall-hung unit's cover, and grabbed a large-sized patch application. The package finally undone, he wrapped the bandage around his wounded arm. The material was pressure-sensitive, and within seconds, it tightly shrunk around the opening of the wound. He knew this was temporary at best—the bleeding was severe. He required serious medical attention immediately.

But there was still the issue of the irritating neighbors outside, bent on blasting him and the ship to pieces. He needed a way to defend himself and the Glasśigh until help arrived; however, *Explorer Eleven* had no offensive weapons. Eno could do nothing unless he could point the ship at the Zakéema and ram them. Ridiculous!

Then it occurred to him. Mosca and DaJees had completed the checklist. The ship was ready for launch. If one can't fight, one should run away, he thought.

"Vací! Begin cryogenic procedure…for my command chair," he ordered as the dizziness rapidly increased. "Run full body scan and…and…administer medical aid…as necessary!"

If he could launch the ship and start the cryogenic sleep process before becoming unconscious, his body could be healed in transit. The medical programs and apparatus built into the constant monitoring system within the chamber would work autonomously.

"Cryogenic procedures beginning for command chamber. Please return to the chair, Commander."

Eno staggered toward his command chair and unceremoniously collapsed into his seat.

He was able to concentrate, just enough to change the main panel view screen to focus on an outside view. The camera on the Zakéema, he could see that the bridge was completely retracted, now one hundred feet away from *Explorer*. The cannon was still being prepped, though it would only take a few more moments before it was ready to fire.

"Vací, engage manual launch procedure!"

"Manual launch procedure executing," she said. *"Twenty seconds until manual launch availability. Course set and locked. Rocket ignition starts."*

As a rumble from below shook the craft, he realized that something was wrong. Yes! The course! That needed to be changed! He couldn't continue with the mission to Earth!

"Vací! Manually override course, set to standard low orbit for—"

"Course cannot be altered during manual launch sequence," Vací interrupted. *"Would you like to pause the launch?"*

"No, no, no! Do not pause launch!" Eno cried. He glanced at the viewscreen. A gunner was quickly taking a position to sight the laser cannon.

"Manual launch procedure continuing. Launch tunnel chambers doors opening."

Explorer Eleven groaned and vibrated as launch systems roared to life.

"Ten seconds until manual launch availability."

Outside, Eno could see the enemy's activity become even more frantic: they realized that the ship was in launch mode. They hurriedly loaded a three-foot-long silver metal power cartridge into the breach of the cannon.

"Five seconds until launch availability. Powering down force field as per launch procedure."

"What? N-no!" he cried.

A glance at the display screen showed the Zakéema rebels swiveling the gun into position.

"Four seconds..."

The Zakéema gunner stared through the cannon's sight.

Eno could see the green targeting beam flash as it passed the external camera.

He gripped the chrome launch lever on the panel to his right.

"Three...force field down."

The Zakéema pulled back the cannon's priming handle, its tip beginning to glow red, its engine whining, the laser about to activate.

"Two..."

The Zakéema gunner waved his crew away to safety. He was ready to shoot.

"One. Manual Launch now available."

A light glowed green, lighting up the entire command panel before him. Straining and in pain, Eno pulled the chrome lever down hard.

"Fire!" Eno cried.

Outside, the rockets roared. The tower and bridge shook violently, knocking a few intruders off the metal decking.

The laser pulse discharged, but the force of the rocket's blast sent the beam off-target, past *Explorer*, and bore a twenty-foot-deep crater into the tar's rock wall.

The ship rose quickly off the pad, propelled by orange flame and black smoke that spewed out from the seven engine nozzles. The inferno quickly rose to a height and width that engulfed the tower and the bridge. Though a few Zakéema ran back to safety within the control room, all others were vaporized.

Explorer Eleven thundered into the sky, racing to exceed Áhtha's escape velocity of almost two miles per second. Glancing out the right port window, Eno could see the surface of the tar wall rushing by in a blur. The ship was still shaking violently as the view changed from rock to ice that shined yellow and gold from the reflection of the engines' blaze. In a flash, Eno saw blue as he rocketed through the fálouse, then—blackness. The ship stopped shaking as it entered near space. Still, the hydrogen fuel-cell rocket engines' rumble continued, increasing *Explorer's* speed.

"Vací," said Eno, somewhat relieved, though struggling to remain alert, "change c-course to, umm…Áhthan orbit test."

"Mission map changes require a secondary command crew member authorization."

"I have no…secondary! I am the only occu—"

Eno stuttered. His eyes loosely focused on the cryo-chamber lid above him. Yes, it was descending. He could hear Vací's voice but could not make out what she was saying. The cyro-lid continued its descent until it locked into position and sealed.

As Commander Eno Ćlaviath lost consciousness, *Explorer Eleven* began its four-hundred-million-mile journey to Earth.

3
Far Side of the Moon

January 6th, Earth year 1942

Once *Explorer* had reached Earth, Vací woke Eno from his four-year-long cryo-sleep. It took a few hours to orient himself, and eventually, he was able to ask for a status report.

"Vací, what has Earth been up to while I slept and recovered? Anything interesting?"

"I have been monitoring broadcasts since we left Áhtha," she said. *"There is trouble, commander. This may explain. A message from the President of the United States of America."*

She played the file.

"...Yesterday, December 7, 1941—a date which will live in infamy—the United States of America was suddenly and deliberately attacked by naval and air forces of the Empire of Japan. The United States was at peace with that nation and, at the solicitation of Japan, was still in conversation with its Government and its Emperor looking toward the maintenance of peace in the Pacific."

"W-what?" exclaimed Eno as he listened to the broadcast. "How long ago was this broadcasted?"

"Just thirty Earth days ago," she replied. *"Since then, there have been over seven thousand hours of broadcasts from over one hundred amplitude-modulated frequencies, from multiple broadcast sites over the globe."*

"Unbelievable," was all Eno could say. "When did this begin? This war? An entire world, as large and prosperous as this? All the peoples at war? Again?"

"Broadcasts have been intercepted since the time of our launch from Áhtha," explained Vací. *"A detailed analysis and text have been created for you. In summary: this was a gradual conflict that began in Earth year 1935 with political unrest in multiple areas. By 1939, shortly after our launch, the nation of Germany attacked and militarily occupied its neighboring nation of Poland and continued acquiring adjoining nations through warfare and other forms of subjugation. German armies currently control most of the eastern portion of the continent named Europe, displayed in red on your map. They are attempting to conquer neighboring nations to the north, west, and south."*

Eno rubbed his eyes. "I can't believe this!"

"It is correctly reported. In the Pacific Ocean and eastern Asian continent, the Empire of Japan has been at war since 1931 with its neighbors, acquiring natural resources and land area. At this time, the war over island supremacy is being waged on the fronts shown in blue on your display. Both theaters have major air, sea, and land conflicts."

Eno just shook his head as he realized the extent of the battlefront.

"We couldn't have chosen a worse time to plan a visit. How could this have happened?" Eno asked. "We had been monitoring news broadcasts via radio waves for the past several Áhthan years! Yes, there was an almost worldwide war, but it had ended via treaty, and the Earthlings themselves had called it the *war to end all wars*."

"They were incorrect," said Vací.

He looked away from his monitor and out the wide, main viewshield above the command panel. *Explorer* was hiding behind Earth's dead moon. Eno adjusted the ship's position to peek over the moon's horizon and observe the blue and white orb beyond. From here, Earth looked beautiful and welcoming, and peaceful. Later, with the telescopes mounted on his ship, he would witness the war's activities in real-time.

While the Glasśigh slept in her chamber, Eno read the full report Vací had created. Earth's civilization might be a thousand years younger than those of Áhtha, he realized, but they were undoubtedly more proficient when it came to dreaming up ways to annihilate each other in outright aggression. And all these resources and space! And this is what they chose to do with it? It was illogical.

Once Eno finished reading, it was time to contemplate his options. Option one would be to return to Áhtha right away, but physics would not allow this. Due to the changing positions of the elliptical orbits of the two bodies—Earth and Jupiter (or Ofeétis as it was called on Áhtha)—they were now well over five hundred million miles apart. The mission parameters had planned on the worlds being in opposition, meaning at their closest points, under four hundred million miles from each other. It would be eleven more Earth years until they were again close enough to make the journey home. The nuclear fuel was all but spent on the deep space trip to Earth. Eno needed to replenish the uranium supply and render liquid hydrogen fuel. Explorer had the devices to accomplish that, but not the materials. They were on Earth's surface.

Another option would be to continue with the mission and make first contact. But with this war going on, Eno decided that was unwise. If years and years of listening to Earth broadcasts had taught the scientists of Áhtha anything, it was that Earthlings were constantly attempting to get an advantage over other Earthlings. They would undoubtedly draw the visiting Áhthans into this new battle. Not them personally, but the technology on the ship would certainly be coveted.

The only course of action would be to land on Earth, remain incognito, start the hydrogen charging and locate some uranium. In the meantime, Eno could observe and document behavior, the natural world, customs, etcetera—so the entire mission would not be a failure. He could then wait until the time was right to return, as planned, in Earth year 1956.

But what to do about the Glasśigh? he thought. I have to wake her, don't I? I can't allow her to sleep until 1956! The extended cryogenic process may have already affected her development.

"Vací, I have developed a plan," Eno announced as he walked to the lounge area of the ship. "I need you to tell me if it is a feasible design. Please access proper AI programs to attend."

"AI programs accessed."

"I have decided to stay and observe Earth incognito. I will gain fuel and supplies needed for return. Opinion?"

"The only reasonable choice."

"Good," said Eno. "I also will attempt to live among the Earthlings, and I will have the Glasśigh do the same. Opinion?"

"Chance of success near zero."

Eno would have expected nothing less, so he fed additional causal factors into the program.

"I will physically alter our appearance to blend in with the Earthlings: minor facial reconstruction, prosthetics to change our nasal appearance. Opinion?"

"Chance of success raised to eleven percent." Vací and her AI were not convinced.

"I will remove digits from appendages as necessary. Opinion?"

"Chance of success raised to fifteen percent," Vací said. *"Your plan for the difference between Áhthan mane and human hair?"*

Eno hadn't thought of that. Neither could walk about Earth with a head covered with what would look to Earthlings like feathers! And if the Glasśigh's mood changed? And the color of the ends went from black to red? In an instant? No, no, no, Eno thought. Maybe…

"I will remove the child's masguliar gland!" Eno triumphantly proclaimed.

Áhthan's were born with curly, ringlet-like hair, all single strands that demonstrated a more bilateral structure that caused the hair to curl. However, as puberty arrived at approximately one Áhthan year, the masguliar gland would produce pasterpeptide, and the childhood hair would be replaced with a more concentric arrangement of different cortical proteins that caused the feathery-like mane and abrupt color changes. A simple procedure for an experienced physician such as Eno Ćlaviath, removing the gland would stop producing pasterpeptide.

"Chance of success raised to eighteen percent."

"I will shave my head," he added. "Daily."

"Chance of success raised to twenty percent," Vací responded.

"Vací! I would think that would be a higher number! What is the issue?"

"Two major issues jeopardize the mission," she said. *"One is where you choose to locate. Most concerning is that the war could spread to your location, and you might be killed."*

"That would be…unfortunate," agreed Eno. "We will choose a safe location, least likely to be in a conflicted zone. Recommendation?"

"America," suggested Vací immediately, *"preferably away from the coastlines or large cities. The area called Northern Idaho would be optimal. It is sparsely populated yet has basic technology and resources. This raises the likelihood of success to thirty-three percent."*

"And the other major concern?" asked Eno.

"It is your skin color. The deep olive-brown skin of Áhthans will resemble Earthlings from the African continent. These people are persecuted in many parts of the world, especially in America. There have been mass exterminations, murder, enslavement and refusal of fundamental rights. Like the Graćenta, they are considered a lower class. Many earthings feel they are a different species."

Eno thought of this for a while. His skin color would make exploring dangerous. And what about the Glasśigh? She too must be kept safe.

"What if…I use daily doses of genetically modified forskolinthain glycerodes to change our skin color," suggested Eno. "It would take a few weeks, but we could lighten our skin by about ten percent? Opinion?"

"At ten-percent you could resemble the Latin and Italian peoples, among others."

Vací displayed pictures on his PDT of lighter olive and brown-skinned Earthlings with dark hair.

"Handsome, I must say," Eno muttered, "though not as handsome as Áhthans, however."

"If you choose Idaho…and complete the alterations and skin

lightening..." said Vací as she continued her calculations, *"this raises the likelihood of success to seventy-six percent."*

"Splendid!" exclaimed Eno. "Moving on! So I may be free to explore, I will have the Glasśigh raised by Earthling parents. She has no language skills yet, so the immersion in the language, culture, and systems will be convincing. I will swear them to secrecy. Opinion?"

"Chance of success lowered to twenty-seven percent."

"As a means ensuring that secrecy," Eno continued, undaunted, "I will pay the Earthlings in gold to raise her, as we have a large store of it onboard. Opinion?"

"Chance of success raised to eighty-seven percent," said Vací.

Eno smiled.

"I also suggest you set the deep space module in static orbit on the dark side of this moon, out of Earth's view," Vací added. *"There are no space-capable vehicles on earth so that it will remain hidden. When you land, hide the crew section of the ship."*

"Vací, I am insulted you even felt the need to say that, but thank you for the guidance. Anything else?"

Vací rattled off several obvious recommendations, such as dressing like an Earthling, not straying too far from the Glasśigh, allowing no one to examine her medically, avoiding any physical confrontations where one could be injured, and avoid the war at all costs.

"Anything else?" asked Eno as he stood to look out the main viewport, observing Earth and its problems.

"Yes," said Vací. *"Deep analysis and the running of over ten thousand possible scenarios conclude that it is imperative you do not tell the Glasśigh she is Áhthan."*

Eno hadn't thought of that.

4
Persuasion

December 21, Earth year 1956

"...and that is why Ganymede, the third of Jupiter's one dozen moons, a dead and lifeless world, could never support life. Thank you."

As Gary bowed and then returned to his seat, the classroom afforded him light applause.

"Well done, Gary," said Mrs. Tiernan, "a fine speech to persuade. I am sure none of us will try to build a summer home on such a dead and desolate moon as Ganymede."

Tiernan executed her cackling, wheezing and annoying chortle, laughing at her own joke, as was her fashion. Some of the more serious senior students politely forced a short chuckle to placate her and gain any advantage from their teacher to obtain a better grade. Coeur d'Alene High School had a little over six hundred students total. That meant that everyone, without exception, would sit through Mrs. Tiernan's public speaking class at one time or another, whether they liked it or not. Many would have preferred death to public speaking, but alas, that was not for them. There were the few oddballs who actually enjoyed speaking in front of crowds—Gary being one of them.

In the back of the room sat Gladys Gallotta. She was certainly considered an oddball, though few used that term. Weirdo was the preferred label.

It was not that she was ugly; she was certainly not. In fact, every girl without exception was extremely jealous of her naturally thick, black hair with uniformly tight one-inch curls that flowed from her head, falling like a mysterious waterfall well past her shoulders. They also hated her eyes that looked slightly larger and brighter than most. And they were so intensely green and framed by thin black brows and thick lashes that never needed liner. Some girls even asked her what makeup she used. She answered, "None." Her beautiful and amazingly clear olive-tan skin made many suspicious. It was dark enough to make some wonder if she, perhaps, was not Italian, as her name suggested. Maybe Gladys had some Negro blood.

Maybe the students thought her odd because Gladys was quite tall for a high school girl—or a boy for that matter: exactly five-foot-ten and one quarter. That certainly made her different physically. And she didn't look the seventeen or eighteen years of age as did the other girls. Gladys looked almost twenty-five.

And as for boys? They were not interested in Gladys in *that way*, or she in them. It was a mystery.

Or was her strange interest in world history, specifically war, that put off her peers? Jee was introduced to the subject by her father, a veteran of the Second World War. He encouraged her to read everything available in the small but well-stocked town library. Once those books were devoured, she dove into her father's extensive collection of notes and documents on strategy and tactics compiled from his time spent in Army Intelligence. And the stories he told! His memories from his two years spent on General Patton's staff, most notably in planning for the invasion of Sicily and subsequent battles, made for fascinating and exciting tales. When dad wasn't available, it was back to books. *The Art of War* by Sun Tzu was kept like a bible by her bedside. Other tomes enthralled her with the exploits of Alexander, Hannibal, Achilles, Leonidas, Napoleon, and George Washington. She chose war or military leadership as a topic for school reports and projects whenever appropriate—and sometimes when not really appropriate.

One Christmas, her father presented her with a relic from his basic training days: the book *Dirty Fighting* by Lieutenant David Morrah, US Army. The World War Two manual was brutal and graphic. Jee begged her father to practice punches and to wrestle with her. At first, he disapproved but soon surrendered and became an enthusiastic and willing teacher. Jee quickly became a strong, intelligent, and skilled little soldier, even practicing in her room on pillows and a giant stuffed giraffe her uncle brought her years ago. It was mostly fuzz and thread now.

The entire school knew she read endlessly about these subjects and wrestled with her father on the side lawn of their home. This did nothing to bolster her acceptance socially.

Was her unpopularity caused by her excellent singing voice? Possibly. High schoolers were an odd bunch, and anyone who could sing anything, let alone opera, was someone who invited scorn as well as envy.

But Gladys didn't behave rudely or obnoxiously. She was quiet and non-confrontational. Even when she had finished singing at last night's concert, and the adults showered her with praise, she modestly smiled, became embarrassed, and responded with a simple and soft "thank you."

It wasn't her clothes that made her unpopular. She dressed conservatively, as did everyone who lived in the rural farm and lumber mecca of northern Idaho. There were no rich people there, or at least not any she knew. Fashion was for those in San Francisco and Hollywood, not Idaho. Kids here dressed in simple, sensible clothes.

Some did think of her to be 'sickly' because, at times, she had trouble breathing, which made her gag and cough, and her face would turn red for a few minutes. Kids assumed she had typhoid fever or some such ailment. On the contrary, Gladys was otherwise very healthy. Had anyone seen her in more revealing clothes, they would have noticed her trim physique and well-toned arms and legs. She would hate for them to think of her as muscular, yet that was the term her gym teachers used. Muscular.

The other students didn't completely ignore her. She actually became noticed one time, in third grade. A mysterious thin feather had been spotted in her hair, seemingly tangled amongst her dark ringlets. Another child had plucked the feather out, and Jee felt pain as if it had been attached. They called her 'Birdie' for a year or so. Soon, they settle on 'Jee,' presumably short for Gladys. 'Jee' never bothered her. It was better than 'Birdie'.

Mostly the verbal one-liners or smirky looks she received from time to time were benign, yet now and again, some childish prank went a little too far. There was an incident when she was a freshman involving two older boys. They grabbed her and then pushed her to the ground. They called her 'nigger.' Jee had gotten back up and put the boys in their place quickly and firmly, as her father had taught her. One received a sideways edge of the hand strike to his Adam's apple. The other, who grabbed her from behind, had a broken shin bone, courtesy of *Dirty Fighting*.

Though there were a few kids that Gladys genuinely didn't like, she did wish that at least the other girls accepted her a bit more. They rarely invited her to parties, sleepovers, or included her in the simple past time of just hanging out, unless their mothers forced them. Oddly, adults, for the most part, seemed to accept her and appreciated her more mature attitude. When assisting her mother after church making sandwiches for the less-well-to-do, she was included in the women's conversations. Gladys liked being there, helping, and belonging.

But most teachers seemed intimidated by her intelligence, even though she was always polite and respectful. This made the other kids dislike her even more.

Gary sat down at his desk next to her, a self-satisfied smirk on his face.

"Well, Golly *Jee* Willikers," he jabbed. "Top that, you darkie!"

Jee shook her head. "It won't be difficult," she replied softly. "I'll just have to wake everyone up first."

A boy sitting nearby tried unsuccessfully to stifle a laugh.

"Gary, you jerk," the other boy whispered. "She ain't no nigger! She's a *I-tral-yan*!"

"Same difference," Gary retorted.

Jee shook her head. "You're both idiots."

"Miss Gallotta?" said an annoyed Mrs. Tiernan seeing the informal conversation taking place in the rear of the room. "Are you volunteering to speak next?"

Jee stood and nodded.

"Then up you come," ordered the teacher. "I hope you do as well as you sang last night. Just beautiful."

"Yes, Mrs. Tiernan. Thank you." Jee blushed with embarrassment. "I-I have some visual aids. I need a moment to set up my slide projector and screen. And my record player."

Tiernan seemed impressed.

Some of the students looked up, awaking from their utter boredom to observe. Visual aids? A record player? Only a weirdo would use visual aids.

The class watched as Jee set up her projector, then pulled down the movie screen mounted above the blackboard. She positioned her Kodak Cavalcade tray containing a few dozen slides and tested an image on the white screen. Then she walked to the light switch and turned off all the classroom lights except the farthest row in the rear. Finally, she returned to the front of the classroom and stood at attention next to the podium. From here, she could easily advance the slides.

Taking a deep breath, she began.

An image appeared on the screen: *Rosie the Riveter* by Norman Rockwell, the cover illustration he created for the *Saturday Evening Post*. Goggles sat atop the woman's curly red hair as she proudly ate her lunch, showing off her muscular biceps and holding a riveting gun in her lap. On her lunch box, the name 'Rosie' was evident.

"Rosie the Riveter," Jee announced in a strong, confident voice. "Have you seen her?"

No one answered, but they stared at the screen. Of course they had seen Rosie.

"While American men were off fighting the Nazis and the Japanese, women—American women—left the kitchen and the nursery and moved to the factories. But we know that."

The slides advanced to show women in the kitchen, women holding babies, a factory floor where airplanes were being built. The music coming from the phonograph was right out of a military newsreel: trumpets, marches, patriotic themes.

"Four million women put down spoons and bowls and took up riveting guns to assemble the skins on fighter planes, warships, and transports that won the war."

The image changed to close-ups of the riveting tools, red hot bolts, and women working with masks on, shielding eyes from sparks and shards. As Jee spoke, the images changed to address her words.

"They did more than place rivets. They built tanks, they tested guns, manufactured ammunition, and some were even spies!"

"Women spies?" laughed a boy. "Right."

"Can it, Richie!" snapped a nearby girl. "Women were too spies, you dolt!"

Jee continued, unfazed.

"Yes, spies, mathematicians, chemical engineers—" the images changed as she continued, accompanied by the *clack* of the slide advancing. "—without women in the workforce, we could have lost the war. It would be difficult to kill the enemy with only a sharp stick—right, ladies?"

Polite laughter.

"Women helped produce over 2,000,000 trucks," Jee continued with proud enthusiasm, "86,000 tanks and 297,000 aircraft! Battleships, destroyers, aircraft carriers, guns, bullets, and other kinds of munitions. 350,000 American women joined the military! They had jobs as nurses, truck drivers, repairers of planes and ground vehicles. Some were pilots! And some were killed performing their duties. They proved—*proved*—" Jee paused for effect, "that women could build these things and make them well. We won, didn't we?"

More laughter. Girls applauded. A few boys, too.

"So, what happened when the war was over? Do you know?" asked Jee. "Anyone?"

The room was silent. There was a moment of thought. Gears whirred in heads. The slide changed. On the screen was a picture of a frustrated woman, in an apron, holding a crying baby. The next showed a woman in the kitchen making a meal, the dog running with muddy feet across her clean floor. Her husband, wearing a neat white shirt, thin necktie, and dress slacks, enjoyed a cigarette as he read the evening paper, oblivious to the turmoil surrounding him.

Some of the girls in the class squirmed in their seats. A few boys chuckled. One murmured: "They went back to where they belonged!"

Jee aggressively pointed a finger at the heckler in the crowd. "Remember that comment, ladies. 'Back where they belong.' Though proven workers," Jee continued, "valuable and precise specialists, they were all fired—fired from their jobs, even the single women. They weren't needed." She paused again for effect in mock contemplation. "No, *needed* is the wrong word. They weren't *welcom*e or wanted in the workforce! 'Thanks, Miss! We used you, drove you like a slave, but get back to the kitchen! The men are home! And you have their jobs!' But…we know that—right girls?"

Some of the girls were leaning forward, paying a little more attention than they had been previously.

The slides changed; the music stopped.

The room was silent.

"Ladies, I speak to you," Jee continued as a slide of a frowning pregnant woman was projected. "You may want to stay at home and be a housewife. That's fine."

Jee paused for effect. Some of the girls fidgeted in their seats.

"But if you want something else—a job? A career? To be your own boss? To be in control of yourself? Ha! Who are we kidding? You have no choice! I hope being barefoot and pregnant and staying at home for the rest of your lives surrounded by this, this *chaos*, is to your liking!" quipped Jee with clear derision.

"Let me ask you, ladies," Jee continued. "Even if you were to get a job—let's say making canoes for Grumman—did you know you would be paid about thirty dollars a week? But when a man gets the same exact job, he starts at almost fifty-five dollars a week! And do you know why? Because he has something you don't—a penis!"

"Miss Gallotta!" cried a horrified Mrs. Tiernan.

The classroom erupted in laughter.

"Sorry, Mrs. Tiernan," Jee said, though she wasn't sorry in the least. She returned to her speech.

"Maybe you can be a teacher? But I know for a fact that our wonderful and caring English teacher, Mrs. Tiernan, gets paid only slightly over half of what Mr. Bates gets for teaching history. And she has been here longer! That's not fair, is it?"

"No!" cried a girl in the front row. Others soon agreed with head nods and whispers.

Mrs. Tiernan was shocked.

The slide promptly showed a sheep being sheared by a farmer—a man.

"Ladies, if we stay silent and tame, like the little sheep the men want us to be, then aren't we to blame, at least partly?"

"What can we do about it?" asked a girl in the back row.

"Ah!" exclaimed Jee. "Someone was paying attention! Well, sister, you can do one of two things. You can lie down and be sheared until you're naked and submissive, or you can stand up for yourself!"

"Y-yeah!" called another girl, enthusiastic but nervous.

"Now, now, Jee—" began Mrs. Tiernan, but the train was rolling.

"Our mothers stood up to the Nazis! And the entire Japanese army! They made some awesome equipment—" Jee continued as the slides changed rapidly from image to image of P51 fighter planes, M4 Sherman tanks, LCM landing craft, and other war machines. "And when the war was over, not a single medal did they win! Oh! Wait! They did get something! This stupid picture!"

Rosie the Riveter re-appeared on screen.

"I will say this, my sisters," Jee continued as her voice rose in volume and fury. "Do not lie down in the field and be stripped of your abilities and your future! Demand a choice! Demand equal pay for equal work! Work in industry and professions, and be rewarded!"

Some girls were clapping, even the shy ones. Jee adjusted the arm and needle on the record player. Marching music began.

"How do we do this, you ask? I will tell you. First, get your mind right: you are as good as a man! Say it! Say 'I am as good as a man!'"

The girls repeated it as one voice, though most meekly and clearly uncomfortable.

"Stronger, ladies! You made B17 Fighting Fortresses!" Jee called as the image changed, first one B17 bomber plane, then another, then an entire sky full.

"I am as good as a man!" they all yelled.

"Right, you are! But we know that!" Jee continued, her voice rising to a fevered pitch, powerful and confident. "You will decide! You will not be forced to take your place behind the kitchen counter, or the diner counter, or behind the mop! You will choose! You will ascend to a place alongside the best men in the world! Doctors, lawyers, scientists, titans of industry!"

Every girl in the room stood, moved by Jee's words, each looking to the other and calling out: "We know that!"

Even some of the boys were caught up in the fervor. Other boys laughed; while a few cowered behind desks.

Mrs. Tiernan sought to calm them down, but she simply could not be heard over the din.

"Good luck!" shouted a boy above the noise. "We will never let you out of the house! Ha ha ha!"

The room seemed to lose air. Some of the girls began to waver and wilt. Faces burned red, abashed and cowed. Eyes looked to Jee.

"Exactly what I expected!" Jee shook her head. She continued unperturbed. "Do you see, my sisters? They will try to keep you down! And they will succeed—*if you allow it!"*

The projected images changed to women picketing for the vote, women protesting, carrying signs demanding rights, and even some photos of women being arrested.

"We have fought for equality before!" Jee continued. "We struggled and suffered for over eighty years to win the right to vote! Now let us win the right to live as equals! How? We will get our due—" she paused until all were looking into her eyes, "—by doing nothing! Nothing! No more cooking and cleaning! No more baby-making machines!"

The girls were re-lit with enthusiasm. They were standing and clapping and calling at the boys to 'shut up!" and 'can it' and to 'back off' whenever any of them tried to speak.

"No more working for peanuts! No more finishing our education with a paltry high school diploma! We will go to college and learn to lead in politics and society! And until we get what is ours, we will do nothing but protest and strike!"

The girls erupted in cheers.

"We know that!" one yelled.

"Yes," agreed Jee, "we know that! Because we are smart and capable! And to get equal treatment, we will withhold EVERYTHING from men, EVEN SEX!"

The girls were standing on chairs, banging books to the ground, chanting: "No sex! No sex!" and "We know that!" One girl kicked over the garbage can. Another slapped the boy next to her when he tried to interrupt.

At this point, the boys were shrinking behind their desks, either from the utter excitement and wrath being displayed toward their kind—or maybe just for fear of the possibility that sex, as mild as it was in sleepy Coeur d'Alene, may be withheld.

Poor Mrs. Tiernan, though somewhat moved by Jee's call and even admitting that a small portion of herself wanted to join the movement, had to put a stop to this. But it was too late.

"Come with me, my strong and capable sisters!" shouted Jee as she thrust her arm upwards, her finger pointed to the sky. "We will ignite our friends and mothers! Our sisters all over America will join us! Equal pay! Equal work! Equal rights! But you know that! We start this very moment! To the streets!"

The doors to the room burst open. Twenty girls followed Gladys Gallotta out into the hallway, stomping and chanting: "Equal pay! Equal work! Equal rights! Equal Choice!" and basically, kicking over anything in their way.

To Jee, this was quite amusing.

"I am not amused," growled Principal Callan as Jee sat in his office. He looked over his desk at the girl with a scowl on his face that made his flabby cheeks wrinkle and flap as he spoke. He looked like a bulldog.

"It was a speech to persuade," Jee said. "I persuaded."

"You started a riot!" Dr. Callan yelled. "Even other classrooms were joining in! What were you thinking?"

"I was thinking, Dr. Callan, that I should receive an A."

Callan increased his scowl. He took a deep breath, ready to let out a string of condemnations and colorful metaphors.

"Dr. Callan?" came a voice

It was Miss Cooper, his secretary.

"Dr. Callan, Gladys's parents are here," she said.

"Show them in!" he snapped.

In walked Mr. and Mrs. Gallotta. Mom was meek and looked embarrassed as if she had been the one called into the principal's office for bad behavior.

Mr. Gallotta was anything but meek. He looked serious and professional as always when there was real business to attend to. He carried himself with confidence. He looked fit as if he was still in the Army.

Taking off their heavy winter coats, her parents delivered a disapproving stare. When she returned the glare as if to say 'you'd better be on my side with this,' they seemed to understand.

Mr. Gallotta spoke first.

"Well, well, what is this about then, Callan?"

"Mrs. Gallotta, Captain Gallotta. Please have a seat," asked the principal, calming slightly.

"Gladys is never in trouble," murmured Mrs. Gallotta as she sat. "Whatever could she have done?"

Callan smiled somewhat evilly. "She started a riot."

The parents turned to their child.

"I was giving a speech to persuade!" countered Jee. "I did an outstanding job, obviously."

"She convinced not only the children in her class to riot," Callan chided, "but she also drew in other girls from all four grades into the mayhem. She held an impromptu rally in the main hall for over two hundred female students, convincing them to join her and her protest. Even some of the younger teachers were swept up!"

"A riot?" echoed Mrs. Gallotta. "Your uncle will not be happy."

"What does Uncle have to do with this?" asked Jee.

"Dr. Callan," Mr. Gallotta continued, ignoring Jee's question and addressing the principal. "A riot? That is a pretty strong word. I mean," he let out a short chuckle, "was there bloodshed? Theft? Destruction of public property? Fire?"

"Hmm," mused Mr. Callan mockingly. "Not the fire, but yes, the rest! Garbage cans were kicked over by the mob. Posters ripped off the walls! A boy was slapped. Plants overturned! Crude messages were written on hallway walls! Kids spit gum at teachers!"

"Hardly a riot, Dr. Callan," said Mr. Gallotta, in his deep voice.

"It was downright communist!" thundered Callan.

Even more shocked, Mrs. Gallotta echoed the principal once more. "Communist?"

Mr. Gallotta seems ruffled by this comment. "Really, Callan, that's a bit harsh."

"Gladys advocated—quite forcefully, I might add—for the young ladies in the class to revolt," Callan accused. "She told them to do no housework until they received equal pay and got their war-time jobs back. If that is not communistic, I don't know what is!"

"Principal Callan," Jee interrupted. "I believe in the phrase *'equal right to life, liberty, and the pursuit of happiness.'* Hmm…" she added, mocking the Principal's previous tone as she feigned searching her mind for the quote's attribution. "Thomas Jefferson, I believe. Not Stalin or Lenin or Marx. Perhaps you have forgotten?"

Callan jumped up from his chair with surprising speed, face red with anger, fists clenched.

"She used the word 'penis' in the classroom!" he yelled.

Mrs. Gallotta shrieked in dismay.

"I see…" said Mr. Gallotta. He turned to Jee. "Gladys, what on Earth started this? How did this speech get out of hand?"

"Dad! Are you not even going to ask me if any of this is true?"

"All right, Gladys," he said. "Is any of this true?"

"Um…" she hedged. Then, softly: "Yes. All of it, actually."

The room was silent for a moment. Jee took a breath and spoke deliberately and clearly.

"Mrs. Tiernan assigned us a speech to persuade, as I said. So I chose to persuade the girls to stand up for their rights, and until they get equal rights and pay, they should withhold all favors from men—even sex—and then some of the girls—"

"Sex?" shrieked Mrs. Gallotta. "Are you having sex, Gladys?"

"No, mom!"

The room fell silent again.

They were all embarrassed, though Jee most of all.

Callan shuffled a few pages on his desk until he found the one he was looking for. After a moment, he spoke. "Ahem, well, here is a list of the damages—"

Jee snatched the list from his hand and read it quickly. "I didn't do any of this! The other girls did!"

Callan looked at her with that bulldog scowl. "But *you* started it. And as punishment, *you* are suspended for three days. You will write an apology to Mrs. Tiernan and every other teacher whose classroom you upset. Are we clear?"

"Clear," Jee replied curtly, her tone more than a little vindictive. "Just keep us girls down, right, Dr. Callan? When we rise up, put your jackboots on our necks!"

"Gladys!" shrieked Mrs. Gallotta in shocked bewilderment.

Mr. Gallotta, however, was smiling, just a bit. Jee has become quite assertive these last few years, he thought. Could that be from all my talk of equality and doing the right thing, even if it means trouble? Maybe I'm spending too much time with her, and some of my *decisiveness* is rubbing off.

In silence, Jee and her parents left the principal's office, walked the hallway to the school's front entrance, and exited into the cold December afternoon air.

They stood at the top of the landing before the dozen steps that led down to the parking lot. Before them were three hundred girls and a good number of boys, all staring. It was silent for a moment. Then, clapping began, a cheer rose up, and the students chanted "Equal Rights! Equal Pay! Equal Choice!" and "We know that!"

Some rushed to shake Jee's hand.

Her parents were overwhelmed.

Jee smiled.

Through the crowd, Mrs. Tiernan approached with a deadpan face. She thrust a paper at Jee, who took it. Tiernan walked away.

It was a score sheet for her speech. Her name was in the upper right-hand corner and below, a large, firm, red letter 'F'.

"Figures," Jee muttered.

As they approached their maroon and chrome '54 Buick Special, the crowd dissipated. Jee waved to a few girls and then ducked into the back seat. Yesterday she was a weirdo, an oddball, a nobody. Today she was a celebrity. She liked the feeling. It was new to her. Maybe she could be famous someday. Of course, starting riots probably didn't pay well, and there was always the threat of jail.

"Sorry, Mom. Sorry, Dad. I didn't think it would go that far."

"Hmm," her father grunted. "We'll talk later tonight."

After dinner and writing letters of shallow apology to her teachers, Jee was ready for bed. Frost had formed on her upstairs bedroom windows, and the light shining in from the streetlamp at the edge of their yard made the crystals glow. It was so cold outside, and that it made being inside and warm even more special.

As she pulled up her covers, her father knocked and entered.

"Time to talk," he stated, sitting on her bed.

"I bet it's not gonna be a war story, is it?" she asked.

"No," answered Mr. Gallotta. "You've heard them all before."

He took a deep breath and looked into her eyes. Jee didn't look like a little girl anymore, or even a teenager. She looked like a young woman. Saying she grew up fast was an understatement.

"How was work at the mill, Dad?" she asked.

"Trying to change the subject? Funny. It was boring. And peaceful. Just the way I like it."

"You've had enough excitement, huh, Captain?" she probed.

Mr. Gallotta was silent for a moment or two.

"Enough for a lifetime, sweetheart," he said, a slight hitch in his voice.

She knew he had seen things in the early days of the war that he would never talk about. Their marathon discussions of the various campaigns he participated in were primarily about strategy and overall tactics, not the stuff of movies and heroes. She knew that his time in North Africa and Italy was initially spent in the 3rd Battalion, 67th Armored Regiment as an intelligence officer. Due to his successful planning in Operation Torch and the invasion of Casablanca in 1942, he was moved into Eisenhower's army intelligence group and promoted to captain's rank.

"It seems," he began, "that based on the reception you had when we left the school, the kids liked your presentation."

"They did," she said. "I got my facts and figures from my books."

"Most of *your* books are *my* books," Mr. Gallotta pointed out.

"I know. That's what convinced them: the facts and figures," she said with a smile, knowing what his response would be.

"Facts and figures convince no one," he said. "Hearts convince."

They were silent for a moment.

"Look, honey," Mr. Gallotta continued. "You started a small-grade riot at school. People, innocent people, could have been hurt. Was that what I taught you? To be careless? To not think about what comes next?"

"I just didn't think...that I could do it. I mean, make the kids do what I was suggesting. But they did."

It was difficult for him to be angry with her. He was proud of Jee's abilities, not just her singing, but her understanding of history, and how things worked and were connected. Ever since she arrived, he knew she was different. Special. But what father didn't feel that way about his kids?

"School is not a place to experiment with your...powers of persuasion, Gladys."

"Dad, women are being repressed. It's like we are slaves. You even said so."

"I used the word slaves?" he asked, somewhat surprised.

"No," Jee admitted, "but Mom did."

Mr. Gallotta nodded. "She's too proper to get angry about it all, but I know her feelings. And I agree with her. And with you. All people should be allowed the same rights and privileges—"

"Well," Jee interrupted. "I just thought I should *do something* about it instead of just *agree.*"

"Gladys," he said, shaking his head. "I approve of that part. Right goal, decent strategy and tactics, but?"

Jee closed her eyes. And let out a heavy sigh. "Wrong timing."

"The 'when,'" he said, standing, "is as important as the 'what,' remember?"

"Yes," she said.

"So, you are grounded. No books, radio, no—"

"Parties? Dates? Sleepovers?" she interjected. "I don't get invited to those types of things anyway."

"That's a good thing, I think," he responded, bending over to kiss her goodnight.

"You are old," she responded. "And a fuddy-duddy."

"Christ, I sure hope so," he sighed with a smile.

"But, even though I'm grounded, we can still wrestle, right? I read about an old Roman-era chokehold I would like to try on you!"

Both laughed.

"Gladys. My fragile flower-of-a-daughter, who acts like a son."

She just smiled widely and batted her eyes.

"I'm too much like you. It must be in the blood."

He smiled uncomfortably.

"Goodnight, Gladys," he said and turned out the light.

At four-thirty in the morning, Mr. Gallotta awoke. That damn pain in his thigh. Still there after all the surgery. Not that the wound slowed him down, his limp was barely noticeable. But at times, it kept him awake with a nagging sting. As usual, he decided he would just get up and start the day.

Once in the kitchen, he turned on the light above the stove and started a pot of coffee. As he turned around to reach for his cup, he saw a face in the window of the kitchen door.

"Geeze!" he blurted out.

The door opened and in walked Eno. He was easily over six-and-a-half feet in height, thin, and completely bald. He had extra-long arms that seemed slim even for his slight body, and his height came from his long legs more than anywhere else. His ears were a little large for his face, his nose was pointed, his lips small, his cheekbones full. It looked to Mr. Gallotta as if no feature actually fit together on his face. And, he acted as strange as he looked.

"I didn't mean to startle you," Eno said, sniffing the air.

"Well, you failed," replied Gallotta as he looked upward at the taller man.

"Sarcasm? Humor? I am getting the hang of it," said Eno in his sing-song voice.

Gallotta sighed, and poured a cup of coffee for Eno. He knew the man's opinion of the brew.

"Ah! Coffee! Thank you, yes. How is Jee?"

"Good. Getting feisty."

"Still enamored with war? Still training her to fight?" Eno asked.

"That's just for fun, Eno. She enjoys the strategy. The history. The Generals. She knows every major conflict since the early Egyptian eras, and many of the tactics executed. She's got a bright mind."

"For war, yes," said Eno. "Maybe it's in her blood? Your blood?"

"Funny. I guess you *are* getting better at humor," Gallotta mumbled as he handed Eno a cup of coffee, no cream.

Eno sipped the drink and paused to smell the aroma. "Coffee. Mankind's pinnacle of achievement. In my opinion."

"Glad you like it. Why are you here at four in the morning?"

"Why are you up at four in the morning?"

"What is it, Eno?"

Eno sighed and took another sip. He leaned against the kitchen counter.

"Remember what I said? At the beginning of all this? That someday I would come to take her away? For good?"

Mr. Gallotta frowned. He broke into a cold sweat.

"That day will be December the twenty-first," said Eno.

"Already?" Gallotta protested. "I-I mean…that's not even three weeks from now…I, we have grown quite fond of her, Eno. She is like our own. She is our daughter—"

"It has been almost eleven years," Eno interrupted, "and I appreciate what you have done for me, *brother*. And for her. But our time has come."

"B-but where will you go?" pleaded Mr. Gallotta." I-I mean I must know. Maybe we could come see her—"

"That will not be possible, unfortunately," Eno said with a slight chuckle. He stood and produced a metal case the size of a shoebox. He handed it to Mr. Gallotta. "This has a time-sensitive lock. It will open itself after we are gone. Please bring Gladys to my ranch by dinnertime."

Eno left the kitchen and disappeared into the early morning darkness.

5
Ga Ya!

Just off Lake Pend Oreille's eastern shore, south of Owen's Bay, sat Memaloose Island. Its five acres of wooded paradise offered a view of the surrounding forest, the water, the Monarch Mountains to the west, and the small town of Sandpoint with Switzer Mountain to the north. Only three structures stood upon Memaloose: the boat dock, a large barn, and Uncle Eno's enormous ranch house. There was also a covered pontoon-style ferry boat Jee's uncle had built to move his car and other goods back and forth from the mainland to the island, a trip of about eight hundred feet.

Uncle Eno owned the entire island. He was rich. Mr. Gallotta had told Jee that Eno was some kind of mineral trader, but he was also a doctor. Since she was a baby, he had been Jee's physician and supplied homemade medicine, vitamins, and even a type of breathing machine she could use if she was gagging too much.

Jee believed Eno was her father's brother, though she couldn't be sure. No one ever discussed the relatives. In fact, as far as Jee knew, she didn't have any relatives besides her parents and her uncle, and Eno was always described as 'distant.' He never talked to her parents much, only at the beginning of each visit. They would go into Dad's shop in the garage or into her uncle's study without her and have a quick discussion. One time, years ago, she snuck close and put her ear to the door to listen. They mainly discussed her health and school and some financial matters that usually ended up with Uncle giving her parents money. Then Eno would sit with her and go over homework and some special assignments he had given.

The special assignments! Lord, she thought, they were simply insane—that was the word. Mostly, he made her learn ancient and lost American Indian languages. He was insistent, and her parents made sure she studied. It also seemed that the better she was at speaking these forgotten linguistic oddities, the more money her uncle gave her parents.

There was always something underneath it all—something surrounding the family—and her uncle was in the center. Why was he even involved? And though Jee had visited Memaloose many times, sometimes staying for weeks when school was out—just her and Eno—she little about him. Eno was different, though that was too mild a word. He was *odd*. Maybe that is where she got her weirdness from?

After breakfast on December the twenty-first, her parents announced that Uncle Eno had requested Jee spend the last bit of the Christmas holiday with him at the ranch. They were going to Spokane to see one of Dad's old army buddies.

"Just me? And him?" Gladys asked dejectedly.

"Yes, that is what he said," replied Mrs. Gallotta.

"When?" Gladys asked.

"Today," Mr. Gallotta answered.

They dropped her off late in the afternoon. Snow covered the scene making the island look like a Christmas card. Her mother hugged her and cried. Her father just kept looking at her, and though always a tough man, he, too, seemed ready to break. Why were they so dramatic? Because she was spending a week with weird uncle Eno? Yes, that would be enough to ruin anyone's holiday, but it was she who would be made to suffer.

But, for some reason, this visit to her uncle's was different. They were clearly upset.

"Gladys," whispered her father as he gave her a long embrace. "Just remember, I love you, a-and I am proud of you. Think of us when you can."

"Dad! It's just a few days! You act like someone has died!"

"No, no one has died," he said with an odd smile. "Here. A present. But don't open it until Christmas morning." He handed her a small box, one that could contain a ring or a small piece of jewelry. It was wrapped in bright holiday paper. "Put it in your pocket. See ya soon."

She watched as her parents waved goodbye from the pontoon boat as it slowly crossed the water to the mainland. They got into the Buick and disappeared down the dirt road into the forest.

Jee now sat alone in the elegant wood and stone mansion. Stained pine beams framed the house inside and out, and finely sanded, honey-stained aspen paneling complemented the dark furniture and wool rugs that adorned the dozen rooms. Jee sat on the large plum-colored leather sofa and looked through the tall glass windows that made up the living room's entire rear wall. The winter sun was setting over the Monarchs, painting the water with golden glitter. It sure was beautiful here, she thought, even prettier than Lake Coeur d'Alene, which was extremely pretty.

She wondered why her uncle had all this property and this huge house—yet lived alone. According to what she had heard from her parents, he was not home very often. He traveled the world for his 'mineralist' job but seemed to collect simple things that dealt with more than rocks. Many of these curios came to rest on the walls and tables of his home as decorations. He had African tribal masks, pottery from China, old weapons from forgotten wars, preserved and stuffed animals of every kind, seeds and beans, weird machines, small appliances—and yes, boxes of rocks, all cataloged and labeled. Years ago, he had shown her his collection of coffee makers (she had counted them—twenty-seven): presses, percolators, and even several steam-driven espresso makers from Italy. He had pounds and pounds of coffee in giant burlap bags.

Yet the majority of her uncle's collection was made up of books he kept in his basement library, a cavernous space almost as large as the public library in Coeur d'Alene. Thousands of volumes, surely, and many types: literature, language texts, science and field journals, colorfully illustrated books of plants and animals and national parks, but mostly history books on civilizations. History was their shared passion. She had devoured almost every history book in her uncle's library over the years while either visiting or 'checking them out' to be brought home. On this trip, Jee had found a new book, *12 Decisive Battles of the Mind: The Story of Propaganda During the Christian Era.*

It was getting late, and the room was slipping into darkness. Jee lit a fire in the massive stone fireplace that made up the entire wall between the kitchen and the living room. After a while, the flames had died out some, providing a cozy light. Along with a large wool blanket, she settled in on a huge leather couch to read while she waited.

One of a dozen clocks chimed the time: eight o'clock. It had been almost three hours since she arrived when she heard a car pull up, pebbles crackling across the gravel driveway and the soft crunch of snow. Running to a side window, Jee could see the vehicle come to rest under the single lamppost that stood next to the driveway. It created a stage-like spotlight on her uncle's new red Jaguar XK 120. He might be weird, she thought, but anyone with the taste for a beautiful roadster like that at least had *some* class and certainly some money. She quickly returned to the couch.

"Ah! My little *Glasšigh!*" her uncle Eno said as he walked into the room.

Jee stared, considering all his features. He wore his reading glasses that were tinted smoky-gray. His olive skin matched her own. No feature actually fit together on his face. But that fact complemented his overall oddness.

"Good evening, Uncle Eno," Jee replied. "*Shayhalla.*"

"Yes, yes," he said as he put down a large box of groceries on the table. "Shayhalla to you as well! So…you have been studying? Your Áhthan accent is perfect, my dear!"

They conversed in the strange Indian language for a few minutes after moving into the kitchen. Eno smiled throughout their exchanges, nodding often. He was proud of her. She had become fluent in the language.

"Uncle Eno, how would you know what the accent would be? You never heard it. It's a dead language and has been for years, at least that is what it stated in the books you gave me. We can only guess what they sounded like and how they pronounced things."

"Yes, yes," he said, "well, more on that later. For now? Let us engage in deep thought and wise counsel."

"P-pardon?" she asked.

"It is a special night, and to celebrate, I have brought one of Earth's most precious gifts! But for coffee, it would be the pinnacle of man's contribution to civilization! Bananas!" he announced happily, "and chocolate, vanilla, and strawberry ice cream!"

As he continued to lift each item out of the box, he announced it: "Also, cocoa syrup, roasted peanuts, whipped cream, and finally…" He paused for added dramatic effect. "Huckleberries from the hillsides east of the lake! To make banana splits! And for me," he withdrew a bottle and winked at her, "a little brandy—also a stunning achievement of mankind's."

Jee could only smile slightly and shake her head. "Uncle, I have never told you this, but you are—and have always been—a little peculiar."

"Hmm," he said as he took two large glass bowls out of a cabinet, "you are not the first person to say that to me."

They prepared the splits and moved to the kitchen table. Eno, once done constructing, had poured his brandy over the entirety of his concoction. Jee could only assume it ruined the dessert completely; she did not want to try any, not even when Eno had offered.

Afterward, they ate dinner, again an Eno weirdness to have dessert first. Still, his cooking was excellent, so this oddity she would allow him. They made a salad with field greens, dressed with ripe cherry tomatoes, sweet onions, and assorted early spring vegetables Eno had grown in his indoor, climate-controlled greenhouse. Sprinkled with peanuts and a few left-over huckleberries, it was tossed in a creamy, peppery, red wine dressing. He also had some beautifully filleted rainbow trout from the lake, lightly breaded and fried in Italian olive oil, much better than the lard or butter used by so many others in Idaho.

Once finished, they both sat back in the heavy wooden kitchen chairs to relax.

"Ah, my little Glasśigh, so nice to be with you," Eno reflected, wiping the corners of his mouth on his fine cloth napkin.

"May I ask, Uncle, why you call me that? My given name is Gladys, not *Gluh-sigh*," she said slowly in a deep voice, stretching out the pronunciation to point out the strangeness of the name.

Eno looked at her disapprovingly. "Your mother told me that some of the other school children call you *Jee*. Would you rather I use that name?"

"That would be okay," she responded.

"Hmm…Jee? Yes. I like it. It's short," he reasoned, "and Gladys starts with a G, and Glasśigh starts with a G, so Jee makes sense."

She smiled. "It does."

"Well then, speaking of names, let us consider *Glasśigh*. Do you know what that means in Áhthan? Can you translate? G-l-a-s-s-i-g-h. Accent on the second syllable. *Gluh-SIGH.*"

"Um, yes," she responded, thinking. "*Gluh-SIGH,* accent on the last syllable…that would mean…well…*gla* is a prefix that means 'special' in Áhthan. And *sigh* is love. So Glasśigh means *special love*."

"Very good," he said. "That is the literal meaning. It can also mean 'everyone's love' as 'love' is used as a pronoun. In this case, it is a love that belongs to everyone. It's special but special to everyone."

"So why do you call me that?"

Eno smiled. He had been waiting to tell her this for the past fourteen-and-a-half years.

"Because," he said, knowingly, "you are *the Glasśigh*, everyone's special loved one. And not just here on Earth."

"Not on Earth?" she muttered. Eno was being weird again. She exhaled loudly. Maybe he meant not on Earth, but in Heaven, as if he thought her an angel or something.

They finished their meal, did the dishes, and made coffee using one of the many coffee-making contraptions Eno had collected from wherever it was he had traveled.

"Please get your coat and come with me to the deck outside, my dear," he suggested, taking both cups.

As the stars were out, they both paused for a moment by the railing of the deck, taking time to look upwards. It was warm, considering that it was only days before Christmas. From this island, right next to the dark lake and the darker forest surrounding, they could see thousands of stars—and eventually, as their eyes adjusted, even their colors: primarily white, some yellow, blue, and even red. The longer they gazed, the more stars they saw, and soon it seemed the entirety of the Milky Way was painted across the evening sky.

"It is so beautiful up there. No moon tonight," she observed.

"Not one you can *see easily*," Eno murmured. "But there are moons up there."

"Uncle, have you ever thought what could be in outer space?"

"Mostly large expanses of nothingness, that's what is there," he said.

"I mean, where there *is* something, like planets… stars… maybe even people. I would love to see everything," she said excitedly, "or at least some of it!"

"Good. I-I mean, yes. All things are possible in an infinite universe," he commented. "Look low on the horizon. Can you see that bright star just above the dead pine? Right at the top?"

Jee nodded.

"That is Jupiter," he said with a sigh. "Not a star, actually. A planet. Some call it *Ofeétis*."

"Ofeétis? Really? Gosh. It has over a dozen moons!"

"Actually, it has over seventy-five, depending on how one defines the term *moon*," he said. "So now, yes, Jupiter is nearing *opposition*. That is when it will be closest to Earth."

"Do you have a telescope? Can we see it?" she asked.

"You will see it, yes. But not through a telescope, Jee."

"I wonder if any of those moons have life on them," she mused.

"I am sure there is life out there," Eno stated. "And we can test the theory! I have a science project we can play with. To the barn!" he announced happily and led the way.

Jee had never been in the oversized barn. Upon entering, Eno flipped a switch and several lights mounted on the ceiling illuminated the area. She was overwhelmed at the amount of *stuff* neatly arranged in rows and upon racks: shelves of odd pottery, jars with some kind of liquid that suspended odd shapes of dark objects, mounted creatures of all kinds, ancient shields and pikes made of wood and steel, a Willy's Jeep, lawnmowers (at least seven), odd and familiar tools, paintings, sculptures, a clay-looking oven, a stone wheel device, boxes and sealed crates marked in Áhthan characters, more books, small appliances, strange clothing from around the world, and more.

"What? There is a lot of weird stuff in here!"

"Yes! These are my collectibles!" Eno proclaimed with obvious pride. "Unfortunately, I will not be taking them with me. But, I have my scans!"

"Scans?" she asked.

"Photographs and movies, let's say," he responded. "All my books have been scanned. Each artifact in the house, the library, and this barn has been photographed and...we will say *electronically stored.* The most unusual specimens I have already prepared for travel."

"Travel? Where are you taking them?"

"Ah, I will answer that in a moment. Come!"

He led her to the rear of the barn and to a small coffee pot on a shelf surrounded by other household items: old pans, dishes, cooking pots, grills, brooms, baskets, and lamps. He took the lid off the coffee pot, reached inside, and pulled out a ring holding a dozen or more keys, all different sizes and shapes. Walking across the wooden-planked floor, he led Jee to the corner of the space and opened a door that looked as if it led to a storm cellar.

"We need to go into the basement," Eno said.

"A basement in a barn?" she asked.

"Why not?" he asked, smiling.

They took the dozen or so creaky steps to the bottom, a single bulb lighting their way. A passage led to a locked door. Eno found a specific key on the crowded ring and inserted it into the lock, which turned with a click, and the door creaked open. He held the door for Jee as he switched on another light.

They entered a small room, about five feet square. Three walls were made of large local stones. The fourth wall was taken up by a massive steel door. It had heavy hinges and several sturdy-looking latches, and a big metal dial in the center.

"A vault?" she asked, surprised.

"Not as such," said Eno. "But this is where my most precious possessions are kept."

Eno moved each latch aside after unlocking them with keys from the ring. Finally, using the big control knob, he dialed a combination of at least twelve numbers, then pushed the massive door open.

Before them was another door, slightly curved at the top and bottom, all white and made of metal. It had an odd, angular silver panel on one edge. Eno waved his hand in front of it, and a handle appeared accompanied by a thumping sound. Eno pulled the handle and the door opened with a sigh.

He stepped into the dark room, Jee right behind him, moving cautiously. He pressed a wall switch, and the room awoke, now awash in a white-green light; not from incandescent bulbs as were found in every building Jee had ever been in, but a more even light that seemed to make things *glow* instead of shine. It looked eerie.

She was in a laboratory of some sort, approximately the size of Eno's living room in the main house, possibly fifty feet long and twenty feet wide. Everywhere, she saw instruments, most made of white metal. Panels of lights and gauges; flat screens that looked like televisions recessed into the walls, and rows of switches and buttons surrounded her. The ceiling also contained dials and knobs, yet not quite as many as the walls

At the far end of the room was a sitting area with three chairs arranged side-by-side. Jee thought they looked like large eggshells, cut in half, their bottoms attached to the floor. Inside, they were padded and covered in a soft, leather-like material. Above each chair, recessed in the ceiling, was the top of the egg, but this half was made of glass with steel edges and clear tubes stuck out in odd positions, running into the ceiling.

"Is this a-a laboratory?" stuttered Jee, trying to take it all in. "Are you a scientist?"

"Of course," Eno answered, obviously insulted. "Of course I am a scientist! I have been *sciencing* for, well, the entire time you have known me, and before that even!"

"Sciencing?" Jee said with a laugh. "Is that even a word?"

"It is now." Eno flicked a few switches, and parts of the room began to hum. "Someone has to make up new words, and I, as a *scientist*, might as well be the one."

Eno led her to the seating area. "Sit."

Jee took a seat at the edge of the row.

"No, not there," Eno corrected. "That is my seat. You can sit in the middle one."

"Okay…" Jee said and moved to the center seat.

Before her was a dashboard, similar to one found in a car; however, this one was way more *involved.* Complicated. Again, small screens faced her, along with something that resembled a typewriter, but the keys were flat, and each contained an Áhthan symbol. There were many more keys here than on the Royal she used at school. Also covering the control board were dozens of dials, gauges, and switches. Right above the panel, at her eye level, was a glass wall, like a car's windshield, except this glass was at least five times thicker and larger by three times. It also curved upward, becoming part of the ceiling for about six feet. Through it, Jee could see the basement's stone wall before her, and above, the ceiling that was the barn floor.

Eno began flicking switches and adjusting levers. Each time he did, some device would light up, make a whirring noise, a flash, a glow, a buzz, or all of these at once.

Jee began gazing about in wonder. "Uncle? What are we doing in here? It's scary, and I don't—"

"Nothing to be nervous about, Jee," Eno said, reassuring her. "I have a powerful radio here, capable of sending and receiving signals strong enough to reach, well, Jupiter. Let us try it out!"

Jee wondered what Eno would do with a powerful radio such as this. Maybe they would listen to broadcasts from Europe? That would certainly be exciting for a little while.

"What will we listen to?" she asked.

"We will do more than listen," Eno answered. "We will communicate! I have an antenna on the roof of the barn, pointed at Jupiter. If we are lucky...here, sit by the microphone..."

Eno pointed to a small metal bump on the dashboard that looked like it had a screen over it. She leaned within a quarter-inch of it and began to speak.

"Come in, London!" she called loudly. "Jee calling London! For the Queen!"

"Not so close dear, it is a very sensitive microphone. Just sit back and speak normally," Eno said as he flicked a small lever on the dashboard. A red light the size of a jelly bean glowed above the microphone. He moved his hand to a large dial the size of a small saucer and turned it a fraction of an inch.

"There! Just say '*Shayhalla Tar-Aśello. Ertog tas Spectortha Lectica. Dutha colleta?*' And repeat it with each turn I perform on this dial."

Jee was confused. Those words were Áhthan. Why would anyone in the world want to hear Áhthan? And why would anyone say such an odd phrase? *Good Evening Canyon Aséllo* (whatever *Aséllo* meant). *This is* Explorer Eleven. *Do you hear us?*

"Uncle," she began, looking concerned, "why would I say that?"

"Humor me, Jee," he replied. "Repeat the phrase, please."

She did. Nothing. No response.

Eno insisted that they wait thirty minutes between each try, and if there was no response, he would move the dial a fraction of an inch, and they would broadcast again. This went on for an irritating and tedious two hours, maybe three, never hearing anything except static, popping and crackling and hissing.

Jee fell asleep between sessions. This meant that Eno would wake her and ask her to repeat the phrase, which irritated her.

"Again," Eno insisted.

"What time is it?" she asked.

"Three-thirty. Again, please."

Jee repeated the phrase.

Then: something. The static stopped, and as perfect as if listening to a radio broadcast from nearby Spokane, a voice came through, loud and clear. It sounded like a man, but maybe it wasn't. It was an excited voice, to whomever it belonged, and it was talking a lot. It sounded as if the person was speaking perfect Áhthan.

"What the heck is going on, Uncle Eno?"

"Repeat the phrase!"

She did.

Nothing.

"It's gone," she said.

"No, no. It takes approximately thirty minutes for our signal to reach them and for them to respond back. We have them. Just wait."

As promised, after thirty minutes, the reply came again, and this time, Jee could understand each Áhthan word.

"Explorer Eleven! Explorer Eleven! Impossible! Can you confirm mission code Etáin twelve? Confirm Mission code Etáin twelve! Can you hear us?"

Jee looked at Eno, eyes wide, and let her mouth drop open.

"Tell him 'Etáin code Ćlaviath one-five-zero-one' please."

"Etáin code Ćlaviath one-five-zero-one. Etáin code Ćlaviath one-five-zero-one," she said as she eyed her uncle suspiciously, then added, "Do you hear us?"

Thirty minutes passed. Then:

"Code received and confirmed. Explorer Eleven, this is Aséllo Station at Targan Base. Glad you are alive, Commander! What is your status? Why did you not alter course and return after the attack?"

Commander? Who the heck is that? Jee thought. Is this a hoax? Though it was not like him, could Eno be teasing? It wasn't funny, whatever he was doing. They had been sitting, alone, in this creepy lab for hours, and it was beginning to be too much.

"Eno, this is really not what I needed tonight. I am tired of your—"

He held up his hand for silence and began speaking in Áhthan.

"Targan Base! I was forced to launch to avoid the laser cannon of the Zakéema. I was critically injured and could only survive by entering the cryo-chamber. Being unconscious, I was unable to change course. *Explorer* continued to Earth. Due to worldwide war activity here, I made no official contact. I repeat: no official contact. Observation only incognito. We are preparing to return as per schedule. Do you hear us?"

Jee stared at him. Her uncle seemed very serious. Then again, maybe he was…

"Uncle," she said, "are you okay? In the head, I mean? Did you have a fall—"

"Jee, we are communicating all the way to Ganymede! Do you know Ganymede?"

"One of Jupiter's moons?" she asked. "Yes. I know it from school. But that is hard to believe—"

"Yes, yes. And you have just spoken to the beings that live there!"

Jee smiled. "You—are nuts. And even if that is true—and I don't believe it one bit, mind you—then why are they listening? How do they know you? How do they know you're here?"

"Because it is time for them to listen. Because I am one of them. They sent me here."

Jee looked at him and shook her head. Maybe there was a way to get him into a hospital in Boise.

"Why wait until today to contact them? Eh?" she asked accusingly.

"The planets were not in opposition," Eno explained. "Ganymede has been too far away until now. Though I have a powerful transmitter, any signal I sent would have been too weak. But today! Today we are in range! It is exciting, isn't it?"

That was plausible, she thought. But still…

"For being from Ganymede, you look pretty human to me." There! she thought. Got him!

"We are similar looking, Áhthans and Earthlings," Eno answered. "And I do *appear* human. I had to perform physical and cosmetic changes to blend in, surgically alter some bone structure in our faces, your nose actually. Your alterations were slightly more…*elaborate* than mine."

"Me? Wait. You—*you altered me*?"

"Umm…yes. I had to convince you and the Earthlings."

"And you are saying that we both are from Ganymede?"

"Yes, Ganymede," he said, "though the beings who live there call it Áhtha."

Jee shook her head in disbelief. "Uncle, I think you need to see a doctor."

"I *am* a doctor," Eno declared, slightly perturbed. "And a geologist and a sociologist. And an astro-*naut*, as they say here on Earth."

"If this is all true," Jee continued arguing, "then why do they speak some old, dead American Indian lang—" she stopped. Wait... Could it be…that Áhthan was not a dead American Indian language? It was true that whenever she mentioned it to her teachers, they had no idea what she was talking about. Even the librarians had no records of the

Áhthan tribes. Could it be the language of some other world? But why had Eno made her learn it?

An uneasy feeling crept into her consciousness.

"It is not an American Indian language, Jee," Eno said. "It is the language of Áhtha,"

Just then, the radio broadcasted a reply.

"Explorer Eleven, this is Targan Base. We hear you are returning per schedule. It is joyous! The Zakéema have been defeated. Is the Glasśigh with you? Do you hear us?"

Jee frowned. How could whoever this was on the other end of the conversation know that Eno called her Glasśigh? He must have told them, as part of the gag.

They stared at each other for a few moments, Jee not wanting to believe anything except that her rich, eccentric, mysterious, weirdo of an uncle had finally lost his mind.

Eno swallowed hard, then addressed Targan Base.

"Targan Base, this is *Explorer Eleven*. The Glasśigh is with me and perfectly well. She has grown into quite a beauty, I must say—"

"Eno!" Jee screamed.

"And as you can hear, she has a well-developed set of lungs and speech capability—"

"Ah! Don't tell them that! Shut up!" she yelled, slapping at him repeatedly. Surprisingly, he did an admirable job of defending himself.

"You are insane," she huffed, standing up.

"Targan Base, can you hear us?" Eno continued into the microphone, undaunted.

"I don't want to play around tonight," she stated firmly. "In fact, I'd like you to take me home. This is not funny."

"I am neither insane nor trying to be humorous," he said, "though at times I can't help it! Ha! I have a *natural humor!*"

Jee just shook her head.

"I know this is unexpected, but this is why I called you here. Listen to me, Glasśigh—"

"Stop calling me that! My name is Gladys! I want to go home!"

"You are not from here!" he yelled, loud enough to stun her into silence for a moment. "Not from Earth," he said more gently this time. "You came with me as an infant. From Áhtha."

"Seriously? An infant astronaut?" she countered.

"There was an…unfortunate incident, an accident that put you on a ship with me. To Earth."

She stood, turned her back to him, and stomped off toward the doorway.

Eno watched her retreat. He knew this would be difficult. She was more obstinate than expected. However, it was good to see that Jee had a scientific mind after all. Up until this point, he thought she was content being an ordinary teenaged Earthling, going to school, reading history, singing, watching movies in downtown Coeur d'Alene, and listening to music. But in the last few years, she had developed a solid argumentative style and a sound structure to her reasoning. Tonight, she defended her position well, as her biological parents had defended their opinions so many years ago, though to no avail.

"Eno!" she exclaimed as she waved her hand in front of the odd panel handle on the door. "Open this!"

How could he convince her? There was one sure way, but maybe not yet. He'd rather she believed his words on her own if that would be possible.

"Explorer, this is Targan Base. We are approaching Ofeétis's far side and communications blackout. Proceed as per plan. This is our final broadcast. We prepare for your return. Good luck, and make the best speed home. Communication complete."

"Received and understood," Eno replied into the microphone, then, flicking a switch that obviously shut down the radio, he sat back in his chair. "Please, my dear *Gladys*," he said, now speaking English once again. "Sit for a moment. Please? I will explain."

Jee turned back to him, crossed her arms over her chest, and stood defiantly. The look on her face said: *If I must! Go ahead!*

Eno proceeded slowly. "I know this sounds crazy, *Jee*, but...I also know that there are things you must have noticed or felt, things that make you feel different from the other children."

Yes, there were things that she felt uncomfortable about, she always had, but what teenager in the fifties didn't feel awkward most of the time?

"What are you talking about?" she asked.

"Things that make you different than the others," he said. "Your height, for example. You didn't get that height from your parents, they are short. Your father is barely five-foot-nine. You're tall for an Earth female, even tall for an Áhthan! And you are not done growing yet!"

"I-I'm going to get even taller?" she seemed shocked at the notion.

"Also, let's not forget your large, deep green eyes. Does anyone you have ever met have such eyes?"

"You told me I had a slightly overactive thyroid!" she argued.

"I had to tell you something, something you could use to explain to others if need be. Large eyes are an Áhthan trait," he explained. "I couldn't shrink them, you know. I tried."

"You tried to shrink my eyes?"

"Ha ha!" Eno chuckled. "Again, a joke! No, no. I left them alone. But the vitamins you have been taking? I formulated supplements to change your skin color to match these humans. It lightened acceptably and will return to its natural shade within a few months. And your hair, well…"

"What about my hair?" she asked.

"Remember the feather? In third grade? I must have missed something during the procedure."

"How did you know about the feather? And what procedure?" she said nervously.

"And that gagging reflex and flushed face that you suffer from occasionally?" he continued, ignoring her question. "It's caused by the extra nitrogen in this atmosphere. It affects you adversely. You have become somewhat used to it, but you might remember the tent I had your parents use?"

"The oxygen tent I slept inside?"

"Yes. It helped you adjust to the richness of Earth's atmosphere. And the strength you have! That! That is an Áhthan trait! And think of this: you are a senior in high school? Eighteen years old? Yet…no menstrual cycle."

"Mom said I'm a late bloomer."

"That's not why," Eno stated. "You will never menstruate. Áhthan females do not. Ever. It is not part of the reproductive process. They can control their fertility by thought. It's voluntary."

"Really?" Jee asked, shocked.

"Yes. Also, you don't have much of a sexual drive or interest in sex, do you?"

"N-no. Not really…"

"That's because there is no chemistry between you and Earth boys, literally."

"Let's change the subject," she pleaded, embarrassed.

"Yes, yes. Then what about wearing sandals?"

"I never wear sandals…" Jee said slowly, thinking about this.

"Why not, Jee?"

Jee flushed red. "You know, *Doctor!* I-I have deformed feet!"

"Yes!" he agreed, smiling. "Strange webbing and, of course, seven toes. On each foot!"

He quickly removed his shoes and socks and lifted his feet off the floor for her to see. Webs. Fourteen little digits.

"Me as well!" he crowed triumphantly. "In fact, there are over three hundred and forty million beings on Áhtha just like us! Toes galore!

We also have seven fingered hands on Áhtha, but that was remedied with a quick surgical procedure—"

"You—*you cut off your own fingers?*" she asked, a look of horror appearing on her face.

"Only two from each hand. Yours as well," Eno said as he began putting his shoes back on.

"That is easily explainable," she asserted. "W-we are related. Both of us have the same genetic deformity."

"Both with seven toes? Really, Jee? That would be extremely improbable. But, all right, if you demand proof, think about this, dear. I am your doctor, as I was on Áhtha. I couldn't let anyone else on *this* planet examine you. They would have seen the irregularities; your physiology is quite different. Do you remember last summer? You were complaining that your heart hurt? But then you would vomit? That's because your *heart* is where the human *stomach* is, and your stomach is where the human heart is. I think you ate a cherry sno-cone? Disgusting! Also, you have three extra ribs on each side. You have different chemicals in your blood. I even had to alter your nose so it would *protrude*. I did that permanently to you. For me, well, I used a prosthetic."

"A prosthetic? What is a prosthetic?" she asked, afraid to hear the answer.

"A fake nose, in this case. Observe!" He grabbed his nose and started wiggling and stretching it.

"Stop, Uncle!" She backed away.

Eno didn't stop. He continued to pull and twist his nose, stretching it as if it were made of freshly-chewed gum. He yanked until it reached over a foot from his face. Then he pulled more.

"This hurts, actually," he said.

Then, it snapped.

In his hand, he held the nose, or whatever it was. With his free hand, he was rubbing where his nose *had* been. Bits of the gummy skin were dropping onto the clean metal floor.

"There!" he said and removed his hand from his face.

Jee could see no blood, just a smooth *nose*, but one much flatter than a human's. There were two nostrils, thank heaven, and the holes were tiny and a bit more vertical, resembling slightly rounded diamond shapes. Taking in the whole thing and filtering it through her shock, all Jee could think of was that Uncle Eno's nose looked like a reptile's.

"You look like a snake!" she shrieked through her disbelief.

"A snake?" asked Eno, offended.

"Well, just your nose," Jee clarified.

"Hmm. Would you like me to take off the rest of my face?"

"The rest?" she screamed.

"No, no, I am kidding! This is it. Ha ha. I really had you there for a minute. Come. Sit. I won't bite."

"I wouldn't be surprised," she quipped. She cautiously returned to the dashboard, though remained standing.

She was more than stunned but somehow curious. If this is a fake, it is an excellent and thorough one, she thought. And why do all this? Could it be true? Eno did resemble a serpent; however, he actually looked more handsome than before. His features finally seemed to fit his face. Slowly, Jee reached out to touch his nose, as it were. It sure felt real. She poked it a bit. Then, she grabbed as much as she could and pulled. Hard.

It wouldn't come off.

"Owww!" Eno yelped, backing away. "Dear, dear, dear, that really was painful! Are you convinced yet?"

"Convinced that you are an alien from Áhtha? Maybe," she said. "Wait…will, will my nose come off like that?" she asked, frightened.

"No, no. Not without surgery. I used some of your hip bone—a bit off each one—to build the two nasal bones. I used some of your ear cartilage for the upper and lower nasal cartilages. You see my ears are long? Yours are not. More human-like ears you have! I think it came out quite well. No one noticed, did they?"

"No. But I still think you're lying. About me, at least."

Eno frowned. He was still not getting through.

"You must have noticed the identical scars on your hips?" he asked rhetorically. "And scars on your hands where I removed the extra little fingers? And around your nose?"

She frowned. Yes, she had always wondered about the marks.

"Give me one last chance to show you something that will convince you? Please! Sit!"

She did, reluctantly.

Jee thought about what she knew: Eno certainly wasn't human, and if he was, he was grossly deformed. She had to admit that she also had a few physical oddities that couldn't be easily explained. As much as Eno addressed her physiological differences, it was the mental and social ones that bothered her most. She had feelings for *something like* romance, but not with these boys, or even movie stars, or even any men or women. Mostly, Jee felt that she never fit in, never was one of the gang. She always felt alone, with no close friends. Even the teachers were aloof. She didn't have in-depth conversations with anyone, no discussions of dreams or futures, no intellectual arguments—except with her father, sometimes her mother, and one other person: Uncle Eno.

That was upsetting.

She decided to allow Eno one last attempt.

"Okay. One last chance, then I am leaving!" she claimed as she sat back down.

"Excellent! Safety first!" Eno pressed a button on the dashboard. The chair in which Jee sat suddenly produced a harness that automatically wrapped around her snugly, like a fighter plane's seat belt.

"Uncle! What is this for? How did—"

"My dear Glasśigh," he said, beginning a frenzied toggle-flicking and button-pressing procedure on the panel. "I am sorry I had to lie to you, but it was necessary. However, once we return to Áhtha, you will return to normal, and your feelings for others will be deeper! You will feel like you belong! In an extraordinary way! And also, of course—"

"W-wait! Áhtha? We're going to Áhtha?" Jee shook her head vigorously. "I'm not going to Áhtha! I'm not going anywhere but back to Coeur d'Alene and back to school!"

"You have been suspended! It's Christmas break!" Eno pointed out as he resumed work, typing in a sequence of buttons on the panel in front of his chair.

"Yes, but only for two weeks! I'm not going anywhere with you!" she yelled. "This is stupid! Undo this belt!"

She struggled, but it was impossible to free herself. She grabbed for Eno to scratch or slap him; however, he was smart enough to lean away, just out of reach.

"Dear! Please! If you want out, fine!" Eno chided. "Stay here, but without me to look after you, you will soon succumb to various ailments and diseases that I have been protecting you from."

"I don't care!" Jee yelled.

"All right then! To release the seatbelt, pull down the chrome manual release lever above the screen in front of you."

She looked above the screen and saw two chrome levers.

"Which one? The one on the left or the one on the right?" she asked angrily.

"The right one…" he said.

Jee grabbed the lever to the right and slammed it down hard. The lights in the lab dimmed for a second. A throbbing sound filled the room, growing louder and louder. The floor shook. The entire room began to tilt upward.

"Or maybe," Eno said, "it's the one on the left?"

She looked at him suspiciously.

"What?" Eno asked defensively. "I don't sit *there*. I sit over here by *these* controls. Mostly."

"What is happening?" she demanded.

"Hoverjets are active! Good thing that belt is on! You're going to need it! If you are ever going to believe me, it will be now!"

"This is no laboratory, Eno!"

"No, no, it's not, my little Glasśigh! This is *Explorer Eleven*, my spaceship, and I am taking you home. This instant!"

The ship began to tip upwards. Looking through the windshield, Jee could see the nose of the ship burst into the ceiling above. Wood and other debris rained down onto the windshield amid a cloud of dust, but the craft remained undamaged. Soon their backs were firmly pressed against the egg chairs, parallel to the barn basement's floor.

More parts of the barn collapsed. More planks of wood fell past the viewshield. Some of Eno's collection of oddities made a short and noisy trip from the barn floor into the basement. Dust flew everywhere.

Eno punched in the last few entries on his panel and leaned back into his seat. He shouted above the noise:

"Vací! Execute mission launch order 15!"

"Order 15...phase one executed," said a soothing voice above the cacophony of noise.

"Who the hell is that?" Jee screamed.

"That is Vací! Our voice-activated command interface! Better hang on!" Eno exclaimed with a laugh. "She's got a led foot! A-ha ha ha!"

Explorer Eleven fired the subspace drive, sending spent solid hydrogen-fuel exhaust through its seven engine nozzles and subsequently igniting all matter in the barn's basement and the barn itself, spewing flaming hot debris in every direction. The craft promptly leaped high into the air. In a single second, the ship rammed through the basement ceiling, then through the remaining planks of the barn roof. *Explorer* stopped, hovering a few yards above the evergreens, melting the snow beneath it and casting an eerie blue light about the area.

Turning sickly pale green from shock, Jee looked to a side window. She could see that the barn was almost flattened and on fire, the main house and the deck were also ablaze, and several trees surrounding the once beautiful home were burning.

"Phase two ready to execute," said Vací.

"Engage!" cried Eno above the noise. Then he turned to Jee and smiled. "And we're off!"

Jee turned to face forward, hyperventilating and shaking her head in disbelief.

The propulsion drive tripled its output in a tenth of a second.

Explorer Eleven leaped into the night air, racing to reach Earth's escape velocity of seven miles per second.

Jee gasped as she stared, eyes wide, straight ahead at the approaching starfield. She was pressed back hard in her chair, the speed ever increasing.

"*Ga-Yaaaaaaaaaa!*" she screamed.

"Exactly!" cheered Eno, "Ga Ya! The Áhthan phrase for 'we go!'"

Explorer Eleven blasted into the dark night sky, leaving a trail of flame and force that observers would later incorrectly claim was a meteor striking Memaloose Island.

"Escape velocity obtained," Vací calmly affirmed.

"Fly me to the moon! Let me play among the stars!" Eno sang as the ship shook the bonds of Earth's gravity. "Let me see what spring is like, on Jupiter and Mars!"

The craft roared into the upper troposphere, the ship's exhaust briefly illuminating the few clouds that lingered in the night sky as *Explorer* passed through them. It blasted through the stratosphere, the mesosphere, and finally into outer space.

"Ga-Yaaaaaaaaaaaaaa!" was all Jee could add.

6
The Taźath

Nag 10, Áhthan year 1023

A sleek, silver-skinned Type-C luxury skyliner lifted effortlessly off the landing pad at Palace City, carrying Pronómio Tok, now the forty-fifth Taźath of Tar Aséllo. The Type-C's pilot held position over the pad for a few moments, adjusted the hover-fans, and then ignited the main jet engines to begin the short trip through the tar to the Síndian Province.

Happily alone, Pronómio sat comfortably on a soft woven couch in the spacious and plush cabin situated behind the flight deck. He took in the view below while sipping an early-morning cocktail and munching on one of his favorite delicacies, *flairnick kernels* dipped in tangy *meríca syrup*. Looking out the window that stretched almost the entire length of the skyliner, he observed the familiar sight of sparkling *Palace City*. Population: four-and-a-half thousand.

Palace City sat on a dark-stoned, rolling-hilled peninsula that grew north from the southern tar wall. It was surrounded on three sides by the blue-green Sea of Etáin. From the northernmost tip of the peninsula, one could look south and see the spectacular, five-mile-wide Falls of Etáin. Its green-tinted ice-water fell from the surface of Áhtha, the journey ending in a crashing, roaring storm of white mist and foam. Looking to the east revealed the massive green fields that served as a park and gathering place for the citizens with a proclivity for the outdoors.

Having all the trappings of a wealthy resort, Palace City was simply exquisite. There were spas, pools, restaurants, museums, art galleries, banks, entertainment complexes, beautifully manicured gardens and parks—precisely what one would expect of a lavish and sophisticated little kingdom where no resident had to lift a finger to do anything. In the center of it all was the *Palace of the Taźath*. This included Pronómio's private estate, several private restaurants and spas, the Palace Leadership Center, and housing for over six hundred members of the upper Koŕeefa: influential ministers and bureaucrats of the government, owners of major industries, and media personalities. All lived with their families in absolute luxury.

To maintain such a place, there were over two thousand Graćenta: the lower class. They were shop workers, gardeners, clothiers, machinists, cooks, and other manual laborers. Additionally, almost three hundred members of Merćenta, the middle class, held high positions as managers and performed professional duties such as running the banks, the restaurants, and various service and medical facilities. They were also doctors, professors, advisors to businesses, designers of all things, artists, legal counsel, government workers, members of the security forces, and high-ranking military personnel.

Of course, none of the Graćenta and few of the Merćenta workers lived within Palace City. The Merćenta who worked there were transported via high-speed water-trains that sped across the Bays of Arimía from Etáin City. The laborers of the Graćenta class came by supply truck or walked the few miles from the worker district of *Tepótah*, north of the Palace. A tall stone wall a mile wide, constructed ages ago, hid Tepótah and its relative squalor from the eyes of the elite.

The Type-C now cruised over *Etáin City*, the tar's largest and most spectacular metropolis, sparkling even in the fullest glow of Ofeétis. Though he had seen Etáin countless times, Pronómio still marveled at its center: a stunningly beautiful and modern district consisting of hundreds of elegantly shaped blue glass-covered skyscrapers, some rounded in design, some angular, but all tall almost beyond belief and standing proud. Lights of businesses and entertainment centers flashed and glowed amid the people-filled streets. Multi-level skylanes managed traffic of a half-million personal and business aircraft as they wove their way between the colossal structures and the surrounding region. Spacious public parks of green trees and turquoise waterways were abundant between the constructs.

Climbing higher into the moist air above the city, the Type-C turned northwest, heading for the farm fields of the Síndian Province.

As Pronómio Tok looked down to take in all of Tar Asėllo, he remembered his path to Taźath. It was over one-and-a-half Áhthan years ago, just before the launch of *Explorer Eleven*, that he and Gákoh Kalífus plotted to take control of the government of Tar Asėllo. At that time, Taźath Hátha Feh struggled with the Zakéema Front crisis and the pressure from trade negotiations with neighboring Tar Éstargon. The last bit of hope for her administration collapsed with the attack on Targan Base by Zakéema terrorists and the accidental launch of *Explorer Eleven*, resulting in the loss of Commander Eno Ćlaviath, and even worse, the loss of the Glasśigh.

Hátha Feh lost her vote of confidence four weeks later. The Yahyéth of Oso-Gúrith Province, Pronómio Tok—who promised strong leadership and swift, overwhelming military action—was handed the reins of the government and the title of Taźath. As his first act, he vowed to hunt down the Zakéema and their sympathizers immediately and eliminate them. He was supported by almost every minister and an overwhelming number of the Koŕeefa class. With that mandate, Pronómio Tok converted the Yahyéth's Special Police force he used in Oso-Gúrith to a tar-wide policing body now referred to as the *Taźath's Special Police*. With Gákoh Kalífus at its helm, the *TSP* accomplished the purge. The Zakéema were swiftly eliminated. Normalcy returned to Tar Aséllo.

However, as time passed with no one to blame for issues or cast as an enemy of the state, many Koŕeefa questioned the need for such a militant and forceful leader as Pronómio Tok. And why spend so many resources on Kalífus's large military complex? There was little threat, after all. In the halls of government, ministers considered calling for a vote of confidence.

And then the *Enária Front* appeared, just in time. News of their becoming the 'next Zakéema' frightened the populace, and therefor ensured Pronómio's position as Taźath.

Unlike the Zakéema, the Enária were far less militant and made no demands. They didn't kill needlessly, mostly stealing food from warehouses and supplies from medical depots and lightly protected convoys. These materials they distributed to the poorest of the Graćenta, winning their hearts and their support.

Of course, the details of their activities were painted in more evil tones when reported by the Taźath-controlled media, and that suited Pronómio.

Today was *Fullglow*, the fourth day of the six-day week, when Ofeétis was brightest in the sky. Golden-orange light reflected down on the spectacular sight of the farming fields passing below the Taźath's skyliner. This area was fertile land, Pronómio knew, and it produced a quarter of the food for all who lived in the tar.

For ten Áhthan years, Tar Aséllo was the most productive food source on all of Áhtha, supplying delicacies and staples to the tables of the civilized tars. So excellent and sought-after was the Asésllian crop that the citizens of Tar Asséllo, especially the Koŕeefa living in the southern regions, enjoyed an unparalleled period of prosperity and splendor. The trade from the other tars, namely its closest neighbor, Tar Éstargon, had made them rich.

And it should have continued! thought Pronómio, had the leader of Tar Éstargon, the Ef Keería, minded his own business and left well enough alone. But no. The Éstargonians became embroiled in Asésllian politics, attempting to impose their belief in social systems and personal liberties. They wanted change in Tar Asséllo—namely a dissolving of the age-old social caste system. If this did not happen, Tar Éstargon would end all but the most critical trade. Some thought it best to capitulate, to give in to the Éstargonian demands. Pronómio Tok did not.

Ties were all but severed. With no trade to Tar Éstargon, production levels fell, and the need for such a large worker class dwindled. Many fell into deep poverty, moving into the overcrowded and deteriorating city of Éhpiloh, in the center of Oso-Gúrith. There were too many unemployed, and that caused trouble. Pronómio Tok dealt with it, ruling with an iron glove. At least he had kept the nation and its class structure intact.

At full speed, the craft had taken less than an hour to travel the one hundred and twenty miles to Farm Field 73 in the north-western region of Síndian Province. It landed on a small ridge where a stone platform met the sheer cliffs of the northern tar wall. The pilot powered down the craft, walked into the passenger cabin, and opened the ventral door for the Taźath.

"A pleasant trip for you, Taźath?" asked the pilot.

The Taźath simply exhaled and gave a quick, forced smile as he left the craft.

Standing outside to greet Pronómio was a uniformed man dressed in battle fatigues of green and slate gray. He was fit, hard of muscle, and grinned widely. He had a spiky, dark gray mane and had recently grown a short white beard in stark contrast to his dark olive skin.

"Gákoh Kalífus, my friend," said Pronómio as he met the Commander of the Taźath's Security Forces. "It is good to see you."

"And good to see you, as always, Pronómio," Kalífus said with a slight bow.

The Taźath laughed a bit.

"You still bow to me? Please!"

"I bow to the leader of our nation, not necessarily to the man I taught how to walk and talk at the same time," joked Kalífus.

"Not too great an exaggeration," granted Pronómio with a chuckle.

After a firm head touch, the two men turned and walked toward the edge of the ridge. Special Police troops were positioned there, watching the fields directly below through VEDs: military-grade binocular visual enhancement devices.

"Would you like to look?" asked Kalífus as he offered the Taźath his VED.

Accepting it, Pronómio looked ahead and downward. He could see workers in a field. They performed back-breaking labor, picking produce, moving bushels of food, loading and unloading small trucks, and, when allowed, drank water directly from a spigot. This is what they are trained for, he thought, and better them than me. They are paid a small wage because they are not members of the Merćenta or the Kořeefa, and they certainly do not take their education seriously. They are where they should be. They must know their place.

"This might be a more involved action, Pronómio," stated Kalífus. "Our intel says two high-ranking leaders of the Front are present. We can tell from our scanners they most likely have no weapons. There is metal out there, but it looks like shovels and farm tools only. Maybe four or five Enária Front soldiers at most, mixed in with the farmhands. Stealing food! How else will they eat? They don't work."

"They must be stealing quite a bit to cause shortages in the south," added Pronómio. "There is no *tobafruit* to be had for under a small fortune! People are angry, asking questions."

"The Enária have increased their numbers since their humble beginnings, Pronómio," Kalífus pointed out. "They are not as powerful militarily as the Zakéema were at their peak; however, they have grown. And these workers are helping them. They do more than steal food; they steal our smaller transports and guncars. I lost a man last week in a minor skirmish."

"Unfortunate, Kalífus. I am sorry," Pronómio said.

It became darker as the clouds gathered above. The blue, swirling fálouse thickened and blocked out Ofeétis's glow. At this point, only the southern tar wall was illuminated with the soft orange light.

In Field 73, workers continued their labor. They were tired, and they were hungry. Many snuck a bite of the fruit they picked from head-high bushy plants—the tobafruit. One could eat the entire bulb: the skin, meat, and pit; and therefore leave no evidence.

A siren blared, sounding like tearing metal. This meant danger. The dictated procedure in the fields was for workers to stand still and wait for an overseer's direction. Sometimes it was a test, as most workers assumed, but at other times there were the insects: the creepy, foot-long red and black *larculls* that would crawl out of damp holes. They burrowed underground by the thousands, and when the time was right, and they had bred to sufficient numbers, they came streaming upward out of the ground. They devoured plants and anyone who happened to be in their way. This was a rare occurrence, thankfully, but it did happen.

Two men stopped working in their assigned row.

One was a thin middle-aged man with a medium length, wispy sand-colored mane and light blue eyes. The other was a heavy and muscular man with a close cut, black spikey mane, and deep-set brown eyes. Both had in common a *krísi*, the mark all Graćenta received at birth. Positioned over the right eye just below the scalp line was a simple, dark blackish-brown ring about one inch in diameter with two lines resting on top.

The thin man looked at the ground. He saw no movement, no tell-tale signs of the larculls. Usually, there would be one or two of the creatures every few feet, appearing as an advance party before the massive feeding frenzy.

"I don't see any larcull bugs," he said. "Do you, Orgo?"

"No, Salǵeea," the muscular Orgo responded as he, too, looked up from the ground. "I see none. This is bad."

They both scanned the immediate area of Field 73. The plants rose almost to their eye level, and through them, they searched for TSP troops rather than insects. It would be hard to see anyone approaching.

"Better signal just in case," suggested Salǵeea to his old friend.

Orgo took two nearby shovels, and banged them together in a series of three strikes, then paused and repeated the signal.

Other workers began to move, even though they were required to hold still. Yet who could see them amidst the tall stalks?

Some of the workers on the edge of the field saw them first: glimpses of camouflaged troops moving in semi-crouched positions, advancing quickly from the surrounding fields.

"This is a Special Police operation," came a firm voice from across the fields, amplified by some unseen device. "For your own safety, do not move, or you will be shot. Raise your hands above your heads."

The field workers had heard stories of what happened during these raids. People were shot when they ran or resisted; people were shot when they complied. If one was indeed an Enária soldier or a sympathizer, or simply someone trying to make a living, the chances of being killed were high. It would be better for one to run and hide in the surrounding fields. Then slowly and quietly, when the glow of Ofeétis dwindled and the clouds gathered, make one's way west, away from the TSP forces.

One worker lowered his hands, and looked about, left and right as if searching for the best direction to flee. A pulsegun fired, the hot charge glowing red as it raced through the darkened field, hitting the man in the face. In a splash of blood, his body fell.

Workers nearby screamed. They fled in random directions. More shots were fired.

"Salǵeea!" cried Orgo. "They know you are here! They are coming for us!"

"Signal the others!" called Salǵeea. "We are surrounded!"

Orgo once again grabbed the two shovels and began frantically banging them together. A red pulse hit one of the shovels, knocking it from his hand. Diving for cover, Orgo hit the ground and crawled to the end of a row of stalks. More pulsegun shots fired, glowing charges striking the ground around him. At the end of the row, he met Salǵeea. They both began digging in the dirt with their hands, next to the row marker. Their fingers finally hit metal. Each unearthed a simple projectile *shortgun*, two of the over twenty they and their team had brought with them earlier. It was a precaution they took whenever Enária Front soldiers, posing as ordinary workers, could get assigned to a farm crew. If needed, they would use them against the TSP. Each weapon could fire a one-inch long ballistic round of soft metal through a barrel about one-and-a-half feet long. The guns were old and not very accurate, but at this close range, they were lethal and sufficient to assist in escape.

Special Police moved in closer from all directions. If they saw movement, they checked to determine if it was TSP personnel. If not, they fired. There were always more Graćenta. In fact, there were too many of them, now a drain on resources. These fieldworkers, Enária thieves or not, were of little value to Asĕllian society.

On the ridge, Commander Kalífus activated his earpiece. "Report, Commander Myren," he said calmly.

Myren heard the request through her Headset Communication Node, or hel-com, embedded in her light-armor helmet.

"Myren here, squad one. We have the entire Field 73 surrounded. Moving in. No TSP casualties. No resistance."

Salǵeea and Orgo loaded their weapons with small clips holding several rounds each. They took a position, back to back, and as Salǵeea led the way to the south toward the sea, Orgo faced north, sweeping his gun left and right to cover their rear. Neither wanted to fight. As always, escape was the goal.

Mixed in with the abrupt coughing sound of the TSP pulseguns, they could hear other weapons discharging with a deep, loud *bang*. The other Enária Front members who had come today had gotten to their shortguns and were returning fire. The innocent field hands continued to scatter.

Still moving south, Salǵeea and Orgo had made it a hundred yards or more away from the fighting.

"We look clear, Orgo. All the way to the sea, as far as I can tell," whispered Salǵeea.

"Keep moving," said Orgo.

"We need to go back!" urged Salǵeea. "We have people back there!"

Orgo shook his head. "No. They know the drill. Run. Make your way back to the falls. My job is to bring you home alive."

"We can't leave them—"

Pulse rounds kicked up dirt and severed nearby stalks. It was apparent the shots were coming from multiple positions.

"I thought you said it was clear!" yelled Orgo.

"It was!" cried Salǵeea. "You know I am no good at this!"

"You better get good fast! We're going to have to blast our way out to the south, cut a hole in their circle! Move it!"

The fighting halted in the center of Field 73. Knowing they were surrounded, the remaining Enária fighters fled from among the workers to several farm vehicles that could provide cover from the pulseguns. They immediately formed a circle, pointing their projectile shortguns outward at the encroaching TSP. Though light on weapons, they had a fair amount of ammunition and worked in teams of two: one firing, one ready to load new clips. As Kalífus's group tightened the noose, the Enária opened fire at close range.

"Under fire! Heavy!" screamed Officer Myren as she ducked into a low ditch between two rows of tobafruit stalks. She peeked over a clod of dirt to get a visual, but the ground erupted with projectile strikes.

"I have two down in squad three!" came a frantic call through her earpiece.

"Three down in squad five!" came another.

How many of the Enária were there? thought Myren. The intel stated only four or so, unarmed. There had to be three times that many, and they were returning fire.

"Pull back!" she called into her hel-com. "Commander! Call in the wings."

"I hear you," acknowledged Kalífus. "Calling in wing support. Make your way back to the ridge."

The Enária team smiled as they saw the TSP troops pulling back. They began to look south and prepare for their escape.

Orgo could see two TSP troopers who had blocked their escape now running to the east and turning north along a tree line.

"Good," said Salǵeea. "Let's wait for the others here."

"No," insisted Orgo. "We move. Quickly. To the south until we hit the water. The TSP, those brown-jacketed *bilgasacs*, might return with a greater force. We must keep going."

Before Salǵeea could begin to argue, a low rumble was heard. At first, they both looked to the north, toward the center of Field 73. The sound became louder, the pitch rising. Orgo realized the rumble was echoing off the northern tar wall. He turned around and looked south. A formation of three Katíga C6 rocket-bombers appeared before him, gaining altitude as they rose over a small ridge.

"Oh no," he said flatly. "Stay down."

They watched as the ships roared overhead, then dove slightly, releasing their payloads on the center of the field. The fireball surely killed everyone within fifty yards of the farm vehicles.

"Well done, Gákoh," Pronómio said as they entered his skyliner. "What are the damages?"

Gákoh Kalífus joined his friend at a small table, taking a seat across from him. Through the viewport, he could see his troops returning to their positions at the makeshift base. The rumble of an incoming *transport ship* could be heard. It would land shortly to take the troops back to their base.

"My reports have just come in," Gákoh answered. He looked at his ABC. "Thirty armed combatants were killed today." Suddenly, his face drained of color, and his mane flashed a deep golden hue. "Those *bargo-licking gore hags* killed five of my troops and injured three others!"

"I am sorry," Pronómio said. "What about non-combatants?"

"We don't count them," Kalífus stated as he watched his armband and scrolled through the holographic report. "We recovered a dozen Enária weapons, old projectile shortguns. Old, but deadly."

The Taźath poured two glasses of *Rongpok Ale*, a mostly clear drink with large silver bubbles. He passed one to Kalífus, who took the delicacy and drank heartily.

"I assume this action today should help with the upcoming vote of confidence," Kalífus said. "I hope this was worth it, Pronómio."

Pronómio took a sip of his drink. "It is worth it, Gákoh. Madam Khileetéra and her small band of soft hearts are always mounting a challenge. But with today's little skirmish, the ministers will be reminded of the Enária activity and my resistance to them. We will win the vote. No one wants a weak leader in these uncertain times."

"Though, we lost good people today," Kalífus countered cautiously. "Explaining our actions to the troops—they wonder why we don't eliminate the Enária once and for all."

"Gákoh Kalífus!" barked Pronómio. Some of the black color drained from his mane, to be replaced by dull blue. "Without the Enária, what is the threat to Etáin? To Tar Aséllo? To the Kořeefa? There would be no threat!"

Kalífus's mane now also tinged blue at the edges, though only momentarily. "The threat of the Enária Front becoming too strong keeps us in power. I am aware. However, the fact of the matter is that this is a difficult position to explain to the troops."

"Then, you must find a way to explain it!" snapped Pronómio. "Do you remember what happened after the fall of the Zakéema? We almost lost our position! We weren't needed! But the rise of the Enária—"

"Yes, it saved us," sighed Kalífus dejectedly.

"We need them," continued Pronómio, cooling his anger. "I thank Aséllo's Ghost every day for the Enária!"

Kalífus was quiet for a moment. He drained his glass and shook a bit from the effect of the fermentation. By the time his hair returned to its usual gray color, he had decided to change the subject. Arguing with Pronómio Tok was never a winning proposition.

"On a more pleasant subject," said Kalífus, "what are your plans for the Glasśigh? She arrives in less than six-hundred days."

"The Glasśigh! Yes! Six hundred days!" Pronómio replied, his serious mood once again changing quickly to joy, a red tinge quickly replacing the blue of his mane. "We have much to prepare! Many events are planned! Tours of the tar, appearances in the halls of power! It will be joyous! Amazing that she, and Eno, are alive after all they have been through."

"They are of the Ćlaviaths and Aséllos. It should be no surprise," said Kalífus with a smile. "Does her appearance change anything?"

"With Tar Éstargon? I do not believe so," Pronómio answered, pausing in thought.

"Internally to Tar Aséllo, then?" asked Kalífus.

"Most certainly!" agreed Pronómio. "And at first, I thought she might *upset* things, not understanding the culture and our history. However, I soon realized that her return could be an opportunity."

"An opportunity? For what?"

"Ah! Everyone will love the Glasśigh!" exclaimed Pronómio. "This is the biggest event *ever* in Áhthan history! She is not only the Glasśigh, but the idea that she was marooned on another planet! How amazing a story! It is like she has come back from the dead! Everyone, regardless of class, will follow her every move! They will treat each word from her lips as if it came from Ásue Asésllo himself!"

"Yes…" said Kalífus in a questioning tone.

"So, imagine having someone who every Aséllian loves…" Pronómio paused for a moment, his hair turning almost purple, "…that would suggest to the masses, for example, that votes of confidence are ridiculous? They should be outlawed! Or might possibly mention we need increased funding for the AMF? Who knows what those devils in Tar Fortus 'might' be planning!"

Kalífus poured himself another glass of Rongpok and topped off his friend's drink. "And she would say those things because?"

"Because we will ask her to," responded Pronómio as he sat back with a confident grin and sipped his ale.

"Why would she listen to us?" Kalífus asked.

"Because she loves being the Glasśigh!"

"Yes. Who wouldn't love to be the Glasśigh?" quipped Kalífus. "Leading a life of privilege? No real responsibility?"

"A life of absolute pleasure and adoration, every wish a command! And most importantly, funded by none other than the Taźath!" Pronómio crowed with an exaggerated evil laugh. "She must know that we are the source of her happiness! And therefore, if she wants to remain wealthy, and the most popular, most desirable, most loved being on all of Áhtha...she must be beholden to us!"

"And we ensure her loyalty by making her life simply wonderful," added Kalífus.

"Yes," said Pronómio. "And we also have the Enária to blame—when we need them."

"And Eno?" asked Kalífus. "What of him?"

"He will be pampered, promoted, and be her keeper! As long as he can lecture to his followers in the scientific community and make documentaries about Earth, he will be happy."

"There is one other issue," Kalífus pointed out. "It will be months before she arrives. And there will certainly be more votes of confidence. Can we survive them? Will the little skirmishes with the Enária be enough? They are not as effective as they once were, you know."

"Oh, they can be quite effective," stated Pronómio with a smile. "I can almost guarantee that the Enária Front is planning something big for the Glasśigh's arrival. It will be enough to make certain we survive any vote of confidence."

Salǵeea and Orgo had run for hours without stopping, at first moving south, then southwest from Field 73. As the new day of Lastglow came, the color of the tar changed considerably. The orange radiance from the planet above waned. A cloud cover rolled in, further diminishing light. Eventually, they turned northwest, and the terrain changed from rolling fields to harsher brush and stone. Soon they were forced to zig-zag their way through the rough, bolder-littered beaches and shoreline of the Síndian Sea. They hid in one of the slightly-sheltered rocky coves, sitting down on the hard ground, hoping for some rest.

Orgo produced two tobafruit, handed one to his friend, then took a bite.

"Stealing tobafruit is illegal," said Salǵeea.

Orgo grunted. "Add it to the list."

Salǵeea squirmed in his seated position. He couldn't really get comfortable, nor had he ever been. He had begun work in the grower's fields at a half Áhthan year of age. Soon, the unrelenting work and horribly low wages he and his family earned had led to his theft of a bag of food destined for the shops in Etáin City. He was arrested, beaten after his judgment, and sentenced to *Gaoule*, an island prison off the coast of Éhpiloh that held thousands of Graćenta—and no hope. The conditions were harsh, and the food even less than he had gotten as a farmworker.

Orgo Talhínsa had been Salǵeea Calćoa's only friend at Gaoule. They met one day, and being of the same age and temperament, they formed a tight bond. Both swore to protect each other as best they could—not from the other prisoners—they were not the problem. They needed protection from the abusive guards.

Together, they hatched a plan to escape and recruited other young men to assist. In the end, once free, they had joined a faction of the Zakéema Front. But after almost a full year of fighting, the Zakéema fell. A new front emerged from the remains—slowly, carefully, with a different purpose: not to overthrow, not yet, but to aid the needy. It was Salǵeea's plan, and he led this new movement with Orgo as his tactical leader.

"We have rested long enough. The TSP patrols will widen, and they will use heat detector scans once it gets darker," Orgo instructed. "We better get going."

Salǵeea nodded, stood, and grabbed his shortgun.

"Remind me to stop leading from the front," Salǵeea said.

"I did remind you," responded Orgo. "You didn't listen. Again."

They moved west toward the Kryménos Falls. These were

spectacular, even by the standards of Tar Aséllo, measuring almost ten miles wide. Hidden behind the torrent of water were caves, created eons ago by the rushing falls that carried ice sheets and dense boulders, scraping and hammering the wall as they fell. The caves could be reached by entering an area to the far southeast, coming behind the water's edge, and making one's way carefully along slippery passages. Through these tunnels, one could access the myriad of caves that was the stronghold of the Enária.

Here were the weapons of the Front, as slight as they were, along with stored food taken by raiding parties from the Síndian fields, and more supplies donated by the supporters amidst the Graćenta. The Enária had technology here as well, mostly antiquated but still useful: scanners to track movement, old armband communicators, a single mobile Torchette missile array, two heavy armor cars—in sections and always under repair. Of course, the most essential resources were the four to five hundred armed soldiers and support personnel housed there at any given time. Some acted as spies, saboteurs, and supporters and were spread throughout the northern and southern cities—even within Etáin itself. There also was a new group of deep-cover operatives on a new mission called *Isos*.

Salǵeea and Orgo found their way to the eastern edge of the Kryménos Falls, where they were met by scouts that guarded the entrance. Joyous was the meeting, and soon communications were sent to the others that their leaders had returned.

7
Four Hundred Million Miles

Explorer Eleven took a bit more than a day to make the trip from Memaloose Island to the dark side of the moon. Eno kept Jee restrained—and rightly so.

She was extremely agitated, calling Eno names in Áhthan and English that no young lady should use, let alone know about. She kicked, thrashed, and twisted to no avail. The safety belts were strong and tight.

The only time she became calm was as they approached the moon and traveled to the far side to dock with the deep space module. Eno had released her then. Looking out the side viewport, Jee marveled at the large, white and gray structure. To her, it looked like a ten-story building. After a few communications from Vací, several lights began to blink on the module, and Eno piloted the ship into position. With a soft clicking sound, the docking was complete. After locking in, Eno initiated the transfer of the uranium he had 'gathered' on earth. It would recharge the deep space engines. Once completed, *Explorer Eleven* headed home.

Watching Earth slip away, Jee became upset. Still free from her bonds, she physically assaulted Eno with a metal dinner tray. He found it necessary to restrain her once again until she calmed down and promised no more violence.

Eventually, she was composed enough to be 'unleashed' and to roam *Explorer's* crew section. She was intrigued by all the equipment and, of course, the view. But after two days spent watching Eno go about his duties—checking supplies, organizing the many Earth samples, fawning over odd and mostly useless trinkets, and re-examining daily logs he kept while on Earth—Jee became depressed. She mostly stared out the main overhead viewport, looking behind the ship as it sped away from the shrinking blue globe, shaking her head and sniffling.

Eventually, she came to the conclusion that it did sort of make sense. She never really felt comfortable with anyone besides her parents. Though Eno was no more comfortable to be around than an irritating high schooler, he did seem to understand her, and she, him, in an odd way.

If I'm an alien, then that's what I am, she reasoned.

Jee had a thousand questions about Áhtha. They would pop into her head at random, but when she inquired, Eno would only say: "After our sleep, we will talk. Vací will wake us in plenty of time."

"How long will we sleep?" she asked.

"Four years," Eno stated.

Again, she became violent. Again, she had gotten the tray.

But, as before, Eno calmed her down. "Jee, it will take four years to reach Áhtha, but to you and me, it will seem like only a day! You will fall asleep, and *voila*, you will wake up a few weeks before our arrival; maybe a bit groggy, but not too disoriented."

As Eno prepared her command seat for the extended period she would be in cryogenic stasis, Jee showered in the lounge area. When finished, she donned a simple robe that Eno had given her, then drank an odd concoction that, to Jee, smelled like shoe polish and tasted like sour orange juice. He then helped her into her seat.

"It will be cold in here, right?" she asked. "Can I get a blanket?"

Eno laughed. "It doesn't work that way. You will be unconscious by the time the temperature drops enough to be uncomfortable. But if you would like a blanket, I will get you one."

"Please," she said, "and when you wake me, will I get some answers?"

"Absolutely," Eno promised. He retrieved a blanket from one of the many storage areas in the *Explorer's* cabin. "One thing I *will* tell you now, in response to a question I'm certain has been burning deep inside that head of yours, is yes, I really am your uncle."

Jee frowned. "I assume that was meant to make me feel better?"

"Goodnight, Jee," he said.

"This is weird," she mumbled, feeling sleepy. A yawn escaped. "I don't know about all this, Eno."

"I guarantee that what awaits you is a wonderful, amazing world where you will fall in love with the people, the cities, and the nature!"

Eno spread the blanket over her.

She grunted. "Really? It's not a creepy place with weirdos where everyone wears space suites all the time?"

"I will tell you this," added Eno. "It is most like a tropical island on Earth, always in twilight, warm and lush. Áhtha is, for the most part, as advanced as Earth. Maybe a little more advanced in the sciences but very similar. And cleaner!"

"Flying cars?"

"Actually, yes," he chuckled.

"Can we have one?" she asked with a slight smile, followed by yet another yawn. It was apparent she was fading fast.

"Of course. Good night, Glasśigh," he said.

"Good night...Uncle. Don't...forget...the...blanket..."

Eno watched as she drifted off into induced slumber, brought on by the shoe polish concoction.

"Vací, begin cryo-sequence on chair two."

The apparatus slowly descended, hissed, and locked.

Jee looked peaceful, he thought. For now. Wait until he told her that she was a...what was the Earth word? There really wasn't one that fit precisely. Her position didn't exist on Earth. Knowing her temper, she would either love the idea of her new role or clang him in the head with a metal tray.

Looking out the main viewshield, Eno gazed at the starfield ahead. Stars were not easy to see from the bottom of Tar Aséllo. The twenty-mile-wide opening at its widest, with Ofeétis in the way all of the time, made viewing them impossible. He remembered taking his astronomy and astrophysics classes and traveling in special craft to the surface to listen to radio signals from Earth. He was required to stay in those horribly uncomfortable observation stations for weeks on end. They were cramped, the food was vile, the wearing of cold gear and rebreathers when outside was unbearable, but the view! When Ofeétis eclipsed, the entire galaxy lit up. Four hundred billion stars. Four hundred billion suns spread out over one hundred light-years.

"Vací," he said, "what is the status of the Glasśigh's chamber?"

"Cryogenic systems at one hundred percent. No issues."

"Is she asleep?" he asked.

"Subject is unconscious. Breathing and heartbeat are slowing. One minute away from full cryogenic hibernation."

Eno stood up and then knelt down next to Jee's cryo-chamber. The outer glass on the lid had just started to freeze the moisture from the cabin, the condensation forming frosty crystals on the surface. As the visibility in the chamber slowly began to fade from the necessary gasses, he could still see her, eyes closed, simply beautiful, just as lovely as she had looked the night of the concert. Yes, she looked human, but it suited her. He thought she was even more beautiful than any Áhthan female. And what would that fact mean once in Tar Aséllo? She would look different than the others. Maybe he should undo what he did that made her look like an Earthling?

Better wait to ask her, knowing her temper.

As he was the only family she had, Jee was also the only family Eno had. That made him think. Would he and his niece return to a world far different from the one he left over eighteen Earth years ago?

"Vací," Eno said, returning to his seat. "Please begin command chair chamber for hibernation."

"Command chair cryogenic hibernation process beginning. When will you wake?"

"I'll need fifty Áhthan days prior to landing," he replied. That would do it. He could listen to some radio wave broadcasts and see what was going on. He planned to wake Jee a bit after that and get her prepared for arrival.

Eno soon drifted off to sleep while *Explorer* silently sailed through the dark, star-filled space-scape, engines still on, approaching the cruising speed of fifteen thousand miles per hour. Once attained, the engines would shut down, conserving fuel for the reentry breaking. It would take four years to travel the three hundred and eighty-eight million miles to Ganymede.

▲▲▲

The first thing Jee could make out was the dull glowing of twenty or so colored spots, primarily green and amber, with one or two red spots also flitting in and out of existence. At first, the spots were fuzzy, seemingly a few feet in front of her eyes. Then, after a few blinks and squints, they became clearer. She recognized these lights, but from where? A Christmas tree?

Or...was it the control panel of *Explorer Eleven*?

Yes, that was it!

Oh dear, Jee thought as the memories of the last few days flooded into her consciousness. It was not a dream. All that insaneness about being from Ganymede, being an Áhthan, Eno and his webbed feet...his nose...

It wasn't the past few days either, she finally realized. It was...over four years ago! That is what Eno had said; that it would be a four-year journey from Earth to Áhtha and that he would wake her before they landed. No wonder she was hungry. Her stomach ached and groaned loudly.

She remained still for almost an hour, or so it seemed. In that time, her vision adjusted to nearly normal, her motor skills returned, although she was weak. There was a slight moistening in her mouth. A tube! *Yuck!* She spit it out.

Jee moved in her chair, attempting to sit a bit more upright.

And where was Eno? she wondered.

"Good morning!" came a sing-song voice.

"Wha...guh," she slurred, slowly turning her head. There was Eno, semi-reptilian face and all. He held a clear tube with a straw-like device protruding from the top.

"Drink," he commanded playfully.

On his head was a wig of some sort but made of dark brown feathers.

"T-there is a bird on your h-head," she groggily pointed out.

"Yes, my mane. Here," he said, holding the drink close to her lips. He tilted the container, and liquid dripped into her mouth. It tasted like chalk and bubble gum. "Not water, but a refreshing concoction of nutrients and sugar-like substances to help you recover from your sleep. The weakness you are feeling is to be expected, but after a meal, your strength will return."

"I hate you."

"Back to your old, charming self, I see," retorted Eno. "Let me start something for breakfast! And let us only speak in Áhthan. You need to get in as much practice as possible. Luckily, I speak the language fluently. As do you, actually. I am simply *more fluent*."

And *more annoying*, thought Jee. But it did make sense. Áhthan it would be.

Soon her uncle returned with a plate of dried fruit and something that looked and tasted like strawberry ice cream. It was cold and refreshing. She devoured it.

"What was that?" she asked.

"Strawberry ice cream. Have you forgotten?"

Eno disappeared into the rear of the ship, then returned with a large flat-screen device similar to a television set but about the size of an open textbook and considerably thinner. He placed it on Jee's lap. It weighed almost nothing.

"What is this?" Jee asked.

"A personal display tablet. A PDT. It can be connected to the ship's central computer to access large amounts of data and even show text, images, and movies if you want to see them. I promised you I would answer your questions when we were nearing Áhtha. This will help. Ask away!"

He seems excited about this, Jee thought. She was really in no mood to learn anything, but what else was there to do?

"All right," she began with a yawn. "Why are there brown duck feathers on your head?"

"They are not feathers. It is called a mane. All adult Áhthans have fine branching fibrous structural protein strands on their head."

"They look like baby duck feathers," said Jee.

"Be that as it may, they are not feathers at all. Since I have not shaved my head since Earth, well, here I am! Mostly, Áhthan's have black or brown or gray manes. But the color changes depending on mood. See?"

As she watched, Eno looked upward in thought, and his mane color changed from dark brown to rich red at the edges.

"W-what in the hell…" she stammered.

"Happiness! I am happy! Happy to be almost home! With you!"

"That is just weird…"

"There are many colors you will see, each representing a mood, if you will. But only powerful moods. You will not have this ability, I don't believe," Eno said, pointing to his mane. "There was a surgical procedure. No more feathers for you. It's a long story."

"I don't want to know."

"A wise choice," he agreed, smiling as his mane returned to normal.

"Where are we?" she asked, still staring at his feathers.

"We are three and a half million miles from Jupiter at this time. But on Áhtha, it is called Ofeétis. Accent on the *FEE*."

"Why Oh-FEE-tus?" she asked, trying the pronunciation.

"In the ancient language, it means "seer" or "watcher." The clan kings and queens worshipped the planet as a god! The great storm? His eye!" Eno laughed. "Preposterous!"

Eno tapped the data tablet. As Jee watched, a diagram was displayed showing the ship's position and distance to Ofeétis and Áhtha. It also showed their path of travel and a few additional odd items Jee could not comprehend. One she did understand was the distance from Earth: 386,859,000 miles.

Jee considered this. The three and a half million miles more it would take to get to Ofeétis and Ganymede would take two weeks, as her uncle had said. That would be a long time to spend with Eno. Alone.

"What day is it?" she asked.

"The Earth date? Or the Áhthan date?"

"What's the difference?"

"Almost twelve years, actually," replied Eno. "An Áhthan year is longer. Ofeétis determines our years. So it takes Earth one Earth Year to travel around the sun. Ofeétis takes almost *twelve Earth years* to complete the trip."

"Hmm…" she responded.

"So, on Áhtha it is…" Eno checked the tablet. "The ninth day of the month called *Geet* in the year 1023."

"Wait…we left Earth on… December 22nd, 1956," she stated.

Eno looked upward as he calculated. "Correct. On Earth, it is

December 7th, 1960."

Jee thought of this. A cold shiver ran down her spine. "Eno? How old am I?"

"Again, in what measurement? If you were on Earth right now, you would be…twenty-three years old."

A wave of disbelief washed over her face. "Twenty-three? Geeze! Eno! I'm an old lady!"

He chuckled. "If it makes you feel better, divide that by twelve, and you get your Áhthan age."

"I'm… not even two?"

"Chronologically correct. But, considering you have been sleeping in cryo-sleep for four years—actually, if you count the trip *to* Earth, you have been asleep for eight!" Eno laughed. "That would make your *conscious* age even less! It is only…"

"Stop! Can we move on?"

Eno laughed uncontrollably for a minute. "Next question!"

"Who were my parents?" she asked, happy to change the subject. "I mean, who were Mr. and Mrs. Gallotta? Why didn't you just raise me?"

Eno shifted his position in his chair and paused for a moment. Jee noticed that his mane seemed to flash a bit whiter, but maybe it was the light reflecting off his feathers.

"I-I couldn't raise you," explained Eno, carefully. "You see, Jee, I needed to explore, and you needed to fit in. Taking an infant with me as I traipsed around the Earth, well, that wouldn't work. I spent a year on Memaloose setting up recharging systems for *Explorer* and searching for surrogate parents for you. I met the Gallottas in a church in Spokane. They were nice people, childless and hard-working. Your father came home from the war in 1944, early in the year. A wound rendered him unable to sire children. Still, he married his childhood sweetheart.

"I chose them to raise you because, being of the Italian race, they had darker skin—like your skin—and I thought it would be more believable. They lived in Spokane, but I convinced them to move to Coeur d'Alene, where no one would wonder where a little girl came from—as Mrs. Gallotta was never pregnant."

"And they agreed?" Jee asked.

"Well, I did pay them."

Jee simply nodded. She stood and slowly walked to the viewport to stare out at the starscape before her. She missed the Gallottas already. She missed the stories and the mock-battles she planned with her father and the late-night reading of history books, the cooking dinner and church visits with her mother.

All of it was over, Jee thought. And nothing to remember them by.

Then, she remembered the box. She ran to the rear of the crew section where Eno had placed her clothes. In the front pocket of her jeans, she found the small package Mr. Gallotta had given her. She hastily unwrapped the paper and opened the box.

Inside was a pin the size of a quarter. On it was a gold Sphinx in front of a skeleton key. Two lightning bolts flashed behind over an azure field. The words 'Always Out Front' were scrolled across the bottom. This, Jee knew, was her father's Army Intelligence Pin, for his planning of Operation Torch, the Invasion of Casablanca in 1942. It was dear to him and now, dear to her. Tears threatened her eyes but Jee forced the emotions down. If she started crying now, she knew she wouldn't stop. It'd be best to change the subject, talk about the future.

Eventually she returned to Eno.

"Who are my *biological* parents?" she asked excitedly. "Can I see a picture of them? I mean, you must have one."

Eno tapped his tablet and handed the device to Jee. In a moment, the screen displayed a very flattering picture of two Áhthans. Both were smiling, posing by a beautiful natural pool, surrounded by flowers and glowing green vines. A waterfall behind them sparkled in white and deep blue. The male's mane was dark, short, and wavy, with a few streaks of bright red flowing through. The slightly shorter female had a long, jet-black feathery mane that fell in waves to her waist. It, too, had red-colored stripes.

"Wow," said Jee. "They're both…so beautiful. And there skin is so dark."

"As is the skin of all Áhthans," said Eno, now pointing to the image. "Tye Ćlaviath and Dypónia Aséllo! See the red in their manes? Very happy!"

"Sy-*PO*-nia? What a beautiful name!" Jee exclaimed.

"To be sure! A famously stunning woman, your mother!" added Eno. "And your father, my brother, well…he was okay."

"Obviously, he got all the good-looking Ćlaviath family genes then," she teased.

"Humph!" pouted Eno. "They were very, very important members of the government and loved dearly by the people who live in Tar Aséllo. They were famous, you could say, as was I. This picture was taken on their wedding day, one could call it. You were born a few months later."

"And my parents," Jee asked, still looking at the picture, "they are still part of the government?"

She stared at him, watching his mane change color yet again.

"Your hair has gold on the edges," Jee said, concerned.

"Jee," he said softly. "Your parents are dead. I am sorry."

Jee seemed to catch her breath. She stared at the picture. Her face turned red, and she dropped the tablet to her lap.

"My dear…" said Eno, moving close to her and touching his forehead to hers, but there was nothing he could say.

Jee stood and quietly retreated into the rear corners of the ship. Eno could hear her sobbing softly. He thought it best to leave her alone.

About three hours later, Jee returned and motioned for Eno to join her in the lounge area.

"Tell me about them," Jee asked.

"This gets into some history," he began nervously, taking up the tablet. "Our tar was discovered and settled by *Ásue Aséllo* and *Jaydí Ćlaviath* over a thousand Áhtha years ago. They created a government structure that has, for the most part, remained unchanged. Your biological mother, Dypónia, was a direct descendant of Ásue Aséllo. Your father's name was Tye Ćlaviath. My last name is Ćlaviath."

"Is my last name Cuh-*lay*-vee-uth?" Jee asked, sticking out her lower jaw and again drawing out the syllables to point out the ugliness of the name. "I hope not. It's simply hideous."

"Hmm," Eno grunted, seemingly insulted, "not very nice. But no, you are not named Cuh-*lay*-vee-uth. On Áhtha, the firstborn is always named after the mother. That is why it would be proper to call you Glasśigh Aséllo."

"So, children take their mother's name?" Jee asked.

"Only the firstborn," explained Eno. "The second takes the father's name, the third the mother's, and the fourth, well, those parents usually are committed into insane asylums. He-he-he! A funny."

"No, not really," said Jee, unimpressed with Eno's humor. "So my great, great grandparents were like Christopher Columbus, the discoverer and…Thomas Jefferson, the architect of the laws in America?"

Eno thought about that for a moment, and though not exactly the same, it was a comparative assessment.

"Yes, that is a decent comparison," he said. "Or it would be…if Columbus and Jefferson mated and had children."

Jee thought for a moment as Eno chuckled at his own joke.

"So, what is all this Glasśigh stuff then? I mean, what is the big deal about me being a Glasśigh?"

"*The Glasśigh*," Eno corrected. "Ancient written history tells that

Ásue Aséllo was so in love with Jaydí Ćlaviath, that he wanted a daughter to love as well, to remind him of her. He also wanted the beauty that was in Jaydí to be part of the Asello family name. So, to accomplish that, he needed a daughter with a mother named Asello to keep the name and a father named Ćlaviath to bring those genes of beauty into the mix, as it were. This child would then have the name of Asello, but the beauty of the Ćlaviath family!"

"So...what happened to you?" she asked.

"W-what do you mean?" inquired Eno, perplexed.

"The Ćlaviath beauty? You didn't get any."

"Oh," grumbled Eno with a smirk. "Your feeble attempt at a humorous insult. Juvenile, I must say."

"That is so sweet of Ásue to want to have a daughter that reminded him of his wife!" said Jee. "How many Glasśighs have there been?"

"That is my point! You are the first! After more than a thousand Áhthan years, you are the only one. Ever."

Jee wrinkled her brow.

"I am the first and only? That is crazy! I mean, Tar Asello is...over twelve thousand Earth years old! You would think that some marriage of an Asello and a Ćlaviath would have produced a daughter!"

"Yes, one would," responded Eno. "But as I said, a *firstborn* daughter with the mother's *last name being Asello* and the *father's last name being Ćlaviath*. There have only been three unions of Asellos and Ćlaviaths in history where the mother was an Asello. But never was there a firstborn daughter—until you. And Asello was correct! Your beauty, even as an infant, is renowned all over the world."

"W-what?" she blurted out. "People know about all this?"

"Of course!" Eno answered with a giggle. "People, as you would say, 'go nuts' over you. 'Famous' would be too mild a word! The excitement of every Asellian during your mother's pregnancy, your birth, and your first few months of life reached unbelievable and unprecedented levels of complete fanaticism! The Minister of Media could never produce enough content to satisfy the citizenry—they were insatiable. I remember being interviewed for a seven-hour documentary focusing just on the day of your birth!"

"Eno...I..."

"Your face adorned endless articles and media files that saturated the tar-wide network," he continued. "News of your favorite food, your fantastic eye color, infant-like hair, not yet a mane, with its black ringlets, your first sounds, your sleep patterns—every conceivable factoid—was regurgitated by the media and digested by the citizens of Tar Asello. People viewed talk shows and documentaries with obsessive curiosity, and everyday conversations were filled with *Baby Glasśigh Talk*. There were dolls made in your likeness, and the Taźath, so overjoyed at your arrival, declared your birthday a national holiday! That is what happens when the first Glasśigh is born!"

There was a length of silence. Jee mulled this over, mostly shaking her head in disbelief.

"There is even a crown," Eno added. "Actually, the *Crown of Aséllo*, made by Jaydí. Only Ásue has worn it, but on his deathbed, he decreed that it is only for his Glasśigh, whenever she would come. I assume you could wear it, but it is *ceremonial* at best."

"I am *not* wearing a crown, Eno!" she declared, now afraid.

"Your head is probably too big! What is important here is that your parents were so fond of you. And proud," said Eno solemnly. "I loved them very much. And, well…you are…okay, I guess."

Jee ignored his tease. She pondered how incredible this had all unfolded. How odd it was. And how unbelievably sad her position. No parents at all? Anywhere?

"Eno, how did my parents die?"

Cautiously, Eno told her about the launch of *Explorer Eleven*, the tour, and the attack on Targan Base by the rebellious group, the Zakéema. He recounted her parents' death, the injuries he sustained crossing the bridge to the ship, and the unlikely events that unfolded in the last few moments that caused her to be rocketed to Earth.

Shocked by the news, Jee once again became quiet for a while. Eno patiently waited until she decided to continue. Eventually, after a few tears and skipped breaths, she began again.

"Zakéema? That means to strike, to hit," said Jee.

"Yes, and very good. They were a violent bunch and given arms supplied by Tar Fórtus, an old enemy of Tar Aséllo."

"So, the Zakéema, are they still…around?" asked Jee.

"According to the conversation we heard over my radio in Memaloose, they have been defeated," replied Eno. "Jee, be comforted in the fact that Áhtha is a peaceful world. War has been rare. Tar Aséllo had its last war against Tar Fórtus over thirty Earth years ago. And before that, there had been peace for over a thousand years. Now, that is not to say there are no issues. However, you, Jee, my little Glasśigh, you could be useful to help calm any strife that exists."

"W-what?" she stammered. "W-why? Why me? What do I have to do with all this?"

Eno reached out and took her hand.

"The Glasśigh is someone every Aséllian—regardless of position—will love and take an interest in. Not only because of your heritage and the love they had for your father and mother, but also, because, well, you grew up on another planet! And now your return will be greatly celebrated! You are an innocent in your own homeland. And a curiosity. People of all tars will listen to your words."

"But I'm no politician or negotiator," she protested. "I can't convince anybody of anything—"

"The riot?" prompted Eno. "Back at school? I would say you are a natural at persuasion."

She had forgotten that.

"Jee," continued Eno. "Worry not. You have no formal role in the government."

That calmed her. "So what does a Glasśigh do? What would you compare it to? On Earth?"

"That—that is a tough question. I have searched for an Earth term, a word that aptly describes it—and to be honest, the closest word appears to be," he paused and took a breath, "princess."

Jee's already wide and colorful eyes became larger and appeared almost luminescent as she considered his words.

"I- I'm a princess?" A disbelieving smirk appeared on her face. "Me?"

"As I explained previously," continued Eno as he held up his hand to suggest some caution, "it is the closest word I can think of in American English. Maybe another term would be…celebrity?"

"I'm a celebrity? Like a movie star? Eno!"

"Yes, yes. And then again, not really. Oh dear," he said, shaking his head. "I have been thinking about this for years, and I knew; I just knew I would fail miserably in the explanation! First, there is no royalty in Tar Aséllo, so though you might be treated *like* a princess, you are not actually a princess."

"What would I have to do? As the Glasśigh?"

"So, you could, if inclined, become an important member of the government. Even the Taźath, if you wanted—"

"Wait. Taźath? What is that? What does the Taźath do?" Jee asked, interrupting.

"To make a loose comparison, the position is like the President of America, but with more power," Eno stated. "The Taźath is the executive, to use the Earth word, but also controls the judges. If you chose this path, you would have to be duly elected. As in America. It is not a birthright, but you, because of your family heritage, *could* assume that office."

"What if I don't want that?" she asked flatly. "Because…I don't want that."

"Then, you, my dear, can simply enjoy the life of a princess," he said, smiling.

The excitement immediately returned to Jee's voice as a smile beamed across her face. "And, and what is that, exactly?"

"It would be expected that you, for example, attend dinners and festivals. Especially the Festival of Jaydí. Jaydí Ćlaviath was your ancient great-grandmother.. Maybe act as an honorary appointee of the Taźath? Maybe travel and be seen by the people? Choose a cause as the First Ladies of the American Presidents have done! People will be interested in your time on Earth. I assume you will be interviewed on the media—"

"Media?" she asked.

"Television," Eno clarified.

"So I just…have fun?"

Eno grinned. "For the most part, yes."

Jee smiled widely for the first time since she had looked at the stars from Memaloose Island that night they left Earth. She stood up and rushed to the front viewport and looked at approaching Ofeétis.

"So, are they expecting me?"

"With great enthusiasm and joy!" said Eno as he joined her. "They will probably proclaim our arrival day as a national holiday—yet another one in your honor!"

"What do you mean *another one?*" she asked, worried.

"Your birthday! It's like Christmas!" Eno exclaimed. "People exchange gifts!"

"Please tell me you are joking," she said, all color disappearing from her face.

"No, I am not."

If Jee was not shocked by all that was said before, this news had the effect of literally making her dizzy.

"I need to sit down."

Later, they finished a simple dinner of breaded trout and potatoes, followed by a dessert of huckleberries that survived the freezing process quite well, they agreed. They returned to the command area and took seats. As Eno worked at his command console, checking systems and the like, Jee wanted to begin the questioning again.

"Does everyone look the same?" she asked.

"For the most part, yes," answered Eno. "We have the same pigments and basic physical features; males and females are roughly the same size, though none of the other males are as handsome or charming as I."

"You're the best looking Áhthan male?" she asked. "That is depressing. What do people eat?"

"Mostly bugs and worms." Eno returned to his work at the main console. "Some fresh dirt is nice."

"Eno!"

"Ha ha! Oh! Had you!" he said with a laugh. "No, no, not bugs! A mixture of vegetable and animal matter, mostly fish. There is a huge ocean in Tar Aséllo, made up of eight connected seas. Bugs! Oh! I am a kidder!"

Jee thought about how long the next few weeks would feel. After a few scowls, she continued. "What is it like there?"

"Well," Eno said, "that is a tough question. Geologically? Biologically? Socially? Politically?"

"Just tell me about it," she urged. "Start anywhere!"

"All right," Eno activated his personal display tablet and tapped a few points on the screen. Images, animations, and movies displayed, detailing the specifics as he spoke. "Áhtha is smaller than Earth, about one-third the size. Almost the same area as America. Just over three hundred and forty million people are living there."

"Where do they live? On the surface?"

"No, no, nothing lives on the surface of Áhtha; too thin an atmosphere, temperatures are hundreds of degrees Fahrenheit below zero. Life exists in enormous canyons called *tars*.

"Tars," repeated Jee. "Big Canyons. Got it."

"The tars have an oxygen-rich atmosphere," Eno continued. "Since there are no seasons in the tars and a constant heat flow from thermal venting driven by the molten iron core, temperatures are steady at about eighty degrees."

"That sounds nice!"

"Yes," said Eno. "I would compare the tars on Áhtha to the lush tropical jungles of the Caribbean Islands. Or Hawaii."

"Wow!" Jee smiled; her eyes were wide with excitement. "Hawaii!"

"Indeed," Eno went on. "There are five major tars, each with its own government and leadership. The largest tar, the nation called Tar Éstargon, is over twenty-one thousand square miles."

"Is that a lot?" asked Jee.

"The Grand Canyon on Earth is about two thousand square miles, so I'd say so."

"Tar Éstargon is ten times bigger!"

"Your math power is truly dizzying," he teased. "To the east of Tar Éstargon, connected via a channel system within the subterranean ocean, is *Tar Asélło*. It is about seven thousand six hundred square miles of surface area. That is where we are from."

"Tar Asélło! Named after me?" she asked.

"Technically named after your great-great-grandfather," Eno corrected. "It is a mostly agrarian nation. When we left, the population was near seventy million. To the east of Tar Asélło is Tar Fórtus, the next largest tar.

"Then there is Tar Gorfínous, a small nation in size and population separated from the other tars and rarely visited by outsiders. It is somewhat of a mystery. Tar Monbíllious, just slightly smaller than Tar Asélło, lies on the western edge of Tar Éstargon. They are a modern society, as we say."

"So, are there robots walking all over the place?" she asked.

"Jee," said Eno shaking his head. "I told you that Earth and Áhtha are very similar in technology. There are no *robots walking all over the place!* People work! And have jobs! Well, most do. They live in houses, they eat at restaurants, they shop. But there are some differences. Obviously, Áhthan space exploration is many years more advanced than Earth's. Jet propulsion is standard for vehicular travel, and we have rocket-powered craft—you are in one! Our medical abilities and communication systems are a hundred years beyond what humans have."

"B-but are there computers and ray guns everywhere?" she asked.

"Yes to the first, and, well technically, yes to the second, but only on military craft."

"And flying cars?" she asked hopefully. "You said they had flying cars!"

"Jee, I have work to attend to with my collections in the rear portion of the ship." He stood and handed the PDT to his niece. "Vací, show the Glasśigh images of Etáin City."

Jee was stunned. On screen was what appeared to be a city built of glass situated within a deep canyon, glittering in the twilight.

"This is Etáin City," Vací said, *"population nine million. It is the capital of Tar Asélło."*

Jee saw that Etáin contained hundreds of elegantly tall skyscrapers made of shined metal and glass, much taller than any she had ever seen, even in pictures of New York City. Each was lit with the most beautiful white, blue, and amber lights. The buildings were mostly thin rectangular shapes stretching high into the dark sky. However, many had curved sections, and some had bridges connecting them to other structures at multiple points, hundreds of stories above the ground.

A video showed various angles and scenes of the city. At one point, floating lights of various colors, shapes, and sizes moved between the buildings in organized straight and curved lines, never intersecting yet connecting smoothly. To Jee, the lights looked like sparkling blood cells flowing through clear veins, twisting through the city at various heights.

"Vací!" she exclaimed in a sudden realization. "Are those the flying cars?"

"Yes," Vací stated, *"they are called skyliners or skycars. Some are autonomous, meaning no operator. Many are personal craft or delivery vehicles bringing goods to markets. On the lowest street level, there are* groundcars *of various sizes, types, and purpose."*

More images and video files showed different angles of the city, from far and near. The most spectacular file showed a view from the water as if taken on a boat, the metropolis growing right to the shoreline, where the most massive collection of towers stood.

The images changed, showing shorter buildings that looked like palaces made of smooth white stone, interspaced with climbing and hanging gardens, manicured parks, and open spaces. Many of the buildings looked as if they were growing out of high cliffs overlooking the city.

"It looks like a fairy tale!" Jee said, mesmerized. "But a *Flash Gordon* fairy tale!"

As the images changed, one in particular caught her eye. "Vací! Stop!"

The image on the screen was so beautiful and alien that Jee's mouth fell open in amazement. Built into a tall precipice of rust and white stone was a two-story mansion made of smooth, uniform, marble-looking blocks, polished and set precisely in place. The outer walls were curved, forming an elegant line that made one portion of the building jut outward to hang over the cliff, with a large balcony out front. There were blue-tinted glass windows almost everywhere along each wall to allow enjoyment of the spectacular view. There were pools and gardens built into the walls of the area; vines that glowed from some inner light crept and wound their way along the smooth stone.

"Where is that? The King's house?"

"The image is of One Palace Place, in the municipality known as Palace City, home of the Palace of the Tażath. It is reserved for visiting dignitaries."

For the next hour, Jee gasped and sighed at the beauty of Etáin and the surrounding villages. It looked like Oz to her, only more real and certainly bigger.

"Eno!" she called.

"Yes?" came his voice from the back of the crew section.

"Where will we live?"

"In a floating castle in the clouds, probably!"

"Eno! I will get the metal tray!" she warned.

"Probably a nice apartment-like structure in Etáin City," he said, now walking to the command deck to join her.

"Are there restaurants?"

"Yes, of course!" answered Eno. "At this little place I know, the fried dirt is especially good—"

She hit him in the shoulder.

"Animals?" she asked. "Are they weird?

"Since you are from Earth, they would seem so. Almost all have the ability to glow, usually a turquoise color. Some glow more than others. Plants too."

"Eno! I swear…"

"I'm serious!" Eno yelped. "Please! I am trying to work! Vací, show her the fields of Yamillia and some of the luminescent plants and animals native to Tar Aséllo."

Jee watched as the PDT displayed image after image, video after video, of the magical-looking Tar Aséllo: wide-open canyons with walls stretching up five miles high into a swirling blue mist that covered the opening; views of the night sky showing Ofeétis in various stages from full to the slightest sliver as it sailed mysteriously into eclipse; the greenest fields she had ever seen accented by glowing flowers and leaves; trees that grew as tall as skyscrapers or out of cliff faces; oceans of turquoise and green and blue; beaches of stark white, deep black and rich red sands—even one with powdery sea-foam green sand contrasted by shiny black boulders and dark palm-like trees that grew a quarter-mile high.

And the animals: countless types of birds that looked vaguely familiar, yet totally alien, some that even changed colors as they flew; pods containing hundreds of whale-like creatures swimming in a placid sea, each animal the length of a football field and looking like earth's dinosaurs; grazing herds of spindly, horse-like creatures with almost human faces and manes of frizzy blonde hair; jumping fish that lived in ponds embedded in the tar walls.

Most remarkable were the thousands of waterfalls, many dwarfing Niagara. Their streams of water traveling from the surface above and roaring past mile-high pinnacles of stone, their bottoms submerged in blueish-purple bays, their tops in the clouds. Mostly tropical, Tar Aséllo appeared to be an Eden.

All Jee could do was gasp at each image or video Vací offered.

"Maybe, this place won't be as bad as I thought," she said to herself. "And, well, I *will* be a princess!"

She laughed at the notion. She had heard that people in Coeur d'Alene used terms like 'pragmatic' and 'serious' and 'unassuming' to describe her. But after the riot, as some called it, and after her singing engagements, she felt that maybe she could enjoy a bit of notoriety. After all, once in Tar Aséllo, she was going to be a celebrity—that would happen if she welcomed it or not. She might as well get used to it. There could be worse positions!

One perplexing subject came from viewing a particular image of Etáin. In the corner of a photograph, amid towering skyscrapers, was a sign on the side of a building. It had a simple black background and an Áhthan letter in the center. It was the letter that represented an English 'T', followed by a phrase. It took Jee a few seconds to translate it: *'Know Your Place.'*

"I wonder what that is about?" she muttered.

"*It is a societal phrase displayed to citizens as a direction.*"

"A direction?" asked Jee. "To get to somewhere?"

"*As a direction for living one's life in a purposeful manner.*"

Jee frowned.

"How many more of those signs are in Tar Aséllo?"

It took a second or two before Vací answered.

"At the time of our departure, one hundred seventy-two thousand seven hundred and fifty-two."

"That…that is a lot," Jee said, surprised, "I didn't see that in any other photos of Etáin."

"They are almost all in the northern area of Tar Aséllo, in the Oso-Gúrith province," stated Vací.

"Why is that?" asked Jee.

"That is where the Graćenta, the workers, live," came the answer.

"And why do the Graćenta need to see this message and the others do not?"

Vací was silent.

"Vací?" Jee probed.

"They need to be told what to do."

"Why? Are they…stupid or something?" asked Jee, now becoming irritated. "Listen, Vací. Tell me about the Graćenta."

There was a silence as if Vací was thinking. Then, *"There is no further information on this subject."*

Over the next few days, Jee spent considerable time with Vací and the PDT. She remained in the more comfortable lounge area on a cozy reclining chair, sipping weird but tasty juice-like concoctions Eno had created.

"How was your time with Vací?" asked Eno as he passed by.

"I still have some questions. What is music like on Áhtha? I can't find any at all."

"There is music!" objected Eno, looking up from his work.

"Vací only found sounds of drums and banging stuff," said Jee. "And people talking over it all."

"Is that not music?" Eno asked.

"No, it's not," she stated firmly.

They remained in silence for long moment.

"Eno…are you telling me…"

"Yes, yes, just drums!" Eno snapped. "But some are tuned!"

"That's it?" she asked, shocked.

"Hmm…" sighed Eno. "Earth is more, how do I say, *involved* in music than Áhtha, I am afraid. Sometimes more advanced music can have a strange effect on Áhthans. They get…they get emotional. Deeply."

"So just drums," she grumbled, looking out the viewshield. "Turn this thing around. Immediately."

"That reminds me," Eno continued. "Singing. I believe it would be best for you not to sing, at least not right away."

"What? Why not?"

"Trust me," he said, holding up his hand to make a point. "Áhthans have strong emotions, and singing can profoundly affect them, much more than how Earthlings respond. Please do as I say? Please?"

Odd, thought Jee. But he was the expert.

"Fine. No singing," she sighed. "At least not in public."

Explorer Eleven began to slow as it approached Áhtha. As they were only days away, there were frequent communications from the ship to Tar Aséllo. Most questions were about the health of the crew (good), the ship's condition (excellent), and requests for news of Earth (boring).

Eno was both surprised and happy that one of the first voices he heard was that of Pronómio Tok, his old friend, who had successfully been appointed Taźath. Pronómio informed him that as of today, he was no longer the Minister of Science but a member of the *High Ministers Council*. Eno told Jee it was an honor and a promotion.

"I will be spending the rest of my life disseminating the trove of information I have gathered from Earth," Eno haughtily explained, adding a wave toward the rear storage compartments where his collection was stored. "I assume there will be other missions, surely to formally contact Earthlings as they couldn't possibly have another war. I will plan the missions, of course."

Even more than these subjects, the communications from Targan Base were filled with requests to hear the voice of the Glasśigh. At first, Jee would only listen; she was too embarrassed to say anything. She doubted her ability to speak the language effectively.

"Eventually, you will have to speak, Jee," he pointed out. "And I can assure you that your Áhthan is perfect. Please, let us call home, eh?"

Jee sat in the command chair and cleared her throat. She nodded to Eno.

"Vací," he said. "Open an audio communication link to Targan Base."

"Link open," Vací stated.

"Do you hear us, Targan Base? This is *Explorer Eleven*," Eno said, aiming his voice to the microphone on the control panel.

Almost instantaneously, the response came.

"Yes, we hear you clearly," said the voice.

"And we hear you," responded Eno. "Someone aboard would like to say hello to Tar Aséllo. Would that be acceptable?"

"Is it the Glasśigh?" the voice asked excitedly. *"Is it? Because if so, we will patch in the Aséllo media outlets to broadcast! Everyone in the world wants to hear!"*

Jee was suddenly uncomfortable again. "Oh, dear."

"That would be fine," said Eno as he placed a steadying hand on Jee's arm. "We will wait for your word to proceed."

"Thank you, Explorer Eleven! Please stand by!"

Jee looked at Eno with a nervous smile.

"What should I say?"

"Start with 'hello' and then maybe how you feel about returning home? That should get things started."

"All right." Jee wet her lips, cleared her throat, and sat up straight. She fussed a bit with her hair.

"They can't see you, dear," said Eno.

"I know, I just want to, you know, be alert," she mumbled.

Targan Base came back on the radio, and immediately Jee could tell things were excited down there. There were voices in the background, all high pitched and sputtering. There was clapping.

"Hello, Explorer Eleven! So exciting this is! Can you hear us?"

"Yes, we can," answered Eno.

"Please wait for the Taźath!"

Jee looked at Eno and smiled as she whispered: "the *Taźath?*"

Eno also smiled and whispered back. "He doesn't bite."

There was a silence, some clicking noises, and then:

"We interrupt your program to bring a message from the Taźath. Stand by."

Another pause, then:

"Greetings, fellow Aséllians," boomed a strong and deep voice. *"This is your humble servant, Pronómio Tok, Taźath of Tar Aséllo."*

"Ooh! He sounds...official!" whispered Jee excitedly. Again, Eno patted her on the arm.

"As you know, we have been in communication with Explorer Eleven, and I am also sure that each of you, in every class, has been watching the programming about this historic mission. You have also heard the great news that not only is Commander Eno Ćlaviath aboard, but the Glasśigh herself! Ah, our little Glasśigh! Glasśigh, the light of Áhtha! She who had left us, presumed dead and lost forever—"

Jee wrinkled her brow.

"—lost in the stars, leaving the entire tar, no, the entire world, in a state of shock and sadness. But now, now she is returning and will actually speak to us for the first time! Explorer Eleven, do you hear us?"

Jee looked at Eno, waiting for him to say something.

Eno shook his head and pointed to Jee, then the microphone section of the radio panel.

Jee shook her head as if to say, *'I'm not talking first.'*

Eno's brown eyes widened, and he motioned again, then leaned back as if to say, *'I am staying out of this.'*

Jee, resigned not to keep the Taźath waiting, took a deep breath, and responded, using her softest, smoothest voice possible. "We hear you, Taźath. This is Glasśigh Aséllo responding from *Explorer Eleven.* Hello to all on the good world, especially Tar Aséllo."

Eno looked at her with an admiring yet surprised face. He nodded his head in approval.

Over the radio, they could hear a noise that sounded, at first, like static, but after a few moments, Jee and Eno realized that it was applause and cheering.

"Ah! Glasśigh! Our Glasśigh!" exclaimed the Taźath. *"It is her! The light of Áhtha! The lyrical voice of beauty and goodness! Raise your voices, Tar Aséllo, raise your voices in celebration!"*

"Dear, dear, dear," muttered Jee softly, now a little nervous.

The cheering went on for a full minute.

"Excuse us, Glasśigh," continued the Taźath. *"We have been anticipating the sound of your voice for too many long years! The people of Tar Asèllo, in all modes of life and duty, the Kořeefa, the Merćenta, and the Graćenta—are joyously awaiting your return! And Commander Eno Ćlaviath as well! But forgive me for my excitement. Are you well?"*

"Yes," answered Jee. "Uncle Eno has been an excellent doctor all these years."

The crowd, wherever they were, cheered again.

"He is the most skilled we have, my dear Glasśigh," affirmed the Taźath. *"Eno Ćlaviath is the best you could hope for."*

"Except for cutting off my fingers, yes, I would agree!" Jee added, laughing a bit.

Eno looked at her with a shocked expression.

Jee realized that perhaps that bit of information could be misunderstood. She mouthed "sorry" to Eno and then stared at the radio for a moment.

"Y-your fingers?" asked the Taźath.

Wincing, she thought that she might as well explain. Better now than when they see, and notice, that she didn't look like a garden snake.

"Yes, you see, dear Taźath, when we were living on Earth, I couldn't walk among the people looking like a, a baby sna—" she caught herself. Not that they would know what a snake was, but why bring that up? She continued, a little more guarded. This was harder than she had thought.

"—I-I mean looking like an Áhthan. So the good doctor had to alter me, and himself, to look more like the people of Earth."

"I see," said the Taźath.

Eno jumped in.

"She is, as she has always been, a beauty, even today looking quite like an Earthling. You will see! Such radiant eyes and flowing—"

"I am so very excited about returning home," Jee graciously interrupted, slapping Eno away from the microphone. "I have seen videos and pictures of Áhtha and Tar Asèllo, and I must say it is a beautiful and wondrous place. I can't wait to see it all—if that is allowed!"

"But of course, Glasśigh. Anything you desire!" assured the Taźath. *"Can you tell us a little about your time on Earth?"*

Jee thought for a second. Where to begin? What was the most significant difference? The people? The planet? What was the most interesting thing?

"That is a hard question to answer," she finally said, "but, I can tell you that my days were filled with learning in a school, and there were other children there, and I lived in a small house with the Earthlings that raised me. Eno was nearby but was gone exploring the great planet often. I liked Earth, though I was a bit taller than the other young women—"

"And stronger!" added Eno, "Why, one time these two ruffians—"

"And I loved to be outdoors and walk in the wooded areas," Jee interrupted, slapping Eno again and frowning. "And the food was wonderful! Delicious!"

More cheers.

"We must tell you that we are planning a little celebration in your honor," announced the Taźath. *"Would that be all right?"*

"Of course, Taźath," she said. "I assume I will be able to meet many people? I would like that."

"Yes! We will introduce you to the most important members of the Kořeefa! And media interviews for all classes. And there will be great feasts and maybe even some entertainment."

"That sounds delightful," replied Jee. She smiled widely at Eno.

"The festivities will be cast across the tar, and I assume in our neighboring countries as well! It should last at least two full days!" the Taźath added.

"Oh! How long, Eno, is that in Earth hours?" she asked, expecting some smaller period.

"Umm…fifty-six hours."

"Wow," she said, dropping all propriety and character to her voice.

Cheering again.

"Wow!" repeated the Taźath. *"Wow! I am not sure what it means exactly, but I assume it is an exclamation of joy?"*

"Um…yes."

"Then, we will let you prepare for the celebration!" said the Taźath. *"And I can assume that I speak for every grateful and excited Asėllian when I say we extend our best wishes for a safe return. Welcome home, Glasśigh!"*

Insane cheering, hooting, and clapping came through.

"Thank you so much, Taźath, and thanks to all on Áhtha," Jee said. "And before we go, is there anything we can do for you?"

There was a pause. Eno looked at her a bit oddly, but then again, it was Eno, and he always had an odd look on his face, especially since losing his nose. After a few more moments of silence, Jee worried if she had violated some Áhthan protocol by asking if she could do a favor for the Taźath. Or was it just that being cooped up on *Explorer* would make doing a favor for anyone simply ridiculous. It wasn't like she could stop at the grocery store and pick up a huckleberry pie for the party.

"You see?" said the Taźath, his voice almost cracking with emotion. *"Gone all these years, and our wonderful Glasśigh asks if* we *need anything! Wow, if I must say so! Wow! Do you see the grace in her? I do! She knows her place, and she offers to do more than her share. That is our Glasśigh!"*

The cheering lasted a full two minutes

Jee thought that Tar Asello might be a bit weird and take a little time getting used to.

"I'll take that as a no, then," she muttered softly.

"Goodbye, for now, Glasśigh! This is Tar Asello ending transmission!" concluded the Taźath, and the connection terminated with a simple *click.*

Jee exhaled loudly. "That was…weird."

"I think it went quite well," said Eno, "except for the part about me cutting off your fingers; however, I assume no harm will come of it. They will find out eventually that you look different." He paused, looking at her. "Maybe we should transmit a picture of us back to Áhtha, so they know what to expect? Your skin is a few shades lighter, and you do have a protruding nose. I can't remove that without serious and probably permanent scarring. Maybe you should keep it?"

"Of course I will keep it!" she said, shocked at the notion. "But I understand. A photo would be a good idea. What do I wear?"

"For the picture? What you have on is fine. I don't see—"

"Eno! Wait! Our arrival and the celebration!" she screamed.

"What of it?" he asked.

"What do I wear? I mean, I can't show up in my school clothes, for the love of Pete! I need something to wear!"

"Oh," said Eno. "I see. Well, not to worry! Formal functions on Áhtha require all parties to be totally nude."

"W-what!?" Jee exclaimed.

"Ha ha ha! J-just kidding! Oh, I had you there, I did! You should have seen your face!"

"Eno, so help me, I will kill you and land this thing myself!"

"Yes, yes, all right," he replied, still laughing. "You will need a formal gown, and though we do not have one, I will call ahead and have one sent to the ship upon our landing."

"I can get dressed quickly!" she assured him excitedly.

"Yes, but you will need to make it very quick. It would not be proper to keep the Taźath and the media cameras waiting."

"I agree. Uh, Uncle? The Tażath mentioned the classes of people. What is that all about?"

Eno paused, and he looked down for a moment. He did not want to have this discussion, not without more preparation. Maybe, he thought, he could water it down a bit?

"Jee, Tar Aséllo is not like Earth, not physically and not socially and not politically. It would take a long time to explain it completely, and most is not really in the history archives. So let us say that the *Koŕeefa* are the most educated, well-thought-of, most important people on the planet responsible for running things. Does that make sense?"

"So the Koŕeefa…they are the government people?"

"Yes, but also industry, military, and education leaders," Eno said. "The names are labels. Koŕeefa, Merćenta, and Graćenta. It relates to their function, their jobs. Merćenta are sort of…the managers of the work people do."

"Okay. I guess that's like Earth then. Some people are educators, some managers, and some…dig ditches," Jee added.

"Yes!" Eno said, relieved. "Very much like America. It is a grouping of people and functions. Is that sufficient?"

"I am not sure, but I will think about that," Jee said. "There's a lot to think about!"

"You have the rest of your long life," Eno added with a smile.

Later, after a meal of mostly dried vegetable matter that Eno explained was a vat-grown compound that resembled real Áhthan food, he announced a surprise for Jee. He handed her a box made of lightweight metal. It snapped open the instant Jee touched the lid with her finger. Inside lay a slender band, less than an eighth-inch thick, two inches wide, and about six or seven inches long. It was silver, with a small glass-like screen and several flat, button-like sections. The metal was etched and cut beautifully, with beveled edges.

"What is this? A watch?"

"It is an *ABC*," Eno corrected, "an Arm Band Communicator, and a very advanced one. At least it was when I left Áhtha. This particular model was made in Tar Éstargon."

"And this silver material?" Jee asked. "It's beautiful! What is it? Steel?"

"It's actually silver," said Eno. "That band was DaJees's, one of the explorers killed before our untimely launch from Targan Base. The Ef Keería, the leader of Tar Éstargon, gave it to her as a parting gift. Wear it well."

"What do you do with it? Here! Help me put it on!"

"You slip it over your wrist," Eno instructed as he assisted her. "There. This one is extra special. It is like a PDT but also has a hologram projector and scanning camera. You can take a three-dimensional picture with it, and it will store that in its core, or send it to Vací."

"It has Vací in there?" she asked.

"No, but it is connected to her. You may access Vací from anywhere on the ship. After we land, you will still have access to her, as she is actually present everywhere."

"You mean everywhere? How?"

"A worldwide radio wave network. Millions of computers are linked together, and that ABC gives you access to all of it. Most of it, anyway. Entertainment, educational data, businesses—enjoy!"

"Impossible!" she exclaimed in disbelief.

Using the armband was fun. It had a high-quality 3D holographic projector that was so advanced, it looked like every video or image shown was physically there. The band also contained a small display screen in case one needed to have privacy in her communications. And the best feature, as far as Jee was concerned, was Vací.

Jee and Eno used the ABC to take over fifty images of themselves, using the built-in holographic scanner. With Vací's help, Jee picked her favorite. Eno transmitted the image along with requests to Targan Base for proper attire that would befit the Glasśigh and himself.

What was this going to be like? Jee wondered. By the way the Taźath acted, spoke of her, and the crowd cheered, it seemed as if they expected a celebrity like Clark Gable—or more accurately, Marilyn Monroe! What would a young woman from Idaho do to impress them? What did her mother—well—what did *Mrs. Gallotta*, tell her to do when she was nervous in front of people? Oh yes: *Take it slow, and if you don't know what to say, say nothing.*

▲▲▲

Behind the protection of the Kryménos Falls, Salǵeea and Orgo, along with five hundred others, went about their lives. This area was originally an intricate series of naturally formed cracks and caves that reached into the tar wall itself, creating small rooms, large openings, and a myriad of twisting hallways. Once power was established and certain sections expanded and modified, this cave city became the Enária Front's main stronghold.

Some relaxed and ate; others planned raids on unprotected shipments of food from the Síndian Fields and medicine from the factories in the city of Éhpiloh. Technicians repaired the few weapons and vehicles that were housed in the caves.

"The Glasśigh is almost here," sighed Orgo as he finished a healthy portion of fruit. "Glasśigh Aséllo. What does that mean for us?"

"What does it mean for us?" repeated Salǵeea. "I am not sure. It most likely will be bad. It is always bad for us, Orgo. The Graćenta and the few Merćenta who support us may become preoccupied with her...doings."

Salǵeea realized that with the return of the Glasśigh, she would take center stage in the life of every Aséllian, regardless of their class. To the rich and powerful, the Kořeefa and Merćenta, she represented the elite nature of their standing. The thought of a member of the two founding families returning was a great joy and a reaffirmation of their position as the leaders and privileged ones of Áhthan society. To the lowly Graćenta, the main supporters of the Front, the Glasśigh was a descendent of the past heroes before the rigid caste system came to be. She would remind the Graćenta of ancient times when there were no laws to keep one in one's place. All were equal then, as was the playing field.

"They will love her," said Salǵeea.

"They already do," said Orgo. "I heard the call from Commander Ćlaviath and the Glasśigh on the media feeds last week. People went crazy. And, the Arena of Asèllo is completed. They will have the landing there. Parades, festivals..." He sighed. "A holiday has been declared."

Salǵeea stared down at the stone floor of the cave. He could only shake his head. "This diversion will kill our recruitment. I can't be one hundred percent sure, but I feel it. Too bad she is not on our side."

"Then," suggested Orgo, "somehow we have to get to her."

Salǵeea took a deep breath and exhaled. "We could use Isos."

"Isos? Isos is untested," countered Orgo. "The whole idea is dangerous. It's too new."

"But in position, yes?"

"*Scheduled* to be in position," corrected Orgo. "But...it would take a major effort to speed things up a bit. We could be ready just before *Explorer Eleven* lands, maybe right after. I don't know...."

Salǵeea was resigned to it, Orgo could see. For all his physical frailty, he was still a tough leader. It was his call.

Salǵeea looked at his friend with determined eyes.

"Do it."

8
The Return of the Glasśigh

Geet 21, Áhthan year 1023

"Ganymede," was all Eno said as *Explorer* rounded the planet Ofeétis.

In front of them was the grayish-green moon, scarred with dark, dull purple cracks and impact craters filled with splintered ice. Jee witnessed blue and gold auroras: shimmering colored curtains, spouting from the northern hemisphere and another to the south, reaching hundreds of miles into space. Though dark and foreboding, Ganymede—or Áhtha, as Jee was now used to calling it—had a mysterious beauty.

Eno slowed the ship almost to a complete stop and had Vací disconnect the deep space module before releasing it in orbit around Áhtha. Once free, he piloted the crew module onward, descending into the thin atmosphere and leveling out a few thousand feet above the surface. Over the gray-white plains of Áhtha they went, past rolling ice dunes, alongside massive stone mountain ranges peeking up through the frozen shelf, and around countless crystalized water geysers that formed an enormous glass forest as far as the eye could see.

A gentle smile of nostalgia crossed Eno's face. "Each slender ice tower is as tall as an Earth skyscraper. Beautiful, isn't it?"

Jee could see an interesting curling at the top of each geyser, a flourish of white and clear crystal. Down each tower's side were rows upon rows of translucent greenish icicles, each the size of the greatest Idahoan pine. They appeared like daggers pointing downward, becoming sharper and thinner as they descended.

"It is as if the moon itself created these frozen arms and hands," whispered Eno, "reaching into the very edge of space to grasp at the darkness."

"Poetic," said Jee, impressed. "Are they dangerous? The geysers?"

"They do fall from time to time," replied Eno. "They are created by the thermal venting caused by Áhtha's molten iron core. At various places in the tar, there are vents of great heat that rise through the mantle, but many times, they rise through the oceans that lay beneath. The oceans literally boil in some areas! Immense heat and pressure cause tons and tons of liquid to be rocketed through gaps in the stony crust, all the way through the surface. Some of the holes are as wide as a city block, and the water can spray up over two thousand feet! That is taller than the Empire State Building! Then, they freeze. As new geysers are formed, they blast into the existing towers from below."

Something caught Eno's eye. "Oh! Look! There is one being formed right now!"

"It is knocking down that big one!" marveled Jee as she watched the spectacle.

"It happens! But do not be alarmed. Just don't go wandering around up here!" Eno said with a laugh. "Ah, almost there!"

Immensely long yet narrow lakes on the surface of the moonscape came into view. An eerie blue glow came from these areas, seemingly a thousand miles long and so thin, like a crack in the ice. As they neared, it was soon apparent that the lakes were not bodies of water; rather, they were large pools of mist, slowly swirling as they hugged the surface of Áhtha.

"Vací showed me! Those blue, misty things!"

"They are called *fálouse*," Eno said. "It is the atmosphere you see; the breathable atmosphere. Below is Tar Éstargon, by far the largest of the Tars of Áhtha. Our home, Tar Aséllo, is over one hundred miles longer than Idaho is from top to bottom! Its width is fifty miles at its widest, but in some areas, it is less than a mile wide! Hard to comprehend, isn't it?"

"That, dear Uncle, is a really big hole," she replied nervously.

Eno looked at her and frowned. "A hole, indeed! What a caution you are!"

Continuing onward, Jee soon saw another swirling fálouse on the horizon, hiding the wonders beneath.

"Tar Asréllo!" gasped Eno, his voice full of emotion. "We are home!"

Eno activated the communication link to Targan Base and was instructed to follow a predetermined course on their approach to Etáin City, located at the center of the tar. Jee gave a start as Eno put the craft in a steep dive. Speed dramatically increasing, the ship's engines whined.

Jee's eyes opened fully as Ofeétis, now above them, reached eclipse; a flash of the distant sun around its edge marked the end of light and the coming of near-absolute darkness. Within this deep shadow, they plunged into the glow of the thick swirling fálouse that covered the entire tar.

Suddenly, they were through.

With no light from Ofeétis, Jee expected the entirety of the tar to be dark. However, she found that Tar Asréllo was bathed in a cyan glow which emanated from the tar itself. In the center below stretched an ocean, spanning from the west to the east as far as Jee could see. The water rippled, sparkling in brilliant hues of blue, although streams of green, silver, and even gold shone through.

"Oh! It's…" Jee's voice caught in her throat. The wonderment was overwhelming.

"It is the bioluminescence!" Eno explained. "Many creatures, especially the microscopic ones, have the ability! They are literally everywhere in the surface layers of the seas. Chemicals in their bodies, under the right conditions, create an illumination. Many plants have the same quality! Look!"

Eno pointed ahead to the far northern shore. Becoming more discernable with each second, Jee could see the land reaching away from the far canyon edge toward the water. The glow from the plants and trees created a silvery-green twinkling blanket of life. Within this land, Jee could make out the shape of precise circles and squares of different earthly hues. Farms? she wondered.

Jee was at a loss for words. Was this the same Ganymede that her schoolmate, Gary, had called a 'dead and lifeless world'? It was anything but.

"We are in the day called *Eclipse*," Eno told her. "The tar's glow is especially colorful today! Ah, I have missed this place."

Jee gasped as she beheld the massive openness of Tar Asėllo, exposed in its glittering, fantastical twilight. The tar was incomprehensible in its depth, width, and height. They seemed to float above it all, motionless, though Jee knew that the craft was still falling at a tremendous rate.

In what could only be cities, Jee saw a more uniform display of lights coming from windows within structures, signs, street lamps, and purposely planted trees.

Eno turned the craft slightly to the right and proceeded toward the city below. As they approached, and more details could be discerned, Jee noticed other vessels in the air: thousands of sleek and mostly silver machines, lights flashing, moving in an orderly fashion along lanes that crisscrossed the air above the cityscape. Eno did not fly in these lanes, however. He proceeded higher above them. *Explorer* was larger than the other craft by ten times at least, and there seemed to be a path cleared for it, leading into the heart of the city.

After a few moments, several different-looking ships approached. Even sleeker than the others, these were mostly shiny chrome and bore two after-burner turbo-fan engines, one under each of two wings, glowing with a hot red-orange fire. About the size of the World War II *Corsairs* Jee had seen at the airshows in Coeur d'Alene, these ships were more streamlined than those, their mirror finish reflecting the city's lights below

Four approached, flying in formation, then split into pairs, taking positions on either side of *Explorer*.

"What are those?" asked Jee excitedly as she unbuckled herself and ran to the viewshield.

"Aréus A4 Fighters!" Eno said. "They are part of the Aséllo Military Forces, the AMF. And these particular ships have a "U" character on their tails, as one can see. These are part of a much larger wing of the highest echelon of our air forces! The *Ultos Wing* they are called! Heroes, all!"

"What are they doing?"

"They are here to escort us home!"

Jee watched as one of the ships drew extraordinarily close, within feet it seemed. She could see the craft in detail, to the point of being able to clearly make out the pilot. He appeared to be a young man. He wore something on his head, like earphones made of thin metal, which somehow emitted a soft, pale-blue glow. She could make out his tiny, flat—yet somehow cute—nose. He smiled and performed a salute: a single index finger to his forehead followed by a smart outward movement in her direction.

She smiled and performed the same salute in return.

The pilot grinned widely, then resumed his position in the formation.

"They look like those Chevy Corvettes," Jee said excitedly, "but they are airplanes! And silver! With really big jets! I would have expected rocket engines and all that."

"They are after-burner turbo-fan engines, to be exact," Eno corrected. "Remember that the tar is only six hundred miles long. For most non-military airships, basic jet propulsion technology is more than efficient to cover our transportation needs."

Again, Jee looked through the main viewshield. The buildings became denser and much taller as they neared the city center.

"Look!" Eno said as he piloted the craft onward. "There!"

Directly ahead, beyond the clustering of a hundred metal and glass skyscrapers, Jee could see a massive oval structure placed in the middle of a spacious, riverfront park. It dwarfed the surrounding constructs except for the tallest buildings. It had to be over three hundred feet high, a bowl-like shape made of white and gray stone. It was topped with golden metal spires of random and various heights extending into the sky, each lit in an array of bright, sparkling colors.

A white light shone from within the arena, the glow projecting into the tar's upper atmosphere, seemingly hitting the fálouse above.

"W-what in the name of..." was all Jee could say, her mouth literally wide open in amazement.

"Ah, the Arena of Aséllo! The Tażath's pride and joy! What a fantastic site! We will land there!"

Jee could see throngs of people waving from below and from windows of the skyscrapers, a sea of bright-eyed, serpent-like faces, smiling and calling out in joy. Unsure if they could see her, she waved back. Looking sideways in both directions, she caught glimpses down side streets of the great city. As far as she could see, people lined the roads.

"Eno, they have dark skin!" she exclaimed. "Will mine get that dark?"

"Eventually. Do you have a problem with that?" he asked.

"Well, no. I guess it may take some getting used to."

Then, something else caught her eye.

Was it raining? Jee wondered. Upon closer observation, Jee realized that falling and fluttering from the sky were flowers, flowers of every color and shape. Thousands of them were being tossed from windows of skyscrapers that lined the streets, each one bioluminescent, glittering with an inner light.

"Eno, I..." Jee began, but no other words came.

"Speechless? That's a nice change," Eno said with a chuckle. "I am sure at least some of this is for me, but yes, *Glasśigh*, this is really all for you. But don't let it go to your head, as the Earthlings say." He laughed aloud. "I love that phrase! I mean, where else would it go? The brain is there! In the head!"

Explorer Eleven reached the stadium, and the craft hovered in the center above the crowd. Jee and Eno could see that to the east, jutting out from the stadium's inner wall, was a fifty-foot-tall stone promontory. Its top was oblong and flat, at least two hundred feet long and a hundred feet across. Around the front half of the structure was a ten-foot-wide ring of water that cascaded over the promontory into a deep pool below. Submerged lights of gold and amber lit the falling water and billowing mist. On the top, embedded dead center into the stone itself, were pulsing red lights that made a perfect fifty-foot circle.

"I would assume," said Eno, flicking a few switches on the control panel, "that must be my parking space! Oh, I am funny. Of course it is!"

Explorer Eleven descended into the bowl. Over the engines' noise and the whine of the hover blades, Jee heard cheering. Looking outwards, she saw what had to be over two hundred thousand people sitting in the stadium.

No, not sitting; standing.

As the ship descended further, Jee saw what looked like television cameras tracking their every move. On the far end of the arena was a massive screen at least three hundred feet wide and almost that in height, displaying the image Eno had taken aboard *Explorer*. Since the original was made in 3D, the view on the screen rotated, allowing a view of Eno and the Glasśigh from every perspective.

"Oh my God, no!" she gasped, horrified. "Look at that forehead! Eno! I look like an alien!"

"To them, you *do* look like an alien," he said.

They watched as the picture on the massive screen changed to display the ship landing.

"Better get to the rear! Be ready to change into whatever gown they bring before those drone cameras poke through a viewport! They are everywhere!" Eno warned with a chuckle.

Jee saw the drones, little flying helicopter things with blinking lights—everywhere—like a swarm of bees. In a panic, she ran toward the rear of the ship, mussing her hair as she went.

All watching the screens in the stadium, at home, or in public display parks across the entire world observed with glee as *Explorer Eleven* steadily hovered over the stage.

"You need to stall!" she called.

"Listen, young lady," chided Eno. "*Explorer Eleven* is not like one of those Earth coffee pots that percolate! I have important and precise procedures to follow in order to shut down this machine! I have a complicated series of actions to complete, including—mind you—the disengaging of the force shield! Otherwise, well, if you tried to walk through it on your way to meet your *subjects*—"

"Stop it, Eno!" came the response.

"—it wouldn't be pretty!" Eno said with a laugh.

"My hair looks like black seaweed! Get my dress, Eno!"

Eno leaned into the control panel and whispered: "Vací, begin automated landing and shut down procedures."

"Procedure underway."

The Tażath stood on the left of the stage, still in view of most of the audience. He wore his official white suit and simple red sash. With his ministers and friends beside him, they applauded and anxiously watched as *Explorer* hovered above them, made slight adjustments to position, and gracefully touched ground. Within seconds, internal power units wound down, lights lowered, hissing gasses left valves, and a flashing light on the control panel informed Eno that the automated landing procedures had been completed. The force shields were now safely powered off.

The crowd went insane. The roar was deafening, and many of the dignitaries—the highest of the Końeefa—covered their ears. There were fireworks and the banging of drums—some even tuned.

Technicians were signaled. They approached the ship with various scanning devices to take readings of the outer shell of the vessel. As soon as all was found safe, more workers came wheeling a small container to the stairs. Two sealed bags were removed and were carried into the now open door of the ship.

In one of the bags was the formal state meeting suit for Eno. The other bag was for the Glasśigh.

▲▲▲

"We currently await the appearance of High Minister Commander Eno Ćlaviath and the Glasśigh," said the announcer, his voice sounding a bit thin and crackling with a slight static. The picture was a bit fuzzy. The display screen in the cave base of the Enária Front was old and in need of replacement. It struggled to receive the signal broadcasted from over three hundred miles away as it bounced off the tar's stone walls, through storm clouds, heat vents, and rain that raged over the seas.

"Never has excitement, I believe, ever been this elevated in the entire history of Tar Aséllo!"

Orgo entered the cave base dining hall and found Salǵeea. He took a chair.

"What does she look like?" asked Orgo. "People say, at least the idiots on the media, that she looks *alien*, but somehow still beautiful."

The display screen showed a picture of the Glasśigh. The dozen or so Enária soldiers present joined their two senior leaders as they studied the image.

"I think that thing on her face is called a *nose*," said Salǵeea.

Orgo considered it, tilting his head a bit from side to side as he studied the image. "Hmm. I kind of like it."

Salǵeea smiled.

"The Graćenta have been doing nothing but reveling in her homecoming for over twelve hundred days!" continued Orgo. "That's a third of a year. You were right about the recruitment. It is at zero for this period. Some soldiers are stealing from our food stores and leaving."

"Our people now have something else to be excited about," said Salǵeea.

"The Glasśigh," said Orgo. "The beautiful Glasśigh, mind you, is more than a distraction. They will love her, and we, my friend, will pass out of their minds."

"They will return once they see nothing has changed for the better," assured Salǵeea as he leaned back in the uncomfortable chair.

"They have dolls made of her already," added Orgo. "I want one."

"Ah! Joyous!" continued the announcer. *"Here comes someone! Someone off the ship,* Explorer Eleven, *that intrepid craft of discovery!"*

▲▲▲

The crowd in the Arena of Asėllo emitted a deafening roar as High Minister Commander Eno Ćlaviath descended the small stairs that led from the side port of *Explorer Eleven* to the landing pad. Dressed in his new and spotless white High Minister's Council suit with a green sash, Eno walked purposefully across the stage, waving and smiling. He made his way to the Taźath, his friend, Pronómio Tok. Cameras followed every move, especially the drone-mounted ones that flew within mere feet of them, at times blocking out other stationary cameras and even bumping into each other.

Everyone knew of Eno Ćlaviath before the mission and was saddened and shocked when his disappearance was reported. As a result of his *rebirth*, his popularity soared. The fact that he was returning the Glasśigh to Áhtha didn't hurt his reputation either.

Throughout Etáin City, in the hills and port towns of the southern tar, and in the resorts and the vacation homes, the populace watched as the event was broadcast. Some viewed from their ABCs. All were beyond themselves with excitement. People screamed and cheered, hugged, and cried with joy upon seeing Eno once again.

In Éhpiloh and the outlying towns of Oso-Gúrith, the Graćenta watched the proceedings in public spaces newly fitted with large display screens. Many field and factory workers were given the day off. All were as equally ecstatic as their southern neighbors, even more so in many cases. Though Glasśigh Asėllo and Eno Ćlaviath belonged to the Kor̗eefa, the members of the lower classes reveled in the dreamlike world in which they lived. Young females wondered what it would be like to leave their poverty and be magically promoted to such a place, such a life, as the Glasśigh's. Young males desired to wed her and hold her hand as they walked along the beaches of Chanteeda shores.

On the screen, the Taźath, in a not-so-rare show of emotion, rushed the remaining distance to Eno and hugged him tightly, completely overwhelmed with joy. The crowd reacted by raising the pitch of their excitement even higher. As the clamor continued, Pronómio placed his arm around Eno, sized him up as if to see if he was well-fed, then smiled with approval at Eno's apparent heath. He then motioned for Eno to move to a podium fitted with a microphone. As Eno stepped up, waving and smiling, the Taźath waited below. This was Eno's moment.

Eno looked to the leader and bowed slightly in respect. After a nod from the Taźath, he turned to the arena crowd once again. The applause continued, and it took a full five minutes for them to calm themselves enough to even hear that Eno was calling, politely, for silence.

"Thank you! Thank you for a wonderful welcome! It is good to be home!"

Roaring cheers, emotional outpourings, and thunderous applause burst forth.

Inside *Explorer Eleven*, Jee watched as a short and thin young woman and an older woman approached and entered the ship. Each was dressed in dull garb that could only be a work uniform. They were holding a tall bag on a hanger.

"Is this my dress?" asked Jee nervously.

"Yes, Glasśigh," said the older woman.

"Are you here to help me? I mean, I sure could use some help. I'm a bit nervous!"

The women nodded, keeping their heads down and avoiding eye contact. Jee thought this was odd, but, well, all of what was happening was the epitome of oddness.

"Who are you?" she asked.

"We are your servants," answered the older.

"Oh…" said Jee. "Do, um, do you have names?"

"Yes," responded the older one as she looked for a place to hang the gown. Jee looked up at a thin conduit running across the ceiling. Neither of the servants could reach it, so Jee took the bag, hung it, and then began the unwrapping. Both women tried to help, but they could not reach.

"I have it, ladies," said Jee. As she removed the layers of paper-like material, she nervously continued talking.

"So, you have names. Can you tell me them?"

The older woman responded again. "Yes, Glasśigh. I am Lágneece Tilka, head seamstress of Etáin City. This is Reǵeena Ahdelfía," she continued, pointing to the young woman. "She will be your personal servant beginning today."

Jee laughed as she continued unwrapping the gown. How many layers of paper did they need?

"Reǵeena Ahdelfía? What a beautiful name! How long do I have you? Forever?" Jee asked with a laugh.

Reǵeena looked up for a moment as she gathered the paper that had dropped to the floor.

"Yes. Forever. Or until you grow tired of me," Reǵeena replied.

"R-really? I-I was only—that's weird," Jee said. "But, well, great!"

It was then Jee noticed the young woman's beauty. Reǵeena's feathery silver mane, the length just above her shoulders, and her expressive blue eyes and deep olive skin made her look…what was the word? Exotic! That was it!

"I have heard of the flashing thing you do with your mane," said Jee. "I see red and orange at the edges, Reǵeena. What do those colors mean?"

"Red means she is excited," explained Lágneece. "Orange means she is scared or nervous."

"Oh!" exclaimed Jee with surprise. "Don't let me get you nervous! If my hair changed color, I'd be completely orange right now! Like a tangerine!"

"Tanger-eene?" asked Reǵeena, sounding out the word.

Jee then noticed an odd tattoo above her right eye. It was a simple dark-brown circle the size of a dime, with two parallel lines on the top.

"Reǵeena, that tattoo you have…I think the Áhthan word is... *krísi?*"

"Yes," confirmed Reǵeena as she continued picking up the wrapping. Her mane now turned pink.

"She is embarrassed," explained Lágneece again.

"Dear! I don't mean to upset you, Reǵeena. Does the *krísi* mean something to you? Or do you just like it?"

"It means," answered Lágneece, "that she is Graćenta."

"Oh," said Jee. "And you do not have one, Lágneece?"

Lágneece rumpled her nose in annoyance. "No! I am Merćenta."

Jee nodded as if she understood; however, she certainly did not. What was a Merćenta again?

Jee stripped away the final layer of cover and beheld the gown. Her mouth dropped open. Her already sizable eyes actually seemed to grow larger. Reǵeena and Lágneece smiled.

"You will wear a replica of the ceremonial gown of the house of Aséllo. Your house," announced Reǵeena.

"It was worn at the crowning ceremony of your most ancient grandfather, Ásue Aséllo," said Lágneece. She began assisting Jee in the removal of her old clothes. "Jaydí Ćlaviath first wore it on her wedding day and then at the ceremony. She, herself, placed the Crown of Aséllo upon his head."

"It's beautiful," Jee said, stunned.

"…And it is with a humble heart that I thank each and every one of you for this most joyous of welcomes!" said Eno to thunderous applause.

If anyone in the crowd could have imagined the scene becoming even more exhilarating—the noise rising to a higher pitch, the dancing and jumping being elevated anymore—it still would have fallen short of the actual moment.

Eno turned. He could see the two assistants descending the stairs, smiling. They saw him and nodded their heads to imply, *'she is ready.'*

"And now," said Eno to the crowd, "yes, there is someone you have all waited too long to see, to see again! My fellow Aséllians…"

He was barely heard over their booming outpouring of excitement.

"My fellow Áhthans, my Taźath…" Eno continued, "I officially present to you…the direct descendent of Ásue Aséllo and Jaydí Ćlaviath…"

The entire stadium was shaking—quite a feat as it was made of stone.

"Glasśigh! The Light of Áhtha!"

Drums rolled.

A thunderous roar erupted.

The Glasśigh stepped down from the ship, descending the stairs with caution and some apprehension. The cameras, even the ones mounted on the dozens and dozens of fist-sized media drones that hovered like insects, zoomed in on her feet. They took in the delicate slippers of white with gold trim. Her ankles were sleek and fair—smooth without a single hair (or feather)—as were all Áhthans. Her skin color was an even light olive-tan.

The image from one of these cameras was displayed on the giant screen inside the arena. The other cameras were broadcasting to additional outlets all over the planet.

The crowd's enthusiasm was heightened. Drums rolled on, fireworks exploded, the roar of the throng sounded like a howling wind. The stadium shook to the point of almost knocking down mounted cameras. The announcers were speechless, many happily admitting that there were no words to describe the joy, letting the image and the crowd's reaction explain this historic moment.

As the Glasśigh descended, the cameras focused on her gown. It sparkled in the light, or maybe was iridescent, or possibly had its own source of illumination. The effect made her looked as if she was adorned with a thousand tiny stars. The gown was primarily made of gold strands falling from off one shoulder, across her chest, to her slender waist, and then draping like a waterfall off her hips to just below her knee. The strands dangled, sparkled, and swayed with each step. As the cameras could see, there was silver mixed into the gold, and the gentle waving of the strands as she moved accented her curves. No crown she wore, no high-winged headdress. Only her jet-black hair somehow set with jewels that shimmered in the light.

One of the cameras had the assignment of zooming in on her face and, in particular, her eyes. Most media outlets chose this feed. The world saw the enormous but delicate deep green eyes of their long-lost love, the flowing black hair of a thousand ringlets, and the smile that would light the world—the Glasśigh.

Jee smiled and waved, and only Eno could tell that she was nervous. Gone was the confident and obstinate little girl, now replaced by a vulnerable but purposefully cautious young woman.

The crowd was stunned—to the point that the cheering lessened, only to be replaced by a collective gasp. Unable to control themselves, many in the crowd rushed the promontory stage. The officers of security had their hands full protecting the attendees from injury.

The cheering soon returned to its previous level of insanity as the Taźath escorted her to the platform where Eno stood.

"Oh my dear," Pronómio said, trying to be heard above the noise of the crowd. He wiped away a tear as his mane displayed streaks of deep gold. "Look at how they love you! We all do! Welcome home! Welcome home, Glasśigh!"

"I guess having a nose didn't scare them," she joked with a nervous smile.

With that, the Taźath turned to the crowd and the cameras. He swept his arms outward, and then both arms to the side, pointing at the Glasśigh. She began to laugh as the crowd roared again. Stepping up to the podium, she embraced Eno, who, she had to admit, looked stunning in his suit. He gently touched his forehead to hers and then surrendered the stage to his niece.

Jee continued to wave. Thank goodness I watched those parades in Idaho to see how the prom queens did this!

She stepped to the microphone, which to her, looked like some kind of multi-spiked weapon the size of a potato masher.

The applause and cheering lasted for what seemed to be five whole minutes. She could see a strange glowing and undulating red wave moving through the crowd, changing and growing. It took a moment for her to realize the color was from the manes of the entire crowd flashing from dark brownish-black to a solid red, with several pockets of purple. Red was for happiness, Eno had said. The purple was still a mystery.

Finally, the applause and hollering subsided, now slightly reduced to a roar.

"Wow," she breathed, the microphone catching her first word.

The multitude, again, went uncontrollably wild. Eventually, they calmed after what seemed an eternity. And though the adoration never truly subsided—the cheering continuing as a constant rumble—the Glasśigh was finally able to speak and be heard, at least somewhat.

"*Shayhalla!*"

The roar increased.

"This is all so overwhelming!" she cried sincerely. "I really have no words to describe what I feel, how thankful I am that you have welcomed me home!"

The cheers rose again.

"Seeing Tar Aséllo for the first time left me speechless!" she continued.

Eno could be seen nodding.

"And the people! All of you who came out to see me! I-I don't deserve this, really!"

Excessive cheers of adulation were now mixed with shouts of "Wow" and "We love you" and "Glasśigh! Light of Áhtha!"

Jee simply smiled with embarrassment and bowed her head. This caused the audience to immediately increase their thunderous exclamations of approval, again shaking the stadium itself.

▲▲▲

Salǵeea, Orgo, and the Front soldiers continued watching the event from the cave stronghold behind the Kryménos Falls.

"Will you listen to that!" exclaimed Orgo. "They do love her!"

"If she was any more beautiful, they would make her Taźath!"

commented Salǵeea, laughing. He looked at the others and noticed that even his most dedicated and experienced men and women stared at the screen, eyes as wide as the smiles on their faces. Even they were enamored by the young woman. The Glasśigh's face filled the screen as she spoke; her authenticity was undeniable, her gratitude sincere.

"I hope that someday, soon, I can visit you all!" she said.

"Maybe she could come to see us in the caves, eh, Salǵeea?" joked a soldier.

"As long as she brings some good food!" added Orgo.

The group laughed heartily.

Salǵeea leaned over to Orgo and whispered. "What is the status of Isos? Positioning is delicate and must be done precisely if we want to be successful. We can't miss this opportunity."

"Isos is ready. Stop worrying," Orgo replied, staring at the screen. He watched the Glasśigh with interest. In his opinion, and that of others who had seen the three-dimensional image sent from the craft, she was genuinely gorgeous. And that thing on her face, the *nose* it was called, really wasn't that bad. In fact, it was somewhat cute. It accentuated her eyes.

▲▲▲

"Thank you, everyone! My love to you!" said Jee, and she stepped down from the podium. She joined Eno, and both gave a last wave to the crowd and walked back to Lágneece and Reǵeena, who escorted them to the rear stage exit. They were greeted in the wings by the Taźath.

The roar of the crowd could still be heard; their fervor was unending.

"Listen to them, my Glasśigh! They are still calling for you!" cried Pronómio.

"It is strange to me," she said, smiling. "All I did was take a trip to Earth! All right, I guess that's pretty special, but I don't deserve this!"

"However, they want and deserve you!" Pronómio said. "When you were thought to be lost forever, there was a full Ófeetian period of mourning. It's like you came back from the dead."

"Oh dear," mumbled Jee, still smiling as she looked toward the entrance to the stage. The cheering from the arena had not subsided one bit. With two hundred thousand people calling her name in unison, it was again becoming overwhelming.

"I think," said Pronómio, "it would be a good idea for you to go out and give them one last wave for the night."

"Do you think so?" asked Jee, biting her lip and taking another apprehensive look back toward the stage.

"Eno, please go with her?" asked Pronómio.

"Of course!"

"We will see you at the Palace? Tonight?" asked Pronómio. "We have a special place for you, and transportation will be made available. Reǵeena Ahdelfía will wait for you and assist. Enjoy, Glasśigh!" He gave her a fatherly embrace and turned to leave.

"Shall we?" asked Eno, holding out his arm to escort his niece.

They walked the few yards down the hallway, up the short flight of stairs, and onto the stage again. The cameras followed every move. Immediately, the live image of the two explorers walking up the stairs was broadcast onto the screens of the stadium and all over the world.

Jee and Eno began waving before they even reached the platform, and the crowd, as expected, went berserk.

▲▲▲

Far to the northwest of Etáin City, a lone technician sat inside a water-tight mobile bunker under the surface of a low-lying marsh in the *Gláysien Lake* region. The console in front of her was equipped with a few simple buttons, a dial, and a targeting display. It was dark in there, cramped and quiet. On a screen, the technician watched the re-emergence of the Glasśigh and Eno at the Arena of Aséllo.

A voice spoke through her head-com.

"We are approved. Activate immediately."

"Confirmed," she said as she pressed the activate button.

▲▲▲

"I still can't believe this, Eno!" Jee yelled over the roar of the crowd. She continued waving her hand as the celebration continued.

"It is quite stupendous, even I am surprised!" Eno shouted.

Still walking arm-in-arm, they continued waving, moving to different parts of the stage to gesture and smile at particular areas of the arena, for individual cameras, even to the sky.

The armband communicator on Jee's wrist began to vibrate. She looked down. The screen was flashing red, and a series of white numbers rolled across. She could barely hear Vací's voice through the pandemonium. She tugged at Eno's jacket and showed him the band.

"What does this mean?" she asked, now breaking from the constant smiling and waving.

"That's odd," yelled Eno over the din. "Red? Red means meteor strike imminent."

They both turned to look at *Explorer Eleven*. Pulsating red light was emanating from every port. A shrieking siren could barely be heard.

Eno grabbed Jee's wrist and held the band to his ear.

"-E7 warning code. Projectile strike in seven seconds. Unable to take evasive action. Repeat-E7 warning code..."

Eno looked into the sky. There. He saw it: a pale red streak arcing across the sky from the northwest. The streak seemed to break apart, but then a brilliant white light exploded behind it.

"That is no meteor! It's a booster rocket!" he shrieked. Eno grabbed his niece by the arm and ran, pulling her to the rear of the stage.

"Eno! What is—"

"Shut up and run!" he called as he dragged her backward.

A quick look over her shoulder and Jee saw the rocket heading straight for them. The hovering media drones scattered. She looked toward the hallway at the rear of the stage. They would never make it. She tugged at Eno; it was enough to make him lose his balance.

"Over the edge!" she yelled.

"No!" scolded Eno.

But Jee had pulled him hard enough. Still holding hands, they leaped over the edge of the fifty-foot promontory. As they fell, the rocket struck square on *Explorer Eleven*. A huge flash lit the surroundings. Jee could feel the heat. Eno was screaming. After a few agonizing seconds, they landed in the deep pool surrounding the stage below.

9
One Palace Place

It was identical to a week of mourning. Throughout Tar Aséllo, and indeed the entirety of Áhtha, people were in front of media screens, tablets, and their armband communicators, watching the news and waiting for every bit of newly discovered information and speculation.

In the Hall of Ministers—a full house of dignitaries, lawmakers, military leaders, and the upper levels of the Kořeefa—were gathered to hear the speech by the Tażath. To say the mood was solemn would be an understatement. The ministers and the people of Tar Aséllo, regardless of social level, were in shock.

Finally, the drums rolled in the hall. The cameras were on. Pronómio Tok entered and walked to a raised platform at least twenty feet higher than the seats before him. Standing before the microphone, he began.

"Let me begin by letting you know that the brave Commander Eno…and the Light of Áhtha, our Glasśigh, are both fine. They are under our best doctors' care. The shock of striking water at that distance was not fatal, though it did cause a few contusions. The Glasśigh's left arm, in particular, was slightly sprained. She must wear a sling for two weeks. Due to her superior bloodlines and bravery, she is expected to make a full and rapid recovery."

There was a collective sigh across the tar, and the members in the hall cheered.

The Tażath smiled, nodded, and then raised his hand for quiet. "I will tell you this: those responsible will be captured, they will be brought to justice, and they will be punished. We know that the Enária, in a desperate attempt to remain relevant, have perpetrated this attack. They have released a statement via an illegal mobile broadcast cube, claiming no involvement whatsoever. I do not believe them."

Those in the hall answered in resounding approval.

"No matter what it takes," he continued purposefully, "I will use every resource and facility in my power to bring them down!"

This was met with the expected cheers and applause.

"And now, Security Minister Commander Gákoh Kalífus will address the particulars."

The Tażath stood aside, though never entirely away from the cameras and media drones. Kalífus, in full combat uniform, took the stage.

"Greetings fellow ministers and dignitaries, citizens of Tar Aséllo, and to the whole of Áhtha. Here is what we were able to ascertain: the ordinance that struck the stage at the Arena of Aséllo was a type-seven automated medium yield explosive device known as a Klaymac. This was mounted on a ten-foot-long class-7 rocket. Together, they make a highly dangerous weapon that can cause enormous damage to personnel and machinery. The trajectory we calculated showed the launch point was near one of the small islands in upper Gláysien Lake. *Explorer Eleven* suffered only minor damage, a scrape on the craft's main dorsal panel. It will be thoroughly examined and then decommissioned. It is apparent that the force field saved that intrepid ship, allowing only a flashy show. We have information pointing to the Enária, and we will investigate and carry out swift retribution. I assure you that we will not rest until those Enária are captured and brought before the Taźath!"

The crowd applauded and stood as Kalífus and Pronómio exited the chamber.

▲▲▲

In the recovery center of the City of Etáin Medical Complex, Jee and Eno sat comfortably in adjustable lounge chairs. An entire wing customarily reserved for high government officials was assigned to them. Their room was plush, had separate sleeping quarters for each, and a small space for Reǵeena Ahdelfía. The recovery area surroundings were beautiful. There was a visiting room, (actually a towering atrium with a glass roof), a swimming pool, and an entire wall of glass that allowed a view of the sky and the city below. It was undoubtedly less hospital-like than the emergency rooms where Jee and Eno had been initially treated.

Reǵeena was there, ever dutiful, and waiting on their every need. Jee felt awkward having a servant, but she reasoned that Eno, and most likely the Taźath, wouldn't allow her to *not* have one. Even so, it made Jee uncomfortable. If they could become friends, that would be all right then, she reasoned. They would be doing things together, not just for Jee. That's what friends did, right?

Still, something was odd about Reǵeena: though always polite, she was distant and quiet. When Jee thanked the young woman or smiled in recognition, Reǵeena would only nod her head and say, "I am glad you are pleased." Her mane rarely changed color, except for pink. Though Jee went out of her way to get close, Reǵeena remained formal and distant, though not in a superior way. Oh well, maybe friendships take a long time to build here, thought Jee.

In addition to Reǵeena and Eno, there stood at least seven doctors at the rear of the recovery room at all times. Jee found them totally unnecessary. Every hour they insisted on re-scanning Jee's left arm to track its progress. The attention and concern of the doctors, all female at Jee's request, was professional and kind, but it quickly became a nuisance.

Then there were the gifts.

Over a period of three days, an absurd number of presents appeared at the door, arriving every few minutes. Some were simple flower arrangements, sweets, or small trinkets from people of all classes, wishing the Glasśigh a speedy recovery. Others were bigger and more involved: ABCs of all types, jewelry for Jee, sculptures, some kind of live horse-like animal that had to be 'sent to the Taźath's menagerie' according to Eno. There were fancy platters, odd machines for cooking who-knows-what, dresses, and pottery. However, the gifts that touched her heart were the simple letters and pictures sent by young school children, all expressing hope that she would quickly recover.

"Eno, shouldn't I send thank you notes to these people?" she asked.

"A staff member will do that," said Eno, as he continued reading something on his tablet.

"But what do we do with all these gifts? Some look expensive—"

Eno looked up. "They are! That glass sculpture of the red fish there? It is a *Garvino* original. Famous! Worth as much as the Taźath's skyliner. A million earth dollars, I'd wager."

"Really?" asked Jee, disbelieving. "Eno! This is just, well, stupid. Dear, dear, dear! There is no room to move around! We can't just throw it all out!"

"I have already called for a staff member to dispose of them," replied Eno, uninterested. "Some will be donated to museums, I assume. But we are keeping the Garvino."

What was even more perplexing to Jee was the multitude of simple white envelopes, at least numbering in the thousands that had arrived so far today. Made of a papery-looking fabric, each was addressed in a flowing, hand-written script, and each contained a silver bracelet encrusted with multi-colored jewels. Along with every bracelet was a photo of a smiling man in an odd pose of some sort and a small card with snippets of personal information about the sender.

These were all addressed to Eno.

"And what are all these? Are these bracelets for you?" Jee asked, holding several in her hand. "And the photos of the creepy men inside?"

"Those are proposals," answered Eno nonchalantly. He returned his attention to the tablet.

"Proposals for…what?" asked Jee.

"For you. You in marriage. These men want to meet you."

"W-what?" she gasped, shocked, so much so that she threw down the envelopes in her hand as if they each contained a large family of spiders.

Reǵeena stifled a laugh.

"It is the custom in Áhtha," Eno explained. "If a man wants to marry a woman, he must first ask her father, and in his absence, her uncle. Me. They are asking me if it is all right.

"W-what? Reǵeena, is that true?"

"Yes, Glasśigh, of course. Minister Ćlaviath is correct."

"Some of them are quite wealthy," continued Eno, "at least according to the few cards I have read. Some quality candidates, certainly. I will have to spend considerable time, so—"

"Don't I have a say?" interrupted Jee, growing concerned.

"Yes, yes, it is an *old* custom. Don't get all upset and in a huff," Eno said. "I will only grant permission to several at a time."

"Eno!"

"I am kidding!" he said, laughing. "I have no intention of setting loose the entire male population of Tar Aséllo on you. I will not respond."

Later, Eno and Jee sat on a balcony of the medical center that overlooked the Bay of Arimía and Etáin City. Using Jee's ABC, they watched the Taźath's speech about the Enária and the rocket attack.

"I thought you said these rebels were wiped out and that we missed the whole uprising," probed Jee.

"I believed so. However, this is a new group I am unfamiliar with," her uncle said. "The Enária, another faction of the discontented! Yet, still, none of it makes sense…"

"What?" asked Jee. "What doesn't make sense?"

"I am hungry!" Eno announced in an attempt to change the subject. "Reǵeena, bring me some *hannea loaf*."

"Yes, High Minister Commander Ćlaviath," replied the young woman as she turned to leave the room.

"Uncle! What manners!" Jee scolded, turning to Reǵeena in apology. "Reǵeena? Not everyone from Earth is as rude and boorish as my uncle. Would you please bring him some of, um, whatever that was he wanted? Hyena loaf?"

"Han-NEE-ah," corrected Eno.

"Shush!" Jee admonished, giving Eno a stern look and a wave of dismissal. "Reǵeena, would you like some help?"

"No," answered the girl. "It is a pleasure, my Glasśigh."

"My Glasśigh? Oh dear. Just call me Jee. Is that acceptable?"

"No, it isn't!" scolded Eno sharply.

Jee turned to her uncle with a firm stance and countenance. "I wasn't asking you, *High Minister…Commodore Eno Cuh-lay-vee-UTH!"*

"She is doing her job!" Eno countered. "Her role. And there is no need to say please."

Jee looked at Eno as if he had somehow changed into some sort of, well *lord.* Shocked at his behavior, she crossed her arms and scowled at him.

Reǵeena left the room in a hurry.

"Reǵeena is my servant, not yours," Jee snapped, "and if you want her to help you, then say please, or *get it yourself!* I mean it!"

Her voice was so loud that the doctors in the back of the room ceased 'observing' and looked away, pretending to read reports and study their armbands.

"Jee," said Eno, unfazed, "this is Tar Aséllo, not Coeur d'Alene."

"Really? I hadn't noticed. They look so similar! Except the people here are more rude!"

"Jee, calm down—"

"And I don't like this place! Too many windows! And people watching us! Can we move?" asked Jee angrily.

"It will be up to the doctors," answered Eno.

"I will talk to them. This place smells too clean! And anyone can just look in here!"

Eno laughed. "Who can look in? We are over two hundred feet above the nearest level of houses and shops! Please!"

"I will speak to the doctors all the same," pouted Jee.

"They will not listen to you."

Within an hour of her request, a team of workers moved Jee and her uncle from the medical center to a permanent abode.

As a gift from the government, they were now the residents of none other than *One Palace Place*. Jee had seen a picture of the stunning structure before their arrival and was ecstatic when told the news. It was a home that many considered second only to the Palace of the Taźath. Built into a grand ridge of reddish-brown stone that jutted outward from a prominent hillside several stories above the sea, Palace Place afforded the occupants a view of the always-sparkling Etáin City to the west, the blue Bays of Arimía directly below, and the Falls of Etáin to the south. All were visible from the massive white-stoned deck that was attached to the main house and living quarters. Gardens were built into the walls of the home with pools of flowing water and tall trees that reached impossibly high.

To Jee, the inside of One Palace Place was as high-tech and modern as *Explorer Eleven*, with massive glass windows from floor to twenty-foot ceilings. It was elegantly simple, mostly white and gray stone material for walls, counters, and fixtures, and a few emerald accents.

She liked it.

Though Jee found her new home more than adequate and said so when asked, Eno noticed a quietness, a sullen mood and darkness to her overall demeanor. Was she missing Earth? Could she be feeling overwhelmed? Were Áhtha and Tar Aséllo too weird for her?

Maybe it was just that someone tried to kill her with a rocket. Or was the adjustment to the day-cycle throwing her system off-kilter? Certainly, the concept of a 'day' was part of it. What Jee used to call a 'day' on Earth was not comparable to what happened on Áhtha. Earth was a planet; it spun on its axis as it orbited the Sun, so the delineation of 'day' and 'night' was obvious.

Áhtha was totally different.

Firstly, Áhtha was a *moon*, not a planet. Secondly, it was 'tidally locked' to Ofeétis, which meant it did not spin on its axis. Like Earth's moon, Áhtha always had the same 'face' toward Ofeétis. The amount of light that reached into the tar changed depending upon where Áhtha, Ofeétis, and the Sun happened to be in relation to each other. That position constituted the beginning and ending of 'days'. And though not technically a true astrophysical day by definition, this term was what made the most sense to Jee, so 'day' is what she called them.

The first day of the week was called *Eclipse*, because Ofeétis completely blocked out the Sun. Therefore, none of the distant sun's light entered the tar, nor did any light reflecting off the ever-present giant gas that hung above. This was the darkest day of the week, like a moonless, starless night on Earth. Ofeétis appeared as a gigantic black hole in the sky, surrounded by a few bright stars. Only the glow from the cities and the bioluminescent sea and plants illuminated that tar. The darkness made Jee sleepy. The chemical *melatonin* was produced in the bodies of all creatures on Áhtha, and, just as on Earth, the production of melatonin was triggered by darkness, causing animals to sleep. That meant Áhthans slept when it was darkest, which was the entire day of *Eclipse*—twenty-eight Earth hours long.

Everyone remained awake for the whole rest of the week.

The next day was called *Firstsun*, which made sense to Jee as she watched the Sun peeking out from behind Ofeétis with a flash of subdued amber light. Áhtha was over eight times the distance from the Sun as Earth, and that meant the direct light was a dim glow at best. The weak sunbeams, filtering in through the fálouse and abundant clouds made the tar seem like twilight on earth, when the sun had set, though its glow remained. As visible through the narrow opening of the tar, Ofeétis appeared as a 'young' crescent shape. As the day continued, it waxed until it reached quarter, when the Sun disappeared over the edge of the eastern tar.

Firstglow, the following day, was logically named, Jee thought. There was no direct Sun as it had moved beyond view from inside the tar, but Ofeétis was well lit and waxing on its way to full. The entire day seemed like a half-moon-lit night on Earth.

The day marking the second half of the week was *Fullglow*, and on this day, Áhtha had its back entirely to the Sun. As always, its face was directly pointed at Ofeétis, causing a lunar eclipse. Again, there was no direct sunlight, but Ofeétis now appeared full and in perfect focus, reflecting sunlight into the tar. This was the most brilliant day of the week and sometimes was as bright as a cloud-covered day on Earth.

Lastglow was the next day. There was still no direct Sun, only the softening glow from Ofeétis as it waned. The crescent became thinner and thinner, and the tar grew darker and darker with each hour that passed. Again, as it happened on Firstglow, Lastglow displayed wonderfully orange hues that lit the tar with harsh shadows, and the bioluminescence was at its peak.

The final day of the week was called *Lastsun*. It was exactly like *Firstsun* with its dull sunlight, except the Sun appeared in the western sky and continued its journey toward Ofeétis. As the day ended, another eclipse occurred, marking the beginning of the new week.

Luckily for Jee, each of these 'days' lasted just a bit longer than an Earth day, and a week of six days seemed understandable. However, the months had to stretch to cover the full Ofeétian year, which was almost twelve Earth years long. So the days and the weeks seemed normal, but the months, all thirty-five of them, with ninety-six days in each, were hard to get used to.

Eno suggested that Jee think of time in days and weeks because that closely resembled Earth's time units. She agreed, also happy to hear that many Áhthans took time to nap during the week, especially on the darker day of Lastsun.

For the next four full 'weeks', Jee struggled to adjust her sleep pattern. The idea of slumbering for twenty-eight hours during Eclipse, and then remaining awake for five days straight was disturbing. She slept at irregular intervals as her body adjusted, and this left her drowsy when awake and restless when trying to sleep. To assist, Eno had gone to a lab and created a 'sleeping tonic' for her. Jee said it smelled like rotting dirt and tasted like rotting dirt—with dead worms in it. After a dose each day, lessening in quantity as time went on, it worked. By the second Eclipse, she began to feel sleepy and could remain awake longer without napping. By the fourth Eclipse, she was almost adjusted.

Hopefully, if the idea that someone had tried to kill her could bother her a little less, life would proceed pleasantly. To assist in this, Eno had requested a telescope.

At first, she was not interested, but soon the 'Aséllo' in her exerted itself, and she began to study and wonder at the beauty of the tar, or at least what she could see from the balcony at Palace Place. When the world was in near or absolute darkness, Jee could see more of the city's shining lights. Eventually, she found her new surroundings beautiful, and the severity of her discontent faded. Even the constant fly-overs—the circling of the city by the Ultos Wing of the Taźath's forces—added to the world's beautiful eeriness.

One Fullglow, as Ofeétis glowed brightly above, Eno 'toiled' in the kitchen, grinding coffee beans he had brought from Earth. Using his pride and joy, a Toastmaster Stainless Steel and Bakelite 8-Cup Percolator, he happily created his favorite brew.

"A cup of coffee, dear?" he called as he poured himself one.

"You enjoy," answered Jee from the balcony. "I know you have a limited supply of beans."

"Ah, however, somewhere in *Explorer,* I have planting beans—called cherries," he announced proudly. "They are green! As soon as I am able, I will retrieve them and begin my cultivation plans! I will introduce the wonders of coffee to all of Áhtha!"

Eno joined his niece outside as she gazed through the telescope. He took a seat in one of the comfortable loungers and sipped his black drink.

"Bioluminescent waves, you said, Uncle Eno?"

"Yes." Eno was staring at his preferred PDT, reviewing the research notes about Earth's political structures. "As the water is gently disturbed, the microorganisms, in this case, the common *sallo luea* become agitated, they bump against each other, and they glow as a result."

"Sallo luea? Sea glows? Sea lights?" she wondered. "Why do they glow?"

"Sea glows, technically. It's a chemical reaction to the agitation of their cell's inner liquids. It is helpful in attracting others for mating."

"Eno! Why must you always—"

"It is! That is why! I didn't just *make it up!*" he said, feigning agitation.

Jee smiled. "This place gets weirder and weirder all the time."

A chime sounded.

"The door!" announced Eno.

Reģeena went to attend.

"And how are we today?" came the booming voice of Pronómio Tok. He entered the balcony with arms wide, smiling. With him were two others, one a woman clothed in an all-white dress, mid-length, sporting a minister's jacket. Unlike Eno's, however, hers was tailored. She had a striking white mane of delicate feathers. Jee thought she was beautiful, except for what looked like a permanent scowl on her face.

The other visitor was a tall, young-looking man. If from Earth, Jee would have guessed he had just turned thirty. He wore a full-length coat of some kind of thickly woven thread. It was dark, and upon further study, Jee could see fine gold threads woven within the black. He seemed a little less lizard-like in appearance, his nose large but not as pronounced as Jee's. He had a dark mane, short, and in contrast to the woman, he had a charming smile.

Jee and Eno hurriedly left the lounges and telescope to greet their guests.

"Please! No! No! Rest! Do not stand for us!" Pronómio pleaded.

"Good day, Taźath," they both replied.

Eno performed a slight bow. Jee copied the gesture.

"Sit! I command it!" Pronómio said jokingly.

All took seats in the comfortable lounge area of the balcony. It was a clear Fullglow, bright for Tar Aséllo but to Jee, it was more like the time during a late sunset on earth. A gentle breeze passed. They happily enjoyed the view.

"Let me introduce you to Minister Khileetéra, our Minister of Finance," announced Pronómio.

"So nice of you to visit," said Jee as she smiled at the white-maned woman.

"Welcome," said Eno. "I assume you have taken the position of Minister Cib Feeberish? He was Finance Minister before I left for Earth."

"Yes," she responded flatly. "He died."

"Oh," said Eno.

"And this," continued Pronómio in a excited tone, "this is the Ef

Keería of Tar Éstargon, Vothíos Valtéra!"

"This man I know!" said Eno happily. "So nice of you to visit, Vothíos!"

"High Minister Commander Ćlaviath! Wonderful to see you again after all this time. And you," he gushed, turning to Jee with a broad smile, "Glasśigh Asëllo! Is that how I address you?"

"'Jee' is what my friends call me," she answered.

"Oh! I couldn't be so informal! It is a true honor! You know," the Ef Keería said in an overly conspiratorial tone, "historians have proven that your ancient ancestors, the Asëllos and the Ćlaviaths, came from Tar Éstargon originally! They migrated through the cave systems that connect our tars."

"We don't like to admit it," Eno joked.

The others wondered at the statement. Of course, every Áhthan scientist admitted this fact. The others looked quizzically at Eno.

"Uncle!" exclaimed Jee, admonishing him.

"Oh! Humor!" realized Eno, now trying to explain. "On Earth, a sort of insulting type of humor! *Sarcasm*, they call it. It is an...acquired taste."

"Oh!" said Pronómio. "I see. Like teasing, but..."

"In a mean way? But not really?" asked the Ef Keería.

"Yes," agreed Eno.

They all laughed together, except for Minister Khileetéra. Jee assumed the woman never laughed.

"A stunning sight you have here!" stated the Ef Keería with wonder.

"I agree," said Pronómio.

"We must thank you again, my Taźath," said Eno. "Truly generous of you to grant us this abode. We are humbled by your kindness."

"You are most welcome, brother Eno! We are so glad you are home. And, your return has made today the Ef Keería's first visit in a long while."

"Now that the Glasśigh is home," Vothíos said, "may it usher in a new era. We opened the tunnels between our tars for this visit. No small feat, am I correct, Pronómio?"

The Taźath laughed. "It was like pulling teeth to get the Ministers to agree, but in the end, success!"

"I know my people are excited to see you and hear from you," revealed the Ef Keería. "I can only imagine the excitement here in Tar Asëllo! We broadcasted your arrival at the Arena across our media outlets. Everyone wishes you a speedy recovery! And hopefully, we can have you for a visit to Tar Éstargon?"

"That would be most welcome," said Minister Khileetéra.

Jee saw her look to the Tażath for a response. He gave none.

"Are you well? Are you feeling better?" asked Pronómio turning his attention to Jee. "I see the arm bandages are off!"

"We are fine, Pronómio," replied Eno. "We Ćlaviaths and Aséllos are from sturdy stock."

"Indeed!" agreed Pronómio.

Reģeena returned and set out colorful drinks, a bowl of tobafruit, and a plate of *sweet seed daffies*. To Jee, each daffi looked like a jellybean, but half the size. She was assured by all that they were naturally growing seeds, small, but each one an intense taffy-like drop of sweetness. They were almost transparent, each having a distinct flavor, regardless of their many colors.

"They actually taste like jelly beans, Eno!"

"A true delight you are," said Pronómio, smiling.

"Oh, my! You are so easily entertained!" laughed Jee. "You must have more important things to do than sit with us."

"Actually, no, we don't," Pronómio responded, smiling, "except for bringing the Enária who are responsible for the attack to justice. We are working constantly and tirelessly. We will find them!"

"I am sure of it, Pronómio," said Eno with a slight head bow. "And as I read in the morning briefing, you have again won a vote of confidence! Congratulations!"

"Yes!" Pronómio beamed. "It is inspiring that so many have trust in me. There is still much work to be done! In the meantime, I have a few requests to make. I don't mean to dictate, however..."

Jee thought that if anyone was allowed to dictate here, it was the Tażath. She almost said that aloud, as a joke, but humor, especially sarcasm, didn't seem to be a strong suit of the Aséllians.

"Please, what can we do for you?" asked Jee.

The Tażath simply looked into her eyes and sighed. "What a dear child you are," he reflected.

Jee blushed.

"I will ask you, until further notice, to not make any announced public appearances. For your safety, yes? Once we have a better hand on the situation, we will, of course, lift that restriction. In the interim, I have the Minister of Media working on some *unannounced* visits to areas where we can protect you, mainly in Etáin City. It will be a way for you to meet the people, Glasśigh, and be seen by everyone on view screens all over the world. I can't keep you away from the Aséllians—they would simply not stand for it!" he laughed.

"We understand fully," agreed Eno. "I am under no delusion that populace is excited to see *me*—" Eno paused mid-sentence, waiting for someone to disagree, but none did. They simply smiled and nodded. After an uncomfortable moment, for Eno at least, he continued. "—so I will allow the Glasśigh to handle all the public appearances. I have so much information to organize from my findings on Earth, I could use the time! Other science ministers demand to see all of it, truly fascinating."

"May I make a request?" asked Jee, sheepishly.

"But of course, my dear," replied Pronómio.

"I will become bored listening to Eno go on and on about Earth," she informed them. "I, too, am somewhat of an expert."

The leaders laughed and nodded. Eno didn't.

"It is Tar Aséllo I want to study," she continued. "I was able to access some information on *Explorer Eleven*; however, it was limited. Is there a way I can get access to the archives here in Tar Aséllo? I can use Vací?"

"Consider it done!" boomed Pronómio. "I will give you access as a *minister-level* historian, will that do?"

"I don't know, but it sounds pretty good!" said Jee, laughing.

"A minister-level? It will certainly do," Eno assured them.

"Then I will leave you. But first—a gift," Pronómio announced. "I have assigned a bodyguard for you, Glasśigh."

"Oh! That is unnecessary! Really Taźath," she began.

"Nothing is too good for you, especially when it comes to your safety," he said in a fatherly tone. "Reǵeena?"

The servant rushed to attend. "Yes, Taźath?"

"Please send in the Commander."

As Reǵeena left to bring in the new arrival, Jee tried to hide her frown. A commander? How high up the ladder was that rank here in Tar Aséllo? Jee wondered. To reach that level, he probably had to be as old as Eno! Maybe older! And what will it be like having a military man as a babysitter? Not fun. Some middle-aged, muscle-bound jarhead!

The job of being the Glasśigh just received its first wart.

"Ah! Commander Alíthe Afiéro!" announced the Taźath.

Into the room walked a young man. His mane was black but glowing slightly red at the edges. It was cut short, in a military-style as if he was in the U.S. Army. His hazel-green eyes seemed to sparkle. Jee thought he looked just slightly older than she and certainly a lot better looking than Eno—or any other Áhthan she had yet seen.

As Jee stood, she focused on the Commander. Something strange happened: her entire body shuddered, she felt mildly but pleasantly dizzy, and she could feel her heart beating a bit faster. Her eyes also seemed to have increased focus. Her breath was short. Oh dear, she thought, he is a dreamboat, even for a snake-boy! Am I attracted to him…or is it the daffies? I did have a few dozen!

He bowed slightly to all there, saving the Glasśigh for last.

"We have met," he said formally.

"W-we have?" stammered Jee. Surely she would have remembered.

"Unless I am mistaken," he continued shyly, "I was the first Asévllian to officially salute you."

Alíthe recreated the single-finger salute.

She remembered! The pilot! The one she saw as they approached the arena in *Explorer Eleven*. He seemed cute then, but now, well, even more so. Why was her heart beating so loudly? Could the others hear it?

"I-I remember," was all Jee could manage.

"He will never leave your side," proclaimed Pronómio.

"That's good!" squeaked Jee. She quickly feigned clearing her throat. "I-I mean *if that is his charge—*"

"His wing of Aréus Fighter craft and their crews are only a few seconds away, always on patrol. Commander, you are in constant communication with your wing at all times?"

"Yes Taźath," Alíthe acknowledged, tapping his armband communicator. "Only a touch away from the entire one hundred-ship Ultos Wing and a direct line to the Special Police and Commander Kalífus."

"Then we will leave you under Commander Afiéro's capable watch," said Pronómio, standing.

They proceeded back inside and made their way to the front door. As they walked, the Ef Keería stayed back with Jee. He reached gently for her shoulder.

"Glasśigh," he said, "I must say how sorry I am at the loss of your parents. I knew them well. They worked with me tirelessly. I want you to know what good people they were. The entire nation of Tar Éstargon was very fond of them."

"Thank you, Ef Keería."

"Call me Vothíos," he said. "If there is anything you may need, find a way to contact me. I will try to help you in any way I can, as I did your mother and father."

Jee thought this was a little odd. This whole world was weird: the people, the animals, the plants, the color-changing manes, the customs, the silver bracelets with accompanying wedding proposals. So what do I say to that offer? she wondered.

"Thank you," she said with a slight bow.

After the guests had departed, Jee, Alíthe, and Eno returned to the balcony. Eno plopped down in a lounge chair, nodded to his niece and Alíthe, then buried his head in his PDT. Reǵeena gathered the few dishes and drinking glasses and exited to the kitchen.

Jee stood still, looking at Alíthe, who stood at attention as if awaiting an order.

He was *more than interesting*, Jee thought. There was a moment of uncomfortable silence.

"I must say," Alíthe managed, "I noticed you certainly have, um, an enormous amount of, ah, *proposals...*" He motioned to the stack of white paper envelopes visible through the window. "I did not think there were even that many men in all of Tar Aséllo."

"Don't worry about those," said Jee, smiling, never taking her eyes off Alíthe.

"Oh? Well...um...Glasśigh...yes, well..." Alíthe stumbled over his words.

Eno looked up and saw the two younger people smiling at each other. He rumpled his brow.

"So, *Gluh*-sigh," he said. "How did you like Minister Khileetéra?"

"Who?" she asked.

"The Minister of Finance? With the white-feather mane?"

"Oh," said Jee, partially pulling her gaze from Alíthe. "Yes! I saw her. She didn't seem to be too happy with the Taźath. She glared at him a few times."

"Ah, well, she is the leader of the opposition ministers," Eno informed his niece. "A small opposition, to be sure. Pronómio Tok is very popular, but there are a few who disagree with him. They call for votes of confidence, and he wins easily. But, it is the law. He must allow them."

There was a moment of uncomfortable silence as Eno looked at the youngsters and they at each other. Alíthe eventually noticed the commander's stare.

"Yes. Well then..." Alíthe stuttered. "I do not want to be a bother. I will let you two enjoy your day. If you need me, I will be outside the main entrance. There I can observe, um, the, the surroundings."

"Must you?" asked Jee a little too eagerly.

Alíthe turned his head a bit as a quizzical look appeared on his face. "Yes, I must observe. That is my assignment—"

"No, I mean, must you sit outside? Why not stay and keep me—I-I mean us—company?"

"Oh! Of course! How rude of me," said Alíthe, a bit embarrassed.

"Hmm," grunted Eno under his breath, returning to his notes. "And I thought the *sallo luea* were overactive today."

10
Wish Upon a Star

As the day of Lastsun broke, Jee grew tired of sitting inside and begged Alíthe to allow her to explore the outdoors. He acquiesced and offered to escort her on a stroll along the eastern beach of the Bays of Arimía, just to the south of Palace City. There was an expansive park of manicured gardens and stone paths that wound through a turquoise-green field to the east of the shoreline. It continued south to a large cliff by the Falls of Etáin. As a safety precaution, Alíthe had the park closed and surrounded by Special Police.

To Jee, except for *Eclipse*, the tar always seemed to be in twilight, like a dark early-morning on Earth when the overcast of black rain clouds forced the sun's rays to peek through the torn canopy and softly stream toward the ground. To bring a true enchantment to the world, every plant, tree, and lawn glowed, as if each had been strung with soft, muted blue and green Christmas lights, with a few gold and white bulbs mixed in for good measure. Aséllo was painted in a colorful kaleidoscope of ethereal light. *A fairyland*; that is what she thought.

"I have a question," Jee said as they walked through this glimmering dreamscape. "The mane colors. Eno explained that red is happiness, and I have seen orange too. What do they mean?"

"Ah, yes," replied Alíthe. "I have heard Earthlings do not have such a condition. Firstly, most Áhthans have a mane of black, dark brown, and a few have silver-gray. That is very rare."

"I think the silver is divine!" announced Jee, then with a cautious tone: "Reǵeena has silver. She is pretty, isn't she?"

"Reǵeena?" asked Alíthe. "I assume so. I haven't really noticed. I mean, you being the Glasśigh—" He stopped short.

"What does that mean?" probed Jee expectantly.

"I-I mean, um," he stuttered, "m-my position as your bodyguard is taking all my focus. That is, um, what I mean."

Jee smiled.

Alíthe's mane turned pink at the edges.

"So, back to the colors?" Jee continued. "Your mane was black, but now it is sort-of pink at the edges. What does that mean?"

Alíthe appeared nervous.

"Let me start by pointing out that only extreme emotions are expressed by a mane color change. Blue, for example, expresses anger. Red is excitement, but happiness as well."

"I saw a lot of red in the crowd at the Arena of Aséllo!"

"Yes, and probably a very bright and rich red," added Alíthe. "Your arrival was the most exciting event in a thousand years. I wouldn't be surprised if the entire world glowed red for several hours upon their first sight of you!"

"What about the other colors?" she asked.

"Orange is confused, for the most part. Even lost, in a way. Green denotes sickness, or at the very least, the person is physically uncomfortable."

"I have not seen green," added Jee.

"Sadness is gold," he continued, "but sometimes is relief or compassion. If one is afraid, they will display white or gray."

"What about purple?" Jee asked as she stretched her arms over her head for a moment. She then bent forward and quickly tossed her head backward, causing her hair to become full and then luxuriously fall behind her. "I saw some purple in the Arena crowd as well!"

"Oh," said Alíthe, his mane showing streaks of pink, then purple, then pink again.

"Yes! Like *that* purple!" exclaimed Jee.

"Um, well…pink means embarrassed. Maybe you can ask Commander Ćlaviath about purple."

"Well, you just flashed a bit of purple. What were you—there it is again! What were your feelings?"

"May I just say how beautiful the day is?"

Jee smiled. He was embarrassed about the purple. Okay, time to let this one go.

They continued down the path and finally reached the edge of the park. A river flowed past, creating a barrier between them and the southern wall. A warm breeze came, bringing air smelling of sweet flowers. The light from the wall sparkled from plants and animals.

"I thank you for the explanations," she said with a smile. "May I ask a few personal questions?"

"More questions?" he asked nervously. Throughout the past week, he learned that the Glasśigh was not as predictable as other Áhthan women. She was more formidable in every way. True, that attracted him, but there was an element of danger about her, which he believed she was unaware of. And how could one tell what she was feeling? With no mane? No color change? He had to be wary. After all, she was the Glasśigh.

"How did you become my bodyguard? Did you interview for the position?"

"I think one could say that," Alíthe said. "Several members of the air and ground command were considered by Security Minister Kalífus, our commanding officer. I believe I answered his questions well. And, to be honest, the Taźath favored me."

"Favored?" Jee asked. "What did you do that was so special that the Taźath owed you a favor?"

"I can only assume that my service and success in the Ultos Wing had impressed him," continued Alíthe.

"Eno told me you are all heroes. What was your heroic effort?" Jee asked, teasing.

"Oh, nothing really heroic. It was during the final conflict with the Zakéema Front. We had discovered they were hiding in tunnels leading to Tar Fórtus, our old enemy. Even though that war ended long ago, Tar Fórtus continued to supply the Zakéema. We were collapsing tunnels between the two tars, using explosives. This was needed to stop the flow of weapons. Are you sure you really want to know the details—"

"Yes! It's getting to the exciting part!"

"All right," he said reluctantly. "There was one tunnel left open between the tars. A squad of twenty-five ground troops remained inside this final tunnel, fighting the last of the Zakéema. I heard that our forces were being overrun. There were more enemies than we had initially thought. Our commanders decided to collapse the tunnel—even though our men were still inside.

"That is…horrible!" gasped Jee.

"I asked permission to fly my gunship into the tunnel to protect our troops," continued Alíthe, "and allow them to escape. My commander refused, saying the tunnel was too narrow. But I thought differently. So…I appropriated an older and partially damaged Aréus A2 Fighter from the repair field. I flew inside the tunnel, scraping the sides walls more than once, went past our troops, dropped into hover mode, and fired at the enemy until our men were clear."

"Golly!" Jee declared.

"Yes, *golly* indeed," Alíthe responded.

They turned right and followed the path toward the bay, where huge red-brown boulders as large as houses lined the shore, some sitting in the deep green water. Beyond, they could hear the roar of the Falls of Etáin. The sun, so distant, had just begun to slip behind Ofeétis, the light creating a slow-growing ring along the planet's edge. They stopped and sat on a natural bench on the edge of a massive stone.

"Then what happened?" asked Jee.

"I shot a few rockets at the tunnel ceiling and flew out just before it was collapsed. That ended the conflict with the Zakéema."

"Did you receive a medal?"

"I did," Alíthe answered proudly. "However, I was reprimanded for disobeying direct orders as well. Luckily, the Taźath saw through it all and rewarded me. Pronómio Tok promoted me to the commander of the Ultos Wing. He also changed my official social status to Koŕeefa."

"Really?" asked Jee, shocked. "So, what happened to your *krísi?* The mark on your forehead?"

"Ah. Unlike the circle and lines of the Graćenta, Merćenta have a small dot below the right eye. You can see the mark left there when it was removed," Alíthe said, pointing to his upper cheek.

"I see it," Jee said.

"Regardless," continued Alíthe, dropping his hand, "that is how I got you. I-I m-mean, how I received this assignment. A-as your bodyguard."

Jee smiled. "Good. I'm glad. But my hair won't turn red."

Alíthe also smiled, his hair changing to pink at the edges. His face, however, turned red. Really red. To the point of evoking Jee's concern.

"Are you all right?" Jee asked. "Your face is really red right now."

"Y-yes," Alíthe replied. "I am red with, um…happiness…and gratitude for this post. May I also say, Glasśigh," he cleared his throat, "that your face is also red."

Now Jee was embarrassed. She did feel warm, and for some reason, her tongue itched whenever she looked at him.

She wanted to bite him.

Wait! Don't bite him! she thought. But then again, his face *does* look delicious. What is this? Is it what Eno meant by *chemistry?* Did Earth women feel this way around human men? And maybe I am now able to get pregnant? This is the most bizarre place in the universe, surely!

The events that occurred over the next few days were exciting for Jee, though tiring as well. The never-ending procession of gifts and creepy proposals for her hand in marriage was still disturbing.

As Jee began to feel better and had satisfied the doctors that her arm was healed completely, Minister of Media, Zola Názma, informed her of several pre-arranged, though unannounced, public opportunities. She was to enjoy the entertainments and delights of being the Glasśigh and be photographed. Also, there would be regular drone-camera videos taken of her in and around One Palace Place to broadcast in an attempt to satisfy the curious.

Jee panicked. Besides the arrival gown and her blue jeans and white t-shirt from Earth, she had only a few simple outfits she received as gifts. Alíthe suggested that Jee go shopping. Using the three-dimensional model created before her arrival, Jee could shop using the city-wide network and Vací. With access to endless providers across southern Tar Aséllo, Vací could display the entirety of the available inventory and project each outfit onto the 3D hologram of Jee via her ABC. That way, she could see exactly how she would look wearing the clothes and be assured of a perfect fit—without ever leaving Palace Place.

After two hours, she had several outfits on the way, with accompanying jewelry, sleepwear, personal items, lotions, and potions.

Reǵeena sat still during all this and tried to hide her emotions. She felt anger. Did the Glasśigh really need any more expensive clothing? Hadn't she purchased enough? Here was the Glasśigh, spending money adorning herself with extravagances, utterly unaware that just one outfit she had purchased from even one of the lesser-known designers was worth more than a Graćenta family made in an Áhthan month. It was sickening. But then again, The Glasśigh didn't really know about all that, did she?

Jee suddenly stopped talking and seemed lost in thought.

"Something feels wrong," Jee looked to Reǵeena. "Wait! Reǵeena, you will be coming with me on these public appointments, right?"

"Yes, if you wish it."

"I do," stated Jee. "Then it is your turn!"

"Glasśigh?" Reǵeena asked.

"Vací," called Jee, "can you scan Reǵeena using my ABC? It must be as accurate as possible!"

"Yes, Glasśigh. Your Armband Communicator is one of only two 12TM-3D scanners in Tar Aséllo."

"Two only?" she asked. "Eno and I are the only ones with them?"

"That is correct," said Vací. *"Both were gifts from The Ef Kéeria of Tar Éstargon to the crew of* Explorer Eleven. *Rare even in that tar, it is said that eye-witnesses cannot tell the hologram from the actual subject."*

"Oh, no!" gasped Reǵeena, standing and backing away in protest. "I couldn't!"

"The best part of shopping," Jee explained, "is shopping with a friend! At least I think it would be!"

"G-Glasśigh? We are friends?" asked Reǵeena sincerely.

"Of course we are! Reǵeena! You are such a silly! Best friends!

Vací! Scan her!" commanded Jee happily. She pulled Reǵeena to a bright spot by the window and removed her ABC. As suggested by Vací, it was placed on a nearby table. "Execute scan!" ordered Jee.

"Scanning," announced Vací.

When the scan was underway, even Alíthe had to agree: it was impossible to tell the difference between the real Reǵeena and the hologram.

Reǵeena now had a new opinion of the Glasśigh: yes, she was still an unaware, privileged elitist, but a kind and generous one. Maybe she should withhold judgment on her for a little while.

Alíthe watched all this, and when asked, gave his opinion. To him, everything looked good on the Glasśigh. Even Reǵeena seemed to look more *classy*. He soon began to enjoy the process, his role being elevated to the 'final decision-maker' if the ladies could not decide. Considering the Taźath was paying for it, there were no wrong choices. However, to his veiled disappointment, there were times that he was dismissed as the ladies chose more intimate pieces, only to be quickly called back into the room to continue his judging of the more general items.

"All this shopping makes me hungry!" announced Jee during one of the longer sessions.

"You know, one is able to order food on the city network, as well as shop for clothing," Alíthe informed them.

"What do you mean?" asked Jee, intrigued. "Like making a phone call for takeout?"

"I do not know what is *take out*," said Alíthe, "however, we can ask Vací to use the network and find you some food. Here."

Jee and Reǵeena stopped shopping and watched.

"Vací," said Alíthe. "The Glasśigh and her friends need lunch delivered. What would be appropriate?"

After a pause, Vací answered: *"The most popular restaurant for the Koŕeefa in this area is* Gaymee's Fresh and Spicy. *It has a government rating of ten out of ten. Famous people who order from here are Commander Barboos of the AMF, Minister Flaymo Melout and—"*

"That's fine," Alíthe gently interrupted. "Please order the most honored dishes and enough for three. And have them delivered to us here at Palace Place."

"Order is complete."

The doorbell rang.

Jee looked at Reǵeena, then Alíthe. "That was fast!"

Reǵeena ran to the door and returned with a small wrapped box. "This is strange. It's not the food, but…it is addressed to me."

"Then open it!" suggested Jee happily.

Reǵeena wrestled with the box and paper, trying to preserve the wrapping. Once the paper was neatly folded, she placed it gently on the table and opened the box. Inside was a delicate ABC, plated in gold metal, as thin as Jee's and just as beautiful.

"Do you like it?" asked Jee. "Try it on!""

Reǵeena froze, mouth open in shock. Clothes were one thing, but an ABC? These were very expensive, maybe over a year's pay for the average Graćenta. Was this even legal? she wondered.

"I-I can't accept this…"

"Nonsense!" insisted Jee. "Put it on!"

Jee assisted her friend in the snapping on and activation of the ABC. "Try it out!"

"All right…um…" Reǵeena put the band up to her face. "Call the Glasśigh."

A voice from the ABC replied. *"That connection is unavailable without permission."*

"I guess it works," teased Alíthe with a laugh.

"Sorry! I'll fix that," Jee said. "Alíthe, how do I fix that?"

Eventually, the food arrived, packaged in a most interesting container. Looking like a rectangular paper box, Jee was reminded of the Chinese food she had on Earth. Inside the largest box were smaller boxes attached neatly to a plastic, tree-like rack, each box containing a different entrée. Alíthe explained the dishes to them, and even Reǵeena was surprised at the variety. As they sampled, Jee's eyes either lit up with satisfaction, or she would display a deep frown depending upon what she thought of the dish. One, in particular, caught her attention.

"Oh! Yummy! This is good! What is this?" she said as she held up a piece of angular white *stuff* on the end of her utensil, a fork-spoon-knife combination. The food was dripping with a reddish-purple sauce that was the consistency of jelly. It was warm, sweet, yet slightly salty and pleasantly chewy, like a perfectly done steak. "Reǵeena! Here! Taste!"

"Oh," Reǵeena purred, eyes growing wide with surprised pleasure. "I like that!"

"Ah," said Alíthe. "That is my favorite as well. That is *candied gorphus*. It's a fish, quite ugly in its natural state, but once cooked, delectable! They eat mostly the floating plants that grow on the edge of the bays of the Sea of Géeves. The sauce is *oray bulbfruit suspan.* Oray grows on the low islands south of the Yamillian Fields."

"I love it. This is like…the best Chinese food I have ever tasted!"

declared Jee.

"Does *Shy-neese* mean…delicious?" asked Alíthe, confused yet curious.

Jee mumbled something unrecognizable as she stuffed another bite into her mouth.

"Where did you say this came from?" Reǵeena asked.

"Gaymee's Fresh and Spicy," answered Alíthe.

"I don't care if it comes from a garbage dump!" laughed Jee. "Let's get more!"

Soon it was time for the *Glasśigh Tour,* as Jee called it. With her small entourage, she attended several events as per Minister Názma's plan.

The first was a play. At least that is what she thought it was. Two men sat on a bench and argued about what it was like to be well-to-do and all the pressures of living a privileged life. They bragged a lot. There was no humor, except in the absurdity of it. Jee found it insanely dull; however, she only yawned once.

There were 'movies' as she would consider them. The theaters were more like lecture halls, and the subjects were all historical in nature. One, explaining the founding of Tar Aséllo, showed actors portraying her great ancestors. Endless 'footage' of them walking through strange and wild landscapes and, well, not doing anything but walking as a narrator droned on and on.

"At least this one has drums," Eno had commented with a laugh. It seemed that after seeing Earth's films, all containing the sweetening of the experience with music, he, too, was unimpressed.

There was a drum concert (boring), then an art exhibition where Jee had to say hello to a small group attending the event (mildly interesting). There was a banquet held in her honor where, for fifty minutes, photographs and short videos were taken of her smiling, posing with attendees, and waving (tiring). Eventually, she was allowed to sit next to Alíthe and eat (pleasant), until the host asked her if she had chosen a mate (embarrassing), and when she answered in the negative, he proposed marriage right on the spot and offered her a box of jewels as was customary (horrifying). She politely declined, then told the over one hundred people in attendance there that her arm hurt and Alíthe would now take her home (relief).

The guests cheered.

The crowds and adoring people fawning over her were fun—at first.

Yet soon, Jee decided that her favorite events were the ones with just Alíthe and Reǵeena and a limited number of cameras. Jee preferred visiting parks, waterfalls, and eating at cute restaurants in Palace City or Etáin. She liked touring the city in a Taźath-supplied skycar and maybe, now and again, waving to people from within the vehicle or on a balcony of some fancy building.

Minister Zola Názma, a somewhat short and portly man with gray hair and eyes that always looked wet, though never teared, came to visit one day. He was pleased to inform the Glasśigh that she was requested to be interviewed on national media. The broadcast would be shown live throughout the tar. It would take place in three days.

In the remaining time before the interview, Reǵeena ushered in an army of makeup and hair artists, clothes designers, and a 'subject coach'.

Jee chose from her extensive wardrobe, and it was 'approved' by the head designer. Her hair was fiddled with but, in the end, left alone—the hairdressers thought it perfect. The makeup staff looked at her for an hour, agreed with 'perfection,' only suggesting a natural lotion to give her skin a boost in hydration, and a sweep of powder to keep her from looking distractedly shiny while on camera. They were dismissed when finished.

The subject coach, a woman named Idrýlla, was the only one who remained. She was tall, though not as tall as Jee, and had an air of formality and professionalism about her. She spoke confidently with a deep, soft voice which reminded Jee of Lauren Bacall. Her mane was comprised of more sandy-colored, singular-looking feathers than she had yet seen. Maybe it was a wig?

"As per government procedure and principal," Idrýlla was saying, "and through years of my own experience, let us discuss subjects to avoid. You are the Glasśigh, and people expect you to act like the Glasśigh."

"I am the first one in history," Jee challenged. "How would anyone have any expectation of how a Glasśigh would act?"

"Though no one has ever seen 'a Glasśigh'—as you refer to the title," responded Idrýlla, "that doesn't mean they have not dreamt of one, or talked about it, or fantasized about her behavior. There are expectations. And you must not offend anyone or call into question your position."

"Position as what?" Jee countered, growing a bit concerned.

"It is only that we want to make sure your image continues to be a good one, and if not good, a *great* one. The people expect a...well...a Glasśigh!"

"All right," relented Jee, slightly confused "How about I trust you on this?"

"Wonderful!" said Idrýlla happily. "I can see we are becoming great friends!"

They sat inside Palace Place at a small table against the main room's towering window overlooking the city. Reģeena joined them shortly, bringing a tray of some tea-like drink called *Cool Tokee* on ice, along with some tobafruit.

"Hmm," Jee mused, considering. "Cool Tokee? This tea is wonderful! And the fruit!"

"I am glad you like it, Glasśigh," said Reģeena with a bow.

"Thank you, Reģeena," Jee replied and bowed back.

"Dear Ásue!" squawked Idrýlla. 'This is what I mean! You bow to no one! Especially her!"

"But she bowed to me first," protested Jee. "I was only being polite! Geez!"

"She is Graćenta! That is why she has the *krísi*," scolded Idrýlla. "That is the way to spot them! You are Koŕeefa! Actually, you are above a Koŕeefa! You are *the Glasśigh*!"

"Sorry, but in America, we don't have such *inflexible* social class rules," Jee said, annoyed.

The smile faded from Idrýlla's face. "This is not America, my Glasśigh."

"If anyone here knows that, it is me," retorted Jee. "Continue with your, ah, *coaching.*"

"Yes," Idrýlla said, satisfied. "Most importantly, do not speak of anything violent."

"All…right," said Jee, surprised that violence was even mentioned.

"No comments about anything against the Taźath or his actions."

"Why would I do that?" Jee asked, perplexed. "He seems like a very nice man, and he is taking care of me."

"He takes care of us all. He knows his place, and we know ours. Also, no taking off your clothes."

"Okay…" Jee responded, even more confused and now embarrassed. "Do people do that in public here? This place is certifiably bizarre!"

Undaunted, Idrýlla went on. "Avoid talking about your love life."

"That will be easy," Jee mumbled. Reģeena smiled and then quickly turned her gaze to the floor.

"And," continued Idrýlla, "no discussion of bodily functions."

"W-why the heck would I talk about that?" blurted Jee. She stood up and placed her hands on her hips in defiance. She had enough coaching.

"I know nothing of Earth," Idrýlla answered, concerned that she had crossed a line. "I am not sure about its customs—"

"Listen, my dear Idrýlla, let's simply say that I will not do anything disgusting. I will not strip or talk about anything unwholesome, all right?"

"But, there is so much that could offend!" Idrýlla protested.

"I am sure! But we can't possibly cover it all. I will be my normal, charming self. You are dismissed," Jee ordered, ending the conversation as far as she was concerned.

Idrýlla stood, bowed, and left the room.

Jee turned to Reǵeena.

"Hmm…can I…can I do that? Dismiss people? And they will leave?"

"I presume so," said Reǵeena softly. "You just did. You are Koŕeefa. She is, well…not. She is Merćenta."

"Reǵeena, you and I need to have a talk about all this someday," Jee said. "Let's get some more of this Tokee and head to the balcony. I need a new outfit for, um…" Jee floundered for an excuse before crying, "Oh, I just need to buy something!"

Quietly, Reǵeena giggled.

▲▲▲

The day of the interview had arrived. Alíthe was to deliver the Glasśigh to the Media Hall of Etáin in Etáin City. He had arranged for security and informed the proper authorities of his escort team's timetable and routes. When he entered Palace Place and saw Jee emerge from her room, he almost collapsed in shock.

She wore a black, flowing, full-length gown. There was a slit on the left side to her upper thigh and showed a little shoulder and most of her bare neck, but nothing too revealing. It was somewhat tight-fitting above the waist, and the material had a silk-like sheen. Jee also wore a unique blue necklace with matching earrings that Eno had given her from his Earth collection. He called it *Tanzanit*e, though Jee had no idea of its source or value.

It's so pretty, she thought.

"By the soul of Aséllo…" Alíthe said softly. He was aware that his skin was turning red, and surely his mane was—

"Hey, Alíthe. Purple mane again?" Jee teased with a smile. She had a growing understanding of the purple.

Alíthe heard nothing. He felt as if he had been dropped from some astounding height, unable to catch himself. His stomach felt empty, and yet, it was an enjoyable feeling.

"Gungh," he croaked.

"What was that commander?" prodded Jee with feigned innocence.

"I just forgot something..." Alíthe stammered.

"Now listen, Jee," said Eno, emerging from his room. "I have just a few last hints." Now really seeing her, Eno paused. "My, you look wonderful—now some advice: don't say anything negative about Áhtha. Don't say anything negative about the Taźath. Just say how beautiful everything is and how happy you are to be home."

"I know all that, uncle," she stated, "but how do I look?"

"Gungh," Alíthe grunted again. "I mean, um, it is time to go."

"You look like a princess, actually," said Eno, eyeing the red-faced commander with disdain. "The Ćlaviath beauty is shining through!"

"I am glad I got all of it," she mumbled to Reǵeena.

Eno shook his head and motioned for them all to move to the door. "It is time. And, Jee, I can say that I am pleased with the returning of your natural skin color. I would say you are about a third of the way back to normal."

Jee glanced at her reflection in one of the large windows. "I like it. No makeup needed! Let's go!"

The Media Hall of Etáin was a large lecture-like space that seated almost one thousand. Located in the center of Etáin City, it was typically used for political meetings and pivotal speeches. It would do nicely for the Glasśigh's first interview. The venue was built for media broadcast with dozens of cameras, both stationary and drone. A curved woven white couch was placed in the center of the main stage. A screen behind the stage as tall as the studio itself projected endless pictures of the Glasśigh at Palace Place. It showed images of her parents, Eno, and the adoring crowds that had been in attendance during her arrival at the Arena of Aséllo.

The audience, all Kořeefa of the upper crust, buzzed with excitement, their manes mostly red with a few purple heads mixed in.

Jee stood in the stage right wing, Reǵeena and Alíthe on each side. She couldn't help but think this was exactly like the Jack Parr show on Earth and that this was the *celebrity* part of being the Glasśigh that Eno had mentioned. Her heart raced.

Drums sounded, and the audience became silent. Some beeping sounds were heard, and then the drums rolled again. A man walked out, dressed formally, much like Eno in his Minister's suit, but this man's garb was colorful, mostly greens and blues in a flower-like pattern. Jee thought he looked silly.

"No one doesn't know our next—our only guest—for tonight," he began.

The audience started cheering, and the drums rolled again. The man waved his hands for silence with little conviction. After a minute, the outcry subsided enough for the man to continue. "So, so…I, Mewnee, your humble host, am pleased to present to you…the direct descendant of Jaydí Ćlaviath and Ásue Asello, also known as—the Glasśigh!"

A roar of approval filled the hall.

Jee walked out into the bright lights, waving. Alíthe and Reǵeena watched from the side wing, smiling.

Mewnee took Jee's hand and held it high, presenting her to the people and the cameras. Jee could see the audience just beyond the lights. Though a little nervous, she smiled and waved. For some reason, she felt comfortable here in front of these people. On Earth, she was an outcast, but here, finally, she was one of them. It felt good.

When the jitters subsided, Jee left her host and moved to each area of the stage, shaking hands with the few audience members in the front row. She had seen politicians do this on Earth, and to her, it just seemed natural. The people did not know what this 'hand-shaking' was all about. Since their hands were already out, with arms extended, ready to touch the Glasśigh anyway, it was a natural reaction for them to hold her hand and move it.

The applause and cheers continued until Mewnee led Jee to the couch where they sat. With the wave of a hand from a crew member, the audience calmed.

"Glasśigh! Welcome, welcome, welcome!" Mewnee gushed.

"Thank you! It's so good to be home," Jee said.

More cheers.

"What was that, that thing you did with your hand?" Mewnee asked, sticking out his hand toward Jee.

She took his hand and shook it.

"That is a handshake," she demonstrated the procedure. "It is a greeting on Earth. Usually, you grasp the other's hand a little more firmly than you just did."

"Like this?" asked Mewnee.

"Not quite that hard," said Jee, pretending to be in pain.

"Oh!" exclaimed Mewnee, a look of concern appearing over his face. "Did I harm you?"

"No, no, no," Jee chuckled. "I am just kidding. Good job."

More cheering. Jee wondered if the audience was going to hoot and holler after everything she said.

"There are so many things to ask you," continued Mewnee, "that it is hard to begin. However, I will start by asking you about your impressions of Tar Asèllo."

"It is so beautiful!" said Jee. "That everything glows is certainly the most amazing thing! There is nothing like that on Earth, really. And the surface of Ganymede is truly stunning. The ice geysers, the fálouse from above—truly breathtaking."

Cheers.

"Ganymede?" inquired Mewnee.

"That is what Earthlings call Áhtha," Jee explained. "And the city of Etáin! Earth also has large cities, but the buildings here are taller and so elegant."

Cheering and applause.

"Now, onto something a little serious," Mewnee said. "I would not be a good host if I did not apologize. We are all saddened by the fact that those horrid Enária tried to assassinate you at the arena, Glasśigh. Were you afraid?"

"Of course!" she blurted, maybe a bit too harshly. "I was afraid, but Eno and I are just fine. I am sure they will find who was responsible."

Cheers.

"And traveling all that time with Commander Eno! That had to be exciting!" offered Mewnee.

"I have other words for the experience," Jee said, "but yes, exciting could be one of them."

The interview continued for a full hour. Jee amazed everyone with tales of her trip, what it was like on Earth, how she lived, what the people were like, and how she spent her days. Jee thought it was mostly silly stuff that she found easy to answer.

As the interview was wrapping up, Mewnee asked her a question that she didn't expect:

"Glasśigh, what do you miss the most about living on Earth?"

It had all been smiles and cuteness up to this point, but now, she had to think. Her Earth parents? The food? The people?

The cameras zoomed in from every angle, hoping to get a close-up of not only her beautiful face but of her reaction.

"That is a hard question to answer," she admitted, mindful of the warnings her coach and Eno had given her. "I certainly miss my Earth mother and father."

"I see," sighed Mewnee, somberly.

The audience applauded politely.

"Besides that, well…the music, I'd say," Jee offered.

Mewnee grinned widely. "We have music! Drums! Some of them are even—"

"Yes, some are tuned, yes, I know," said Jee. "But Earth music is more *elaborate*. There are drums, but also other instruments that make sounds, beautiful sounds…" Her voice trailed off as she remembered.

"Instruments?" asked Mewnee.

"Yes," she said. "They mimic the voice in a unique way."

"They talk?" asked her host.

"No, not really, they vibrate, like they are singing."

"Singing? We sing!"

Mewnee then started making odd puffing noises with his mouth and added in a *boom-boom*. He sounded like a child doing an impression of a drum kit.

The audience cheered.

"That's, um, that's nice," Jee managed to say. "But the Earth instruments have more of a *lyrical* sound."

"Could you sing for us, Glasśigh? The way you did on Earth?"

"Really? Sure! I used to sing quite often at school! I even can use Vací to play the Earth instruments for me. Would that be good?"

Insane cheering.

Mewnee turned and looked off stage. "C-can we connect the studio sound system up to the Glasśigh's ABC?"

Eno, watching from the rear of the hall, thought the interview was going well up to this point; however, his mane was trimmed in white as he began to worry. She was going to sing? Looking at the audience, he saw manes flashing red with excitement at the prospect of the Glasśigh singing.

They had no idea.

Only a few of the privileged ministers and scientists who had listened to Earth broadcasts knew of their music. They studied the effect it had on Áhthans. It had a *strong* impact, very emotional and profound, and it confused them. After much thought and further experimentation, everyone agreed: Earth music should not be released to the masses, especially the Gracénta.

Eno knew that Jee could bring Earthlings to tears with her beautiful voice. And he also knew how it affected him. The waves of emotion he had never felt before. Sadness, longing, motivation – it was a gamble as to what a song could do to a person. Dear, dear, dear! Eno thought. I hope she sings the silly carol about the reindeer.

The crew in the studio, amid the cheers of anticipation, had successfully connected the sound system to Jee's ABC. They also set up a microphone toward the front of the stage. She rose from the couch and walked to that spot, cameras following every move from every angle.

Everywhere, people watched with raw excitement and eagerness, not knowing what to expect. Even in the far hidden caves behind the Síndian Falls, they waited. In the break rooms of factories in Éhpiloh and the surrounding industrial houses, in the Yamillian Fields to the east, workers and their supervisors gathered around screens to observe. In the shops throughout Oso-Gúrith and in the sprawling slums, workers were riveted to displays and projectors. Families watched temporary video devices mounted in public squares and parks.

The Taźath also watched from his official residence. He was worried. He had heard the Earth broadcasts of music and knew what could happen. As a precaution, Pronómio used his ABC to open a call to Zola Názma. He might have to end this broadcast. There could be a chance that the Glasśigh, however unintentionally, might choose to sing one of those protest-like songs he had heard. What was that one? *We Will Overcome?*

Dear Ásue! He thought. That would be horrible!

"Minister Názma?" Pronómio said as his armband made the connection, "we may have an issue here."

"We are ready, my Glasśigh," announced Mewnee.

The crowd cheered. All leaned forward in anticipation.

Once Jee reached the microphone, the studio lights dimmed, except for a few spotlights that shone directly on her. The screen behind, displaying a close-up of her stunning eyes, faded to black. The crowd was clapping wildly.

Jee turned to the side and spoke into her communicator. "Vací? Can you hear me?"

"*Yes, Glasśigh,*" came the soothing voice.

"I am going to sing a song! Are you connected to the studio?"

"*Connected,*" Vací confirmed.

"Can you play the third song in Eno's personal list, the London Philharmonic instrumental version, not the movie version, okay?"

"Yes. Would you like appropriate Earth images displayed?"

"Please!"

"Images and song sent to Media Hall studio system."

The strains of violins, sad, yet magical filled the room. The audience was stunned to silence. They had never heard such sound. It seemed like a group of people speaking, yet so uniform and precise, but separate. The tones were unexplainable.

Jee stepped to the microphone, head bowed, and waited. Then, raising her head, looking straight ahead, and with her crystal clear, soft, young voice with perfect pitch, she began.

When you wish upon a star,
Makes no difference who you are.
Anything your heart desires,
Will come to you.

On the screen behind her, an image of a small snow-covered town at night appeared. It faded into a new image of a night sky filled with twinkling stars, mountains silhouetted in the foreground. As she sang, more pictures of Earth and its wonders were projected; some with shooting stars, some of mountain lakes reflecting points of light from above. Some were of Earthlings watching the heavens, pointing, holding hands.

If your heart is in your dream,
No request is too extreme.
When you wish upon a star,
As dreamers do.

At this point, there was no one watching who was not in tears. They had never heard such a thing or felt such a feeling. While almost all of it was incomprehensible, they each felt something: longing, hope, beauty. Manes flashed between orange, gold, and red, the colors of confusion, sadness, and excitement.

Even Pronómio trembled with emotion. He needed to react quickly before this escalated out of hand. Wiping his eyes, he immediately spoke into his armband communicator.

"Názma! Shut this down! Immediately!"

He saw that the Glasśigh had stopped singing, but the music continued. Would she sing again?

"Minister! I said, shut this down!" Pronómio yelled.

"I can't, Taźath!"

"Why not?"

"It is Vací! She has taken over the entire broadcast! I-I don't have the code. Only the Glasśigh has the code! She is a senior minister! I-I can't override!"

"Use my code!" yelled Pronómio.

"It is voice imprinted. You would have to be here in the studio!"

The Taźath could only watch.

Jee continued in an unwavering voice, no vibrato, no embellishments—just clear, precise, and beautiful tones ringing through.

Fate is kind.
She brings to those who love,
The sweet fulfillment of,
Their secret longing.

Like a bolt out of the blue,
Fate steps in and sees you through.
When you wish upon a star,
Your dreams come true.

After a few seconds of stunned silence, the studio's audience erupted in applause and shouts of praise. If anyone who had watched the reception at the Arena of Aséllo thought *that* cheering was something…

Many had tears; many pressed hands to their hearts. Others looked about, completely lost. Mewnee stood, rushed to Jee, and embraced her as the cheers continued. His mane was completely orange, then turned gold as he sobbed uncontrollably. Finally, it turned red with happiness. After a world of emotion flooded over Áhtha, they spoke again.

"Did you like it?" Jee asked hopefully.

"I have no words to describe…" Mewnee began. The crowd reacted in agreement. "I am confused, I think. I don't know what I am. Or how I feel, but I feel…like…my troubles may be…gone?"

"That is what the song is about!" said Jee with a sigh. "So you did understand!"

Mewnee smiled. Everyone on Áhtha smiled.

"One last question, Glasśigh. Do all Earthlings sing as beautiful as you?"

Jee blushed.

"I—well, to be honest, no. I am pretty good!"

▲▲▲

"What in the name of…I don't know who to invoke here!" fumed Eno as he walked into the dining area of Palace Place to confront his niece. His mane was completely blue.

Jee and Reǵeena sat quietly while Alíthe stood in the corner at attention.

"The Taźath is coming tomorrow," scolded Eno, "and it won't be for a polite discussion on your choice of fingernail polish! Why in the world would you decide to sing a song on that televised program?"

"They asked me to, Uncle!" Jee shot back defiantly.

"The Taźath is not pleased!" Eno continued.

"I don't see why you are angry with *me!*" Jee challenged, rising from the table.

"You don't see?" Eno's voice was full of disbelief. "I asked you *not* to sing! Remember? These people have never heard Earth's music! It has an enormous effect on them! Look! Your bodyguard's mane is still orange! I can see it under the purple!"

Alíthe shrunk further into the corner of the room.

"How could you be so careless?" Eno admonished.

Jee took a step toward the window that led to the expansive balcony but stopped and turned to face her uncle.

"Let me see, Mister, M-minister…" Jee floundered, furious at her Uncle. "Minister of the, *the high science men*, or whatever the hell your title is! Maybe *you* should have said something! *You* used to live here! *I* just showed up a few weeks ago—whatever a week is on this gray ball! How was I supposed to know they would be so emotional? This is your fault!"

"Jee—" Eno tried to interrupt.

"What else should I *not* do? What if I blink? Does that make them crack like glass?" Her anger continued to rise. "Maybe if I sneeze, they sprout an extra eye in the middle of their snakeheads! Let me ask you about a million things that I could possibly do, and you can tell me if I can or cannot do them! Oh! Let's see. That would take about…fifty Ófeetian years!"

"That's true…" agreed Alíthe from his corner, trying to defend the Glasśigh.

"All right," Eno surrendered, holding up his hands. He walked to his niece. It seemed that the feisty, argumentative Gladys was back. "Yes, yes, you are right! I just didn't think you would sing on tar-wide media! It is my fault! I apologize."

They stood, face to face for a moment. Eno's mane returned to its normal shade of brown.

Jee relaxed with a sigh.

"It's all right, Uncle," she breathed, reaching for him and holding him in a close embrace.

This shocked Eno, as Jee rarely offered hugs, at least to him.

Grateful, he hugged her back, patting her shoulders gently with his open hands as one would to soothe a child.

"I am truly sorry," Eno said, slowly and reluctantly breaking the embrace. "I will explain this to the Taźath when he arrives."

The next day, the Taźath appeared at Palace Place for a morning meal with Jee and Eno. Also in attendance was a very quiet and respectful Minister Zola Názma. After the mostly silent meal, Jee excused herself, as was the plan created by Eno. This would give him time to explain what had happened.

"Pronómio," Eno began, as soon as Jee was out of the room, "this incident has been most unfortunate, and for that, I am sorry and take complete responsibility."

"That singing…" Pronómio whispered softly as if trying to remember. "It is too emotional for Áhthans. It makes people…anxious. She must know that it is unwise."

"Yes, yes," agreed Eno. "But we must remember that for all practical purposes, the Glasśigh is an Earthling! Raised by them! Educated by them! On Earth, the arts are the most popular form of entertainment. And singing with music! It fills the air constantly. That is to what she has been exposed."

"Does this singing have a strong effect on the Earthlings?" asked Pronómio.

"Yes, but not as strong as it has on Áhthans," answered Eno. "I ask you, Pronómio, my friend, to have some patience with her. She has only been here for thirty-six days."

"Taźath," interjected Minister Názma, "possibly we keep her a little more structured? But we need to show her to the public, and at the same time, have her on our side."

"Our side?" asked Eno in a suspicious tone, his mane turning a pale orange at the edges. "What do you mean by that?"

"Nothing nefarious, Minister Ćlaviath," assured Názma. "Our research shows that the Glasśigh is extremely popular with the Kořeefa and Merćenta. She is—pardon my saying this—the most 'approved of' person in Tar Aséllo and probably in the educated societies of Áhtha as well."

"So?" queried Eno, not understanding.

"So it would be a good thing," suggested Pronómio, "if she would do a few favors for our government, just a kind word or two, to show support. That is all."

"Oh," said Eno with some measure of relief. "That is not at all unreasonable. In fact, I am sure she would be thrilled to support you,

Pronómio."

"May I suggest," offered Názma, "as a first step of showing support for the Taźath, that we have her adopt an AMF air wing?"

"An entire wing?" Eno was stunned. "Has that ever been done? I know of small groups of our forces being 'favored' by citizens and even corporations who donate time and money—"

"It has never been done before," interrupted Názma.

"And there has never been a Glasśigh," Pronómio pointed out, "until now."

Jee was called back to the balcony. Reǵeena brought refreshments, including small, round things called *gimpoos*, a burnt donut-like delicacy that floated on a thick, black liquid. They smelled smokey. Jee happily skipped them.

"Glasśigh," Pronómio began. "I can't imagine how difficult all this is for you. It must be simply impossible. Give it time. Learn about our society."

The Taźath paused a moment to give Jee a chance to absorb what he said. Then he resumed.

"I must say—I have big plans for you! You are a doer, someone who needs a purpose! You can give the people something to occupy their minds instead of the drudgery of day-to-day living. Let them see you enjoying yourself! And see your support of the things we are trying to do for them! And I have just the way to start. Reǵeena, call Commander Afiéro to us."

Alíthe appeared within moments and stood at attention just to the side of the table.

"Here in Tar Asèllo," said Pronómio, "we have a custom of sponsorship for certain military arms and groups, isn't that true, Commander?"

"Yes, sir," replied Alíthe. "There are the Fifth Security Troop Fílliaths sponsored by the Fílliaths family of the far eastern Girth Sea Islands. Then there is the Diletta Pulsegun Infantry Group, of course, sponsored by the aircraft manufacturing concern of the Diletta Group."

"Not every branch has a sponsor," the Taźath explained "Namely the five wings of our air force: Artos, Eptos, Raltos, Lantos and, of course Ultos, being the most famous and esteemed."

Jee wondered where this was going.

"I have decided to grant a sponsorship the entire Ultos Wing," said Pronómio, pausing for effect. "I think you will agree, Commander Afiéro, that the wing would benefit by being renamed the *Wings of Glasśigh.*"

Alíthe was stunned. He croaked a bit.

Jee's mouth fell wide open. Though not sure of its meaning, she could tell by the look on their faces and their widening smiles that this was a good thing. She was to have her own air wing? Even if it was just honorary, it was still amazing.

"That is—really fab!" was all she could say.

"F-fab?" asked Pronómio.

"I believe it is like *wow*," explained Eno. "Short for *fabulous*."

"Oh! Yes! *Fab!"* Pronómio repeated with gusto. "The adoption is ceremonial, of course, but still a source of pride for the pilots! You would be expected to visit from time to time and bring special supplies. Personal things like sweet seed daffies and other confections, maybe some additional gifts like special meals, or hold a dinner or an event with entertainment. B-but just drums, please!"

They all had an uncomfortable laugh.

"I could do that," agreed Jee, "though I have no money, Taźath. I-I don't even—"

"The Palace will fund this, Glasśigh," said Pronómio. "Just be seen there regularly, allow the media drones to photograph your visits. It will be good for those pilots and their families."

"You will need a new symbol for the rear tail!" Alíthe happily informed them.

"I can assign an artist to help," suggested Názma.

"The ceremony will be in four weeks," said the Taźath as he stood, flashing a broad smile. "So get to work!"

11
The Wings of Glasśigh

The following Firstsun, Jee sat in the main room of Palace Place in front of the vast, ceiling-high windows that looked out over the Bays of Arimía and the sparkling city of Etáin. She was frowning. From a tablet, she studied the first holographic rendering of an emblem for the Wings of Glasśigh. She motioned for Reǵeena to sit next to her, who observed and immediately frowned. The artist, Veegill, who was standing nearby, had a nervous look on his face.

"N-no…" was all Reǵeena could say.

"It looks like a pinup poster," Jee commented.

"A *pinip?* What is that?" asked Veegill.

"Pin-up," corrected Jee. "It's a poster to hang on a wall that is, well, suggestively, um, sexual in nature, showing off a woman's body in a—" she stopped. "Let's just see the next one, Veegill."

"Yes, Glasśigh," said Veegill, appearing somewhat deflated. He leaned over and swiped the screen.

A new image appeared. The women almost screamed.

"Is that me?" asked Jee.

"Dear Asèllo!" Reǵeena squeaked.

"You like it?" asked Veegill, smiling.

"I'm naked!" shouted Jee. "On a bed with an ax!"

"Don't you have anything that is not so…" started Reǵeena.

"Horrible?" suggested Jee, bluntly.

Veegill was visibly near tears. Soon, he was weeping.

"I'm sorry, Veegill," Jee began. "It's just that the work is good. I mean, you have a talent for realism, and, um, the colors are very nice. It is my fault. I should have met with you first."

"Let me just show you another one I made, one that is a little different." He swiped his finger again, and a new image appeared. It was some kind of wild beast devouring a shark-like monster. The Glasśigh was riding the beast.

"Ah, better, I think," said Jee. "At least I am not naked!"

"Veegill, the Glasśigh does not stand for anger or…*gore,"* explained Reǵeena. "She is compassionate. She is full of love and charity. She is more like a beautiful *filbierta bird* watching over her young than a *Treágor chorb lizard* slaughtering a *cargout* for a meal."

"I have no idea what those things are, but I agree," said Jee, taking up a sketch pad that Veegill had brought with him. She also chose a few colored pen-like tubes from his supply. As she sketched, the other two watched. "Let's try something a bit more *neutral*. It doesn't have to be a *realistic* image of an animal or me about to hack someone's head off—"

"While naked," added Reǵeena.

"All right!" snapped Veegill. "I understand!"

"It should have wings, surely, and with something *Glasśigh-ish*—" Jee offered, sketching her idea.

The door chimed. Reǵeena and Jee both called out simultaneously: "Come in!"

Alíthe entered, carrying some food from Gaymee's Fresh and Spicy.

"Alíthe!" said Jee, lighting up. She stood quickly to—well, she didn't know why she was standing, but her heart leaped, and the redness in her face matched his mane.

In response to seeing her, he stumbled into a low chair. Reǵeena stifled a laugh.

Yes, she looks fantastic, as always, thought Alíthe. Her smile is infectious, and now I feel dizzy again. How long will this last? It had been over seven weeks, and still, he was more like mushy green water moss when around her than a bodyguard.

"Sorry…ah…I bumped into your chair…I…" the commander said, silently cursing himself for being that affected and for his clumsiness. He took a breath and slightly recovered from his embarrassment. "I know the path to a woman's favor, however. Shy-nees food!"

"*Chi*-nese, but yes, you do," she replied, touched at his attempt to please her.

"Ah! Veegill," Alíthe called, striding over to the artist. "An honor to meet you! I have seen your work in the media and some of the preliminary emblems you have done for the *G-Wing*, as we like to call it. I am a huge admirer. We are lucky to have you. How goes it?"

"Not well, I am afraid," answered the artist. "So far, nothing seems to be appropriate."

Alíthe appeared shocked. "Really? Not even the one with the ax?"

The young women looked up, sighed, and returned to the sketch.

After a moment, Jee held up a rough rendering of a red letter 'G' from the English alphabet, somewhat stylized, with green wings sprouting from behind. The entire image was surrounded by a golden-hued circle.

"I-I like it!" said Veegill. "I really do! A bit rough, but yes! What does it mean?"

Jee turned and proudly showed it to Alíthe.

"The red character is a letter 'G' from Earth," Jee explained. "It is the first letter of my actual Earth name and also the first letter of the way Earthlings would spell Glasśigh."

"I also like it," agreed Alíthe. "Are those wings of a bird or leaves of green behind the G?"

Jee smiled. "Yes."

"Yes?" asked Alíthe, confused.

"They could," suggested Veegill, "represent both the wings of the Aréus Bird *and* the crops of the beautiful and fertile fields of northern Tar Aséllo!"

They all nodded in approval. A few suggestions were offered on color changes, larger or smaller wings, and Veegill suggested adding a flame shooting out of the bottom of the G, which was vetoed. In the end, they agreed that the original sketch was fine, and Veegill should work on making that look perfect. He seemed happy, took his tablet, sketchpad, and pens with him, and sat in the corner on one of the plush couches.

"I still liked the one with the ax," mumbled Alíthe.

"I will fire you as commander!" chided Jee with a laugh. "It's *my* wing, you know."

"Oh, I see how you have worked this! You move in and take my wing!" he said jokingly, now moving to her. "I will not stand for it!"

Jee laughed out loud, stood, and put up her hands as if to begin a boxing match. She moved from foot to foot, jabbing her fists outward and upward.

"Come on then," she taunted.

"What…is…that supposed to be? Is that how Earthlings dance?" Alíthe asked, taking a conservative, crouching stance as a wrestler might.

"These are my *dukes*," she told him as she looked at her fists, "and you better put yours up, or else!"

"What do you do with them?" he inquired, moving in.

"Get him!" urged Reǵeena, laughing out loud.

Jee moved in quickly, and just like that, *pop-pop-pop*, she landed three light and playful punches on Alíthe's face.

He went down.

"Oh! Alíthe!" she gasped, rushing to him, all kidding disappearing in an instant. "I'm sorry! I didn't mean to—"

Reǵeena also screamed and ran to Alíthe's side. "Is he all right?"

"He's unconscious!" screamed Jee. "Alíthe! Alíthe! Oh no! I didn't mean—I mean he's a war hero, and I just thought he'd be tougher—"

As she leaned over to check his breath, she turned her head to the side and pressed her face close to his.

Alíthe's eyes opened. He smiled at Reǵeena. Before she could warn Jee, Alíthe snatched his assailant, quickly wrapped his legs around her waist, pushed up from the floor with his left arm, and flipped Jee around on her back. Now he was on top.

"Hey!" Jee called out, surprised.

"Nice punches, Earth-person!" he conceded. "But no match for the *actual* Commander of the newly renamed and elite Wings of Glasśigh!"

"Get off of me!" Jee squealed, struggling and laughing.

He did not. Alíthe found himself staring into her eyes, falling into them. Every time she breathed, he felt her move beneath him. Everywhere their skin touched, he felt the heat. Was she feeling the same? he wondered. It was hard to tell. A moment passed.

"Your mane is purple," Jee whispered breathlessly.

She slowly reached up to his neck, wrapped her arms around him, and kissed him. On the mouth. For a long time.

"Um…" murmured Reǵeena, uncomfortably. Obviously, there would be no change in the situation on the floor for a while. And what were they doing anyway? They certainly liked each other, but usually, Áhthans simply touched foreheads, looked into each other's eyes, and maybe *breathed a little deeply.* This action with the mouths was rather…unsanitary.

"Veegill?" asked Reǵeena, walking over to the artist, "h-how are you doing?"

"I have finished!" announced Veegill, standing up in victory.

"Get off each other and look at this!" urged Reǵeena.

Reluctantly and somewhat embarrassed by their public display of affection, Jee and Alíthe extricated themselves from each other and stood.

Veegill faced the others, slowly turned the tablet, and proudly displayed his masterpiece.

"I increased the vibrancy and saturation of the colors; they are more in contrast, and I stylized the 'G' a bit. Oh, and I made the green wings longer and more elegant to reflect your own elegance, Glasśigh."

"That," Alíthe pointed to the design. "That will look most excellent on my machine! Well done. Glasśigh?"

"Simply beautiful!" she insisted and gave Veegill a hug. "You are hired! I have other ideas that will need your skills. Send that to the Taźath and get his approval."

"With pleasure, my Glasśigh!" chirped Veegill.

Of course, the Taźath loved the emblem and approved it immediately. Veegill was sent to the maintenance depot of the Ultos Base and supervised the re-painting and image transfer of each vehicle of the Wings of Glasśigh, not just airships, but the delivery trucks, maintenance vehicles, and fuel supply trailers. The walls of the main hangar were also to be adorned with the new artwork.

The day of the ceremony was a perfect Fullglow: bright, for Áhtha, a medium-blue fálouse, and a mostly clear, cloudless sky with no rain in the forecast. The dignitaries, ministers, and many other ranking officers of the AMF and TSP forces attended, all in formal dress. Jee wore a flight suit that looked somewhat similar to the ones the pilots wore, except that instead of dark gray, itwas white and more form-fitting.

She arrived just in time to observe the pilots' opening physical exercise routines, complete with chants and clapping.

Next on the agenda was the inspection. Jee was to personally inspect the pilots as they stood in formation in the hangar, walking up and down each row, checking for *something*—she had no idea what. She remembered Mr. Gallotta saying that these 'inspections' were more about raising spirits, not really inspecting, so she decided to take the opportunity to make a personal impression on the over one hundred pilots and support people. As she walked through the formation, she made eye contact with each troop and gave a wide smile. To some, she stopped and said a few words, like 'thank you for your dedication' or 'nice uniform' or just a simple 'hello, thanks for inviting me.'

None spoke, of course. It was against protocol. But if they tried, nothing would have come out of their mouths but gibberish. She had that effect on all of them. This was more than an honor. This was *the Glasśigh!* And by the end of the inspection, each and every one of them loved her more, if that was possible, and would do anything for her. Besides having a difficult time simply standing still, the pilots, in various levels of excitement, flashed several different colors in their manes, mostly of red. A good number of male pilots had trouble hiding the sparkle of purple.

When finished, Jee returned to the front of the formation, followed by the ever-present media drones, and stood before Wing Commander Alíthe Afiéro. He stood at attention. Jee made a show of doing a thorough inspection, checking every inch of the uniform, and over-articulating her feigned dismay. At times she frowned in disapproval or put her hands on her hips and looked to the sky, frowning. In the end, she simply looked into Alíthe's eyes and just shook her head. His maned turned an embarrassed pink color at the edges.

The pilots loved it, and more than a few broke their stance and laughed. Pronómio was ecstatic with the performance and clapped loudly, as did the others in attendance. The dozen or so drones buzzed and jockeyed for position, capturing the scene for posterity and transmitting it to the Minister of Media. It would be on the nightly broadcasts across the tar.

Jee was then taken on a guided tour of the rest of the facility. The Wings of Glasśigh emblem was visible on every wall, floor, and door. Veegill did a fantastic job. He was odd, Jee thought, but he was good.

Of course, there was an air show. Dignitaries sat on stands set up just outside of the main hangar. Aréus A4 Fighters, each airship proudly sporting the new artwork, performed formation flying, simulated strafing runs (on the crowd), and complicated aerial maneuvers.

After a short meal break on the parade grounds, the crowd returned to the hangar where a stage had been set up in front of the large door. Jee sat in a simple chair close to the middle and next to Alíthe and Eno. A podium had been placed at the center of the stage, the new emblem already emblazoned upon it. Flanking the rostrum were chairs occupied by other ministers and security force commanders, including Gákoh Kalífus. He had said nothing to Alíthe or Jee and just gave a slight nod when their eyes met.

From the side of the hangar, the Taźath appeared, taking the stage. Polite applause was given as he began his speech. The drones and other media cameras whizzed and flashed as the festivities continued.

"Today, ministers, citizens, and heroes of Tar Aséllo, we take a formal step in celebrating the society and traditions of Tar Aséllo. All citizens, regardless of social status, can revel in the excitement of our very own, *our first*, Glasśigh, and in her decision to adopt the most decorated and celebrated group in our entire security network, the Ultos Wing of the AMF air division."

Applause.

"We require a symbol of our great heritage," the Taźath continued, "a symbol of our commitment to country and people and a symbol of virtue and, yes, love. Though we sometimes do not agree on everything, we agree on our admiration of and the dedication we have to our Glasśigh."

The deafening applause lasted a full minute.

"The adoption of this wing, by our Glasśigh, signifies the *support* she has for our people," he paused for effect, "our government," again a pause, "and most of all, for our *way of life*. So, with great pleasure, honor, and anticipation," the Tażath continued, "I present to you this prestigious wing's new ceremonial commander and sponsor, Glasśigh Asėllo!"

Thunderous applause and cheers filled the room. Jee stood and walked to the podium where she gave the Tażath a simple embrace, which he played up expertly, seeming to be touched and honored and even a little embarrassed. The drones and floor cameras clicked and buzzed, capturing every moment.

What a ham! Jee thought.

She smiled and waved to the adoring crowd and delivered her approved, pre-written, and rehearsed speech perfectly—until the end.

"Thank you, Tażath, for this honor!"

Applause.

"I never thought in my wildest dreams," she said, "that I would come to a strange land, be welcomed, and then command a wing of over one hundred airships—with my name on their sides!"

Laughter, and then applause.

Jee continued, "I am not sure, Tażath, if I need to be voted for, or in, or whatever?"

The Tażath, according to plan, simply shrugged as if to say 'I don't know' and gave an obviously overstated and fake quizzical look to the camera.

"So, I will ask the pilots and their support staff: is it acceptable that I command this esteemed wing of the Asėllo Military Forces?"

Hoots and hollers and some kind of chant that included her name rose up. This was followed by applause and cheers.

"I will take that as a yes!" Jee declared with a laugh. "As my first command, I will appoint Commander Alíthe Afiéro to take my place in all the administrative functions of the wing, leaving me...to just have fun!"

Laughter and more applause.

The Tażath could see how professional and valuable the Glasśigh could be. She was performing perfectly! There were now hours of excellent video and audio clips that could be used for various purposes. This is working out well, he thought. Just keep it close and controlled.

"Seriously," Jee continued, once the applause had died down, "I could not think of a better way to say that I am honored and proud to be one of you and proud to support—"

This, thought Pronómio, will be the best part of the entire day. The Glasśigh was to say how proud she was to support the Tażath and his policies.

But she didn't.

"—the new Wings of Glasśigh! Thank you!" Jee finished. She smiled at the crowd, thanking them again and again as the crowd continued to roar with cheers.

The festivities were over. It had been a long day, and all agreed it was successful. A car waited to take Jee and her friends back to Palace Place. However, before they could leave, the Taźath and Kalífus appeared.

"A word, Glasśigh?" asked Pronómio.

"Of course!" she replied happily.

The others went to the car to wait. Kalífus remained nearby, listening from a few feet away.

"Taźath," she chirped excitedly. "I thought that went so well!"

The Taźath frowned. "It was fine, except for that last part,"

Jee looked sincerely surprised. "The last part? What was that?"

"The speech was to end with you stating your support for me," Pronómio said in a fatherly but serious tone.

There was an awkward silence.

The smile faded from Jee's face. "I-I didn't say that? I thought I did."

"No," said Pronómio flatly. "You did not."

"Oh! I'm…I'm…" she stammered, her face turning red with embarrassment. "I am so sorry. I-I could have sworn…I can't seem to do anything right…" She began to tear up.

Immediately, Pronómio felt pity for her. After all, he thought, she did correctly perform everything else he had asked. Maybe this was a simple mistake. It had been a long day, and, seeing her cry…it was a shame to see such a pretty thing in distress.

"Now, now," he conceded. "You did a fine job. Let's just try a bit harder next time."

"I am deeply sorry, Taźath," she said and embraced him. "Maybe we can redo that part? For the videos?"

"That is unnecessary," he said, surprised at the affection she showed. "I-I can fix it."

"I can't thank you enough for such a wonderful day," she continued, still sniffling. "It meant a great deal to me. I felt, for the first time, that I belonged here."

"Go," said Pronómio with a smile as they separated. "Enjoy your evening!"

With that, she nodded, wiped away a tear, then ran to the car.

The Taźath watched her. What a dear she is! he thought. Patience is what is needed here. After all, she is an alien!

What the Taźath did not see was the immediate dissolving of her anguish, to be replaced by a thin smile.

"What did she say?" asked Kalífus as he joined Pronómio.

"She made a mistake, that is all."

"And you believe her?" pressed Kalífus.

"I do," said Pronómio. "Don't you?"

"I know she affects us emotionally," warned Kalífus. "And she says she is sorry and confused. But I don't know if I believe it. She has a way of making some people…want to please her."

They both watched as the Glasśigh turned and waved before entering the car.

"She is beautiful," said Pronómio.

"She is dangerous," said Kalífus.

"She has value," countered Pronómio. "We must be patient and nurture her."

12
The Playing Field

Due to her mostly successful performance at the Wings of Glasśigh dedication ceremony and the collection of excellent media files obtained during the festivities, Minister Názma had a surprise for Jee. Another series of unannounced public events—some with large crowds!

There was the visit to the Hall of Ministers (boring and uneventful), the Society of Guild Financiers (more boring and even more uneventful), the Manufacturing Hall of Fame (really boring), and the Field Crop and Livestock Trade Association Exposition (besides the interesting animals and fruit, boring and a bit smelly).

One trip that actually delighted Jee was to a local school. Surrounded by a detail of fourteen TSP troopers, the entourage arrived via private transport at the Etáin Tertiary Learning Center, located in the heart of Etáin City.

Once inside the main building, Jee and her companions could hear growing squeals and cheers of delight: word had passed that the Glasśigh was in school for a special visit. The students, maybe half Jee's age, could hardly keep to their seats. Some couldn't and ran down the halls, in tears, searching for their Glasśigh.

As Jee started the tour of classrooms and laboratories, it was all Alíthe and the security detail could do to prevent the students from mobbing her. Once the masses had calmed down and cheered themselves out, Jee was able to observe. Each student sat at well-appointed desks. The advanced technology on display surprised Jee: computers for each student, high-tech laboratory equipment, all beyond anything she had seen anywhere on Earth. The facility looked more like a modern, expensive, exclusive ivy-league school, but from a *Flash Gordo*n movie.

Jee also addressed an assembly of students, said a few words and thanked them "for allowing me to interrupt your day!" Of course, they loved the interruption and cheered for a full ten minutes as she and the entourage left the building. The entire visit had been captured for video by the ever-present hovering drone cameras.

Once in the luxury transport, Jee sat with Alíthe and Reǵeena, and could only shake her head in disbelief.

"We had no technology like that on Earth," Jee told them. "And the kids here are so smart! Was your school like this one, Reǵeena?"

Alíthe shot Reǵeena a look as if to say, 'be careful.'

Reǵeena looked away, watching the city streak by as the transport sped along the main highway of Etáin City. How could she answer? How *should* she answer? She took a breath and sighed.

"What?" asked Jee.

"No, Glasśigh, my school was not like this one. Not at all. I went to a work-program school in Éhpiloh, a city across the water."

"All schools are free," added Alíthe, still looking at Reǵeena.

"That's true," the servant said. "But they are not all the same."

"Your school did not look like that school?" asked Jee.

"No," stated Reǵeena, with a quiet laugh.

"Each school teaches for different purposes," countered Alíthe.

"And for what purpose is a work-program school?" asked Jee in a suspicious tone.

Reǵeena turned back to Jee. "We were taught how to farm, load trucks, and clear roads of debris, and other manual labor. Some were lucky, as was I. We learned how to serve the Kořeefa as maids, gardeners…Maybe a visit to a work-program school could be scheduled," suggested Reǵeena sarcastically.

Jee noticed her tone and frowned. It seemed odd to her that each school was different. Still, back on Earth, there were private schools, which were supposedly expensive and better than public schools. Maybe that is what this was about, Jee reflected.

A day later, Media Minister Názma announced he would personally escort the Glasśigh to her next public appearance. On the upcoming Fullglow, The Glasśigh was to enjoy a private, luxury accommodation seating room for a favorite Tar Aséllo sporting event: the Adéekos Rush Championship. Of course, Jee knew nothing about the game of Rush, but the fact that it was to take place in the Arena of Aséllo had her thrilled.

"This will be most exciting," assured Alíthe. "I have never been to a game of Rush!"

"It is for Kořeefa only," said Názma. "Not for honorary Kořeefa, I am sorry to say. But you will attend because of your assignment."

Alíthe visibly looked deflated but recovered immediately. "I am honored," he responded. He had seldom been reminded of the fact that he was not born Kořeefa. Then again, he did primarily associate with Ultos Wing members, and social engagements outside of that all-Merćenta sphere had been rare until now.

Reǵeena was not at all excited and seemed sullen about the whole affair. However, she did see this as an opportunity to obtain a glimpse into what the Glasśigh was really like. Would she enjoy the game? Or see it for what it really was? For that reason alone, she agreed to go when Jee insisted, much to the chagrin of Minister Názma.

"It's a package deal," Jee stressed to him. "Both of us or none of us."

The Glasśigh chose to wear an Earth-fashion outfit, as she called her choice: shorts, a plain white t-shirt, and the closest thing to tennis shoes to be found.

The plan was for their appearance to be kept secret until they arrived via groundcar, had entered the luxury room, and taken a moment to relax. At some point during the game, Jee was to walk out onto the balcony overlooking the playing field and wave, smile, and then enjoy the rest of the day. The media drones would capture the entire event.

That is not what happened.

Jee and her companions drove into the private parking area beneath the Arena of Aséllo, followed by the security team. They walked inside through a private entrance then through vacant halls to the luxury room. Jee was surprised at its size, larger than her school gymnasium in Idaho, but with luxurious chairs and lounges that faced a wide and tall glass window looking outward to the field. To one side was a door that led to a small balcony where Jee assumed she was to execute her wave. Along the other sides of the room were ornate restaurants with table seating for at least two hundred.

"I thought it would be smaller," was all Jee could say.

"I thought it would just be the four of us," said Alíthe. "Why such a large—"

His words were interrupted by the sound of a door opening at the far end of the room and the immediate appearance of two hundred other guests, mostly all men. They ran immediately to Jee.

"Hold! Hold back!" called Alíthe, but it was a stampede.

Within seconds they were all around her, on all sides, all talking at once, smiling, handing her cards, and basically jockeying for position. They tried to get a few words in before they were pushed or yanked away by another.

"Glasśigh! How beautiful you are!" giggled one. "I am a fine Áhthan of considerable wealth!"

"That's...nice," Jee said, forcing a smile as she was jostled a bit. She looked at the card he offered her. It was just like the ones Eno received with the gifts: a goofy picture of the man before her and a bio, mostly detailing his fortune.

The crowd continued to press inward.

"I say back away!" growled Alíthe forcefully, his mane flashing deep blue.

"You do not order us around, Merćenta filth!" scolded a slightly rotund man with an angry scowl. His mane, as well as the others, flashed between blue and purple.

"I am the Glasśigh's bodyguard, and you *will* back away!" repeated Alíthe, his mane turning an even deeper blue. The crowd did not heed his warning.

"Please, good people!" Názma called to the crowd. He also was ignored.

"I am wealthy!" trumpeted the rotund man, easing his scowl as he stared at the Glasśigh with an ogling expression complete with one raised eyebrow. "Not a promoted *sloggin* that crawled up from the gutter like this, this *loweworm!"* he grumbled, pointing to Alíthe. "Look at my clothes, my ABC! It is worth as much as the Palace itself! I can provide for you!"

"You are obnoxious!" snapped Jee.

"Please, sirs, give the Glasśigh some room!" cried Reǵeena. The men ignored her.

"My name is Sumgee," announced a smiling young man who had made it to the front of the crowd. "I am a worthy mate if I must say so!"

"What?" shrieked Jee, horrified. "Gross!"

"He is a *gobish targi!*" snarled the man next to him. "Look at his lips!"

"He has no lips," observed Jee.

"My point exactly. Now *my* lips, on the other hand—"

Alíthe pushed his way in front of Jee and called out as loud as he could, "I said back off or be fired upon!"

This dulled the roar and lessened the pushing for a few moments, but then, with renewed energy, the mayhem began again.

Jee began to panic.

Reǵeena was knocked to the floor.

"Glasśigh! Get behind me," Alíthe commanded. He bent down to help Reǵeena to her feet. As he stood, he exposed a small hand-held pulse gun, pointed it at the ceiling, and fired three shots.

"I command you to back away, you *bloated, guarf-sacs!"* Alíthe shouted as he pointed the gun at the crowd, swinging it repeatedly left and right. Do you understand? Get out! Now! Go!"

At the sound of gunfire, seven TSP security detail men positioned outside poured into the room.

"Empty the room! Get these people out of here!" Alíthe ordered sharply.

It took several minutes, but the crowd was 'escorted' away. At Alíthe's insistence, the security detail took up positions outside each entrance. No one was allowed entry without Alíthe's permission, and unless it was the Taźath, the answer would be 'no'.

After some time to recover, the four of them took seats by the window, looking out at the field.

"T-thank you, Alíthe," Jee stammered, still a bit rattled. "What was that all about?"

"It was about you," said Alíthe, embarrassed. "They were suitors."

"I figured as much," sighed Jee. "They were disgusting, I can tell you that!"

"I apologize," said Názma. "I will speak to Commander Kalífus as soon as we return about the 'secret' that someone let out."

"My main concern is the safety of the Glasśigh," Alíthe fretted, then turned to Jee. "At the first break, you will wave at the crowd, and we leave immediately."

Jee nodded in agreement.

Drums rolled and pounded, and they looked out the window. Jee could see that the cheering arena crowd was much smaller than the one that welcomed Jee and Eno home. She turned her gaze to the playing area. It was clear that it was made of some kind of lumpy, green grass, and twice as large as an American football field. Then she noticed the oddest thing.

"Minister," she asked, "is the field *tilted?*"

Reǵeena smiled. What would the Glasśigh think of the rules to *this* game?

"Yes, it is tilted," Názma responded happily. "Ten degrees!"

Again, the drums rolled. Two teams entered the field, causing the crowd to cheer once again. One team of thirty or so individuals wore gray, rag-like clothes that really didn't match. The other team had bright red padded uniforms and sturdy-looking helmets.

"The idea," explained Minister Názma, "is that the gray team will try to run uphill into the black area at the top of the field. The red team will try and stop them. If a gray gets to the top, he or she can stay off the field for the rest of the period."

"I see…" said Jee.

"This red team is actually the *Norgana Wilgoes!* They are the highest-scoring team in the league!"

"That must be why they are in the Rush Championship," suggested Jee.

"Right you are," confirmed Názma.

"And the gray team?" asked Jee.

"They are just the opponents for today," answered Názma.

Jee wrinkled her nose. "Do they have a name?"

"No," replied Názma.

"That is *odd,"* Jee wondered aloud. "But so is this whole world—to me at least! I assume the grays are the second-best team then?"

"No," said Názma. "As I said, they are just the opponents for today."

"Wait…what?" blurted Jee, still confused.

"The grays are randomly selected," added Reǵeena. "They are everyday Graćenta; maybe some are out of work."

"B-but they are in the championship! They must have played the game before though, right?" asked Jee.

"No, Glasśigh," Reǵeena informed her. "Only Kośeefa and Merćenta can play in the league."

"So…they are just people someone picked up off the street?" Jee asked bewilderedly.

"Yes," answered Názma and Reǵeena simultaneously.

"I must be missing something," mumbled Jee. She continued studying the field and could see that the surface was not only tilted but had obstacles in the form of tall mounds and holes spread all over in an uneven way, not in any pattern at all. She also noticed several members of the red team carried poles of ten feet or so, about the width of a broomstick.

"Why does the red team have sticks, but the gray team doesn't?" Jee asked.

"That is the rule," said Názma.

"Hmm. How do the teams score points?" Jee asked warily.

"The red team gets one point for every gray they knock down and put into the holes you see!" explained Názma excitedly. "Sometimes they use the poles to slow the grays!"

"Really? All right…then I assume at some point they switch sides, and the gray team gets to score points."

"No. The grays do not get points," stated Názma, as if it was as natural a thing as the glowing of Ofeétis. "Only the red team."

Jee looked at him for a moment, then looked to Reǵeena, then to Alíthe, who only shrugged.

"So, only one team is allowed to score points?" asked Jee.

"Yes!" said Názma. "Very good, Glasśigh! You are gaining an understanding—"

"How…So the reds always win?" Jee probed.

Reǵeena nodded.

"It is not *winning;* it is *scoring points,*" clarified Názma. "You see, it is the *number* of points they score that is important. All the teams in the league play against a group of grays and collect points! Whoever scores the most points in the season goes to the championship, in this case, the *Norǵana Wilgoes."*

"So the Wilgoes, the reds, never play against any of the other red teams? Just randomly selected…amateurs? Who they beat with sticks and throw into the holes?"

"That is correct," said Názma. "One point for each! Oh! It is starting!"

Jee looked on. She could only believe she was missing some key element of the game. It might be better to watch for a bit, she thought.

On the field, the red team rushed downhill with incredible speed in a formation of sorts. The reds with the poles led the way. The gray team clumsily scrambled, trying to hide behind the mounds on the field, or each other.

Jee watched with the rest of the arena crowd as a red team player pummeled an unlucky gray with a pole, causing him to fall to the ground, seemingly unconscious. A different red team member without a pole grabbed the fallen gray, dragged him to a nearby hole, and threw him into it. The hole looked to be ten feet deep.

"A hole point already! Amazing!" cheered Názma.

Jee gasped in horror.

Another gray was thrown savagely into a hole, then immediately, another was tossed in after him.

"Double hole!" yelled Názma, along with the crowd.

"This is stupid!" Jee exclaimed. She looked to Alíthe to see if he had an opinion. He was embarrassed, his mane turning a pinkish hue around the edges. "Reǵeena, why in the hell would the grays volunteer for this? Do they get paid at least?"

"They do not," whispered Reǵeena into Jee's ear. "They are forced to play, and there is an endless supply of grays. Most are from Oso-Gúrith. All are untrained Graćenta."

The crowd roared ecstatically. Another gray had been struck hard in the face by a pole. The gray stumbled, and a red Wilgoe slammed into him in a football-like block that knocked him into a hole.

Názma stood with the others in the crowd and applauded. "That was a great hit! Did you see that? He wacked that gray right in the face, and Jarvinktis butted him right into the hole!"

"This is ridiculous!" shrieked Jee. "People are being hurt!"

"They are only Graćenta, my Glasśigh!" said Názma dismissively. "You will grow to love it!"

"I doubt it! I mean, if the grays had a chance to start from the top or score points! Or defend themselves…if the playing field was even, then it would still be idiotic, but—"

"Why would the reds give up their advantages?" asked Názma, pulling his attention away from the game. "They want to score points!"

Jee's face grew red with anger. "Reǵeena? Do you like this—"

"No!" Reǵeena answered quickly. Her resentment was apparent. "It is demeaning and unfair and, most of all, cruel."

"Reǵeena Ahdelfía!" chided Názma. "Know your place!"

"She is right!" protested Jee. "This is sick! I'm not watching anymore."

Jee stood up. Alíthe immediately rose, as did Reǵeena.

"Nor am I," added Reǵeena with a smile. It was becoming apparent that the Glasśigh *was* the kind of person Reǵeena had hoped she was.

A drum rolled, and play halted.

"But the match has only just begun!" Názma pleaded. "It is just the first rest time! There are nine more sessions!"

Reǵeena and Alíthe followed the Glasśigh to the exit.

"Aséllians of the Arena of Aséllo!" boomed a deep voice over the audio system within the stadium. *"We have a special guest attending the game today!"*

"But Glasśigh!" called Názma. "It is time for you to wave! Come back!"

Taking the cue, a swarm of drone cameras appeared by the window. They recorded the Glasśigh, clearly angry, shaking her index finger at Názma, and then dismissing the Minister with a rude wave and a few unheard words. Finally, she stormed out of the room.

13
Tepótah

Jee, Reǵeena, and Alíthe returned home immediately after the game. It was only a few minutes before Eno blasted into the main room at Palace Place, dismissed Reǵeena and Alíthe, and lit into Jee. She could see his mane had changed from dark brown to almost entirely blue.

"I have been officially reprimanded by the Taźath! I had to literally get on my knees and apologize! And all you had to do was wave!" Eno growled. "How hard could that possibly be?"

"Have you ever seen a game of Rush?" she fired back, hands on her hips and ready to fight.

"Of course! It has been part of our society for—"

"It is an abomination! Poor, defenseless Graćenta being beaten by bullies with sticks? Thrown into holes? It is barbaric!"

"Earth had boxing!" said Eno in defense. "Barbaric could be an accurate word to describe that sport!"

"So what? It *is* barbaric! I don't like that either!" Jee angrily pointed out. She continued, counting out her reasons on her fingers. "One, boxers choose to compete! No one is forcing them like they do the Graćenta! Two, they can quit if they want to! Three, boxers get paid! And four, boxers are on equal footing with their opponents!"

"It is just a game!" Eno shot back.

"It is not just a game!" she countered. "Games are supposed to be fun! Maybe you could play it sometime—"

"I have!" blurted Eno. "In school!"

"Really? How about you try playing it as a Graćenta! Would you trade places with them? On that uneven field?"

"All you had to do was wave!" he snapped.

"Answer me!" she demanded, taking a threatening step toward him. "Would you trade places with them?"

"Why would I trade places? Give up my—" Eno stopped short.

"Your advantage?" Jee barked. "Your unfair advantage? You're just like all the other Kořeefa bullies! You didn't work for what you have! You were born into this! And the Graćenta were born out of it! I'm not going to smile and wave like a trained *poodle,* as if everything is ginger-peachy!"

She stormed off into her room.

Eno was dumbfounded. Usually, any argument where screaming

occurred and threats were leveled yielded nothing. No person changed their mind or had an epiphany about the wrongs of their position. But at this moment, doubt began to grow. Eno's time on Earth permitted him to see much of that world's inequality. He read of the riots in the American south, the violence between races all over the globe. He saw evidence of the extermination of Jews during the war. All were based on greed for power, fear of anyone different, or from wrongs perpetrated so long ago that the reasons for hatred were forgotten, though the hatred remained.

His niece had a point, he had to admit. Eno was born into privilege, but he did work hard for his position and fame. Yet, if he had to trade places? Especially at the beginning of his life? Growing up Graćenta? Nothing he had accomplished would have ever been possible. He never would have seen the surface of Áhtha, never traveled to orbit Ofeétis, never been to the rings of Gayída. And as insane as it all was, he never would have gone to Earth. Where would he be today? Perhaps Asèllo's class structure was just wrong. Maybe a life of ease built on the backs of injustice was a tainted prize – if you had a conscience. Earth and its ways were part of them both now, and possibly, he was more human than he realized. No, he did not wish to trade places with the Graćenta. For that, he felt ashamed, and a knot began to grow in his stomach.

Jee canceled all public appearances. Though Eno spent time going through his collections, he mostly looked out the window in the kitchen and murmured to himself.

On a clear and unusually bright Lastsun, everyone's mood lightened. Eno actually said 'hello' to everyone, then returned to his cataloging of the collection of Earth files and images on his PDT. Jee, Reǵeena, and Alíthe remained on the Palace grounds, enjoying the scenery and the warm, clear weather. With not a single cloud in the sky, the fálouse was a deep blue, undulating above them as if they were underwater in a Caribbean sea, the surface slowly twisting and whirling above. No matter how insane this whole situation was, Jee realized that the beauty of Tar Asèllo always astonished her and, at the same time, put her at ease.

Later, Reǵeena prepared a light dinner of simple mixed fruits and white, pretzel-looking things that tasted like cheese. Jee just hoped they *were* cheese, and not some odd grubs or worms—they certainly looked like worms.

"Do you require anything else, Glasśigh?" asked Reǵeena when they had finished eating.

"No, I am fine," Jee replied. "Though I would like to ask a favor? From you both?"

"Of course, Glasśigh," said Alíthe, automatically.

"Oh Earth, people called me Jee. Please call me that. No more Glasśigh—it is so formal. Is that understood?"

"Yes, Glasśigh," they both answered.

"I-I mean, yes—" Alíthe strained, as if he was unable to form the correct sounds. "J-J-J—Jee."

"Yes, J-Jee," echoed Reǵeena.

"Why is it so hard?" asked Jee, laughing.

"It is not my place," said Alíthe. "One must know one's place and treat people with the respect to which they are entitled."

"It is also not my place," added Reǵeena.

"You are Koŕeefa *and* the Glasśigh," explained Alíthe. "I can't think of anyone who deserves more respect than you. Our place is to serve you."

"Our class dictates it," continued Reǵeena.

Jee shook her head, agitated. "And I am frustrated and sick of all this. You know, I asked Vací about the classes, and everything she told me seemed to be…watered-down."

"Watered?" asked Alíthe.

"I mean, not all was described thoroughly," Jee clarified. "Vací implied that everyone, in all classes, was happy about the structure of the society. But I don't think that's true. I want to know the whole story. The real story."

"What do you want to know?" asked Reǵeena.

"These classes," continued Jee, "they mean more than what *job*s people do; it is how they are treated, right?"

"No," replied Alíthe.

"Yes," countered Reǵeena.

Now Jee was scowling.

"All classes are needed for society," instructed Alíthe. "All have a function."

"So who decides what class you are in? What function that you are to perform?" Jee asked.

"We are born into a family," offered Alíthe. "And that family is in a class. Certain classes perform certain functions."

"My point is that no one has a choice, correct?" asked Jee.

Neither spoke. And that made Jee wary.

"I think I see what this is," she said softly, though there was a pit in her stomach. "Let me ask this—and Reǵeena, you answer first: What if you wanted to stop being a Graćenta and become a Koŕeefa? How would you do that?"

Reǵeena looked to Alíthe, seeing his stern look. She hesitated.

"Don't look at him!" snapped Jee. "Answer me!"

Reǵeena jumped, startled at the outburst.

"I-I'm sorry, Reǵeena," Jee said, reaching out to her friend and stroking her arm gently. "Please?"

After a moment, the girl answered softly. "It is not allowed. It is against the law to change."

"We know our place in the world," offered Alíthe. "And no class is really any worse or better than any other."

"That is not true," objected Reǵeena, now with some conviction.

"I saw that game of Rush, Alíthe," Jee objected. "I would say those people on the gray team were not better off."

"Kośeefa and Merćenta—they live better," added Reǵeena. "They have better lives. Better schools, better health. More choices. They can go anywhere they want and do whatever they want. This is not true for Graćenta."

"That's not fair," said Jee. "It seems like you are being kept down, Reǵeena. That is not freedom."

"Freedom is for the Merćenta and Kośeefa," said Alíthe. "That is just how we have lived for a thousand years."

Jee noticed that now Alíthe's statements were made with a wavering—a weakness in his voice—and he knew it. It was time to test him.

"And you are all right with that?" asked Jee. "With scoring points on an uneven playing field? With the rules stacked in your favor?"

"Yes. I-I mean no! Um…" stuttered Alíthe. He now saw her point, as uncomfortable as it was.

Jee waited for a better answer; however, Alíthe just sat there, staring at her. She rose from the table abruptly.

"I am tired," she announced, somewhat formally.

"That is good," sighed Alíthe, standing. He was happy to change the subject. "You must be adjusting to the phases of Ofeétis and—"

"Good night, Commander," said Jee, coldly. "Reǵeena?"

"Yes, J-Jee," Reǵeena said, standing.

Together, the two women walked briskly into the house.

Alíthe, still standing, seemed shocked, then embarrassed.

"All right then," he said to no one. "I will just stay here…and guard the, ah…the flowers."

Reǵeena entered Jee's room, and immediately was stunned by its size and opulence. It was as large as the main room and kitchen of

Palace Place combined, with a soaring ceiling that rose twenty feet or more above the polished stone floor. A massive closet was off one side, almost nine hundred feet square. Colorful and delicate stone inlay artwork adorned the walls in beautiful, flowing patterns. There was a large bed against the far wall, facing the floor-to-ceiling windows. Next to it was a lounge that could hold two people, easily, positioned to take in the view: a private garden-balcony, the Bay of Solcey to the south, and Shay Point to the east, the home of the G-Wing. Reǵeena could see Aréus A4 Fighters taking off and landing, their lights sparkling like miniature stars in the darkness, like the *DeeDee* bugs she used to chase as a child, glowing on and off in different colors as they fluttered about.

By contrast, Reǵeena's room at One Palace Place, was more of a medium-sized closet, though still larger than the entire apartment she and her brother had shared in Éhpiloh.

"Come here, please," said Jee as she hopped up on the bed and crossed her legs under herself. "Time for girl talk."

Reǵeena complied, though uneasily. Jee was not acting like the entitled Kośeefa *snart heege* that Reǵeena had initially presumed. Still, it was not right to be so informal with the Glasśigh. Then again, there seemed to be a special friendship developing. And, she was ordered to join her for this, what was it called?

"What is girl talk?" Reǵeena asked.

"Ah! It is an Earth saying," explained Jee happily. "We talk about whatever we want, with no boys around."

"Ah, I see," said Reǵeena. A smile appeared on her face. "Let us talk as Earth girls do."

"Great!" started Jee happily. "So I have a question for you. The *krísi* you have? When did you get one?"

"I did not *get* one," said Reǵeena. "It was put there by a doctor when I was two months old."

"Why do doctors do this?" asked Jee as she studied the mark.

"All Aséllians look the same, yet are not the same. This way, those above us can identify us quickly."

"For what purpose?" Jee asked, fearing she already knew the answer.

"So they know how to treat us. Keep us from doing what we are not allowed to do. To keep us in our place."

"At the bottom?"

"My *krísi* explains it all," said Reǵeena. "The circle is me, a Graćenta. But the two lines above the circle signify the upper two classes, the Merćenta and the Kośeefa."

Jee nodded. "I understand. Let me ask, are you allowed to vote? On anything? Go to a school of your choice? Choose your job?"

"None of those things," Reǵeena replied.

Jee thought of this, then after a moment asked, "What is it like for you, Reǵeena? You and the other Graćenta? Really? How bad does it get? I'd like to hear the truth, for a change."

Reǵeena appeared uncomfortable. She knew what the treatment of Graćenta was really like—she was one, after all—but she also knew the bitter truth was never exposed to the upper classes. Besides, even if they knew, they wouldn't care. They thought themselves better than the Graćenta—and they were—as far as they were concerned.

"It would be hard explaining it to you," Reǵeena finally responded. "You are the Glasśigh. You live in *this* world." Reǵeena motioned with her hands to mean the house, the closet, the view. All of it. "You wouldn't understand."

"I see," murmured Jee thoughtfully. She sat back on the bed and considered the point. With a slight grimace, she leaned closer to Reǵeena and began speaking softly and thoughtfully, yet deliberately.

"When I lived on Earth, I wasn't the *Gluh-sigh.* I lived in a small town in a place called Idaho."

"Eye-duh-ho?" asked Reǵeena.

"Yes. It was cold there but beautiful. My Earth parents were not wealthy by any means. We led a simple life. I went to a school, not a fancy one. We had some good teachers, and I studied as hard as I could. My parents worked hard. They called me by my Earth-name, Gladys."

"*Glay-diss*?"

"Close enough," Jee said with a smile.

"And you had many girl talks? With the other children?"

The Glasśigh seemed to have a sadness wash over her, and Reǵeena became concerned.

"Glasśigh? I-I mean *Jee*?"

"I-I never had a girl talk. I did see them in the movies—'videos' you would call them. I really didn't have close friends," Jee went on. "I was an oddball. That is what the kids called me. A weirdo."

"Odd-ball? Weer-doh?" asked Reǵeena, not understanding.

"I was not well-liked, and I spent much of my time alone, reading. Eno said it was because there was literally no chemistry between the Earth people and me."

Reǵeena thought of this for a moment. The Glasśigh must have been lonely. "I am sorry," she said.

Jee gave a helpless shrug. "I never understood it. I was just a little girl. No one liked me except my mother and my father. He was…very special to me. I miss him."

Reǵeena just looked on her with pity. Considering what this woman had been through, Reǵeena realized that being the Glasśigh was not what everyone dreamed it would be. Yes, it could have been if Jee had been raised here, taught to accept a life of privilege. She might have then believed it was her right as a Kořeefa to take everything to which she was entitled.

But the first Glasśigh—no one could have imagined her childhood, her years *on another planet*, living as…well…like Graćenta, based on what she just revealed. That made her different. And special. Maybe she could understand the real Tar Aséllo.

"And now, here I am! The Glasśigh!" Jee rolled her eyes. "And I am still an oddball," she added with a laugh. "So maybe, instead of explaining this place to the *Gluh-sigh*, you could explain it to the little oddball weirdo girl from Idaho? Named Gladys?"

Reǵeena smiled. "I could do that, *Glaydiss*."

Jee smiled and gave Reǵeena a hug. It was strained for a moment, but soon, Reǵeena hugged back, tightly.

"What is really going on here, Reǵeena?"

She thought for a moment, wondering where to start. "Maybe it would be better if I showed you?"

▲▲▲

Jee and Reǵeena left Palace Place early, the breaking of Newsun still hours away. Reǵeena insisted that even at this time, there would be Graćenta about in Palace City, on their way to work, or on their way home. To avoid being seen—or worse—mobbed by adoring crowds, Reǵeena dressed Jee in some of her clothing brought from Éhpiloh: a simple gray cloak and a veil to cover her face. Of course, the garb was too short, but it worked.

They silently left Palace Place by the back servant's entrance. The guard there simply nodded, assuming both women were servants, probably out to obtain fresh food for the daily meals. They descended stone stairways covered in ivy-like vines that led five stories downward. There were few lights, and that made the descent difficult, but after some time, they arrived safely at the lowest level of the city.

Reǵeena led Jee to the north, walking along quaint streets. They passed shops, service buildings, and cafes. None were open, yet they were manned by workers preparing for the week.

"I hope they get paid well for the early hours!" commented Jee laughing.

"They do not," Reǵeena replied, shaking her head. "All Graćenta get paid the same wage, regardless of position or hours worked. It is barely enough to put food on the table. That is how they keep us in our place."

The young women walked in silence, heading down the main street. Small trucks rambled past, driven by their sleepy drivers. Workers dressed in all types of uniforms hung onto the sides of these trucks or rode uncomfortably in the back amid boxes of goods and baskets of food, destined, according to Reǵeena, for Palace City.

Jee noticed that the further they were from the Palace, the less maintained were the streets. Every so often, there were potholes and puddles of odorous water. The buildings and park-like areas became less frequent. There were a few grungy restaurants.

"Who lives in this area?" asked Jee.

"This is an industrial district," explained Reǵeena. "Not many live here. It stores food, medical supplies, and other wares in support of Palace City. Areas like this are everywhere in the southern tar, mostly by the larger cities."

"How much further do we need to walk?" Jee asked.

"Another five minutes. We will go to the transport station, then take a worker's car north to *Tepótah,* our destination."

No one noticed the tall woman or her small friend as they continued north along the ever-narrowing streets. Soon, Jee could see the Sea of Etáin ahead and a small island out in the bay. The faint glow of the *sallo luea* in the water was in contrast to the dull but orderly structures that lined the streets. Soon the road began to curve around small hills, large rock formations, and larger plots of undeveloped land. They rounded a corner where there were few lights, though up ahead was a dark building with a single amber-colored bulb on the outside which marked an entrance. A crowd of workers suddenly poured out of the building, filling the street as they walked toward the palace.

"This is the transport center for workers," Reǵeena said as she led her friend inside.

To Jee, it looked like a subway terminal, though she had never seen one in person. Workers were streaming past them, silent, heads down. No one looked happy, though some talked among themselves quietly.

A worker's car sat still by an open archway within the terminal. Reǵeena led Jee inside the bus-like vehicle, and after dropping a few coins in a slot near the door, they took seats along a side bench. A few workers now filed into the windowless transport, but it was mostly empty. Soon, it rattled and lurched and moved forward.

"The workers who use these cars live in Tepótah, a worker's village," explained Reǵeena softly so as to not attract attention. "They must pay to ride the car. But many who have children can't afford the passage. They walk the miles and then leave their children in a village home or a workhouse. Many sleep somewhere close to Palace City, sometimes on the streets."

A few other passengers began to notice the tall lady with the large green eyes. Some whispered, a few stared. Jee could only turn away. Soon, the car stopped, the door opened, and the passengers walked out into the darkness.

"Where to now?" asked Jee. She was getting uncomfortable. This area was not like anything she had seen in Etáin or Palace City. The streets were dark, the buildings bland and in disrepair, and there was an odor of rotting food. Few vehicles were on the streets, and the ones she did see were delivery types, looking more like garbage trucks than anything else.

They walked a short distance and soon stood before a brutal-looking building, barren of any ornamental constructs. They went inside. It looked like a warehouse, dusty and strewn with junk. Children, maybe a hundred in total, were playing at tables piled with what looked to be toys. Yet, as Jee watched them, she noticed not playthings, but old machines, piles of metal, and strange devices.

"This is a workhouse of a kind," said Reǵeena. "This is where Graćenta must leave their children while they go to work. They pick through discarded things, looking for valuable and reusable pieces. It is owned by Kořeefa business people and run by Merćenta managers."

"At least they earn some money," said Jee.

"What they earn pays for their place in this workhouse."

"Oh," sighed Jee.

Reǵeena took her by the hand and led her to the rear of the large room. A drape was hanging over an opening in the wall, with a single hand-written sign on the left side. It read 'caution.'

"This is the health center for children," said Reǵeena. "If you want to see what it is really like being Graćenta, then this will give you an idea."

They went inside. What Jee saw shocked her: row upon orderly row of cots, fifty or more, each with a reclining child. Several people were attending who appeared to be nurses or doctors. Some cots held small, motionless patients with thin gray manes, tinged green at the ends. What could only be concerned parents knelt by some children, or held a hand, or stroked a brow. Some cots had sheets covering the occupant completely.

Reǵeena led her friend through the rows, slowly. Jee stared in disbelief at the conditions. Things were clean and orderly, yet there wasn't any equipment as she would expect in a hospital located in a nation as wealthy as Tar Asélło. Rags were used as bandages and washing cloths, blankets were torn, and the beds had the thinnest mats as cushioning. The cots were so close together that it was a wonder anyone was able to move between them to check on a child without leaning over another patient. The lighting was stark and insufficient to see clearly.

She took off her veil and loosened her cloak as she walked. It only took a few moments until some of the children noticed her.

"The Glasśigh!" one called in a loud whisper as she passed. Soon others called out her name with weak voices. Smiles began to appear, a sight that seemed out of place in this dingy, gloomy room.

"Children," instructed Reǵeena in a loud whisper, "quiet, please! Yes, this is the Glasśigh. She has come to visit. But stay in bed, and she will come to you. And keep quiet! It will be our secret! Yes?"

The children excitedly nodded their heads, and some that were able to sit up did so in anticipation of their visit.

All Jee could do to keep from falling apart was to concentrate on their smiles. She asked their names, what they like to do when they played. Sometimes, she just smiled and held a hand.

"Are these doctors?" asked Jee, motioning to the attendants.

"Not all of them, no," said Reǵeena. "Most are volunteers. They have learned a few things to ease the pains of the children; however, schools for medicine are not open to Graćenta. Only Merćenta."

"You must be a Merćenta to be a doctor?"

"Most are, yes," replied Reǵeena. "It is not the law, but schooling is so expensive, no matter what one wants to study. And you must have a Koŕeefa sponsor. That also is expensive. No Graćenta have that amount of money."

"But there must be Graćenta people that have some money—and maybe own a shop or a small business?"

"Again, this is not the law," explained Reǵeena, "but there *are* laws requiring license fees, and fees to pay to Koŕeefa sponsors. With the low wages and all businesses owned by the Koŕeefa, none can afford to go to different schools or start a business. Some have tried; few have ever made a living."

"But you said you went to school," countered Jee.

"Yes, but most are only taught service skills, like how to pick food, fish, or work in a factory. I was lucky—I was able to learn a servant's job."

"That's not right. Tar Aséllo, especially Etáin City, is so…rich. It shouldn't be this way."

"Yet it is," responded Reǵeena "We cannot do as we wish. We learn to do what the Kośeefa and the Merćenta do not want to do for themselves. The difficult work. The dangerous. We are mine diggers, chemical plant workers, factory workers, bricklayers, maids, gardeners. Most are slated to be manual laborers, like farmhands and packers of food."

"They are keeping you down, Reǵeena," said Jee. "You are slaves."

Reǵeena stared straight into Jee's eyes. "We are trapped, and there is no way out. This is why there is a rebellion, as small as it is. It has been our only hope. Until you came."

This seemed to resonate with Jee: as Reǵeena watched her eyes, the Glasśigh looked on the verge of tears. She even shook, as if she had the chills.

They continued their visits. Jee stopped at a child's bed where she sat and stroked his brow. Another child was unbelievably hot, and even to Jee, that seemed a bad sign. Others had coughs that sounded raspy or full of fluid.

After a while, Reǵeena advised that it was time to leave. Jee refused. She would visit every child, even if it took all day to accomplish.

Eventually, they reached the rear of the room, where one particular bed was attended by a weeping woman, who could only be a mother. A tall man stood nearby, placing medical tools into a finely woven bag. They stood over a pale child of approximately the earth equivalent of five- or six years old. The child had thin gray hair, half-open hazel eyes, and was struggling to breathe. Otherwise, she didn't move.

"Who is this?" asked Jee, kneeling beside the mother. The woman regarded her, seemed surprised, but then immediately fell back into her depressive state.

"This is Pathéce," whispered the mother.

The girl turned her head slightly toward Jee. A weak smile appeared on her face. Her breathing was raspy.

"Glasśigh?" came the airy voice.

"Hello, Pathéce. That is a beautiful name. You have the prettiest eyes I have ever seen."

"Not as pretty as yours," whispered Pathéce. "Everyone loves your eyes."

"What is wrong with her?" Jee asked as she held the girl's hand.

"She has lung fluid," the man responded, "brought on by exposure and malnutrition. It is common."

"Are you a doctor?" asked Jee.

"Yes," said the man.

"What are you doing for her?" asked Jee.

The man looked a bit concerned by the question. He took a moment, then answered. "She has simply run out of medicine. Her allotment was used. The child has had several relapses. There is nothing more to do."

Jee frowned. "What do you mean? Is there a shortage of medicine?"

"No," Reǵeena explained, stepping in to ensure the truth be told. "Only a certain amount is available to Graćenta. It is very expensive."

"I used all I could," muttered the mother, her voice catching. "I spent all I had, even on the illegal markets, but it was not enough."

"That was most of the problem," needled the doctor. "The illegal markets have old medicine. It is mostly impotent and does more harm than good. You, madam, should not have used illegal goods."

Jee's anger grew rapidly, though she managed to hold her temper. "Listen, I will pay for whatever medicine this girl needs. In fact, I will pay for whatever medicine all these children need. Can you get the right medicine here?"

"He cannot," said Reǵeena, answering for the doctor.

"Each person is only allotted a certain amount," responded the doctor. "It is the law."

"But Kośeefa and Merćenta have a higher allotment," added Reǵeena.

"That is because they can afford it," expounded the doctor as he finished packing his bags.

Jee stood. "A word with you, doctor?" she commanded and walked to the corner of the room, out of earshot of the children. He followed.

"My Glasśigh?" he asked.

Jee turned from a beautiful princess to a scowling horror in an instant.

"Listen to me. I will bring you before the Taźath, or I will pick you up and drag you through the streets if you don't get medicine here immediately!"

She grabbed his hand and squeezed as hard as she could. Her strength was astounding. The doctor winced and tried to jerk his hand away, but he was unable.

"I-I can't," protested the doctor. "It is against the law!"

"I don't give a pile of horse shit about the law!" Jee hissed.

"Horse what?" the doctor asked, afraid.

"Do it!"

"It will do no good," he yelped, still in pain. "She is too far gone! Even if I did have the medicine, it would be ineffective at this point. She will be dead in an hour at the most. Please, you are hurting me!"

Jee released him, though she held his gaze. "Get out of here," she snapped, "you useless piece of cow—"

He rushed away.

Jee's anger subsided, though she vowed to speak with Eno about this. She returned to the cot where Pathéce lay and kneeled down once again, cradling the girl in her arms.

"Would you like a song?" asked the Glasśigh.

The girl's eyes lit up. The other children gasped.

"This is a song about sleeping," said Jee. "So you rest and listen, all right?"

"Yes, Glasśigh," whispered Pathéce.

Jee began softly:

Swing low, sweet chariot,
Comin' for to carry me home;
Swing low, sweet chariot,
Comin' for to carry me home.
I looked over Jordan,
And what did I see,
Comin' for to carry me home,
A band of angels comin' after me,
Comin' for to carry me home.

Swing low, sweet chariot,
Comin' for to carry me home;
Swing low, sweet chariot,
Comin' for to carry me home.
If you get there before I do,
Comin' for to carry me home,
Tell all my friends I'm comin' too,
Comin' for to carry me home.

As Jee finished, Pathéce shuddered, then stopped breathing, releasing her last breath as a gentle sigh, her expression content and serene. Jee began to cry, as did the girl's mother. Reǵeena knelt to console them both.

Above them hovered a small media drone, barely noticeable—only the size of a small child's hand.

14
Éhpiloh

For the next two weeks, Jee kept to herself, staying in her room. The child's death upset her greatly, and only Reǵeena was allowed to enter or bring her food, maybe supply a hug or two. All public appearances were canceled with no explanation except for Eno's suspiciously stated excuse: the Glasśigh is still adjusting to the Áhthan time scales.

She had told Eno what she had seen, about the useless doctor, and her plan to speak to the Taźath about giving aid to the children. Eno agreed in principle and admitted that he was beginning to see some 'unfairness and undue hardships' forced on the Graćenta. However, he expressed that the Taźath would do nothing for the children. It was the law.

Jee slapped him repeatedly and pushed him out of her room.

Even Alíthe was shunned.

Reǵeena, however, knew that Jee had changed after their trip to Tepótah. At times when they were together, Jee would mutter things like "I hate it here," or "Poor Pathéce" or just "What can I do?" then shake her head in frustration. Reǵeena was now convinced that the Glasśigh was not the spoiled rich girl she had thought initially. Jee was compassionate, fair, and beautiful on the inside. People should know this, the girl thought.

In reality, there were times Jee would sob uncontrollably; other times, when not so distraught, she simply sat in a comatose state. Eno had seen this behavior on Earth, and the Gallottas had informed him that after a few days, maybe a week at the most, she would recover and return to her usual self.

One overcast and dark Lastsun before the eclipse, Eno was out cataloging his Earth collections. Reǵeena sat on a lounge chair by the window of Palace Place. Alíthe sat in a stiff back chair by the front door, looking morose, his black mane slightly gold at the edges. It had been a long while waiting for Jee to overcome her sadness. She wouldn't even talk to him, and even the frequency of her conversations with Reǵeena seemed to dwindle.

Suddenly, a door opened, and Jee emerged from her room, wearing a stunning dark wine-colored dress sequined in the bodice, off one shoulder with an asymmetric mid-thigh hemline. Upon seeing her,

Alíthe and Reǵeena stood quickly, though they remained silent.

"I want to eat," Jee announced. "No delivery. I want to get out of this place."

The *Scaffer's Nook* restaurant in the far north of Etáin City was frequented only by the elite of Kor̗eefa. Obtaining a table there was near impossible unless one's last name was Tok or had the word 'minister' in their title.

Luckily for Alíthe, his date was *the Glasśigh*, which trumped all others, possibly even 'Tok'. Unluckily for Alíthe, the invitation also included Reǵeena—not that he thought the girl unpleasant. However, he was looking forward to spending some time alone with Jee, hopefully, to ascertain if her sour mood was brought on by him or something else.

They arrived via luxury skyliner borrowed from the Taźath's pool of vehicles, along with a small security detail that, thankfully, took up positions *outside* the restaurant. As Jee entered the building, wearing that dress—actually one of her less flashy outfits for 'going out'—the room went silent.

"Excuse me," said a staff member as they entered. "Your servant? She is not allowed in here—"

Without a word or a look, Jee grabbed Reǵeena by the hand and walked onward past the stunned man.

"How dare you," growled Alíthe. "Do *not* address the Glasśigh or tell her what she can and cannot do. Escort us to our table immediately. In silence."

As they followed the embarrassed staff member, Alíthe noticed that everyone present was looking at the Glasśigh. Many stopped eating and drinking, stood, bowed, applauded, or performed all three. Some others—younger ministers, or the sons of older ones—smiled at the Glasśigh and tried to make eye contact.

In no mood for any *Glasśigh worshiping*, Jee ignored them as she walked to the table. Regardless, as a defensive maneuver, Alíthe positioned himself between his date and the stares of his competition.

Smartly, Alíthe had arranged for a private table in the outside garden on the large balcony facing north, the sea below clearly and splendidly visible. Vines with delicate green and glowing white flowers, some twinkling, climbed decorative black stone walls were. Tall, slender trees with weeping willow-like branches had been manicured to provide a natural umbrella-like covering for each outdoor table. They swayed in the gentle breeze as they friends sat.

They ordered drinks, *sparkling teefer* for Jee, and a pink *sisty-fizz* for Reǵeena. Alíthe ordered a double *Topkick* on ice, the preferred libation of his air wing. When the meals came, they ate in silence, only Reǵeena and Alíthe trying polite conversation that fell flat. They both noticed Jee's distant, watery-eyed looks and the fact that she didn't touch her meal. She mostly took in the view.

Abruptly, Jee stood and moved to the edge of the stone wall that bordered the balcony. It was low enough to lean on and view the sea and beach below, alive with glowing creatures both small and large swimming in the surf. Further out in the bay, sleek and brightly lit watercraft cruised past lazily, some with sail-like structures, some with unseen means of power.

Jee rested her elbows on the edge of the balcony and looked up and down the beach. White buildings, probably houses of the rich, were built into the cliffs, some with stone stairs reaching down to the water and sand below. She soon turned her gaze across the vast glowing sea. Only a few lights twinkled on the far shore. Beyond stood the great Northern Tar Wall, glowing along its lower portion with light from the turquoise vegetation that clung to its side. The dark red rock of the wall reached upward until it became black, invisible. At the top of the tar, the swirling blue fálouse crowned the scene.

Alíthe stood and turned a stern eye toward Reǵeena. She took the hint and remained seated.

"Jee, I am sorry if I did anything to upset you," he began as he approached her. "I am clumsy and say things without thinking. I also—"

"You have done nothing to upset me, Alíthe," she said and looked at him with a kind smile.

This was a relief to him, and he simply nodded.

"This place is unbelievably beautiful," she continued, "yet there is so much wrong here. I don't think I will ever get used to it…" Her voice trailed off, and she turned her attention to the north again.

"I will do what I can to help," he said.

"If it weren't for you and Reǵeena, I don't know what I would do."

They stood together. Alíthe reached out his hand, and she took it. After a moment or two, she seemed to lighten her mood and began to talk once again, as if she had come to grips with something, though Alíthe could not tell what exactly.

"What are those lights? The ones across the sea?" she asked.

Alíthe turned and scanned the horizon. "The amber-colored ones?"

"Yes," said Jee. "They remind me of street lights on Earth, in Coeur d'Alene, where I lived. It was peaceful there."

"That is Éhpiloh, the largest city of the northern region," he replied.

"Éhpiloh?" she repeated, considering the name. "Éhpiloh means *shame*."

"Yes. The city was renamed for the people that live there. Its ancient name was *Jaydí City.*"

"Jaydí? As in Jaydí Ćlaviath?" she probed. "Why? Why rename it?"

"Jaydí City was all but destroyed in an uprising, many years ago," he explained, "by the people that lived there. The new name is a reminder to those that had a hand in the city's destruction."

Jee stared at the city, so quiet and peaceful it seemed. It reminded her of home.

"Éhpiloh is an ugly name," she announced. "I will call it Jaydí City."

"*Juntberry Liquor?*" inquired a waitperson, tray in hand.

Each took a tall thin glass filled with a thick yet bubbly honey-colored liquid.

"Juntberry Liquor," stated Alíthe. "Strong and sweet, just like—"

He stopped short.

"Like what?" asked Jee, knowing what he meant. A slight smile played on her lips.

"I salute you, Glasśigh!" Alíthe said, holding out the glass toward Jee.

Jee laughed and then motioned for Reǵeena to join them.

"On Earth, we have a tradition called a *toast,*" Jee said, raising her glass high. Alíthe and Reǵeena mimicked the movement. "To my friends. I wish you happiness, and please, have patience with me as I try to find my place."

"Yes," agreed Alíthe.

"I will," Reǵeena assured.

"You sip it slowly," instructed Alíthe with a smile.

They all sipped.

"This is wonderful," Jee cooed as she hugged Reǵeena. "I thank you…my friends."

After a few moments, the sky visibly darkened as Áhtha moved behind Ofeétis and the tiny Sun. With no sunlight and Ofeétis moving toward eclipse, night, true night, began to envelop the tar. Even the plants and sea creatures dimmed their glow.

It was then that Jee heard a whirring sound from above. She looked to each side of the balcony in turn. A fluttering buzz could be heard echoing off the surrounding buildings, the noise becoming louder with each second.

Over the trees they came, a few feet from the topmost branches:

lights, moving fast, pale red glows and white flashes emitting from metallic craft.

"Gunships!" shouted Alíthe in alarm.

There were at least fifty of them. Jee stared in wonder, but soon dread overtook her. The gunships continued past them, past the sparkling city across the bay, then angled north, then again slightly east. A siren could be heard far in the distance.

"What is happening?" asked Jee, fear twisting her insides into knots.

Other patrons ventured out from inside the restaurant and rushed to the stone wall of the overlook. They, too, had wondered about the flight passing overhead.

"They are A4 Aréus Fighters!" Alíthe told them excitedly. "I-I see C7 Katíga Rocker Bombers! That means they are from The Wings of Glasśigh!"

"My wing?" asked Jee, startled.

"They are h-headed to Éhpiloh!" fretted Reǵeena, panic evident in her voice, her silver mane now pure white.

Indeed, they watched as the ships, still in formation, converged on the small amber lights of the city across the water. The sirens continued to wail.

"Why are they headed to Éhpiloh?" Jee asked, turning to Alíthe, a look of fear on her face.

"M-my brother, Náyos!" gasped Reǵeena.

Jee saw the anguish on her friend's face. "Does he live there?"

Reǵeena could only nod as she looked on.

"I have a communication," said Alíthe, staring at his armband. "Yes, it is The G-Wing! Minister Commander Kalífus has located the members of the Enária who fired the missile at the arena! They have refused to surrender! He is attacking."

"But, won't they hit innocent people in the city?" yelled Jee over the sirens.

"We are Graćenta," sobbed Reǵeena. The edges of her silvery mane were now flashing between the stark white of shock and the deep gold of concern.

"Reǵeena!" cried Jee, immediately holding the girl tight. They strained to watch the attack across the water. They could see red and purple beams fired from the gunships as they strafed a portion of the city. Another section of ships headed to the low hills directly north and fired at the base of the tar wall. Huge balls of fire exploded, lighting up the night. Soon the sounds reached them.

"*Exrizi* thermal vapor rockets!" Alíthe gasped, concerned and anxious. "They ignite all but stone. They are used to set fire to cave-cities and drive out any who reside there."

"Cave cities?" asked Jee, horrified.

"That is where the Enária hide," informed Alíthe.

"Not all caves are filled with Enária Front forces," clarified Reǵeena, crying. "Many p-poor families and crippled people move there t-to take care of each other!"

A series of fiery explosions could be seen against the tar, soon followed by the rippling sound of the rockets' detonations. The strafing continued in the city as well.

"Alíthe!" shouted Jee. "Tell them to stop!"

He looked at her helplessly. "Jee, I-I cannot. I have no control over the —"

"Then get them on that armband!" she demanded. "Tell them—tell them *the Glasśigh* commands them to stop! It is *my wing!"*

"Jee, we cannot command them. There is no way to contact them, nor would they listen—"

"Vací!" Jee yelled into her band. "Vací!"

"Yes, Glasśigh," came the calm voice.

"Contact the Taźath! Tell him to halt the attack on Éhpiloh! Hurry!"

"That connection is unavailable," responded Vací.

Jee let out an exasperated scream that scared both Reǵeena and Alíthe. Two security officers from outside burst into the garden area, pulseguns leveled, searching for threats.

"Stand down!" commanded Alíthe. The guards stood their ground but in slightly less threatening postures.

All watched from the opulent balcony of Scaffer's Nook as wave upon wave of gunships raked the portion of Éhpiloh nearest to the water's edge. The larger rocket-bomber airships that had attacked the caves were now headed to the east, moving at incredible speed. A few yellow tracers from hidden ground weapons streaked from the cave areas toward the sky, missing the retreating gunships, a futile attempt by surviving Enária.

The air attack was over. The remaining gunships followed the path of the rocket-bombers, and within a few seconds, streaked out of sight as the sirens ceased.

Reǵeena was inconsolable. She tried to run away, to do anything to get to her brother.

"Please, sweetheart, wait!" Jee begged as she held her back.

Alíthe looked at the two women, both in tears. Even he thought the attack was overpowered for a simple police action against a weak and mostly defeated enemy.

Jee suddenly grabbed ahold of Alíthe's arm, and with the other, she took Reǵeena's hand. Pulling them aside, away from the other patrons, she turned to Alíthe with a commanding look.

"Take us there!"

"T-to Éhpiloh?" he asked in disbelief. "Right now?"

"Yes, now!"

"I can't do that!"

"Why not?"

"It is a battle zone. It is restricted," Alíthe explained. "No craft are allowed in the air during a military mission. It will take at least a day to finish. This is only the air phase."

"What does that mean?" asked Jee angrily.

"There will be a ground phase following that air attack! AMF and Special Police Troops will be in the city, looking for Enária. It is standard procedure. Éhpiloh will be restricted for a few days at least."

Jee looked at her armband. "Vací, arrange for a skyliner. I need a ride."

"No!" protested Alíthe. "They will shoot you down!"

"I won't just stand here, doing nothing," Jee persisted.

"Wait!" Alíthe said. "I have an idea."

▲▲▲

Getting onto Ultos Base, home of the Wings of Glasśigh, was easy. Alíthe had the highest access levels, and merely showing his face to the guards outside was enough to get the three of them into the building. Using a designated Taźath groundcar didn't hurt their chances either. Explaining their visit as a 'snap inspection' by the Glasśigh herself was accepted by the few troops on duty. After a few pictures with the Glasśigh, the ground crews were happy to assist in any way possible.

They entered the outer field where a sleek yet deadly-looking chrome craft sat idle on the runway. The Wings of Glasśigh image was apparent on the tail and side; a stark black number *501* graced the visible side.

"Is that yours?" asked Reǵeena.

"It is the Taźath's ship, officially," whispered Alíthe. "But it has been assigned to me; an Aréus A4 Fighter. Fast. And room for only two, so you both will need to double up. Please, do as I say, and we might be successful."

They began walking swiftly across the landing field, directly toward Aréus 501. Upon reaching the craft, Alíthe set his palm on a hand-plate, and the ship's lights came on. Numerous glowing bulbs and tubes emitted a pale greenish-white glow from under the wings. Something inside the gunship started to hum. A door opened on the ventral side, and a ramp-like ladder extended to reach the ground below.

"Please follow me," Alíthe said as he climbed the now fully descended ladder.

Jee and Reǵeena sat in the rear seat. They scrunched in, following Alíthe's direction on securing the safety belts and his especially firm instructions not to touch anything. In the front command seat, Alíthe donned his head-com, a simpler headset than a hel-com, lightweight and less encumbering. He flicked a few switches on the control panel in front of him. More lights glowed inside the ship, and the soft whine of the after-burner turbo-fan engines began. Within seconds, Aréus 501 lifted off the ground and held position several feet in the air.

"Commander," came a voice. *"Flight Control Officer Breegan Arkéta here. Are you aware of the flight restrictions during the current operation?"*

"Yes," answered Alíthe. "I am taking the Glasśigh to Chanteeda Shores. Just a quick sightseeing flight. At her request."

"The Glasśigh? Can I meet her?"

"It is a bad time. We are in a hurry, actually," said Alíthe.

"Oh! I can see her! Hello! Hello! Over here! In the tower!"

They looked upwards. Through the tower window, Jee could see a small figure waving frantically.

"Please, Jee. Just wave?" asked Alíthe.

Jee smiled as she waved. "Hello there!"

"Can we depart now?" Alíthe asked through his head-com.

"She waved at me!"

"Yes, she did," acknowledged Alíthe. "We are cleared then?"

"I think so..." said Breegan. *"I mean, it is her wing. I assume it is allowed?"*

"It is. Thank you," Alíthe said curtly. He knew it was *not* allowed; however, it was true that she was the Glasśigh. A likely excuse, though not actually one that would hold up.

With explosive speed, the sleek chrome craft blasted off the field and into the black-eclipsed night, immediately climbing vertically into the low clouds.

Both rear passengers screamed.

Alíthe only reduced speed on Aréus 501 when he had cleared the airspace above Palace City and had reached the shores of Etáin. A quick glance over his right shoulder confirmed what he expected: Jee was white with shock, mouth open. Reǵeena's mane was completely white; she was scared to death. Alíthe chuckled to himself before returning his gaze to the control panel. He quickly entered a flight plan, showing that they were headed west to Cheltor's Horn via Farvis, then turning south to Induláy and returning east over the smaller farms and Etáin City.

"I have filed my flight plan. It will only take the security team a few minutes to detect us once I vary our course."

Alíthe turned his gunship west. Jee leaned forward in her seat and reached for him, holding his shoulder.

"Thank you, Alíthe," she said, now calmer. "That was *fast.*"

He could not answer. The chemistry between them was now at such a level that he could barely concentrate. Her hand is on my shoulder! he realized. Hold it together!

"Alíthe, will you get in trouble?" Reǵeena asked.

"More than likely, yes," he answered.

What a fool I am, he thought. They will hang me by the feet until I am dead!

"I will speak to the Taźath," Jee said confidently. "He will listen to me."

"Listening and heeding," Alíthe pointed out, "are two different things."

Alíthe banked the ship in a tight right turn. They had reached the northern shore of Etáin City and were now headed north toward Oso-Gúrith Province and Éhpiloh.

▲▲▲

Kalífus sat in the *Dark Room* at the Taźath's Palace Leadership Center. Its floor was twenty feet below the main conference room, and its area over one hundred feet square. Here is where the Taźath's Special Police Intelligence Team monitored the activity of the citizens, the police, and the military. His team could watch hundreds of video camera feeds at countless workstations. There also were twelve large display screens mounted on the walls, each over twenty feet wide and the same in height. The screens showed live feeds from cameras around the tar.

The room was buzzing with excitement. TSP Intelligence troops sat in front of displays that lit up the immediate area. The large wall screens were alive with activity, displaying images of gunships, rocket bombers, and support ships in or above Éhpiloh.

"Commander Kalífus!" came the voice of a flight technician.

"Report," ordered Kalífus tonelessly.

"A gunship from the Ultos Wing has altered from the filed flight path."

"And?" pressed the Commander. That was out of the ordinary but not a dramatic event.

"It is Aréus 501. Commander Afiéro."

"It can't be," argued Kalífus, "unless someone else took it. Maybe a maintenance run?"

"Negative. The flight plan was filed by Afiéro himself."

That was strange.

Maybe. Wing Commander Alíthe Afiéro knew the rules, including that flying during an active mission was against procedure. However, Alíthe was no simple pilot. He was a wing leader, *the* wing leader, of the most prestigious wing. If he was out there, it was probably all right—as long as he stayed away from Éhpiloh and Kalífus's final clean-up operation.

"And, sir?" added the technician. "According to notes from the base foreman, the Glasśigh is with him."

"That is his assignment then. The Glasśigh," Kalífus said, relieved. "Probably out for some sightseeing. We all want to please the Glasśigh. Let them be, as long as they don't fly over Éhpiloh. Track him in case he needs assistance. Where is he presently?"

The technician glared at his panel, then made a few adjustments to the tracking system. He zoomed in on the actual path of Aréus 501.

"On screen," he said.

Before Kalífus and the entire room, a map appeared on a large display showing the center of Tar Aséllo, with Etáin City and the Palace in the south and Oso-Gúrith and Éhpiloh in the north. Alíthe's flight plan was shown in a yellow line, sweeping directly from the hangar due west toward Cheltor's Horn. A blue line with a leading flashing dot showed his current position: off his flight path, indeed, heading north of Etáin City.

"Probably just circling the city," reasoned Kalífus.

They watched as the blue dot turned east, toward Éhpiloh.

Still, nothing to worry about, thought Kalífus. One could turn right or left to make a circle. He had work to do, the reports and video of the mission needed to be filed and prepared for the Taźath. The media needed to be prepped. This was a distraction.

He took one last glance at the screen. The blue dot was not altering course. It continued, now heading northeast. It then slowed. It was now apparent that Aréus 501 was heading to Éhpiloh, right to the heart of the operation and the Taźath's ground security forces. The blue dot stopped blinking.

"They are in a landing cycle," announced the technician, "hovering most likely."

"Prep my ship," Kalífus ordered as he rushed outside.

▲▲▲

From the balcony of Scaffer's Nook, Éhpiloh had appeared to be a cozy hamlet, a soft glow radiating from the city in contrast to the glittering and ostentatious Etáin. However, approaching from the air, the dream was slowly shattered, making Jee all the more apprehensive and repulsed. Éhpiloh was not like Coeur d'Alene as she initially thought.

Instead, it was as if a smothering thunderstorm stretched directly above the city, although no rain had fallen. Buildings ignited by the air attack burned, casting a thick, gray smoke across the scene. The glow from Éhpiloh that had been visible from the restaurant was now all but extinguished. Harsh light beams sliced the dusty air like daggers, shining down from dark machines that hovered in the air and hunted on the ground.

When the smoke cleared for a few moments, Jee caught a glimpse of the poor city: a collection of ghostly dark industrial-looking buildings, brutal in design. The squat structures were arranged in uniform blocks, creating several large courtyards. The only relief was the taller cubed gray buildings, some with no windows at all, reaching several stories into the smoky mist. What appeared to be haphazardly placed tiles of various rectangular shapes on the ground were actually make-shift roofs of huts, many either burning from the raid or smoldering. The huts seemed to spread like a cancerous growth, arms reaching everywhere between the taller constructs. It reminded Jee of the over-crowded slums she had seen on television news shows back on Earth, or one never-ending prison compound, complete with sharp wire barricades.

Almost every building displayed a 'Know Your Place' banner like the ones Jee had seen on Eno's PDT. Many were defaced and stained with what could only be some kind of liquid that had been harshly pelted against it, leaving a spattered and dripping stain of brown.

As they neared the city center, the streets widened considerably. Aréus 501 was in hover mode, forty or so feet above a highway, moving slowly and cautiously forward. Smoke wafted before the ship in waves of gray and black, obscuring their view.

Jee and Reǵeena leaned forward, one on each one side of Alíthe. All looked ahead.

In an instant, they saw something large coming from a side street and turning to the left, onto the main highway, heading away from them. At first, it seemed to be a swarm of insects running on the pavement. Yet soon, as the smoke dissipated almost entirely, it was obvious: not insects, but people. Soon, another group entered the highway from another side street, just ahead of the first.

"There must be two thousand or more," observed Alíthe. "Where are they going?"

"What are they running from?" asked Jee.

The answer came quickly. As the crowds of children and adults alike ran down the highway, a dozen vehicles entered from side streets. They looked like stubby little wheeled tanks to Jee, painted black, each having several machine gun-like weapons mounted on the front. The tanks sped out from side streets, and formed in a line abreast. Then, with a belch of dark smoke from their top-mounted exhausts, they rushed toward the fleeing crowd.

"W9 guncars!" Alíthe called out as he halted his advance.

"Alíthe!" Jee called hysterically. "What are they going to do?"

"No, please, no!" sobbed Reǵeena.

The guncars opened fire. The slaughter lasted all of thirty seconds. Some surely escaped, but in the end, the bodies lay in thick mounds. The street ran red with blood.

After a full minute of shocked silence, Jee was the first to breathe.

"Oh my God!" Jee cried. "What just happened?"

Reǵeena's mane now flashing blue streaks through the silver. Her horror left her stunned a moment longer. As her senses returned, she began to scream and cry out in anguish.

"Did you see that, Alíthe?" Jee asked, still horrified. "D-did you see it?"

"I-I did. T-they must have been Enária!" he reasoned.

"All of them? I saw children in there!" Jee protested. "Get us the hell down there! Now!"

"Hell?" asked Alíthe, confused.

"Land this thing! Anywhere!"

"Over there! By the park!" said Reǵeena, pointing ahead and to the left.

In the center of a large square created by the surrounding squat buildings was an open dirt field, large enough to land a full flight of twenty Aréus A4 Fighters. It was mostly clear, only a few people rushing through it.

"My brother!" called Reǵeena. "He lives on the outskirts of the park!"

Aréus 501 landed in the center of the field. Upon seeing the ship, the few people remaining nearby ran, fearing a second wave of attack from the air.

"They must think we are part of the massacre," said Jee.

"This is too dangerous," warned Alíthe. "I can't allow you to leave the ship. You could be hurt, even if by accident."

Jee turned to him with a scowl. It was clear she was not going to obey. She grabbed Alíthe by the shoulder and leaned into his face.

"Open the door! I command it!"

"That doesn't really work, Jee," he protested, trying to appear formidable. "Not with me."

They stared each other down for a moment. Suddenly, a tear fell from Jee's eye. Alíthe immediately began to lose his resolve. Seeing her in pain was enough to make him do anything for her, though he fought the urge to open the door.

From within the ship, they could hear sounds from outside: pulseguns, officers barking orders to troops, and people crying in pain. Reǵeena was glued to the window.

"On Earth, Alíthe, there are no real classes," Jee pleaded. "Governments have laws protecting all people, regardless of their position. But when something happens, something where people are being hurt or kept down, others rise up, from all walks of life, to defend them—"

"This isn't Earth, Jee," he countered softly.

"But those are still people out there!" Jee implored. "What if your family was in that crowd? About to be gunned down? Wouldn't you go to help?"

"It is against the law, Jee. I would be arrested as a criminal!"

Jee thought for a moment. She had to do something and do it quick. She did know a trick. Not fair, she thought, but it could work. It was time to test their feelings for each other.

"What if it was your family down there in the street?" Jee asked. "What if it was me?"

The ladder of the Aréus descended. Alíthe exited first, holding his short, handheld pulsegun.

"Stay immediately behind me. We will move slowly," he commanded. "Keep your eyes up! On the rooflines."

The women proceeded down the ladder's rungs, then stood for a moment under the wing of the craft looking about and into the shadows of the dark town. Now and again, military vehicles resembling small tanks could be seen rolling along slowly through side streets, their searchlights probing. Somewhere nearby, a pulsegun fired a short burst, sounding like several deep coughs from a large, predatory animal. Another sound, more of a popping noise, answered.

"The Enária are still fighting," Alíthe observed. "That second sound was a projectile weapon."

"My brother, Náyos, has an armband, one of the few in this city," said Reǵeena, studying her ABC. "Here, this way!" She pointed to the east of the park, "He is two miles down the main road."

"Two miles?" echoed Alíthe. "That will take forever!"

"And I bet it's not a straight line," Jee replied. "We best be going."

They moved from the protection of the ship and out into the dirt field.

"Stay hidden," Alíthe warned as he pointed upward. "Those black machines up there are Bot Copters—unmanned preprogrammed policing vehicles."

They were everywhere. Lights on the ventral sides were sweeping the streets and building tops, searching as they passed in and out of the smoky haze that drifted through the city. Jee and her friends took cover under an awning as one bot hummed past slowly overhead, the markings of the TSP plainly visible.

As they neared the edge of the park, a pile of debris blocked their way. Carefully they climbed over the mound of stone blocks, metal beams, and other materials that could have once been a home or a small business. Jee stumbled and fell to her knees. To her horror, mixed in the debris were bodies, several of them bloody and dead, faces twisted grotesquely. She screamed an ear-piercing wail.

"Alíthe! What the hell is this?" she cried, scrambling away from the carnage.

"This is not right for you to see…" muttered Alíthe. He shook his head, clearly angry with himself. "I never should have allowed you to talk me into this!"

It took a moment for Jee to calm down. Reǵeena was just as horrified and began to weep again, her mane completely gold once more.

"Jee, we are leaving. Now," ordered Alíthe.

"No, we are going to find Reǵeena's brother!"

Alíthe realized Jee's mind was made up, and he knew there was no way to change it. He couldn't leave her alone. Reluctantly, he helped the women to their feet, and they continued on.

At the top of the mound, they peered through the debris and

surveyed what lay before them. Several dozen armed AMF troops, wearing their dark gray urban uniforms, were standing by in rows. Some turned to them and quickly began to fire pulseguns.

Alíthe grabbed the women and threw them to the ground behind the mound.

"Who are those guys?" whispered Jee.

"The gray uniforms are worn by the AMF, the Aséllo Military Forces. They are ground troops," Alíthe answered.

"The brown we saw earlier were TSP, the Taźath's Special Police," added Reģeena. "They are the Taźath's thugs and killers."

"They are not thugs and killers!" Alíthe protested. He stood up with his hands in the air, calling to the troops. "Cease fire! We are friends! Stop firing!"

"Identify yourself!" came a voice as the firing ceased.

"Wing Commander Alíthe Afiéro! Cease firing, you ground bugs!"

Alíthe waited a moment, then, with hands still raised, walked forward.

"Commander Afiéro? What are you doing here?" inquired an officer from below. "The air mission is over!"

"Ah! First Officer Gollon," said Alíthe as he recognized him. "That is hard to explain. Please have your men stand down."

"Stand down, you brain-dead, puss-dripping *cargouts!*" Gollon snapped. The troopers lowered their weapons.

"Thank you, Officer." Alíthe turned his head back to the mound and called out. "Jee! It's safe. As safe as it can be anyway."

"Who is Jee?" asked Gollon. He turned his gaze to the top of the mound to see the Glasśigh, dressed in her short, glittering wine-colored evening dress, clumsily crawling over the pile of debris. Another young woman followed her.

"Is that the Glasśigh?" asked Gollon, happily surprised. "It is, isn't it?"

"Yes, it is, officer. Thank you for your—"

"Is she here to sing to us?" Gollon's face lit up with excitement. "The troops would love to hear that!"

"Yes, sir!" agreed the nearby aides. They were smiling.

One of the aides called out, "Can we say hello?"

"I am sorry, Gollon," apologized Alíthe. "We are looking for someone in particular. Carry on here."

Some troopers announced the new development, their voices echoing off of the surrounding buildings.

"The Glasśigh is here! She will sing to us!"

A cheer rose, but Jee ignored it as she stumbled to the bottom of the mound.

“At least wave,” whispered Alíthe. “These troops are here to serve. No matter what you think, they are not the enemy.”

Jee turned and quickly put on an exaggerated smile and gave a hurried and overdone salute, mocking the one she had received from Alíthe upon her arrival.

The troops gave a hearty cheer.

“Not nice, Jee,” Alíthe fumed, “or dignified.”

“Can we go now?” asked Reǵeena, her anxiety mounting.

The troops were awed. Many continued talking amongst themselves, discussing the remarkable event they had just witnessed. The Glasśigh visited us! Personally! In a dress! The other forces will be so jealous! She loves us, *and* we received a salute!

Soon Jee, Alíthe, and Reǵeena had passed beyond the lower buildings on the outskirts of the city and entered the center of Éhpiloh. Upon reaching the crest of an old, rusty metal walking bridge, they looked down onto a short street that ended in a courtyard, surrounded by three ugly gray and black structures.

Brown uniformed Special Police were everywhere.

There was a long train-like vehicle with a series of attached compartments being towed behind the main engine. The police pushed children into the compartments through cage-like doors. Women and men, who had to be parents, surrounded the troopers, frantically trying to get past the armed men. They were reaching and clawing for their babies, trying with all their might to pull them from the compartments. Jee saw one mother almost get to the door of a cage when she was grabbed by a trooper. He held her by the mane and slapped her face hard, driving her to the ground. A man swung his fist at the trooper and was immediately grabbed by another. He then was forced at gunpoint into a line with others against the nearest brick wall.

A wheeled military armored vehicle roared into the square. An officer of the TSP quickly jumped out of the doorless car. He received salutes from the troops standing by.

“Who is in charge here?” he demanded as he walked to the center of the square.

“Welcome, Commander Hartell, sir. I am in charge. TSP Second Officer Nernel.”

“The situation?” asked Hartell.

“Enária, captured in various areas. Children that were with them are being detained, in accordance with mission orders.”

“Excellent. Proceed with the executions,” said Hartell.

“Squad!” called Nernel. “Raise weapons!”

"No!" came a cry.

The two officers turned in the direction of the call. The squad, guns immediately raised, hesitated, some sneaking a glance to the figure running toward them.

Jee was rushing down the bridge toward the center of the square as fast as her feet could carry her.

"Glasśigh!" Alíthe cried, running after her. "Jee! By the power of Ofeétis's Eye, stop!"

Upon hearing Alíthe's call, Commander Hartell focused on the running figure. Seeing clearly now, his formal stance slackened, and his expression changed immediately to one of wonder.

Jee had now reached the center of the square. Reǵeena followed, as did a small media drone.

"Stop this!" Jee cried. "Do not fire!"

"The Glasśigh?" Hartell blurted. "Here?"

The TSP officers stared in amazement as the Glasśigh streaked past them, directly to the firing squad. Standing immediately in front, just inches from the guns' barrels, she spread her arms wide in an effort to prevent any firing.

"I command you to stop!" she screamed, moving from left to right.

Some of the squad immediately pointed their weapons to the ground, only to have others yell for them to aim at the line as ordered. It was complete confusion, guns being raised and lowered, Jee running up and down the line, frantically calling for the squad to hold fire.

At the end of the line, one prisoner took advantage of the commotion and broke away in a desperate run. A trooper fired. The man fell.

"I said stop!" Jee called, running frantically toward the trooper who had fired. "Put the guns down!"

Reǵeena joined her, standing as did her friend, arms wide, within point-blank range.

"Reǵeena?" a voice called weakly.

The girl turned to face the prisoners, searching the line to the left and right, until one face caught her eye.

"Náyos!" she screamed and ran toward him. He was injured, a bloody rag over his right eye. He could barely stand.

'Reǵeena!" her brother called, shocked. "What are you doing here?"

"Hold fire!" yelled Alíthe, running past the officers. "Hold fire!" He caught up to Jee and grabbed her in an attempt to take her out of harm's way. She quickly twisted his wrist and broke free.

Alíthe followed, raising a hand to the squad. "I am Commander

Alíthe Afiéro of the Wings of Glasśigh! Hold your fire! Lower your weapons!"

The TSP troopers, still completely confused, looked to First Officer Nernel, then to the woman in the wine-colored dress. Stunned, the entire line of troops lowered their weapons. They couldn't point a gun at the Glasśigh, could they?

"Commander Afiéro?" asked Hartell as he approached. "Is this…is this really the Glasśigh?"

"Of course it is!" snapped Alíthe angrily, pointing to Jee. "Who else would wear *that* to a war zone?"

"Release those children!" ordered Jee.

"Glasśigh—" Alíthe began.

"I said now, Officer!" continued Jee as she stood in front of Hartell. "Well?"

"I-I don't have the authority, my Glasśigh," he insisted apologetically. "Mission orders."

"I don't care about your orders! I am giving you new orders! Release these people and these children! Reǵeena, help them out of those cages!"

"Yes, Glasśigh," Reǵeena replied. She quickly touched foreheads with her brother, then rushed to the train.

"Can she order us?" asked Nernel.

"She is the Glasśigh," shrugged Hartell. "But—oh, I have no idea!"

The men guarding the train stared in awe at the Glasśigh. Some smiled; others just remained shocked in disbelief. Here was the most famous, most loved Áhthan, in person, running about in a fancy evening dress, helping Graćenta children out of a prison train. Many called to her, smiling, waving. Others just stared in awe. Some took photos with their armband communicators.

"Help her!" Jee commanded, pointing to Reǵeena. The train guards immediately stopped gawking and began to assist in the removal of the children.

"You troops there," Jee went on, pointing back to the firing squad, "these people are to go free!"

"Jee," pleaded Alíthe, again coming to her side. "You can't—"

A loud whine and beating noise filled the square. Something approached through the smoke. Above, a winged, four-bladed craft appeared, beating away the thick gray mist that shrouded the sky. Large and black, the craft displayed the TSP emblem on its ventral side. Bright lights flashed from under stubby wings and immediately began searching the area. A few beams found the Glasśigh and Alíthe and remained fixed on them. Several guns mounted on each side and below the craft pointed to the ground, moving about, pausing on areas, then moving on to a new target. The craft hovered for a few moments just above the roof level of the nearby buildings. It then dropped down in a rush of wash and dust, landing on the far side of the courtyard.

Jee shielded her eyes from the blowing debris. A door opened on the vehicle. A figure in a black and blue camouflage uniform, swiftly exited the craft: Gákoh Kalífus. Following him were several troops similarly dressed, pulseguns raised. They immediately took positions in front of the line of prisoners.

"Kalífus!" Jee called, running to meet him. "Tell them to stop! They are shooting people by the hundreds! We saw tanks on the road back there and—"

"Glasśigh, please," he implored. "Let's calm down. Are you all right? You shouldn't be here. This is a war zone, a dangerous place."

"Really?" Jee retorted incredulously. "I hadn't noticed! Maybe I was thrown off by the killing and screaming and gunfire and smoke, and that pile of dead bodies I tripped over!"

"Is that sarcasm?" Kalífus asked.

"Make this stop!" Jee cried. "Now!"

"Dear Glasśigh," Kalífus said in an even tone. "I am not sure what you think you are doing here, but you have no business in this operation. It is against the law to interfere with a police action. I know you are new here, and this all may seem very strange; however, we know what we are doing."

"I know what you're doing!" she snapped. "You are murdering people in the streets and abducting children!"

"These people are Enária, Glasśigh," countered Kalífus. "They are criminals, enemies of the Taźath and Tar Aséllo. They have caused violent acts—they tried to kill you and your uncle! Let us handle this. Return to the Palace, please. I beg you."

"I am not going anywhere! Reǵeena! Have you freed all the children?" Jee moved quickly back toward the train. Kalífus and Alíthe followed.

"Glasśigh!" Kalífus called. He was beginning to lose patience. "Halt!"

She turned, hands on her hips, and glared at him. The media drone hovered nearby, recording.

"What are you going to do, Minister Kalífus? Shoot me?"

"For your own protection, Glasśigh, I will take you into custody and return you to the Palace. Do not resist." Kalífus held up a hand and made a motion toward his squad. Three TSP troops approached.

"I will take her!" protested Alíthe. "She is my charge."

"No one is taking me anywhere!" blurted Jee, rejoining Reǵeena in helping children out of the train and shooing them off into the city.

"Commander Afiéro," said Kalífus, the condescension clear in his tone. "I am not sure you can be effective in managing this situation. After all, it was *you* who brought her here. What were you thinking?"

"I do not command the Glasśigh, Minister," Alíthe clarified. "I guard her. She is a free citizen, she is the Glasśigh, and my job is to protect her, not order her about."

"And protecting her means bringing her into a war zone?"

"As you can see, Minister Commander," Alíthe countered, "she has a will of her own. A free Áhthan of the Kořeefa class. Even you can't control her."

They both looked on as the last of the children were released. Jee and Reǵeena then returned to the line of prisoners.

"Go!" Jee yelled, gesturing them away. "Go now! All of you!"

"Glasśigh!" Kalífus called out, raising his gun, firing it into the air. "Back away!"

Jee continued, unfazed, grabbing a man from the line and placing her own body in position as a shield. She rushed him to the edge of the wall and around the corner of the nearby building.

"Run, quickly!" she urged the man, then returned to repeat the process with the others still in line.

"Those people are Enária!" Kalífus called, angrily striding over to Jee. He attempted to hold onto the woman from behind. Jee instinctively stomped on his foot, grabbed his left hand, spun about to face him, and twisted his thumb backward until he dropped to the street. Free again, Jee moved off.

Recovering, mane flashing blue, Kalífus pulled his weapon and aimed it at the Glasśigh. "I order you to stop!"

Immediately, Alíthe was behind Kalífus, his short pulsegun's tip pressed hard against the man's temple.

"I will kill you where you stand, Kalífus! Lower your weapon! What are you doing? This is the Glasśigh!"

The entire squad and the officers now raised guns, not sure at whom they should aim. Guns were pointed at the Glasśigh, Reǵeena, Alíthe, and the remaining prisoners.

Reǵeena noticed that almost half of the troops aimed at Kalífus.

The drone pivoted to face the scene.

"Let her finish!" added Alíthe. "It won't matter, Kalífus!"

"Commander Afiéro," grumbled Kalífus angrily. "What in the name of the Tażath do you think you are doing?"

"I am doing my duty," Alíthe barked, "as *directed* by the Tażath—

protecting the Glasśigh! And the fact that *you* raised a *weapon* and pointed it at her—"

"I would not have fired, dear me!" Kalífus slowly lowered his gun, aiming it to the ground. "Be smart! I was trying to scare her, to get this under control!"

A minute passed as they watched Jee take each person in line, one at a time, and escort them to safety.

"This is not going to end well for you, Afiéro," warned Kalífus. "I will have you both arrested and brought before the Tażath."

"Really?" asked Alíthe with an uncomfortable laugh. He kept his weapon aimed at the minister's head. "Maybe you can arrest me, but you cannot arrest the Glasśigh! Be serious!"

"Get her out of here," Kalífus hissed.

As Jee escorted the last of the lineup to safety, Alíthe finally lowered his gun. Climbing over the rubble in the square, he went to Jee and grabbed her forcefully.

"You are done here, Jee! You have done all you can! We need to leave, now, before you and Reǵeena and I get hurt! Do you understand me?"

Jee looked around. The line of prisoners was gone; they had run back into the city. The children were also freed. Surely there would be more atrocities committed today, but she was feeling confused and overwhelmed. What more could she do? She was breathing hard and began to tremble.

"Jee, please," Alíthe said, his voice soft and pleading. "I need to protect you, and I can't if you don't trust me. Do you trust me?"

She nodded, the confusion apparent on her face.

"Reǵeena," he called. "Let's go."

All three turned back the way they had come, struggling over the rusty bridge at the end of the street. The mysterious media drone followed.

"Hartell?" called Kalífus, "collect ABCs from the men. I want them all wiped clean before these images get to the network."

"Yes, sir," said Hartell. He then pointed toward the Glasśigh. "And Minister Commander Kalífus, that drone—is it yours?"

Kalífus looked, noticing it for the first time.

"Oh, for all the sprays of Caymana's Falls…" Kalífus said, sighing. He raised his hand pulsegun, aimed, and fired.

Jee and the others heard a short bang just above their heads as they climbed the old bridge steps. Looking up, they saw what was left of the drone falling in pieces to the ground, only a puff of smoke hanging in the air.

15
The Frying Pan

The short flight from Éhpiloh back to Ultos Base was made in silence. Reǵeena wept softly, mane alternating between a worried gold and an angry blue. Jee sat in the rear seat next to her, comforting the distraught girl.

Alíthe stared blankly ahead, listening to idle chatter over the radio as he piloted the craft across the Sea of Etáin. He felt a mixture of emotions, mostly frustration and confusion. He had always been in the air during AMF and TSP operations—he had never seen the results on the ground as he did today. Alíthe saw people gunned down in the streets. True, the commanders had the power to judge situations and deal out punishment; however, it all had happened so fast, as if they didn't care about who they were killing. The crowd of people running on the highway—they could not all have been Enária.

The ship's radio emitted a clear, beeping tone. Alíthe flicked a switch and responded.

"This is Aréus 501, Commander A—"

"This is Ultos Wing Station," interrupted the reply. *"Proceed directly to Palace Field number one. Await instructions there. Do you hear?"*

Arriving at the Palace, 501's hoverjets held the craft motionless above the landing pad, then began descending slowly. Alíthe could see a group of ministers in their white suits standing in a line just to the right. To the left, an entire TSP squad, armed. Out in front of them, staring grimly, was the Taźath.

"The good news," said Alíthe, "is that I see Minister Commander Eno present. That may help us."

Jee peered through the viewshield to see the greeting committee. And yes, there was Eno as well. He did not look happy.

The Aréus set down, engines were shut off. Alíthe wasted no time opening the ventral door and leading the women out of the ship. He then walked to the Taźath, dropped to one knee, and bowed his head low.

"My Taźath—" he began.

"Silence," demanded Pronómio evenly. "Is the Glasśigh injured?"

"No, my Taźath," answered the pilot.

"Then, Commander Afiéro, your life will be spared. Produce a report, detail everything, and have it to me within the hour."

Two TSP guards appeared. As Alíthe stood, they took him by the arms, though not too forcefully, and escorted him into a reception building behind the landing pad.

The Taźath and Eno quickly approached Jee.

"Are you well?" asked Pronómio firmly. He had a scowl on his face, yet he spoke softly.

"I am," answered Jee. "Please don't harm Alíthe. This was entirely my fault."

"Of that, I have no doubt," added Eno sheepishly.

"He will not be harmed," Pronómio said tersely. "Let us move inside the Leadership Center to my conference chambers. Bring your girl, Reǵeena Ahdelfía, as well."

The Taźath walked purposely toward the reception building. One by one, the ministers followed—except for Eno.

"Jee, this is not going to go well," Eno informed her, now standing in front of his niece to block her way.

"They slaughtered over a thousand people right before my eyes!" she hissed in a harsh whisper.

"Enária, most likely," he stated.

"No! Just regular people in Éhpiloh, and children were being taken from parents—"

"Jee!" Eno yelled, his voice carrying out across the complex. "You must—"

"I saw it!" Jee shot back. "So did Alíthe and Reǵeena!"

"Jee," Eno pleaded, struggling to regain his composure. "For your own good, calm down!"

Jee shoved him aside and stomped angrily past armed guards to the reception building. Eno and Reǵeena followed closely behind.

The Palace Leadership Center's outer walls were made of massive dark red stones, all cut in various geometric shapes, fitted tightly together. Only a few tall, thin windows stretched from the ground level to the roof, fifty feet above.

As she approached, Jee couldn't help but notice another building standing adjacent to the Leadership Center. Made of light gray stone and standing a hundred feet tall, the gray building was more an ominous monument than a functional structure. There was a massive black door at its base, and above, stretching thirty feet or more high, was a dagger-styled four-point star carved directly into the stone. Placed in front of the dagger were three letters made of some shining red rock: TSP. This was the headquarters of the Taźath's Special Police. The oppressive insignia made sure everyone knew.

Continuing on, Jee was led through two substantial ivory-colored doors and into the Leadership Center. Inside was an atrium-type area filled with a manicured, glowing flower garden and intricate water features. Beyond was the entrance to the Main Conference Room. Once inside, Jee saw a large oval table made of polished green and blue marble-like stone, surrounded by cushioned seats for at least two dozen. At the far end of the table was a slightly larger chair. The Taźath's throne, she thought. In front of each chair sat a PDT.

The room rose to almost four stories tall, topped by a glass ceiling where Ofeétis, though now in full eclipse, was usually in view. Three walls of the room were adorned with what could only be considered art of some type, made of inlaid stone tiles and gems that resembled galaxies of stars.

The fourth wall contained a chest-high railing that looked down into The Dark Room. Jee walked to the railing. It was busy down there. Most of the screens showed images of the TSP and AMF troops' ongoing activity in Éhpiloh. To Jee, the room looked like a space-aged version of the war rooms she had seen in movies, only filled with more electronic gadgetry.

"Let us be seated," said Pronómio as he entered the room. His ministers followed and quickly took their seats. Eno sat just to the left of the Taźath. The right seat remained vacant. Jee turned to Reģeena to ask her where they should sit, and noticed that she was not present.

"Where should I sit?" Jee asked the room.

"At that end of the table, across from us," said Pronómio. He was looking at his tablet, moving his fingers across the screen as he worked, frowning.

As she waited for whatever the Taźath and his dour friends would decide, Jee couldn't help but reflect on her actions in her first one hundred days on Áhtha. She had insulted the entire arena and the country by not waving at that stupid game of Rush. She had threatened to drag a medical doctor through the streets, convinced a hero to break the law and take her into a war zone, stood in front of a firing squad, and had her boyfriend pull a gun on the High Minister of Security. Forget about the singing that made the entire plant mentally unstable; that was the least of her transgressions.

And what had Tar Aséllo done to her? So far, she had almost been killed by a rocket, she was stampeded by creepy weirdo men, watched a beautiful child die needlessly in her own arms, and witnessed hundreds, maybe thousands of people murdered in streets that now ran red with blood.

As utterly beautiful and wondrous as Tar Aséllo looked on the outside, it was something else under the surface.

Jee again focused on the minsters, working at their terminals, serious and grim. She could only sit and wait for the other shoe to drop, as Mr. Gallotta used to say. What would he suggest? She knew: gather intel. Find your position and advantages before taking action. Sound advice, but it couldn't stop the fear growing inside.

Her face turned red with worry, and her eyes welled up.

This was not missed by the Taźath or the ministers.

"Are you well, Glasśigh?" Pronómio asked, genuinely concerned. He turned away from his tablet.

"Yes," she managed, her voice wavering.

She noticed that the Taźath seemed concerned, almost choked up. And the ministers? To a one, they seemed on the verge of... tears! Manes flashed gold at the edges. Wasn't gold concern? Sorrow? Is it because they see me upset?

Interesting, she thought.

"Glasśigh," said Pronómio, now regaining control of his emotions, "let us discuss." He continued in a soothing tone. "It seems you are having some difficulty understanding how this society operates. We need to set things right."

"I can agree to that," said Jee. "This place is very strange to me."

"Áhtha is not like Earth," Pronómio continued. "And though you are more of an expert than I, or any of the ministers—save Commander Eno, of course—we do know a little of Earth's history and current societies."

"You listened to their radio wave broadcasts?" Jee asked.

"Yes," confirmed Pronómio, "and I have seen video as well. We learned there is a difference in social structure between America and Tar Aséllo. This is the root of your trepidation and unrest, isn't it?"

"That, and the fact that I was a simple girl on Earth," Jee explained, "and here, I am some kind of celebrity princess."

"*The Glasśigh*, you are!" said Pronómio, smiling.

"If I may, Taźath?" asked Eno.

"Please, Commander."

"As a means of explaining social structures in Earth history," Eno began, "going back five thousand Earth years, there has always been class structure. The building of great empires was achieved by the work of class structure—"

"An example, Uncle?" interrupted Jee.

"The Chinese Dynasties, being the most ancient of Earth, had multiple class levels, each with a purpose. The Egyptian, Greek and Roman Empires as well, fueled by the effort of each class, working as prescribed by doctrine."

"Interesting," said Jee. "Each of the empires you just named was built for the select few, on the backs of slaves."

"There were no slaves in the British, Spanish, or French Empires, or in the late Indian empires," he countered.

Jee laughed. "Wrong! They did employ slaves, and even in more modern history, they had them, and still do! They don't call them *slaves* anymore, but the lower working class is a legalized slave class, unable to rise, kept down—and that sounds like this place!"

"Please, please!" interrupted Pronómio. "The point is that the class structure here works. Everyone knows their place and contributes and is rewarded—"

"Not evenly, as I have seen in Éhpiloh," interrupted Jee, trying to control her anger with little success. "Little children taken as slaves?"

"I have heard that before," said Pronómio. "They are not. They are taken to government-run schools. Those stories are lies, spread to discredit the system. They are sent to homes to be taken care of by people who are not criminals."

"Criminals?" exclaimed Jee. "Like the thousands I saw shot in the street by tanks? I saw it! I saw it happening! Did they get a trial? Do you even have judges here?"

"It is not Earth, Glasśigh!" stated Pronómio, somewhat sharply, his mane showing a tinge of blue. "Equality is within each class. It has been that way for years!"

"And," rejoined Jee calmly, "for years, there has been ongoing resistance to the rules, the class rules. Why don't you just give them a little freedom?"

"Freedom?" echoed the Taźath, exhaling loudly. "Leave us for a moment, ministers, please."

A few concerned looks crossed the faces of the ministers in the room before they slowly stood and exited quietly. Even Eno was dismissed.

"Glasśigh," said Pronómio, standing. "Let us start again. Earlier today, according to my conversation with Commander Kalífus, you entered a *warzone*. You interfered with our ground operation in Éhpiloh. Besides being dangerous, it is against the law, even for Kořeefa. If you were not who you are, you would be jailed and facing death."

She wondered if he could actually put her to death, her being the Glasśigh and all. That's scary, she thought. But wait. No, no, he couldn't. I'm too…popular. That's interesting…

"Not to mention your other issues and transgressions," Pronómio continued. "So far, I have been able to keep many of them out of the mass media."

"I didn't know, Taźath," she said. "There was no malice in my actions."

He held up his hand for her to stop.

"I know that," he said. "But these things must remain controlled. Listen, dear girl, your parents, they also felt a need to assist, to give the Graćenta more freedom. They wanted to do away with most of the rules of our class system. They were seen as friends of the Graćenta, and yes, we all need the Graćenta, as they all need the Kośeefa and Merćenta."

"I never knew my parents," Jee whispered solemnly, her eyes welling up.

The Taźath moved to the other side of the table and took a chair next to Jee.

"I knew them," he said. "Your father and I were like brothers. And though I disagreed with his ideas from time to time, I respected his heart. But what he never realized is that the Graćenta are not like Kośeefa. They do not appreciate what we all have here. Some want more than their share, and they don't want to work for it. They do not know their place. And your father and mother, they saw the Graćenta differently. And these Graćenta support the Enária, and before them, the Zakéema, the ones who killed your parents. That is what your father and mother received for their kindness."

Jee began to cry steadily.

"I don't tell you this to upset you," Pronómio explained as he reached for her hand. With his other hand, he offered her an elegant cloth towel for her tears. "I tell you this because I see a fine young woman, one who could do great things for all of Áhtha, who is struggling to understand our way of life. After all, you *are* from another planet!"

They both laughed. Jee handed him back the towel, her tears driven away by the lighter mood.

"Now, this towel," said Pronómio, jokingly. "I could probably walk out to the main square in Etáin City and sell it for a small fortune!"

Again, they laughed.

"I am so sorry, Taźath," she said, though she knew she wasn't. "I-I am just having a difficult time. It is all so strange."

"Then let me help you. Here is my plan."

The Taźath went back to his chair, and using his console, called for Alíthe and Eno to join them. Once they arrived, he continued, laying out a simple plan. First off, there would be a formalized schedule for her, created by the Media Minister's office, to cut down on the impromptu visits and the like. Secondly, there would be formalized education for her, explaining the culture, all steeped in the history of Tar Aséllo.

"Most exciting of all," Pronómio announced, his mood lightening, "is this: as a means of learning the history and development of Tar Aséllo, we have arranged for a three-week excursion! You will explore every corner of the land, most of them anyway, and begin with a trip to the founding areas, the first areas discovered by Ásue Aséllo, in the far western tar!"

They could not believe what was happening. An hour ago, they thought a firing squad would be their next adventure, and now? A vacation?

Jee was suspicious; however, she was gathering intel. How should she react?

"You will see the blue-green Aséllian Sea," continued Pronómio, "the Thousand Towers of the *Pégra Pygréez* beyond the Caymana Strait, the Falls of Jovia and of course Aséllo's Well—and the most fabulous sight of them all, Aséllo's Spire! The views are stunning, not only of the tar but also of Ofeétis as he rises and sets! You will stay, of course, at the original Garden Resort at Aséllo's Spire and visit Aséllo's Tower and Hall, where your great-great-grandfather lived and married your great-great-grandmother, Jaydí Ćlaviath! Commander Alíthe and Reǵeena will accompany you."

"Really?" she asked, "I am shocked, Taźath."

"We will allow," Pronómio stated, overdramatically, "an escort to attend this trip as well. I will send your Uncle Eno!"

"Oh," said Jee, with a bit of a frown. "We would be perfectly all right without him. I am sure he is busy—"

"Nonsense!" declared Pronómio happily, "he will be a fountain of information! A personal tour guide!"

"Thank you," Jee responded unenthusiastically.

"You don't seem excited," said the Taźath, disappointedly.

Jee looked at the Taźath, staring into his eyes. Something was wrong with all this. Why is the Taźath letting me off so easily? She wondered. I am a pain to him. And he is constantly afraid I will do or say something to upset his popularity! I thought I was going to jail, not on vacation! So, why *not* put me in jail if I'm such a nuisance? Is it against the law? But he is the law!

Wait…what would happen if he did imprison me? Or worse?

Then it dawned on her.

Pronómio Tok will not jail me because…he can't! He can't

imprison Tar Aséllo's sweetheart! What would the populace think? And the ministers? He would lose his next vote of confidence in a landslide! My popularity is my protection—and my power.

But what to do with it?

Jee had no answer, not yet, though she decided on one thing at that moment: she would no longer be part of the cruelty perpetrated by the Taźath and the Kořeefa who supported him. Somehow she would help the Graćenta. On the outside, she would behave and curtsy and bow, but on the inside, she would formulate a plan. In the meantime, she would become best friends with Pronómio Tok and play along.

"My Taźath," she finally said softly. "I don't know what to say. I believe we are all completely stunned with your generosity."

She gave a wide beaming smile.

"Ah," he said, returning the smile.

All were dismissed. As the ministers and guests filed out of the conference room, the Taźath reached for Eno.

"A word if I may?"

After the others had left the building, the Taźath remained with Eno in the atrium. They moved to the center of the room and stopped at a refreshment center filled with select liquors. Most of them were rare and expensive. The Taźath poured two glasses of dark red-black *Sour Smaggous*, the most expensive of the collection. It was so sweet that it was not. And the harshness was not for the weak.

"I must say, my Taźath," said Eno as he sampled his beverage, "that was very kind of you. On Earth, we have a saying: 'out of the frying pan!' Then again, the phrase finishes with 'and into the fire,' a bad thing."

"I believe I get the meaning," said the Taźath.

"Thank you again for your kindness and your patience and your wisdom," said Eno with a bow.

The Taźath looked at him with a smile, but it quickly faded, turning into a frown and glaring black eyes. Pronómio's mane flashed a deep blue. Eno was taken aback.

"Let me tell you this, High Minister Commander Ćlaviath," snarled the Taźath. "Keep that woman under control. She will know her role *and* her place, or by the powers I possess, I will see to it that she is placed *into the fire.* Am I clear on this?"

Wounded and afraid, Eno nervously left the conference center. Immediately, Gákoh Kalífus appeared and sat with Pronómio Tok.

"I told you she was dangerous."

The Taźath sighed. "You did," he agreed. "But she has power over people, and we may need that."

Kalífus shook his head in opposition. "She is like a Spearbill Blood Bird, my friend. Small, fragile-looking, and beautiful. So many colors, those large, deep amber eyes, and that song. It is hypnotic. One would think they were gentle and passive. Until…"

"Yes, yes," said Pronómio, annoyed, "until they pick up the scent of blood. I have seen swarms of them attack *góhmar goats*. The frenzy is simply disgusting."

"My point, my Taźath," continued Kalífus, "is that one should not be fooled by beauty. It can be perilous. If one sees a Spearbill, one must kill it before it calls to its flock, before they attack and suck your blood away."

"Poetic, Gákoh," said Pronómio. "But the benefit of capturing this little blood-sucker could outweigh the risk."

"Blood-suckers make poor pets," countered Kalífus.

Pronómio simply sipped his drink.

As Jee and her entourage were driven the short distance to Palace Place, all were quiet. Though stunned and grateful for their good fortune, a sober mood still prevailed.

Eno was especially quiet.

Alíthe and Reǵeena stared out the window at the passing parks and grounds.

The car pulled into Palace Place. Everyone exited and walked to the door, except for Jee. Standing at the side of the drive looking at the opulence of her home, she paused and then turned around. She gazed north, to Éhpiloh. She could see the dull gray city on the far shore across the sea of Etáin, still smoldering.

16
Aséllo's Spire

After the unfortunate event at the Taźath's Leadership Center, Eno kept to his room, watching videos. He was quiet, morose, seemed saddened, and at times angry. Jee worried about him. Whenever she poked her head into his room, he would smile weakly and just say: "A lot on my mind, dear."

During one interruption, Eno informed his niece that he had taught Reǵeena how to grind and prepare a decent pot of coffee and asked if she could bring him a cup.

"Thank you, my dear," Eno said to Reǵeena as she delivered the brew. He took a sip and for a moment, came out of his mood. "A fine cup. I believe you have passed me in expertise."

He immediately went back to his videos and dark disposition.

The trip to the western tar was greatly anticipated, mostly by Alíthe and Reǵeena, and even more so by the public. The media channels were filled with content. The Taźath and Minister of Media Názma had things perfectly planned with exclusive reports of the most minuscule of minutiae for the distraction of the masses. It made for excellent viewing: a detailed analysis of the historical sites the Glasśigh and her escorts would visit; the relationship of her ancestors to each other including the extensive lineage of grandparents going back a thousand years; exposés on each of the Glasśigh's travel companions; speculation as to what the Glasśigh would choose to wear on the skyliner, what she would wear when she arrived at the first location, what she would wear for dinner on most nights. There was even an auction for limited edition Glasśigh dolls and artwork by famous artists, including some from the *Official Appointed and Approved Artist of the Glasśigh*, Veegill. The 'approved' part was most important, according to Jee.

Most insane was the embarrassing seven-part special scientific analysis broadcast addressing the Glasśigh's skin. A time-lapse animation was used showing the gradual changes in her skin color since she had arrived, ending with her current state, just a few shades lighter than the rest of the population. Insanely close-up images were shown of her skin from nearly every square inch that had been available to cameras. Arguments surfaced between medical professionals, famous artists and experienced fashion and make-up designers, each claiming a different 'segment' of the Glasśigh's skin was the most perfect. Yes, there was much praise for Eno's chemical ingenuity that transformed the Glasśigh's skin color in the first place, though there was even more praise for the Glasśigh's unparalleled beauty.

On a brighter than usual Fullglow, the sky was clear of clouds, and the fálouse was in a state of thinness, allowing more of Ofeétis's light to bathe Tar Aséllo. Alíthe arrived at Palace Place with an escort of twelve security men and a box of *kimie cake*s from Gaymee's. The cakes were like a muffin but much lighter, even lighter than a donut, and they had a type of berry sauce in them.

To Jee's delight, she and Alíthe had been spending a good deal of time together. Even in preparing for the trip, they showed more affection, in a *physical* way, within Palace Place and the surroundings: holding hands, a quick embrace, and sometimes, disappearing for a few moments. Their kissing had been observed by Reǵeena, Eno, and eventually would be seen by the ever-present drones. Today, Jee and Alíthe had to sneak into the kitchen to be alone, as the security escorts seemed to be everywhere.

"The skyliner is here," said Eno flatly as he poked his head inside the kitchen. "And stop kissing that boy."

"Eno!" gasped Jee, surprised and embarrassed, breaking away from Alíthe.

"I am not a boy," protested Alíthe as he straitened his uniform and stood at attention. "I am almost three years old, Minister Commander."

"What is your problem?" asked Jee. "You have been moping around for three weeks! You have hardly said a word!"

"I just said nine words," he responded. He stared at them blankly for a moment, then left the room.

"He has been like this since the meeting at the Leadership Center!" complained Jee. "He is upset. I have never seen him so distraught. It's creepy."

"Creepy?" asked Alíthe. "Some of the Earth words you use…"

"Creepy. It means something makes me afraid. He just mumbles and works on that tablet. He won't use Vací or his armband anymore. He said something about it not being safe."

They went to inform Reǵeena that it was time to go and found her in Jee's room. The younger woman had insisted on packing for Jee and herself. The pile of crates and baggage required two security men and a kitchen cart to transfer to the skyliner. As always, Reǵeena did more than her share, probably because she was a trained servant. Jee didn't like it. She was a friend, not a slave.

The trio made its way to a side door of Palace Place, accompanied by the assigned security team and the rolling cart. They could see Eno ahead of them, talking to his tablet as if it were alive. Some images could be seen on its screen, but at this distance, who knew what he was looking at? Probably more of his artifacts from Earth that had been scanned into his database.

When they reached the skyliner pad at the Palace, they all gasped.

"Oh!" exclaimed Reǵeena excitedly. "Look! Is that our skyliner?"

On the pad sat the most beautiful craft any of them had ever seen. It looked like a sleek, elegant, silver dagger, with the hilt being the wings set back under two enormous silver engines. Its skin was a polished metal of some sort that gleamed in the muted sunlight like the Lockheed *Constellations* Jee had seen in Spokane. Though the length of a passenger airliner, this was thinner and more streamlined than any Earth ship. Instead of dozens of small windows, the entire top half of the plane's passenger area was a single piece of glass. Best of all, it had the G-Wing logo on the tail structure.

"*That* is a nifty set of wheels!" Jee squealed as she ran toward the craft.

"There are no wheels," said Alíthe, confused. "Not even *nif-tée* ones."

"It looks like a bullet with short, stubby wings," Jee said as she ran to the craft. "But I love it!"

Drones followed her, capturing it all for the media. Jee even smiled for them purposefully. She had a reputation to uphold, at least for now.

A ramp had been lowered from the ventral side, and a woman in military uniform confidently strode down to the landing area, crossed over to Alíthe, removed her helmet, and saluted. She had a short, dark, feather-like mane, deep golden eyes, and a square jawline. Standing just a bit shorter than Jee, she seemed all business.

"Second Officer Breegan Arkéta, sir," she announced saluting Alíthe. "I am assigned as your pilot."

"Our p-pilot?" asked Alíthe, looking somewhat hurt by the fact that he would need someone to pilot the ship.

"N-not that you need one," Arkéta stuttered, trying to recover. "I-I mean, you are a pilot. Also a pilot."

"I see," Alíthe relaxed a bit, then swallowed hard. "Breegan, I apologize for *involving* you at the base the night of the Éhpiloh mission…and the, um, blasting off like that. Completely against protocol and procedure."

"Do not mention it, sir," she said, also relaxing. "You are wing commander. And no harm was done."

"That remains to be seen, however..." he turned to the ship in an attempt to change the subject. "What is it? It looks like the Diletta prototype."

"It's a modified Type-F Diletta Skyliner, yes sir," confirmed Arkéta as they walked closer to the ship. "The modifications are pretty extensive. This craft has much the same defensive equipment that the military version had, just not the offensive."

"So no guns but tracking and warning systems?" asked Alíthe.

"Yes, sir. It is officially called the *Skyliner Type-G Luxury Aircraft*," Breegan announced. "G for Glasśigh."

"I have a plane named after me?" giggled Jee, flattered.

"Yes, it appears so," Alíthe said. "Mechanical specifications?"

"The Type-G has four hoverjet lift-off modules, replacing the hoverfans of previous models," explained Breegan, "two fixed under the cockpit and two under the tail to ensure smooth hovering and semi-vertical take-off. Mounted above the tail, we have two M44 forced fuel cell after-burner rocket engines"

"M44s?" asked Alíthe, not sure if he had heard correctly. "They were developed for the military but deemed unnecessarily fast."

"Yes, sir. Instead of scrapping those engines," continued Breegan, "the Air Works Group of Diletta slapped them on this one-of-a-kind ship. It is over luxurious and overpowered and capable of speeds well over four hundred miles per hour."

"I like it," said Alíthe with a smile.

Reǵeena had run ahead, almost flying into the cabin through the open door on the belly of the Type-G. Shortly, she re-appeared.

"Oh, wow!" Reǵeena called. "You have to see the inside! It's gorgeous!"

The interior of the skyliner was opulent. It was not the Taźath's personal craft; oh no. The Diletta Group had gone beyond that, designing it specifically for the Glasśigh. With only four passengers, it was beyond spacious. Seats were of a cushioned silken weave in a muted orange with dark brown accents. There was a small kitchen in the back along with screens for viewing entertainment, sleeping areas, and small dining tables. No luxury was overlooked.

Alíthe returned to the passenger compartment after conferring with Breegan on the flight deck. He was pleased with the route to be taken and suggested a few additional waypoints that would give the Glasśigh a better glimpse of the wonders and beauty of Tar Aséllo.

"Second Pilot Breegan Arkéta is well trained. She has been in my wing for a long time. I knew her from my early days in the AMF. We will be in good hands," assured Alíthe. "And with this machine, we can outrun anything on Áhtha! I will fly it eventually, of course," he said, taking a seat next to Jee on a reclining couch.

"Not with me in it," quipped Jee. "I prefer to live."

"Is that Earth humor?" asked Alíthe with a grin. "Ha," he said unemotionally. "I believe that is the correct reply."

Reǵeena found the refreshment stand and attempted to retrieve drinks for the passengers.

Jee stopped her immediately. "This is my trip, and I get to call the shots."

"Shots?" asked Alíthe.

Eno barely paid attention; he turned his gaze away from his portable tablet and stared at his niece blankly.

Jee stared back. "So that means that no one gets waited on by Reǵeena, except Reǵeena. Understood?"

Eno nodded and returned to his pad.

Reǵeena frowned.

"Great," said Alíthe. "Then *Jee,* would you get me a tobafruit cocktail?"

"No," she replied sweetly, "but you may get me one!"

The Type-G Skyliner lifted off from the Palace Pad in view of a group of waving ministers, then continued lazily onward over Palace City and then to Etáin. A few dozen media drones followed the craft closely, trying to capture a view of the occupants, but thankfully, the windows were mirrored and one-way. The media drones saw nothing.

"Can we get out of here?" Jee asked. "I am tired of everyone looking at us, especially through those nasty drone bats!"

"Breegan," called Alíthe, aiming his voice to the flight deck, "Let's see what this thing can do. Next waypoint, please!

"Yes, sir," she responded over her hel-com. *"You better sit down and secure yourselves!"*

The Type-G, all engines on full, streaked away, leaving Etáin City, the crowds, and the remaining pesky drone bats behind.

En route to the Resort at Asébllo's Spire, Eno did little of the aforementioned 'tour-guiding'. Instead, Alíthe and Breegan did their best to take on the role. They pointed out the six-foot-tall *Pillbint Birds* below, their white feathers glowing red the faster they flew, the flock numbering in the thousands.

They passed Cheltor's Horn, an incredible two-mile high promontory of jet-black rock that curved like a horn of some great beast that had fallen into the sea, its final resting place.

Heading westward, they approached Jaydí's Arch. Alíthe explained that the mile-high natural structure had once been a connected semi-circle, but years ago, a piece fell from the center.

"If a pilot is proficient enough," Alíthe called, again directing his voice to Breegan, "a craft could fly through that small opening, maybe sixty feet wide, at the zenith of the natural stone formation."

"I am a proficient pilot," Breegan said over the com and set to prove her point. Increasing speed, engines roaring, she threaded the Type-G through the small opening. Her passengers screamed in delight.

"Now that was fun!" squealed Jee.

Over the Síndian Sea, they marveled at the fertile farm fields below and the gentle waters that lapped on the sandy shores. Soon, they reached the Aséllian Farms, located on the southern tar. Another arch, Dirga's, separated the farms in two. Breegan gave another exciting pass, almost scraping the top of the skyliner as she flew underneath.

"It was named after Dirga Ćlaviath," said Eno, almost in a trance. "Ásue Asésllo and Jaydí Ćlaviath's second-born…he discovered it."

The others turned their heads to him, surprised that he was speaking, but he immediately drifted back into his tablet.

Breegan had slowed the craft to a leisurely one hundred miles per hour, allowing the passengers to take in the beauty of the dark blue Aséllian Sea, and in the distance, the Falls of Kryménos.

The western tar was becoming cloudy. Ofeétis was waxing. Knowing the weather could turn ugly, especially in the far western tar where the canyon walls were close together, Breegan headed northwest, directly toward Asésllo's Spire. Within minutes, they were just a few miles from their final destination.

"Oh my!" gasped Jee as the next feature came into view.

Before her to the northwest, was a vast peninsula, twenty miles long and at least three miles wide, jutting out from the southern tar wall. It seemed to float between the Sea of Jovia and the Aséllian Sea. In the center of the land were mossy green and light brown stone mountains that reached at least two miles high in some places. At the water's edge, Jee could see rich jungles, sandy beaches, and inlets of deep lavender and turquoise waters.

"Delaina's Pool," said Eno wearisomely as they approached an unusually large inlet on the shore of the peninsula. "Very purple," he commented before again returning to his tablet.

Jee rolled her eyes and continued to look at the scene unfolding before her.

After another few minutes, Breegan tilted the Type-G upward, climbing into a thin layer of clouds. *"I suggest looking out the left window,"* she called over the com.

The passengers could see that the Type-G was entering an expansive, gray, rain-filled cloud bank, and as they rose, the haze began to break away. Suddenly, they were above the mist, peering down onto an ocean of orange-tinted clouds that stretched as far as they could see. And there, thrusting through the whiteness and lit by the vivid glow of Ofeétis, was Aséllo's Spire. It glistened as if wet, a black and blueish stone tower rising at least eighty feet above the cloud-sea in the sky.

Jee saw that the tower was mostly a single stone with veins of blue and black rock striping the sides. However, on top was a gray construction of almost perfectly hewn blocks stacked high, creating a three-storied monument. There were arched windows and balconies on the upmost layer.

"Are we staying there?" she asked.

"No," laughed Alíthe. "That is the Crown Room. It is a revered monument. However, if anyone would be allowed to reside there, it would be you and Commander Ćlaviath. We will stay at the Aséllo Garden Resort on the western side, right at the beach. We have the entire place to ourselves. Except for the security team."

"And the media drones," sighed Reǵeena unhappily.

They circled the spire and then dove down to the surface of Spire's Bay to land at the resort. There was a security detail already in place, and a media crew was unloading cameras and supplies.

"Let us find our rooms," suggested Alíthe. "I will have the staff move this luggage inside. We will need to rest, for tomorrow we will hike Aséllo's Spire. There are over one hundred steps to the top—and that is after you climb the mountain!"

"I'm up for it," said Jee.

"I hope you two enjoy the hike," Reǵeena announced with a laugh. "After my long nap, I will find the beach."

"I will stay with Reǵeena," Breegan added. "I also could use a day at the beach as well."

The staff rushed to attend to the arrivals. After a few pictures were taken with the Glasśigh, the travelers were shown to their rooms. Jee and Reǵeena were the first stop in the entirely empty resort. Breegan was shown to the suite across the hall. The men continued on.

Alíthe noticed that Commander Ćlaviath's room was directly across from his own. Eno paused in his entryway and stared blankly at Alíthe.

"Minister?" asked Alíthe, concerned. Eno had ignored him this entire trip. In fact, they had barely spoken since they first met. Could this be about me kissing his niece? wondered Alíthe.

"Commander Afiéro," Eno said softly. "I will also hike the spire tomorrow." He glanced at the TSP guard at the end of the hallway. The guard looked at Eno sternly. Eno sighed and returned the stare. After a moment, Eno called out. "May I assist you, officer? Or must you stare at my family and me like an old *scabeenious crab* from the Thermal Desert?"

"I am sorry, Minister Commander," responded the guard.

"Then stop looking at me!" Eno snapped angrily.

The guard continued to stare for a moment but felt uncomfortable and moved down the hallway, out of sight.

Eno removed a small clip-like device from his pocket. He showed it to Alíthe as he depressed a little button on the top of the device.

"Do you know what this is?" asked Eno quietly

"A jamming clip?" Alíthe offered.

"A *programmable* jamming chip," Eno corrected as he flicked another switch on the bottom of the device. A small purple light on the side of the chip blinked twice. "I have recorded me discussing something with you. If anyone using detection devices is listening, they will think I am admonishing you for kissing my niece. Which, by the way, I am."

"Oh," said Alíthe, slightly deflated. "If I may, Minister, why are we masking our conversation?"

"All in due time. Tomorrow I will start my hike early, before you and the Glasśigh. I will arrive at the top long before you. I want Jee to walk into the Crown Room on her own. Find a way to make that happen. Let us have some time alone."

Alíthe was about to ask why when Eno anticipated his question.

"And no, Commander, I will not tell you why. But you will do as I say, or you will be re-assigned. Am I clear?"

Alíthe nodded. "Clear, High Minister Commander."

"Then have a good rest," said Eno, a bit more cheerfully. "And stop kissing my niece."

As Jee and Reǵeena entered the room, their mouths dropped open. The luxury that surrounded them took their breath away. The main area of their suite was larger than all of Palace Place. In the center was a pool, complete with live aquatic plants that glowed under the water, colorful sparkling inlayed tile, waterfalls, water jets, and multiple seating areas above and within the pool. At the edge of the pool stood a man in a red suit holding towels. There was a bar complete with a servant, and a kitchen with two chefs. The room displayed glass artworks, a floor to ceiling aquarium on one side with a forest of colorful plants on the opposite wall. There were two separate seating areas and a series of marble tables surrounded by plush seating. To the rear was a door that opened to a bedroom, sporting a view of the sea beyond and a private balcony that made Palace Place's dwarf in comparison.

"This is..." muttered Reǵeena, but she had no words to describe the opulence.

"This is not right," said Jee.

"Glasśigh?"

"After Tepótah and Éhpiloh...I-I just can't...understand this. I feel...guilty." The Glasśigh turned to the servants and looked at each one in turn. "Leave. Now. Don't come back."

The hike up the mountain took the first four hours of Lastglow. The light of Ofeétis added a shimmering twinkle to the surrounding rock faces, the silica and quartz flakes catching the rays and reflecting them in flashes of white and gold. Alíthe and Jee stopped for a meal and rested often. It was nice being alone with her, thought Alíthe, but he knew that somewhere up ahead, Eno Ćlaviath was most likely watching.

The terrain was hilly but smooth, and the incline, though steep, was more of a hike and less of a climb. Someone, probably ages ago, had figured the easiest way to reach the spire and installed gray, flat stone steps where needed. The path had been paved in places, making the walk more pleasurable. There were gardens of wildflowers and tall, slender trees with budding white and red striped pods. There were pools filled with *Trogue Marogue*: wonderfully strange antlered fish that glowed every color imaginable as they jumped great distances from pond to pond. When clouds blocked Ofeétis's light and the day turned darkest, hundreds of *DeeDee Bugs* simultaneously blinked their tiny bioluminescent tails in coordinated color flashes of yellow, then blue, and then red. This attracted the various jumping fish looking for a colorful meal, and Jee laughed at the fantastic spectacle. At times there was a misty drizzle of rain coming from so far above it looked as if the fálouse itself was weeping; still, it refreshed their sore muscles and parched throats.

After several hours, they had made it to the tower's base, an expansive flat terrace over ten thousand feet square: the Prominence of Asėllo. Here they rested again and took some nourishment. In each other's arms, they looked up at the tower. It reached another one hundred feet into the sky, literally touching the clouds. They could look north and see the mist of the Falls of Kryménos rolling in waves over the surface of the sea.

Jee thought that of all she had experienced in these past few weeks, the horrors, the strangeness, the confusion; if she could just have this moment, forever, it would be worth it. Somehow, she knew Alíthe felt the same. When their eyes met, they both smiled knowingly, as if they could read the other's minds.

When they entered the tower, they found a circular staircase that wound along the interior's outside edges. The tower's width had to be at least sixty feet in diameter at the bottom. Every twenty or so steps, there was a landing that opened to a small balcony. These became places for the weary to sit and rest.

"Here are the last one hundred steps," said Alíthe. "Are you too tired to continue?"

"Yes," replied Jee. "But I will go on. I must go on."

"I am also tired, so I will rest a bit. But you," he waved a hand vaguely upward, "you should go on ahead. It would be good for you to enter the house on your own. It is a singular experience, and it should have special meaning to you," he advised, "being that you are both an Aséllo *and* a Ćlaviath, I mean."

Jee smiled and shook her head.

"Whatever you say," she said. "Lazy is what I think."

With that, Alíthe smiled and turned away. He walked to the edge of the Prominence and looked toward the green fields and the northern Sea of Aséllo. The cloud layer was just above him, glowing orange.

Jee took a deep breath and began to climb the steps, winding upward yet again. Her legs ached, but not as severely as she would have thought. Step after step she took, the air becoming colder with each riser. She could see an orange light above her as she neared the end. Ofeétis was glowing overhead, no doubt. Since she was now above the clouds, it was brighter than usual.

Stepping up to the final landing, she took a deep breath. The air smelled sweet here, and the oxygen content was richer. She felt awake. Soon the aches in her legs left, and she felt alive and vibrant again.

Jee stepped up the last four stone risers and entered the Crown Room. The area was circular, the diameter about eighty feet. Its stone ceiling was lower than any of the previous rooms, and if Jee hopped just a bit, she could easily tap the top.

There were four large openings equally separated around the circumference, each leading to a balcony. Jee walked straight ahead and outside.

The first balcony was about ten feet wide and five feet deep, facing northwest. It was constructed of the same gray stone as the rest of the tower—there were no ornamental structures or fountains of any kind. They were not needed; the view was incredible. Jee walked to the edge and placed her hands on the chest-high wall.

Two-and-a-half miles above her roared the curved Falls of Jovia, its width spanning over two miles. She felt dizzy from the height but could not look away. White and green-tinted water rushed over the icy edge of a surface glacier. It thundered past and continued falling until it disappeared into the cloud layer below.

"Beautiful," she whispered to herself.

After some time, she moved back into the Crown Room and went to the second balcony. Identical in size to the first, she faced northeast. Here, the cloud cover ended abruptly, just past the tower, and beyond its edge and beneath was the Asèllian Sea, roiling with every possible hue of blue and turquoise. The far shore of the northern tar sat peacefully on a field of green. Above it were small waterfalls, so many that they remained unnamed, each creating a river or stream that ran to the ocean. Even further off was the misty white haze of the Bay of Ramos and the Kryménos Falls.

She sat in wonder, gazing at Ofeétis spinning above, the plunging water, the deep greens of the distant Treágor Delta to the south, with its blue and brown rivers flowing through the jungles to empty into the awaiting sea.

The third balcony faced to the southeast, showing the land that held the Spire and the turquoise sea bordering. Also visible were the small jungles along the edge of the peninsula and the deep violet-glowing Pool of Delaina.

But it was the fourth balcony that took the last of her breath away. Before her, to the southwest, the cloud layer had moved to reveal the calm water of a glass-surfaced emerald green bay, the small entrance flanked by tall stone walls on either side. From her position, Jee could easily see over the walls and into the inlet beyond. It was the shape of an almost perfect circle, at least three miles in diameter. It resembled Idaho's beautiful mountain lakes, except this water glowed brilliantly, and in its center was a deep black hole a half-mile-wide, a well, where water flowed steadily inside.

"Asèllo's Well," said Jee to no one but the sky.

She leaned on the edge of the balcony wall and tried to comprehend this strange world. Did she love it? Or fear it? Maybe it was both at the same time. Though this was her birthplace, she still felt little connection, yet something made her want to belong here, to be part of it, and in a particular way. But within all this physical beauty, there was still a horrible social ugliness, one that needed to be stopped, just as it needed to be stopped on Earth.

After an hour, Jee turned back to the Crown Room and went inside. Only then did she notice an alcove on the back of the stairwell wall. It was lit by some type of light that came from a long, narrow shaft just above. Within the space, glittering like a miniature galaxy of vibrant stars, sat a jeweled crown upon a dark fabric-covered cradle. The crown had five spikes, several inches long, each with a diamond-shaped colored jewel on its peak. The frame was mostly silver but had veins of gold running through it in thin curved lines, and it seemed to sparkle on its own.

"It is the Crown of Aséllo," came a soft voice from behind her.

Startled, she spun around. "Eno!" she gasped. "You scared me."

He smiled. "I have that effect on many people."

"What are you drinking?" she asked, noticing a dark liquid in a clear container.

"Coffee. The last of it, I am afraid," he moaned sadly. "And with my seed cherries on *Explorer*, which is still in repair, who knows when I will be able to retrieve them? I believe I will need to go back to Earth for more. A hundred pounds was not enough."

"It is nice to hear you joke a bit!" Jee said after a short laugh. "You've been so *mopey* and dull these past weeks. Are you all right?"

"I am fine. I see that your skin color has returned to normal, finally."

"It is like a milk chocolate brown now," she observed, looking at her arm. "I like it."

"As do I. You actually look more like an Aséllo, like your mother, than a Ćlaviath."

"A relief," Jee teased.

"The Crown of Aséllo," he said, ignoring her joke and pointing to the relic. "It has never been worn by anyone, except Ásue Aséllo. Many believe it is wrought out of the purest of silver and gold, infused with silica and iron dust for strength."

"Really?" asked Jee, looking at it once again in wonder.

"Who knows?" answered Eno. "No one is allowed to touch it."

"No one? So it has been sitting here all this time, and no one has even—"

"Yes. No one has touched it for almost a thousand years, let alone inspected it," he confirmed, moving to his niece's side. "There has never been a full *rightful* heir of an Aséllo and a Ćlaviath—until you. But even you can't put it on. To do so would be to claim the whole of Tar Aséllo, and that is for the Taźath."

"Then why doesn't he put it on?"

"He is not an Aséllo or a Ćlaviath, let alone the offspring of both," continued Eno. "Ancient custom demands that the next wearer be of both families."

"That is a strange custom," Jee said.

"Yes, the ancient ways seem strange today," Eno agreed, still looking at the crown. "Mystifying, really… People love to hear the lore and read about the olden days. Of course, you are the first Glasśigh; you are the offspring of both a Ćlaviath and an Aséllo."

"I-I don't want to put it on…"

Eno only nodded.

"Does it have any, you know, superpowers or stuff like that?" she went on, half-joking.

"No, no," Eno answered with a laugh.

This would have been a perfect time for one of his idiotic jokes, but somehow he restrained himself. Jee turned to give him her full attention. He appeared older now, standing slightly slumped, wrinkles around his eyes.

"The Crown of Aséllo has no magic," he continued, "but it is a statement of leadership and authority. Whoever wears it would rightfully command the tar…in the minds of many."

"It seems hollow. I don't mean physically, but the idea of just putting this crown on my head would make me a leader. That's just crazy."

"A wise man once told me that authority must be taken through duty—it can't be given—or it is worthless."

"I agree. Who said that?" asked Jee.

"Your father, Tye Ćlaviath."

Eno walked out to the balcony facing Aséllo's Well. Jee followed him, wondering why Eno climbed all the way up here to just give her a history lesson. There had to be more to it than that. He was a complex man, and as weird and uncomfortable as he was to be with, he was undoubtedly brilliant and accomplished: Eno Ćlaviath was a medical doctor, a scientist, a political minister, an explorer, a historian, a naturalist, an astrophysicist; however, though, he was not himself lately.

"What is the matter, Uncle?" she asked as she joined him. "You have been behaving oddly for quite a while. I'm worried that you may be ill."

Eno smiled as he continued looking outward. "Have you ever watched the media file of your parents' death and the events at Targan Base?"

"Yes," Jee answered softly, somewhat saddened by the subject.

"When?" asked Eno.

"When I first was granted access to Vací with my historical minister level."

"Vací, yes," Eno said. "As a side note: no using Vací for any research. Use disconnected tablets and the files I can load for you."

"What? Why no Vací?" she asked, surprised.

"She is part of the tar-wide network. It is monitored. All of it."

"Are you saying the Taźath is spying on us?"

"He spies on everyone," Eno stated as if it was common knowledge. "You saw those screens in Kalífus's Dark Room? At the Palace Leadership Center?"

"Hmm…" she mused. "I guess I am not surprised."

"Let me ask you this," Eno continued. "You have only seen the *prepared* files of the incident at Targan Base, correct? You have never seen the raw media file? Or the files from *Explorer*'s cameras?"

"No," she said. "I have not. Are they different?"

"A little. But just enough. Sit."

They sat on a stone bench. It cooled their bodies as they listened to the rush of water falling into Aséllo's Well. They watched the flocks of orange and red *grígora birds* soaring and diving through the mist that rolled west from Spire's Bay. Jee again thought of the beauty of this place and of the horrors she had seen. Now, more than ever, it reminded her of Earth: the beautiful cities, the open wilderness of the Idaho panhandle, the starry skies that appeared each night. That beauty was in dark and depressing contrast to the evil of the last war, the killings of Negros in the southern states of America, the torturing of dissidents in the deserts of Arabia, the mass genocides taking place all over the globe. There was no Garden of Eden, not anywhere, she thought. Civilization had destroyed it, even here.

"I have seen the raw media files," Eno said, after a while, "from the security cameras in the tower at Targan and, more importantly, from *Explorer*. I have an exact copy. I have been studying it."

"Is that what you have been doing on that tablet?"

"Yes. On my disconnected tablet," he said. "It is not part of the network. I made my copies from the archive computer in the Palace Library. I merged them with the original files from *Explorer*."

"Why did you do all this? What did you find?" asked Jee.

"Things are not as they seem," he whispered. "We must be careful, Jee. After the meeting in his council chambers, the Taźath directed me to control you, or he would control you himself. He has only once before directed me to do something, and that was a few weeks before the *Explorer Eleven* launch."

"What did he want you to do?" Jee asked.

"He asked me to encourage your father and mother to cease their campaign to assist the Graćenta."

"They were advocating for Graćenta, yes. The Taźath mentioned that to me," she said.

"You must remember that at the time of the launch, Pronómio Tok was not Taźath. All knew it was his great desire! But Pronómio and your parents did not see eye to eye. Your father and mother had studied the Earth broadcasts and learned of the many governments of that planet. They became great proponents of a free Áhtha for all classes. Being direct and popular descendants of Jaydí Ćlaviath and Ásue Aséllo, they had a great deal of support in the Ministers' circle. They also had the support of the leader of Tar Éstargon, the Ef Keería."

"I met him in Palace Place," Jee said. "There used to be trade between the two tars."

"Yes, negotiated by your parents," added Eno. "Mostly your mother."

Jee mulled that over for a moment. "Vací told me there was great prosperity. Then it stopped because Éstargon thought Tar Aséllo was going to have too much advantage, having all the food and—"

"No," interrupted Eno. "Not true. There was no issue with food. The issue was that the Ef Keería agreed with your parents about a more free and equal society for the Graćenta. Like them, he disapproved of the rigid class structure and the mistreatment of many. Pronómio, and many other Kośeefa, did not want to give up any power or wealth."

Eno took a breath. He seemed to gain a bit of energy, or maybe, thought Jee, it was anger. His mane glowed slightly blue about the edges.

"The result?" he continued, his voice tight. "With the death of your parents, Pronómio Tok solidified his power and ascended to Taźath. The treaty was dissolved between Tar Asello and Éstargon. The Éstargonians had to find food from other sources, ration what they had or could grow. Tar Asello was left behind in technology of all kinds. The last joint venture between the two tars was *Explorer Eleven*. And that, as you know, was almost a *complete bust*, as the Earthlings say."

"Well, it wasn't a complete bust. I got a real nose out of it," said Jee.

"Of course," continued Eno, "the Taźath saw your parents, and you, possibly, as a threat. And threats need to be dealt with."

"Are you saying the Taźath had something to do with…with what?" Her nerves felt electric at his words. He couldn't possibly mean…

"I am afraid for you, Jee. Pronómio Tok is a very powerful Taźath—arguably the most powerful in the modern age. We must be cautious. We mustn't antagonize him."

"I don't believe half of what the Taźath says," Jee said angrily. "I know he was lying about the children in Éhpiloh, the killing of people in the streets—I was there!"

"Yes, I think we know little of the truth. But there is more to this, and the key is in the raw files I have of the events at Targan Base. They are disturbing; however, it explains so much. I am not sure if you are ready to see—"

"I want to see the raw files," Jee stated without hesitation.

▲▲▲

Eno took Breegan aside after he had returned from Asèllo's Spire. They stood in a garden near the far edge of the resort, admiring the landscape and meticulous attention to its grooming. Here, Eno took a serious tone and asked about the pilot's dedication to the Glasśigh. He informed her that they were to discuss life and death matters, and that many of her beliefs would be shaken.

"The Glasśigh is in danger," Eno went on. "I need to know if you can handle the truth and could possibly walk away from your current life. If not, please allow the rest of us some time together."

After a long moment, Breegan nodded her head. "Is Commander Alíthe joining you?"

"There no way to not allow him to join us," Eno sighed. "The Glasśigh is quite attached to him."

"I trust Commander Afiéro with my life," Breegan confessed. "And my love for the Glasśigh is strong."

"Your love of the truth, no matter how inconvenient, must be stronger," insisted Eno.

"I have seen things, Minister Commander," she said nervously. "I saw the gun films from the A4s that attacked Éhpiloh. I know there is something wrong in Tar Asèllo."

Eno smiled. "Then join us in my room for a game of Bowilberweeks."

The game of Bowilberweeks was challenging to follow, and though almost everyone in the tar had heard of it, only a few ever took the time to actually learn the rules and play it. It involved a complex set of stone tiles, a book of odd rhymes, and a three-dimensional rack of sorts that housed the three tokens assigned to each of the five players. It was boisterous, funny, and almost impossible to follow unless you were well learned in the rules and strategies.

The Special Police guards who were eavesdropping on the Glasśigh and her group were confused completely. The language, the frequent spells of silence, and the almost moronic chants and sayings that were part of the game made it difficult to listen to, let alone follow. In the end, it was just background noise to the guards. The Glasśigh and her party were indoors, in her suite, and having a good time. That was all that mattered.

Of course, no one would win because they were not even playing the game. Eno had used his jamming chip to record a long and program-generated dialog of mostly nonsensical phrases, using words that he, Jee, Reǵeena, Breegan, and Alíthe had spoken since the beginning of the trip. The only understandable words in the whole program came at the beginning when Eno recorded himself saying, "How about a game of Bowilberweeks?"

The group was actually sitting at the main table in Jee's suite, gathered around Eno's portable tablet. They watched the file of the Targan Base attack, starting at Eno's elevator ride to the top of the control arm tower.

Eno looked so young, Jee thought.

"There were two different video systems that made up this file," said Eno, "one from the control tower cameras and one I added from the cameras on *Explorer Eleven*. This part is from the control tower."

The video file continued, showing Eno's discussion with Tye Ćlaviath and Dypónia Aséllo. What shocked Jee was the fact that this version, unlike the ones she had seen with Vací, clearly showed her mother holding the infant pod, and in it was Jee.

The next few minutes of the file had actions that moved hectically: the alarm sounding, the scramble for cover, the lift door blasting open, the smoke, the cries, and the gunfire. The Zakéema, in their black rags, were clearly visible.

Jee lost her breath as she witnessed the fall of her father. She could see her mother running with Eno from the tower toward the bridge. Then, projectiles were being fired, and her mother was hit. She cried as she watched her mother collapse.

Eno paused the file. "Let's stop for a moment."

"No," Jee said. Her friends could see that her face was contorted with sorrow and anguish, though she was trying not to cry. Her voice was rough, her breath short. Eventually, she was able to take a deep breath. "I'm all right."

Eno nodded. The video played on.

They watched the killing of DaJees and Mosca, the desperate jump from the bridge to *Explorer*. The injuring of Eno's arm.

"That was most unfortunate and painful, I must say," Eno added. "If I had escaped injury, I could have altered the ship's course. I am sorry, Jee. But here is a new part, not seen by the public. The file point of view now shifts to the images taken from *Explorer Eleven.*"

The screen showed the laser cannon being moved into position by the Zakéema. Eno swiped the video forward and paused at a particular frame.

"Alíthe, what is that weapon?"

"It is a multi-fiber optic laser cannon, an MFOL. It is a war-class weapon. One was stolen from an unguarded transport by the Zakéema years ago," he said. "They never were used by the AMF or the TSP."

"Oh, it was used by the TSP, I can assure you of that," Eno assured them. "Odd that the convoy was unguarded, with such an expensive weapon, eh?"

"What are you meaning?" asked Alíthe.

"Watch," directed Eno, and the video continued. The events played out as Eno remembered: the scrambling of the Zakéema to put the weapon together, the frantic rush to get the ship's cryo-chambers in order, and the launch sequence started.

They watched in horror as the gun almost fired, but the rockets of *Explorer Eleven* flared and—

"Let's go back to the gun being taken out of the crate," said Eno. "No one, except me, has ever seen it before. Allow me to enlarge this section here."

They watched again as the gun was unloaded from the crate by four large men in full Zakéema gear.

Eno paused the video. "See here? The man on the right. The sleeve on his arm has an emblem. What is it?" He zoomed in tighter on the man's flexed arm. "Anyone?"

"It is a Zakéema emblem," observed Alíthe. "It was their symbol. The flaming letter Z."

"And on this man?" said Eno as he moved the image zoom to another portion of the screen.

"The same," replied Jee.

"It is not right," corrected Reģeena. "Zakéema soldiers had to work in the fields by day or hide from the Special Police. They would never wear a badge like that."

"Yes, Reǵeena. How interestingly perceptive of you. Let's move ahead a bit," said Eno.

The men in the image struggled with the cannon. Two more men came to their aid. They struggled still, six soldiers clumsily bumping into each other, swaying back and forth a bit. After much jostling, the gun was free. Eno froze the image again. "Look at their arms."

Alíthe took control of the pad and zoomed in.

"The sleeve on the man's arm is now rolled up," said Jee, "moved by the struggle with the gun."

"And now we see a tattoo, or something," Alíthe commented.

Alíthe moved the zoom to the other man. His arm's sleeve also was raised and partially displayed the same tattoo.

"What is most interesting," continued Eno, "and confirmation for my theory, is the image that is *under* the sleeve, the tattoo that the attackers *wanted to cover*. Alíthe, copy the two images, boost the gold and black hues, and paste them one on top of the other, then delete all the other color."

Alíthe worked as directed. When finished, he gasped at the grainy but unmistakable image. "That's not right. It's impossible. It just can't—"

"Yes, it can," interrupted Eno as the others gathered nearer to the tablet.

There on the screen was an image of a dagger-styled, four-point black star behind three Áhthan letters. It was much like the symbol Jee had seen on the Special Police building at the Taźath's Leadership Center.

"It is…like the Taźath's Special Police insignia," Jee said. "But the first letter is different."

"Very good, Jee," said Eno. "The first letter is an Áhthan 'Yeh'. The letters read Yeh Seh Peh. It is the emblem of the Yahyéth's Special Police."

"The YSP?" asked Breegan. "That force became the Taźath's Special Police when Pronómio Tok became Taźath!"

"I wish I was wrong," Eno said. "I have tried to explain this away—"

Jee was shocked into silence. Reǵeena could only nod her head. To her, this made sense.

"A rogue element of the YSP?" suggested Alíthe.

Eno shook his head. "Some would argue the YSP *was* a rogue element—created by Pronómio Tok for his own use. No oversight was allowed. It is *possible* the team at Targan Base was a subgroup of the YSP. Maybe they were acting alone. But consider this: there are only four hundred troops making up the current TSP ranks, and only one hundred are actually gun-carrying soldiers; the rest are support. I assume the YSP was much smaller at the time of the launch. And Kalífus knew each member personally. The idea of a splinter group acting without his knowledge? Impossible."

"The YSP all had tattoos?" asked Jee. "Does the TSP also?"

"They do," confirmed Breegan, "but the old guard, the initial members of the YSP, kept their original tattoos. It is an honored mark of distinction. At least it *was*…"

Eno began to pace. "I seriously began to suspect the Taźath when he threatened me after the meeting in his council chambers. "But even before, while still on Earth, it nagged me. How could the lowly Zakéema, who were just a bunch of *vandals*, pull off a plot where they overwhelmed the AMF and base security forces, carried out an attack with a sophisticated plan, and got their hands on exactly what they needed: a one-of-a-kind cannon and a laser drill?"

"They would often steal things," said Alíthe, still not convinced.

"And to what end?" asked Eno in protest. "If it was the Zakéema, they killed the only friends they had in power: Dypónia Aséllo and Tye Ćlaviath! They lost everything! It did not happen the way Pronómio and Kalífus claimed, saying that the Zakéema wanted to show they still had power. And there is one more recent item.

"I refer to the arena attack," Eno continued. "I have studied that video as well and found two anomalies. One is a flash of concentrated red light glistening off the *Explorer* in several images. Look," he instructed as he took over the tablet again. He fumbled a bit but soon displayed the file of the attack, taken by a stage-side camera. Zooming in on the ship, it was evident that there was a red laser cross on the top of *Explorer Eleven*.

"What is that?" asked Jee.

"A laser beam," answered Alíthe, "not a weapon, but a low power beam meant to direct missiles and such."

"According to Kalífus," continued Eno, "it was a Klaymac device mounted on a class 7 rocket that struck the *Explorer*. But here is the other anomaly: there is too little damage. A Klaymac is a nasty thing, isn't it, Alíthe? It should have split the *Explorer* in half."

"The force field!" offered Alíthe. "Kalífus said it protected the craft from even the Klaymac—"

"If it were engaged, yes," interrupted Eno. "I know I am a silly old man; however, I completed every shutdown procedure when we landed, including turning off the force field. How could we have exited with the field still active?"

They were silent.

"But Minister," protested Alíthe, "a Klaymac would have blown the *Explorer* to bits! That didn't happen. You must have turned it back on, or someone else did!"

"Or it wasn't a Klaymac on that rocket," stated Jee.

"Ah, my inquisitive and perceptive niece is on to it! Alíthe, do you know what a *flash shell* is?" asked Eno.

"It's a practice round," he answered. "It makes a big noise and is bright and a bit hot, but not very powerful. Of course, if it struck you, then it would be lethal—but are you saying that the ordinance fired at the stage was a flash shell? How did it get there then? Those are not guided. They are usually fired out of a gun or dropped from a Katíga Rocket-bomber."

"It was on a class-7 rocket," said Eno. "I saw the red trail of its discharge gasses as it came in, and I saw the second stage ignite. How accurate would a class-7 be?"

"Without the usual weight of the Klaymac," offered Breegan, "and the lack of electronics required…maybe to within ten or so yards."

"But it was laser-guided," Eno reminded her.

She thought for a moment. There, on the screen, was the red laser cross shining on the top of *Explorer Eleven*, and that could be no accident. Someone had lit up the ship. But why hit the ship? Weren't they, whoever they were, trying to kill the Glasśigh and Eno?

"How close, Breegan?" prodded Eno.

"The laser-guided class-7 rocket has accuracy to within a few inches—less than the width of my hand."

"And the scar on the *Explorer* is right here," Eno said, showing the explosion on the tablet and then the scarring on the ship. The image showed a small dent, no bigger than an Áhthan hand.

"So, wait," said Alíthe. "With no shield up, the explosion looked horrible, but—it was just a firework? Why? Why would the Enária fire a Flash Shell a, a laser-guided one, at Jee?"

"Not at me!" cried Jee, the realization dawning. "At *Explorer!* If it's that accurate, they *could* have hit Eno or me easily. They aimed at *Explorer* on purpose but wanted it to look like it was a Klaymac on the rocket, intended to kill me."

"But it could not have been the Enária," said Reǵeena. "They have neither the luxury of a firework or laser-guided systems. If they steal weapons, wouldn't they steal a useful one?"

"So who fired it then?" asked Jee.

"Who would stand to benefit if the Glasśigh was threatened but not killed?" asked Eno. "And who would want to make it look like the

Enária were to blame?"

The answer hit Jee. "…and so he could win a vote of confidence! There was a vote just days after we arrived at the arena! You discussed it with Pronómio Tok when he visited!"

"Yes," said Eno.

"Wait," protested Alíthe, holding up his hands to forestall them. "This is all supposition. Coincidence. You don't know that for sure, nor do you know that it wasn't a rogue YSP team that attacked Targan Base. Not really."

"Until there is another valid explanation," countered Jee, "it is more than plausible."

"What we *do* know as fact," continued Eno, slightly irritated at the pilot, "is that *someone* attacked Targan Base as well as Jee and me at the arena. They disguised their identity on both occasions. The tattoos—and the laser-guided flash shell—point to the YSP and TSP forces, rogue or not. We all must tread lightly."

It was time for them to think, understand, and decide on their course of action. Each returned to their rooms and tried to come to grips with what they had seen.

Jee and Reǵeena sat on the balcony of their suite, looking out over the grounds of the resort. They were silent for a while, but finally, Jee spoke.

"Have you ever been so angry that you just didn't know what to do?"

"I scream a lot," admitted Reǵeena.

"Really?" asked Jee, surprised. "I just can't picture you screaming. You are always so *reserved*. 'Cool' as we say on Earth."

"I am cool?" asked Reǵeena. She blinked in mild confusion. "It is never cool here on Áhtha, except in the highest elevations."

Jee smiled. "I am so glad to know you, Reǵeena. I don't think I would have made it this far without you."

"It is my honor to serve you, but even more of an honor to be your friend," said the girl. "Everyone loves you."

"That's about all I have going for me," Jee sighed. "I mean, yes, the Kořeefa, they just love the idea of having a *princess* around. But the poor Graćenta…" she paused, now in thought.

It was clear to her that it was time for action. Could she change things? How had real change happened on Earth? These people in Áhtha were not humans, nor was she. But many were just as cruel, selfish, and evil. Others were kind, gentle, caring, and loving. Like Reǵeena. Like the poor mothers in the day school in Tepótah.

"This place is a cruel, messed up, crappy little dictatorship," Jee said. "And the Taźath..." Her voice trailed off.

"He is a bad man," stated Reǵeena. "And the Kořeefa enable him. But the real people, the Graćenta and the Merćenta, they have goodness. And they love you. There is no need to know why. Even some of the troops in Éhpiloh—they pointed guns at Commander Kalífus instead of you! You represent a dream they all have, a dream of a better day. A wish on a star that just might come true. You can use what you have to help."

"Help?" asked Jee thoughtfully. "Yes. Ha ha! Maybe I could join the Enária Front, if they would have me! Just to talk to them—that would be an experience! And it would really make the Taźath fume!"

They laughed for a while but soon grew tired as it was now Eclipse. In Jee's room, they slept in the large bed together, as they did most nights. Tonight, however, Jee's tossing and turning kept Reǵeena awake. At one point, she left the bed and sat with her ABC, trying to keep the light from the hologram away from Jee.

Poor thing, Reǵeena said to herself. Poor thing…

17
The Captive Truth

Nearing the end of their trip, Jee prepared to go on a short hike alone. On the shore of Spire's Bay just south of the resort lay a beach of white and gold sand, fine to the point of almost being powder. Reǵeena had found it first and reported the amazing jungle surrounding the beach, the gentle trickle of the waves, and the view across the bay to Aséllo's Well. It was peaceful there and private. This is where Jee had come, avoiding the drones and the media crew, and hopefully, the security team. She arrived as the pale light of Firstsun, its source a half a billion miles away, silently lit the edges of Ofeétis in a sparkle of light. Watching this, she sat in quiet contemplation.

Jee accessed her ABC yet stayed off the network. Stored on the device was a series of pictures she had found with Vací while aboard *Explorer Eleven.* They were of her parents, Tye and Dypónia, and she scrolled through them, studying each line of their faces, their smiles, their eyes. She sadly wondered what they would think of her. Though she never knew them, she suddenly felt an overwhelming wave of emotion—she loved them and needed them. And what she would give to speak to Mr. Gallotta again! The realization of that never happening pushed her into a deep melancholy as she listened to the waves gently breaking onto the beach.

After an hour or so, a voice came.

"How are you?" Alíthe asked gently. "Would you like some company?"

"I wanted to be alone, with my thoughts, but I don't believe that is working too well…"

"Do you feel any better?" he asked.

He sat down on the sand, then reached for her hand. She gave it willingly. They remained silent for a moment. The waves made a gentle sigh as they lightly fell onto the sand and retreated. The sound was soothing, in contrast to what they both felt: anger, loss, betrayal, and helplessness.

"Have you decided upon anything?" he asked.

"Since I have been here on Áhtha, I have felt lost," Jee said finally. "On Earth, as silly and backward as it was in Idaho, I belonged. I knew where I stood. I had parents. Now, here, I am just a misfit. I feel afraid. A stranger."

"You are *the Glasśigh*, Jee. That is something to be proud of,"

Alíthe said. "That makes you special. In the hearts of us all."

"Alíthe, I did nothing. I do nothing to deserve this life. I could just sit in my palace, literally, and enjoy parties every day as people suffer and injustice rules the tar. It's overwhelming, and, and I don't know what to do about it."

Alíthe looked down into the grains of sand by his feet. He thought of the multitudes of people who loved her. Jee was a bright spot not only to the Kořeefa, those privileged ones, but to the rest of the people as well, the poor and the abused.

"Tar Asélło would be a darker and colder place without you," he said. "No matter how you feel about Tar Asélło, Tar Asélło feels an attachment toward you. They love you. You are their light in dark times: the light of true Áhtha. You, and Reǵeena, you have opened my eyes to what is going on here. And I'm ashamed."

She recognized Alíthe's love for her, and she knew she loved him. To see him now, vulnerable, had a new effect on her. This was more than physical.

Poor Alíthe. Poor Tar Asélło, she thought.

"I haven't decided what I will do, Alíthe. I don't even know what is possible. When I was on Earth, I had an assignment in school to persuade people to do something. I gave a speech to my class about the injustice women suffer in America. With just a little effort, I was able to convince almost the entire school to revolt. I didn't want it to go that far, but it just happened. It was amazing and scary and wonderful…though I did get into a lot of trouble, but I felt a power, Alíthe. Not a selfish one, like the Taźath's, it was a giving power, you know? Like when you give to someone, and they really need it."

"I understand," he said. "When I saved the troops in the tunnel, I felt the same. I think."

"That is all I have: my empathy and my power to persuade. Not much, really, compared to the Taźath and his forces."

"Your empathy is a greater thing than all the might of the armies of the Taźath," he said. "You give people hope."

Jee lapsed into silence again. Alíthe held her close. They waited for something to happen, some sign of where to go, of how to proceed. Not just for themselves, but for their purpose, if there was to be one. The waves continued to spill onto the beach, the water sparkled with a thousand tiny stars, and they sat in the beauty of it all.

"No matter what," Alíthe spoke softly as he held her, "I will stand by you. I believe, ahem, that you love me, and though I do not know why you have selected me, with all the men of Tar Asélło to choose from…"

"You, Alíthe, are a gem no matter what planet I happen to be on," she said with a smile. "And…the bar is set quite low if you consider the other men I have met here."

Alíthe took a deep breath and smiled. "I do not know what a bar being set low has to do with anything," he replied, "but I also have chosen you. I love you, *Glay-dis*. Not as the Glasśigh, but as Jee, the girl from another world. The one who has dukes and likes Shy-neese food. And the one who saved all those children. I certainly don't deserve you, but I will always be here for you."

She looked up to him, into his hazel-green eyes, and smiled. "I love you, Alíthe, and I know we deserve each other."

They didn't need to kiss; they were close enough as they were, breathing as one, stroking each other's hand, living quietly and joyfully in a single moment of peace and clarity. If it could only stay like this forever.

"Hey!" called a small voice, light and full of excitement. "The skyliner is ready! We are going to the Kryménos Falls on the way back to Etáin! Hurry! And stop kissing!"

"Reǵeena! We were not kissing," Jee objected. "Why must you always assume we are kissing?"

"Just hurry!" came the answer.

Flying the skyliner toward the first waypoint, Breegan piloted the Type-G through a series of pale green cloud banks and light but steady rain. Within moments, the skyliner was surrounded by three TSP Gunships—for protection or control, depending on one's opinion. The formation circled Asélло's Spire then turned south to take a slow cruise over the top of Asélло's Well. All then turned northwest and increased altitude comfortably to almost five miles in preparation for a stunning view of the crescent-shaped Falls of Jovia, then on to the Kryménos Falls.

After a half-hour, the Type-G Skyliner and its escort A3s emerged from the clouds and slowed to a hover. Breegan had turned the craft sideways so the passengers could see all of the Kryménos Falls.

The falls were stupendous. Over ten miles wide, they were the largest in Tar Asélло and the most colorful. Streams of green and blue, but also pale orange stripes fell miles to the sea. The ice-cold water crashed amidst boulders as it reached its destination, the Bay of Ramos, creating a mist and foam that glowed in several spots, swirling and drifting about.

"The glow is caused by light creeping in through the fálouse," said Eno, "and the chemical composition of the mineral particles in the mist. I remember—"

The blaring of a siren interrupted him.

"Threat detection. Projectile launched," the Type-G's threat system called out. *"Please return to your seats and secure yourselves."*

A resounding and deafening *BANG!* reverberated through the ship. A flash of white above and to their left startled them, causing all to duck. One of the hovering A3 Gunship escorts was in pieces, falling to the sea, miles below.

"Arkéta!" called Alíthe, "Get us out of here!"

"I don't see where it is coming from, sir!" called Breegan through her hel-com.

"I see a ground cannon!" shouted Alíthe. "In the water of the falls to the far right!"

"Threat detection. Second projectile launched."

Another flash, clearly seen in the darkness, fired from a different position. The second escort disintegrated.

"What is happening?" cried Eno.

"Threat detection. Third—"

But that warning was drowned out as the darkening sky lit up again, the last of the TSP escorts exploding in a thunderous clap, pieces falling again into the mist.

"Threat detection—threat detection—threat—"

Another flash, then another, then another, as red tracer projectiles streaked past the window, missing the skyliner by mere feet, the glow from the shells lighting up the inside of cabin.

"They missed!" cried Eno.

"Those are warning shots," said Alíthe. "They don't want us to move!"

"Commander Alíthe!" Breegan's voice came over his armband. *"I have a communication!"*

"Hold your position," Alíthe ordered. "Put them through."

Alíthe and the others ran to the command deck.

Breegan flicked the main com switch. "Go ahead," she said, her voice firm.

"This is Salǵeea Calćoa of the Enária Front. Do not attempt to flee. We have a tracking clamp on your hull and surface-to-air missiles locked on. Proceed to the far eastern edge of the falls, at an altitude of exactly twelve-point one-three."

"And if we don't?" asked Alíthe defiantly.

"We will blow you out of the air," came the reply. *"No matter how fast you believe that barge of yours can move, Commander Afiéro, it*

can't outrun a Torchette Missile."

"I really, really, really want to go back to Idaho," Jee groaned.

Breegan maneuvered the Type-G into position. Once hovering, they stared straight ahead out the viewshield at a light velocity stream of a minor waterfall, barely ten yards wide. Through the stream, they could make out the tar wall behind: dark, almost black. Then, a section of the wall came forward from behind the flow and disrupted the fall's path. Soon, it blocked the plummeting torrent, spraying water in all directions. Revealed beneath the stone was an opening sharply carved into a square, leading into a cave large enough to fit the Type-G.

"Proceed inside," came Salǵeea's voice over the radio. *"Welcome to our home."*

Hoverjets on full, Breegan piloted the craft under the light spray and into the dark cavity.

Once past the falls, it was clear that this was no ordinary cave; it was a small city. The open area they entered was dark, but sections were lit in a yellow glow by portable fixtures and lights strung across the two-hundred-foot-wide expanse. Curved arches of stone supported the natural rock ceiling above. Against the cave's rear wall was what looked like a stone apartment building, seven or eight stories tall, carved right out of the existing rock. Jee could clearly see the distinct layers and the cutouts, like windows and balconies, each emitting a greenish glow. Light also rose from the lowest level, coming from dozens of display screens that sat on rock outcroppings, makeshift desks, and crates that seemed to be everywhere. Wherever she looked, Jee saw people walking, working on some machine or computer device, or driving small trucks carrying containers and boxes.

In the center of the cave sat stacks of supplies, vehicles of every type, and groups of soldiers wearing ragged black outfits. A man holding red beam-lights signaled for them to land in a clear area nearby.

The Type-G touched down. Engines shut off. Soldiers in black appeared from every corner of the cave and surrounded the skyliner immediately. Jee counted at least fifty armed Enária fighters.

"What do they want?" asked Jee nervously as she looked out the viewport.

"You, I would assume," suggested Eno. "The Glasśigh will make a fine bargaining chip."

"Let's hope that is all this is," said Alíthe.

Breegan quickly came to the cabin and stood with the others. She had a hand pulsegun out and ready.

"I don't think we can shoot our way out of this, Breegan," Eno said. "Diplomacy and caution will be our best tactic. Alíthe, they already know who you are, but that is no surprise. You have been seen with the Glasśigh all over the media. You, and Breegan, must be extra careful, being members of the AMF."

"You are a Minister of the Taźath!" cried Jee. "I don't think you will be too welcomed either!"

"Caution and patience!" urged Eno. "Breegan, leave the weapon. Let us go."

They walked to the rear of the skyliner. Breegan pressed the door lock. It hissed open, and the ventral ramp descended.

A group of Enária soldiers stood waiting. One was large and muscular, though his face was hidden by a scarf-like black rag. He held black cloths in his hands.

"These are hoods," he said, thrusting them forward. "Put them on."

"Why?" asked Alíthe. "We know where you are located already. What is the purpose?"

The soldier walked up the ramp and stood within inches of Alíthe, face to face. "Listen to me, Hero of the Taźath, I would like nothing better than to take you outside and toss you off the nearest ledge. Put the hood on, or we will take that walk."

"Just do as he says, Alíthe!" pleaded Jee.

"Ah, the Glasśigh!" said the soldier. "It is good to see you. It is an honor. Truly."

Jee took a quick look around. It was hard to tell what expressions the Enária soldiers wore under their masks, but their eyes seemed lit up, and any visible mane seen was tipped in red. A few dozen people in the back area of the stone hangar peered out from dark hallways and behind storage crates. They seemed to be jockeying for a look.

"Hello," she called to them warily.

More than a few called back words of welcome. Some even waved.

The captives placed their hoods over their heads, and each was escorted by a soldier out of the ship. After several turns, Jee realized the noise from the footsteps had lessened. As she concentrated, she could hear only her footfalls and those of one other.

"Alíthe? Eno? Reǵeena?" she called. There was no answer.

"Please keep moving, Glasśigh," said a voice. It was the same voice from before. The large man was her escort. He handled her with care, a firm grip, but not a rough one. He moved slowly and cautiously as he guided her onward, up stairs, and around corners. Then, the sound of a door opening, a metal door. They walked ahead.

It was warm in this room, Jee thought. And there was a humming sound, low pitched. Their footfalls echoed less than before.

"Please, sit," came the voice.

Jee complied and felt the softness of a padded chair with armrests as she sat.

"Please be patient," said the man. He removed her hood.

She was in a large room with walls of stone. The wall to her left had a wide opening a few feet from the floor, and through it, an eerie green glow came. Chairs were set about the sides, all facing her seat in the middle. A display screen was hung on one wall with a camera on a stand and a computer below on a small table.

She turned to see her soldier, but she only caught a glance of his back as he exited. He locked the door behind him.

▲▲▲

"Please. Sit. What is the report for today?" asked Pronómio as Minister Názma entered the Palace Leadership center's main conference room. A mid-day meal had been prepared: *pheril sage* cakes with extra thick *byrumpet sauce* and a tart and crispy *ghurnee bird* stuffed with *jhodie peppers* and *solcum nuts*.

Názma sat quickly, and began filling a plate as he spoke.

"The test statistics are in," Názma stated. "As expected, the Glasśigh was the most popular figure in all of Áhtha and the next closest? Afiéro, the pilot! One survey of all the classes revealed that ninety-seven percent of Aséllians would rather have dinner with the Glasśigh than their own family or love interest!"

Understandable, thought Pronómio. He also would rather spend an evening with the Glasśigh, alone preferably, than with any other person.

"And the Glasśigh's five-week trip to the resort at Asélló's Spire?" offered Názma, "It produced a rich trove of photos, videos, and tidbits of interest! There are images of the stunning views, the dinners, the Glasśigh hiking and laughing—oh, that face! And that cute nose! If there was only a way to productize the nose! Maybe sell replicas for wearing at dinner parties? Children would love them! I'll make a note of this! The populace will be giddy with excitement!"

"Good," said Pronómio, sounding less than interested. He was thinking of the Glasśigh, her beauty, and her nose.

"Then there are the, ahem, personal developments," Názma whispered. "The kind no one can resist!"

Pronómio sliced a portion of ghurnee bird, dragged it through the red byrumpet sauce and plopped it into his mouth. "Such as?"

"The sisterly friendship of the Glasśigh and the Graćenta girl, Ahdelfía. Maybe not the best copy, that, but interesting and controversial without being too shocking. But the most luscious piece of news…is the budding romance between the Glasśigh and the handsome hero pilot, Commander Alíthe Afiéro."

This seemed to peak the Taźath's interest, Názma noticed, but in an odd way. He noticed that Pronómio's mane changed to an odd color: a muted Bluish- green and orange. The minister knew this as the colors of jealousy.

Later that evening, Pronómio contacted Commander Kalífus. He ordered the removal of Afiéro as the Glasśigh's bodyguard and demanded he be sent to the Girth Sea, Degas Point, to be the Security Commander of the Ground Forces Base.

▲▲▲

It seemed as if hours passed. Jee heard no sounds except for her own breathing. Nothing to do but worry and wait. And think.

She hoped Alíthe was all right. Being a member of the Taźath's forces, who knew what could happen? Breegan also would be in danger.

At least Reǵeena would be safe…she hoped. Being a Graćenta, she could be forgiven for working for the Taźath. She had to eat! Even the Enária would understand that.

Eno was a problem. He was a Minister. What if they were torturing him? Trying to get information? Or would they use him as a bargaining chip? A hostage? The only comfort she had, and it was little, was that no one had harmed her as of yet.

She heard footsteps. The door opened. Jee turned to see a dozen Enária soldiers enter, none with weapons. They escorted Eno, Alíthe, and Breegan inside and motioned for them to stand against a side wall.

"Where is my friend, Reǵeena?" she asked, but no one answered.

After a moment, a tall, slender man with a sandy brown mane entered. He wore a scarf, black, as was the rest of his clothing. He moved with quiet confidence to within a few feet of her. A soldier brought a chair for him, and he sat. He removed his mask.

He was older than Jee imagined, looking almost sixty if he were a human. His face was tanned, his skin dark olive and wrinkled, his eyes were light blue.

"Welcome, Glasśigh Aséllo," said the man. "I am Salǵeea Calćoa. I heard you wanted to speak with me."

Jee was surprised at that. After a moment, she responded with a question. "I assume you will kill us?"

"Why would we do that?" Salǵeea responded. It was his turn to be surprised.

"We know the location of this base," Alíthe interjected. "If you let us go, that would jeopardize your position."

Salǵeea laughed. "Is that an insult?" he asked. "Do you think this is our only base? There are several from when we had a different name. We often relocate, so do not worry. We will not kill you; at least that is not the plan."

"Thank you," said Jee.

"You are welcome," responded Salǵeea. "First, I would like to ask you about your intentions."

"My intentions?" Jee asked.

"Yes," continued Salǵeea. "You are a hard one to figure out. Whose side are you on, if any? I wondered. I was especially confused when we captured this video via one of our drone cameras."

He motioned to a screen on the back wall of the room. As they turned, Salǵeea tapped his armband, and the video began. It was of Jee, Alíthe, and Reǵeena in Éhpiloh. There she was, walking the streets, Aréus 501 in the background.

"The media drone," said Jee calmly. "It was yours?"

"Yes," Salǵeea replied, "a small gift from one of our few Koŕeefa supporters."

The video continued, faithfully chronicling the events, including Jee's reckless act of standing in front of a firing squad, her arguing with Kalífus, and freeing children from the train.

"Unbelievable," breathed Eno when the video ended, shaking his head in disbelief.

"How did you get that?" asked Alíthe. "We saw the drone destroyed."

"It was a live feed drone. Near-live," said Salǵeea.

"That's expensive technology," Breegan pointed out.

"We have a few rich friends," Salǵeea stated. "We have another video, almost as dramatic. The Glasśigh singing to dying children. Very moving."

All watched the video of Jee in Tepótah. Few could keep from tearing up.

"What do you plan to do with these videos?" asked Jee.

"That depends on the outcome of these conversations," said Salǵeea.

"What do you want from us?" Jee pressed.

"I ask you that same question. You are the one who wanted to speak to me. What is it *you* want?"

"What makes you think I want to talk to you?" she asked.

Jee realized that he knew more than he was revealing. The video of Éhpiloh was a surprise, she had to admit, but the video of the hospital in Tepótah was a real shock.

Yes, she did want to speak with him, but how did he know?

"So," said Jee after a moment of silence. "You had a spy, didn't you?"

"You mean Isos?" asked Salǵeea. "Yes! Once we knew you were coming, we had a need to know what you were up to and how your arrival would affect things. So we did some enlisting. It was Isos who was responsible for capturing the visit to the hospital in Tepótah. She had a small, hand-sized drone."

"Isos?" asked Eno.

"Brave Isos!" Salǵeea called with exaggerated grandeur, "come forward."

From the corner, a small soldier walked forward. She removed her scarf. "Hello, Jee,"

"Reǵeena Ahdelfía." Jee nodded and smiled wryly.

"Please, do not be angry with me!" Reǵeena pleaded, falling to her knees. "I was approached by the Enária Front immediately after I was assigned as your servant. I-I just wanted to help my people, I just wanted to—"

Jee ran to her. Soldiers moved in to restrain the Glasśigh before she could do any harm, but they were too late. They were shocked when the Glasśigh embraced her friend.

There was a collective sigh and some laughter as well.

"A day of surprises!" chuckled Salǵeea with a laugh.

"How true," Eno agreed.

"Reǵeena, do not worry," Jee insisted. "I knew there was more to my new friend ever since Éhpiloh. You were brave then and dedicated, and you knew a lot about the Zakéema and the Enária Front for someone who was a mere servant."

"You are not angry?" asked Reǵeena, her voice shaking.

"No. Relieved is a better word."

"I am your friend, Jee," said Reǵeena, "and will always be. When I first was assigned to you, I wanted to hate you and your privilege. But quickly, I saw who you were. Gla-diss!"

"I'm just a girl like you, Reǵeena," Jee responded.

"I would not have brought you here if I didn't think you would be safe," Reǵeena continued. "I believe your heart is in the right place, though you are lost here on Áhtha. Maybe Salǵeea and the Front can give you purpose."

Food was brought in, and most of the soldiers departed, except for the large one who had been Jee's guard.

"And who are you?" she asked.

"This is Orgo Talhínsa," said Salǵeea as they sat to eat. "He is in charge of our military arm."

"A pleasure to meet you, my Glasśigh." He removed his scarf and bowed slightly.

"And to meet you, Orgo Talhínsa," Jee replied.

"Let us think of the next step if there is to be one," suggested Salǵeea. "Reǵeena tells us that you know much of the truth. We do as well. Your uncle's tablet! He wouldn't let us see it. He locks that up pretty tight—and we weren't going to torture him to get at it! No need. Reǵeena told us what you discovered. That Taźath! He is one nasty little *droll poker!*"

"I agree!" said Jee with a nervous laugh, "and I don't even know what a droll poker is."

"Tok is the murderer of your parents," Salǵeea reminded her. "Not the Zakéema or the Enária Front. He orchestrated the *Explorer Eleven* disaster and the arena attack, blamed us, and then used the ploy to pass his votes of confidence."

"It was not the only atrocity he committed to remain in power," added Orgo. "Before almost every vote of confidence, there was an attack on field workers or an accusation of sabotage by simple people working in factories for their minuscule wages. They were gunned down, then accused of being Enária operatives."

"So he was able to keep power under the guise of dealing with the rebellions," said Jee. "As long as there was a threat, and he was the strong military-type, able to keep the Kořeefa and Merćenta safe, he remained Taźath."

"Exactly," agreed Orgo. "He is a power-hungry oppressive dictator and a murderer. To put it nicely."

"To the Kořeefa," said Salǵeea, "Pronómio Tok was always a gentleman, always *acting* the part of the dedicated servant, but he was manipulating everyone. Even us. Our only option was to survive until something changed. Until something tipped the balance."

"You," said Eno, speaking to Jee. "You tipped the balance."

"So it is now a choice for you all," said Salǵeea. "Return to your life of privilege and remain part of the Taźath's regime, or disappear somewhere in the wilds of Tar Aséllo, or…join us."

Salǵeea had prepared rooms for the 'captives', really just caves carved out of the surrounding stone and filled with as much comfort as was available: beds, blankets and food. Salǵeea asked them to rest and to discuss their next move. He would come for them later. No matter what their decision, it would be honored.

Jee and her friends discussed their options deep into the night—or whatever time it was in the cave.

Reǵeena spoke of her recruitment, what the Enária were trying to do for the Graćenta. She said, no matter what, that she would remain in the Front.

Alíthe and Breegan spoke of their careers. They had worked for their entire lives and loved their fellow pilots. Could they give that up? Should they? What would they do if they returned to the AMF? Continue on with a murderous Tażath at the helm?

Eno, though angry, had much to lose—privilege mostly. He also was older and was used to the Tażaths and their power; he was used to the class system. But he told them that even though his life could not continue as it was, joining the Enária might not be the best idea. He needed more time to think.

The question they kept asking themselves and each other was: What will we do if we did join the Front? Rob trucks for the rest of our lives?

Jee kept her thoughts to herself.

They retired for the evening, though Jee struggled to fall asleep. Her thoughts drifted to Earth and its history, its people, and how the actions of a few could bring great change. After a time, she had decided on one thing for certain: if she didn't act, the Graćenta would never be free.

That night, sleep never came.

After a few hours, Salǵeea came to them.

"I am sorry to wake you; however, a situation has presented itself," he explained. "I would like you to come with me. Please. And hurry."

They each were given a waterproof coat and led to a guncar capable of fitting them all inside. Once seated in the cramped vehicle, Orgo drove them through a long tunnel that began at the rear of the large main room. It went on a winding set of switchbacks through tunnels that had been bored into the tar wall. Soon, they emerged through an arch that led under a small waterfall. Though the new day of Fullglow had begun, they emerged into a dark world. Heavy clouds covered the tar in this area, and it was raining steadily. The fálouse was completely shielded from view.

The car continued onward, its bulbous tires allowing the vehicle to move effortlessly through the low brush, mud, and rocky hills. There were no roads.

"We are heading beyond the edge of the falls, to the forest near Folvos," said Orgo as the passengers were moderately jostled about. "We patrol this area often. It is our eastern flank, and usually, it is thick with AMF and TSP patrols and search flights of some wing or another. The weather stopped the flights, as visibility is near zero. The ground patrols have moved east."

"What are we to see?" asked Jee.

"We told you earlier that the murder of Tye Ćlaviath and Dypónia Aséllo was not the Taźath's only atrocity," said Orgo.

"Maybe this will help you plan a course of action," added Salǵeea.

The car began to climb up a rocky rise made of dark stone, then stopped along a ridge covered in gnarled trees and brush, but barely glowing, unlike much of the plant life in the tar. As they emerged, each saw that the vegetation was mostly dead. Only the slightest bit of light came from some kind of moss that was devouring the rotted trees. It smelled of damp and decomposing wood.

The car stopped. Orgo and Salǵeea assisted the rest out of the vehicle and led them deeper into the decaying forest.

"This forest was used as a test site for weapons, mostly thermal rockets and bombs. No doubt you know of it, Commander Alíthe? Second Officer Breegan?"

The two pilots said nothing but continued onward. The group moved carefully as the terrain was uneven, making their way down a steep ravine. Here the plants grew more densely, yet something had stunted then, and they were barely bioluminescent. Once at the bottom, the darkness was suffocating, a low gray mist floating along the soft, wet ground.

Salǵeea took off his pack and removed a bag. "Here. Air masks. Put them on."

Orgo assisted Jee and Reǵeena. The others knew how to use them, and soon all were wearing the protective gear except Salǵeea and Orgo.

"Why aren't you wearing one?" asked Jee.

"We have seen this already," said Salǵeea. "It was discovered about a tenth-year ago. We don't come here often. The TSP, however, visits it with some regularity."

"Visits what?" asked Eno through his mask.

Orgo took a few steps forward and reached down into the low rolling vapor. He pulled up a few handfuls of dead and wet branches, leaves, and other debris from the floor of the ravine and tossed them aside. Then, he grabbed something that made a metallic sound, like a chain. He pulled on it as he walked to the left. A massive door made of some lightweight metal appeared out of the fog, and as it opened, the mist rolled inside what had to be a cave or a sunken burrow of a large animal. Orgo moved backward, several feet, staring at the opening in the ground.

Jee watched his face. Orgo, a man who appeared strong and confident, wanted nothing to do with what was down there. He was frightened and suddenly moved away as if something might reach out and grab him.

Though Jee's heart began beating faster, she walked closer to the opening even as Alíthe reached to hold her back.

"What is this place?" Jee asked.

"There is a ramp that descends into a chamber," said Salǵeea. "Walk carefully as it is wet. Your masks have a light on the tip of the mouthpiece. Just tap it."

Jee turned to look into the cavity. A dark brown haze seemed to rise from the hole, but soon, it stopped.

"This is something you must see for yourself to believe it, for many reasons," Salǵeea said. "Mostly, to know the depravity of the Taźath and his followers. Few know of this place. The Kořeefa do not. They live in blissful ignorance. Go inside."

"How far do we go?" asked Eno.

"You will know," said Salǵeea. "We will wait here. The stench is overwhelming, so do not take off your masks. This is where the Taźath, and those who came before him, dispose of things they no longer need or want. It is safe to enter, do not worry."

Jee's hair stood on end, her skin tingling.

Alíthe moved to her side, and held her hand. Together, they entered, and the rest followed closely behind, descending into the fog.

Like the entry door, the ramp was made of metal, and as they walked downward, they could only see what their lights revealed. The floor had marks on it, the type tires or tracks would make. Some kind of dark grease, or thick oily liquid, had stained it. About fifteen feet high, the side walls and ceiling had scrapes and gouges in their stone surfaces as if some machine had run against it numerous times.

"I don't like this," announced Breegan.

They continued because Jee stubbornly pushed on. After forty or fifty feet, they saw a stone wall barrier ahead, about waist high. It was stained from some dark, dripping liquid, though now it looked dry.

All five of them approached the wall at the same time. There was nothing but blackness ahead, maybe some far wall in the distance. Then they looked down.

None could tell the depth of the pit that lay before them, but it was at least fifty feet or more. A thin mist rolled over dark shapes. At times, they could make out scurrying creatures by the thousands.

"Breediss rodents," gasped Eno. "Blind."

"They are feeding on something," observed Jee.

They focused harder. The faint mist cleared. Then they saw.

Thousands of bodies, all children, all dead, in various stages of recent decay, dumped in a massive heap. It covered the floor before them, as far as their lights could penetrate.

Jee thought she was going to be sick.

After leaving the pit, they rejoined Salǵeea and Orgo, who had waited by the car.

No one spoke for the first half of the return trip. At times, all save Jee had manes displaying a sick greenish-orange color, and after a while, a deep blue.

"I am sorry to show you that," said Salǵeea. "We watched convoys of trucks coming to the area for years. Initially, we assumed it was just typical waste. Then we realized there was a pattern. Usually three or four large container trucks appear about once every six weeks. This coincided with reports of children being taken from various cities and farm camps. Like the ones you freed from Éhpiloh, Glasśigh."

"Not all are taken into slavery as many believe," said Orgo. He stopped talking and stared at the road ahead, driving steadily westward the way they had come.

"Why?" asked Alíthe, still stunned. "Why kill children?"

"Population control," answered Salǵeea. "The Taźath knows just how many Graćenta he needs to support the other classes. Any extra are just burdens on the system."

"Adults live long on Áhtha," Eno said.

"They work long hours," added Orgo. "The children are not needed. And, they can be produced, like any other commodity, when required. Maybe some taken are spared…"

Reǵeena simply held her eyes shut, trying not to think of her sister missing all these years. Salǵeea nodded to her, seeing her mane's golden tint and knowing her agony.

"We found other sites," Salǵeea added. "Sites where the bodies of countless Graćenta were dumped, possibly totaling in the millions. The decay showed they had been there for years. This is not just Pronómio Tok's doing. It has been going on long before his reign."

Alíthe was dumbfounded.

Breegan looked angry and wouldn't take her gaze off the Glasśigh.

Seeing the young pilot's stare, Jee took a deep breath. Her mind was made up. What she needed at this point was a plan. And if she learned anything from Mr. Gallotta, and the thousands of years of Earth history she studied, it was how to strategize and plan.

▲▲▲

Upon their return, Jee and the others sat together, watching the Front members pack for the relocation. Orgo had stayed with them, answering what questions he would. Eventually, Jee asked to speak with Salǵeea—alone.

Orgo led her through several passageways of the cave complex and up a series of steps, too many to count. At the end was a low-ceiling cave room, sixty-or-so feet wide and less than ten feet deep. On the wall directly in front of them was an opening, a crack actually, that looked out into the tar. On each side, Jee could see a rush of water from the falls, but in front of them was a clear gap, and the view into the tar was stunning. Before them lay the bluish-purple Bay of Ramos, the dark blue Aséllian Sea, and on the far shore, the Treagor Delta with its green, bog-filled fields and deep jungle.

In the center of the room, close to the far edge, was a long stone bench, and there sat Salǵeea.

Jee approached him as he stared outward. Orgo left them alone.

"May I join you?" Jee asked.

"Please do," said Salǵeea. "I come here to think and sometimes wonder at all this." He gestured to the view.

They sat for a minute or two, just looking at Tar Asélło, listening to the water rushing past, and feeling at peace.

"But I am sure you didn't come for the view," Salǵeea said, finally turning to her.

"Had I known of it, I surely would have," she replied. "I need to think about my options, Salǵeea Calćoa. I have questions."

Salǵeea nodded. "I was hoping you would be close to taking a course of action. Whatever you decide, you must decide quickly. The Taźath is missing his ships, and with no communication from you, he has already begun a search. We will evacuate this base in a few hours, no matter what."

Jee nodded, took a breath, and exhaled slowly.

"There are three possibilities as I see it," said Jee. "I return to being the Taźath's puppet, I join you and we continue robbing transports and doing a little good whenever we can, or…What are your chances of winning a war against the Taźath?"

Salǵeea laughed. "Now that last option, well…as we stand now, our chances are non-existent. We have less than five hundred ground soldiers and support personnel. The Taźath has four thousand battle-ready and armed AMF ground troops. If you count the Special Police, he adds another hundred. Plus, he has fourteen thousand support personnel. He has vast sources of arms, ammunition, and materiel, not to mention his airpower: five AMF Air divisions totaling over five hundred craft. If we engage in open conflict, we would be wiped out in a single day."

"I see," said Jee. "On Earth, there is a phrase for such a scenario: a lost cause."

"It is not lost, not completely," objected Salǵeea with another laugh. "I know that all our disadvantages can be overcome. We only need time and one more thing."

"Me."

Salǵeea smiled widely. "You could bring thousands to our cause."

"And some of those could be part of the Taźath's war machine," Jee said. "In time, we could even the playing field."

"Many will die for our cause," he warned. "Can you live with that?"

"If I do not act," Jee answered, "they will die in the streets of Éhpiloh or end their lives in the cave at Folvos after years of abuse and captivity. In the cause of freedom, I think no sacrifice, mine or that of others, is too great. Yes, I can live with that."

"So you have thought this through?" Salǵeea asked. "You are willing to give up a life of comfort and privilege, trading it for blood and hardship. If you get caught, if we lose, they will take us all out to the thermal dessert, bury us in the sand, alive, and laugh as we are eaten by *hargus-horned bloodworms*. If we are lucky, they may just execute us in the streets of Etáin."

"Can we win?" she asked. "Even if we swell the ranks?"

"Probably not," he sighed. "Not without some unforeseen edge. Some magic, maybe."

"To the ignorant, *knowledge* may seem like sorcery," Jee said with a smile.

Jee paused, then stood and walked to the edge of the opening. She thought of the Graćenta and their plight. They were *her people.* She never felt as if she belonged to the Kořeefa, those who enjoyed a birthright of privilege, not earning it, not even through compassion for others. They had none. It would be impossible for her to live in a world like this, knowing that injustice and abuse continued every day, and the servitude of Graćenta was disguised as an ancient class system.

Her body shook as she began to cry.

Who would help them, if not me? she thought.

Maybe all this was more than just a trip from Earth to Ganymede. She was supposed to be here. Fate? Possibly, but at least for the opportunity to fight for freedom.

"I know things, Salǵeea," she began after catching her breath. "Earthlings have been perfecting the art of war for almost five hundred Áhthan years. My Earth father was one of the warriors. A planner. And he taught me. The Taźath has no knowledge of this."

"An advantage already," said Salǵeea with a smile. "Loved by all *and* bringing a singular knowledge of the deadliest military campaigns of Earth."

"I will not let Pronómio Tok control me anymore."

"Controlling you has been harder than he thought," added Salǵeea, still smiling. "It is your influence he will fear... How deep the people's dedication is to you—that is the unknown."

"Then I must speak to them. Let me begin by speaking with your soldiers."

With a nod of assent, Salǵeea led her back down into the main hangar of the cave and called the present members together. Eno and the others also joined. Jee walked to a side wall, then climbed atop stacked crates, looking out over the crowd of soldiers, five hundred-strong.

"I must ask you," Jee began, "do you love me?"

This shocked the room into a profound silence. "Do you love me?" she asked again. "Because I love you, and I am saddened by your plight. I have seen—" she had to stop, remembering the sight last night. "I have lost my parents to the Taźath and his henchmen, and I know you have lost people you love. So I ask you again, do you love me?"

The crowd remained stunned, but soon they answered with a resounding "Yes!"

"Then," Jee said, nodding, "I will join you."

Orgo laughed loudly. "I knew it!"

The crowd erupted in cheers of approval.

Alíthe was stunned. Reǵeena and Breegan smiled broadly.

"Jee! No!" objected Eno.

Her uncle knew her best, after all, and had witnessed how she could affect people. He knew her powers of persuasion: that crazy riot she caused at school! That had been a great piece of work, convincing people to do her bidding—and they'd thought she was a weirdo! What could she accomplish if the people *loved her?* With all her time reading and studying Earth's thousands of years making war, and all that Mr. Gallotta had taught her? Jee was smart in ways the Taźath and his military could never comprehend! She was learned, and yes, she could be dangerous to the Taźath. However, she could also be killed!

Eno leapt up on the make-shift stage and stood in opposition to his niece.

"Are you insane? Joining the revolt?" he yelled as the crowd settled. "Why so, so *drastic?* Why not just hide? Yes! Hide! Let us seek asylum in Tar Éstargon! We can work from there!"

"I *will not* run away from this, Eno!" she snapped at him. "Have you been listening?"

"So we join the Front?" he exploded. "To do what? To rob transports and, and toss wrenches into gears?"

"That is the very least I will do," she said loudly, now turning to the crowd. "I will not live under the thumb of Pronómio Tok another second. You suggested that we tread lightly, presumably to 'get along.' I will not. I will use *my foot* to *stomp him out!"*

The soldiers loudly agreed.

"Listen to this! Listen to what you are saying, Jee!" Eno implored. "The Taźath holds sway over many, and he has power and resources! What could we do? He has all the advantages!"

"Except being righteous," argued Jee. "Let me ask you, Orgo. What do you need? If you could have anything for your forces?"

"Numbers," he said without hesitation. "Many of us are untrained. And we don't have enough weapons to supply five hundred."

"Do Graćenta outnumber all other classes?" Jee asked.

"By at least three or four to one," replied Salǵeea.

Jee stood with her hands on her hips, looking at the faces of those in the room. She stared coldly as if simply calculating her options.

"Reǵeena," Jee said, turning to her friend. "You know the Graćenta well. You have been one of the people in the streets. Let me ask you—what do they think of me?"

Without hesitation, Reǵeena answered as if she had rehearsed the response. "The Graćenta love you. They see you as a ray of hope and goodness, a dream of a better life. You are their only light in a dark and desperate world. To them, you are everything."

"If I asked for their help, do you think they would give it?" asked Jee.

"I am sure," Reǵeena stated confidently. "I believe they will help you in any way they are able."

Salǵeea smiled and let out a short and quiet laugh. "I think they would jump into the Falls of Jovia with stones tied to their feet if you asked them."

"The Graćenta love me, and I love them," Jee continued. "So I will ask them to join me as members of the Enária Front."

"That would work," said Orgo loudly.

"My dearest," Eno cried. "Even if you could enlist help, the Enária have no weapons! Orgo here has admitted there is no matériel to outfit a sufficient force!"

"Tar Éstargon," said Jee.

"Tar Estar—what about Tar Éstargon?" Eno stammered.

"The Ef Keería of Tar Éstargon told me about his friendship with my father and mother and that if I needed anything from him, to just ask."

"Jee," Eno groaned, "I am *sure* he was not offering military aid to help you overthrow the Taźath!"

"I think he was!" she countered with stubborn force.

"Wait! Wait, why—why not just accomplish this politically?" pleaded Eno. "Peacefully? Announce your desire, your birthright to be Taźath! The ministers could be persuaded! That would be a more direct and less dangerous way to bring change—"

"Pronómio Tok will not give up power willingly," interjected Salǵeea.

"He has murdered thousands just to keep control," added Orgo. "Do you think the Taźath will simply retire to the shores of the Óhzásó Sea and…fish for the rest of his life?"

"He murders children!" Jee continued, fire in her voice and in her eyes. "That bastard killed my parents! He killed your brother! No, Uncle, this will not be put to a goddamn *vote!*"

The crowd cheered again.

"And how will you convince the Graćenta to join?" continued Eno, almost defeated. "Bat your eyes?"

"With propaganda," she responded.

"Propa Ganda?" asked Alíthe. "Who is that?"

"Not a *who,* Commander," Jee said.

"Propaganda is an advanced form of political persuasion,"

explained Eno. "The Taźath uses it! He has convinced an entire population to follow him, as did the Taźaths before Pronómio Tok!"

"He is an amateur!" countered Jee as she forcefully returned her gaze to the excited crowd. They looked at her with fire in their eyes, the fire that hope brings and that a leader who holds power and knowledge promises. "The people of Earth are *masters* of propaganda! They know how to persuade masses to do amazing things, things both horrible and beautiful, things even against their own self-interest! One man convinced a peace-loving people to take their rightful place at the top of the world order and begin a conquest of the planet! He made them commit heartless atrocities! And they did it willingly! The war lasted half a Ófeetian year!"

"Yes, Adolf Hitler!" cried Eno. "The most vile dictator Earth had ever produced! And he *lost!* So think before you cast yourself as a madman!"

"Hitler was a monster," Jee agreed, "but he lost because he was an *idiot!* He lost because he offered *less freedom!* He lost because he knew nothing of making war! He wanted to direct armies! He should have left it to his generals, but he didn't. Opening a three-front war? In the Russian winter? He learned nothing from Napoleon!"

The room was stunned at her passion and anger.

"My Earth father was a warrior," she continued, "and a strategist for the mightiest force on Earth. He taught me well! And I studied for years. Using that knowledge…that is how I will help you become free!"

The Front soldiers cheered once again.

"You scare me," said Eno, slowly resigning to the fact that the course had been set, and he was powerless to change it.

"She scares the Taźath as well," said Salǵeea as the cheering died down.

"If this is our moment," urged Jee, shaking with conviction as she addressed the room, "and we let it pass by, if we just go back to the fields or Palace Place, and let this injustice continue, then we do not deserve to take another breath!" Jee raised her hand, pointing a finger to the sky. "I know your place! It is at the top, where freedom lives!"

As the crowd roared again, Reǵeena raised her right hand high over her head, finger pointed.

Alíthe and Breegan copied the gesture.

Salǵeea followed suit, smiling.

Orgo hesitated. He looked around at the others, then slowly lifted his hand.

The soldiers of the Enária Front lifted their hands as the cheer rose.

"You are asking for war," Eno warned. "Many will suffer."

"They suffer now, Uncle. I need you. I need your wisdom and counsel."

Eno sighed. After a moment, he surveyed the now silent crowd. All eyes were on him.

He felt beaten. *Trapped* would be a more accurate word. The Taźath had moved him into a corner, and to defy him meant to give up all his privilege and status. But to remain part of the Taźath's regime and serve him still, Eno would be casting himself as a willing party to the injustice and horrors perpetrated against the Graćenta. And how long until Pronómio found him a nuisance? Then what?

Salǵeea and Orgo were correct: Pronómio Tok would never give up power due to a vote. For Eno, it was to be war or acceptance of the impossible. He looked at his niece, into her eyes, and saw a powerful force, but also the child he had known and cared for—and worried about—throughout their travels through space and their time on Earth. He could not abandon her. Because she needed him, and because he loved her.

"Then, my niece," declared Eno, "let us travel to Tar Éstargon and acquire some guns."

18
Tar Éstargon

Gákoh Kalífus had sent one hundred ground troops to the base of the Kryménos Falls, the last known location of the Aréus escort and the Type-G. Scanner teams quickly found the remains of the three Aréus A3 escorts, now submerged in the water by the falls. Deep scans also showed that behind the falls lay an intricate and expansive cave system, possibly an Enária base of operations.

Standing in the Dark Room, Kalífus watched various screens mounted to the walls showing scans of the geological structure of the tar wall behind the falls. Eventually, the way in was revealed: the ledges on the far eastern edge of the falls led to several entryways. His team moved into the caves.

Upon searching the area's elaborate passages, the TSP teams found evidence that someone had been in the caves hours before. Food remains were still fresh, a power unit was still active, but no sign of the Glasśigh and her party or a wrecked Type-G.

"I have something here, Commander," came the voice over Kalífus's head-com. It was Jovús, his commander of the ground team. *"In the center of the hangar room. It's a display of some sort, playing a file—"* His voice cut short. Then he muttered, *"Oh no…"*

"What is it?" demanded Kalífus, watching intently.

"I'll put my ABC on it," said Jovús.

Kalífus could see a dangling tablet and Jovús's hand turning it toward his ABC's camera. The tablet was powered on. The fuzzy image it displayed slowly came into focus. There was a media file showing the face of a man. He was talking, but it was too difficult to hear. After a few moments, the image changed.

Kalífus gasped.

▲▲▲

"A message?" asked Pronómio. "From whom?"

"Salǵeea Calćoa," said Kalífus. *"The leader of the Enária, I assume."*

"Can you transmit it to me?"

"It is on the way, Pronómio."

Sitting on his garden patio, the Taźath put down his drink of *Black Kuffo*, a thick, warm liquor that had a salty-earthy taste, and ceased eating his midday meal. His ABC displayed a clear holographic image just to the side of his table.

"Start file," said Pronómio.

"Greetings Pronómio Tok. I am Salǵeea Calćoa of the Enária Front." The man in the video smiled evilly and leaned closer to the camera. *"We have your little girlfriend!"*

The Enária leader's image faded into a picture of a bound and gagged Glasśigh, lying on the floor of a small cell. She struggled, she was in tears, and she was dirty, her clothes torn a bit and stained with what could only be blood.

"She is unharmed, more or less, and she is safe for the time being." Salǵeea laughed, then continued in a condescending tone. "The Glasśigh! Who would have known she was such a tough fighter? Tougher than her uncle!"

The image changed to Eno, much in a similar state as his niece. After a moment, the picture turned back to Salǵeea.

"I could show you the pictures of the servant girl, the two pilots of the Wings of Glasśigh, *but I think you get the idea. You are probably thinking, 'What do these miscreants want?' I will tell you."*

The image changed back to a struggling Glasśigh.

"Our first set of demands requires that you collect the items on the list attached to the end of this message. It is all food and medical supplies. Deliver the items to each of the twelve different locations on the included map. We will be watching those areas. Any booby traps or little mechanized TSP baddies you leave behind will mean we kill the Glasśigh. Painfully. We are not messing around anymore, Pronómio.

"Any attempt to harm us, or any Graćenta in any way—especially during one of your pre-staged skirmishes so you can win another vote of confidence—will result in one of the hostages being killed, or worse. Maybe we will cut off a few appendages, send them to you, and let you guess who they used to belong to, eh? Or better yet, we can send them to the rogue media groups! Try winning a vote after that!

"And if you think you want to sacrifice the Glasśigh—Asèllo's Ghost knows she has been nothing but a pain in your side— this entire message could be sent to the opposition! They would probably leak this out to a broadcast cube. And they will blame you personally for any harm that comes to her."

The image changed back to Salǵeea. He had a stern look on his face, his eyes cold.

"Do not test us, Pronómio, unless you want to find out just how brutal we can be. We have nothing to lose. You have everything to

lose. We will let you know our second set of demands...soon."

Pronómio used every ounce of his being, fighting to control his anger—his fear—that someone would hurt *his* Glasśigh, *his* desired mate. But in the end, he failed. His scream was heard throughout the halls of the Palace.

▲▲▲

To ask the Ef Keería for assistance would require a visit to Tar Éstargon. Theoretically speaking, traveling there from Tar Aséllo could only be accomplished in one of three ways.

They could fly out of Tar Aséllo over the surface of Áhtha, then down into Tar Éstargon. Unfortunately, no Aséllian craft had that capability except *Explorer Eleven*, which was in the repair dock, heavily guarded.

Another way would be to take the tunnels that ran through the miles of thick stone walls connecting the tars. Unfortunately, they were the most heavily guarded areas in Aséllo, staffed by AMF teams since trade cessation.

There was only one other possibility. They would have to go through the ocean underneath Tar Aséllo that connected to the seas of Tar Éstargon. The AMF had five vehicles capable of this feat. Getting one would be dangerous and impossible.

They sat in the main hangar of the temporary Enária stronghold, the Front having completed a move that consolidated the majority of their military personnel and supplies to a secluded cove within the labyrinth created by the Pégra Pygréez. The location was deeply recessed between the towers and twisted tar walls south of the main channel and was pocked with small caves. Though barely visible from above, any exposed equipment or disturbed land had been covered with makeshift netting made from rope and nearby foliage. They were safe—for now.

After some time, Eno smiled, stood and raised his hands in triumph. "We could call the Éstargonian Navy!"

"What?" blurted Orgo.

"How would we accomplish that?" asked Alíthe. "Any communication is monitored by Kalífus and his listening devices. Even the oceans are monitored by the AMF's submersibles."

"Yes," agreed Eno excitedly. "But... one may hear, though still not understand!"

"Uncle?" questioned Jee.

"We will use spectrogram technology!" Eno said triumphantly.

"We create a communication file made from sound frequencies! When complete, it produces a kilohertz-time analysis of the sound waves as a visual representation of the spectrum of frequencies. Utilizing hyperspectral imaging, for example, spectrograms will represent the data as a three-dimensional communicable data cube. This application would create a stenographic state, concealing information within a digitized audio media file!"

They stared at him, dumbfounded.

"It means you can put pictures inside soundwaves," Eno simplified.

"Oh," said Orgo. "T-that's what I thought."

The others laughed.

"Commander DaJees, who was to accompany me on *Explorer Eleven*, was in the Éstargonian Navy," Eno explained. "She told me that the Éstargonian Navy added a twist to *their* messages during their war with Tar Fortus: spectral imaging! They embedded text images within simple and innocuous soundwave messages. For example, the Fortus Navy would hear 'we are going to dock.' But a higher frequency within the message carried the real message as an image, a text image that read 'attack at first light.' Their ships had both an image-audio encoder program to make messages and a wide-band sonic visualizer that looked at all frequencies, even in the ultra or subsonic range. It simply showed the message on a screen."

"Can this work?" asked Salǵeea.

"We will need a simple radio wave broadcaster—but a powerful one," said Eno. "And we need to have it operate underwater, five miles deep to reach the subterranean sea."

"That's easy," said Orgo. "We picked up an old underwater drone in a convoy raid a few years back. The squad didn't know what it was, but it looked interesting, so they took it. I can fit a broadcaster in that."

"Will they hear it?" asked Breegan.

"The submersibles listen constantly and diligently for messages from their commanders," ensured Eno. "We will broadcast at multiple frequencies! They will pick it up!"

"But how do we make sure they come?" asked Jee.

"We don't. *You do*," suggested Salǵeea. "This message must come from the Glasśigh, personally."

"And maybe send a picture of you as well," added Reǵeena.

"That would do it," Alíthe agreed.

By the pools near the Falls of Amée Allin, heavy clouds shrouded the already dim light of Lastglow. This little-visited and secluded area had a series of miles-high folded stone walls created by the fracturing of the southern tar wall. Like fingers intertwined, a maze of sorts existed, ensuring the pools were always the darkest and most secluded portion of Tar Aséllo. The absence of light combined with the heat of many thermal vents made the glowing of plants and animals more noticeable, especially where the falling water met the pools.

The central pool was considerably wider at over two hundred fifty feet. It was also the deepest and one that led directly to Éstargon. It was on these rocky shores that a small team of Enária soldiers and Jee's entourage waited on the sandy, rock-strewn beach. They had taken both a fastboat across the sea and flew the Type-G to this location. Then, the message was sent via submersible drone broadcast to Tar Éstargon. They had been waiting two days for a reply.

"They would be here by now if they were coming," said Jee, deflated.

"The trip is long and treacherous," explained Eno. "There are many obstacles. They may be late."

Three hours later, the pool, usually quietly gurgling, became active with massive air bubbles coming from below breaking the still water. Amid this disruption, the dark gray nose of a seventy-foot submarine broke the surface. To Jee, it looked like a metal whale with no tail. It was devoid of any exterior windows. The nose was covered with dark metal-looking blocks, antenna-like probes, and other equipment that stuck out like small branches or quills. More of these protuberances were along the sides as well.

The sub made a few hissing sounds, and finally, a hatchway opened on top, sliding backward, letting out a pale amber light. After a moment, a person appeared. He took up a VED and scanned the area, quickly finding the group.

The Glasśigh waved.

"So! It is true!" called the submariner across the pool, excitement in his voice evident as it echoed off the surrounding stone walls. "Is that the Glasśigh? Really?"

Eno spoke first, calling out to the ship. "Yes, it is. And there are others with her, as you can see. I am Eno Ćlaviath, a friend of the Ef Keería. May w—"

The submariner turned his head toward the inside of the craft. "Hey! Mowaca! You owe me a *carbanco-fizz* in a tall, frosty glass when we get to port! I told you it was really her!"

"You are lying!" came the voice.

"I'm looking right at her!"

A cheer of excitement rose up through the open hatch.

Eno shook his head, dumbfounded. "It's like you were—"

"The Glasśigh," Jee boasted, smiling.

Once the excitement wore off a bit, Captain Pilot Josáy, who had greeted them, sent a small raft to the shore to retrieve the passengers. Carefully, he assisted the group aboard and welcomed them.

"It is an honor, Glasśigh!" he said, beaming with a wide smile. "We just couldn't believe the message was really true!"

"It is true," said Eno as he boarded the craft. "And Captain?"

"Yes! Commander Ćlaviath?" asked Josáy, still smiling and watching the Glasśigh as she happily met the crew, thanking them and admiring the craft.

"We come here at great peril to ourselves and others," Eno stated. "I must ask you and your people to keep our presence secret. Can you do that? And take us to see the Ef Keería?"

"Of course, Commander Ćlaviath!" Josáy assured, now serious. "We knew as much from the Glasśigh's message. We immediately opened it using the spectrometer. Great picture of her, but aren't they all?"

"Yes, yes," said Eno, a bit annoyed.

"I will alert the Ef Keería of your position and request for secrecy, and I will order the men to hand over any video capture devices. It will take over twenty hours to reach Tar Éstargon, so please, let me make you and your party comfortable."

▲▲▲

After the docking of the submersible in a small eastern port in Tar Éstargon and an almost tearful farewell from Captain Pilot Josáy and his crew, Jee and the others were taken to the old Aséllian Ambassador's quarters in the Capitol. Not quite as opulent as Palace Place, it was more than comfortable and lacking nothing they required. They took turns bathing and then changed into more suitable clothes. An aid arrived moments later and informed them that the Ef Keería had requested they meet at his residence as soon as they were ready. A meal was being prepared.

They arrived at the Ef Keería's Capitol Complex and were shown to a lush balcony. The area was beautiful, surrounded by a manicured garden of exotic plants and streaming waterfalls. Where the trees parted, a view of the landscape beyond was visible. It was similar to that of Palace Place, except that the city of *Envemíro*, far below them, was twice the size of Etáin and home to over eighteen million citizens. The sky traffic was stunningly complex and busy, the buildings considerably higher, some reaching into the clouds. The eclipse had just begun, and they sat in near-darkness, the only light coming from the far off metropolis and the nearby artificially-lit waterfalls that graced the walls of Tar Éstargon. There also was the same blue-green bioluminescent glow of the surrounding flora and marine life. The tar was almost three times the size of Tar Aséllo, and one could not see the far shore or any of its cities' lights. The sea seemed to go on forever.

"Ah! Commander Eno! Welcome," exclaimed Vothíos Valtéra, the Ef Keería. He walked to them, smiling, and with an air of authority and astonishment. Behind him came servants with dishes and tureens, which they arranged on a nearby table.

"This is a surprise!" continued the leader of Tar Éstargon. "And Glasśigh Aséllo! My dear! When we received your message, I was stunned! I-I don't know what to say, except," he struggled for the right words, but after a moment, he chose a simple, heartfelt "welcome!" and touched foreheads with each member of the group. "I hope you are well and refreshed?"

"Yes," said Eno. "Most gracious of you, Ef Keería. Thank you for receiving us. We are in your debt."

"Nonsense!" replied the Vothíos. "Your brother, Tye, and Dypónia were my close friends, and that makes you very special. All of you."

"I thank you again," said Eno. "One other request, my dear friend. We are here in a capacity that is not condoned by Pronómio Tok. We would like to keep this visit, um, personal."

"I have been informed of the visit's secrecy," said Vothíos. "I will make sure it remains a secret." He turned to Jee, bowing slightly. "It is a great pleasure to have you here and an honor."

"The honor is mine," Jee said, bowing in return. "Let me introduce my friends. This is Commander Alíthe Afiéro of the Wings of Glasśigh."

Alíthe bowed his head in respect. "Ef Keería."

"Commander Alíthe?" echoed Vothíos. "I remember you from my visit to Palace Place. Welcome."

"This young lady," said Jee, "is my friend and guide, Reǵeena Ahdelfía."

"I remember you, Reǵeena. Welcome."

Reǵeena bowed her head in thanks and greeting.

"And this is Second Officer Breegan Arkéta also of the Wings of Glasśigh," said Jee. "She is our pilot."

Breegan smiled and also bowed.

"And this gentleman..." Jee paused, looking at Orgo. "This may take some explaining. Shall we sit down and eat? I'm starving!"

They did sit and eat with little discussion. Eno asked politely about the state of affairs in Tar Éstargon and was assured that things were very well. Conversation inevitably drifted to the Taźath, and that made the guests visibly nervous.

Vothíos Valtéra sensed the uneasiness and politely waited as his guests finished their meal before speaking again. "Glasśigh, you promised you would introduce your final friend," he said, taking a sip of clear water from his glass and then looking to Orgo.

"Yes," said Jee. "Here we go! This is Orgo Talhínsa, the military leader of...the Enária Front."

Vothíos almost gagged. It took a few seconds for him to regain his composure. Finally, after refusing help from Eno and Jee and the servers, he was able to take a breath. "You, Glasśigh Aséllo, are full of surprises. The Enária Front? What an odd coupling. I would assume you would be somewhat hostile to each other," he paused for a moment, "being that the Front tried to kill you at the arena."

"Vothíos," Eno began, stepping in. "To say that the reality we once knew has been completely shattered would be an understatement. I have evidence that proves Pronómio Tok and his Special Police are responsible for the attack at the arena and the death of Tye Ćlaviath and Dypónia Aséllo."

Eno took a portable mini drive the size of a coin from his pocket and placed it in front of Vothíos. "The Taźath is also responsible for the death of two of your citizens, Commander Mosca and Commander DaJees of the *Explorer* team."

Vothíos was shocked into silence. He looked at Eno, then the Glasśigh, then at the other guests. Finally, he cleared his throat. "T-this is unbelievable! The Taźath? Pronómio?" Vothíos held up the drive. "This is proof?"

"Yes, I am afraid so," Eno confirmed. "He has also threatened the Glasśigh and me, and we have decided, well, we really had no choice, however, here we are—"

"If I understand you, Eno," said Vothíos, interrupting, "you are seeking asylum?"

"No, no," said Eno. "That—ha! *That* would be a great idea, but also too easy for my niece, I am afraid."

"Uncle!" exclaimed Jee.

"Yes, yes, let us relax, dear," said Eno, taking a long breath. "Vothíos, it is a little more complicated than that. You see, we have joined the Enária Front."

Vothíos, now even more in a state of bewilderment, immediately excused all his aides save one, whom he waved to join them. He was tall and thin, looking almost ancient. He had a delicate chin, a set of deep blue eyes, further accentuated by his gray mane. As he approached, he gave a thin smile.

"Even more privacy is in order," Vothíos said. "This is Amani Plagósia, my Security Chief and Minister of Inter-tar Relations."

Amani nodded and then took a seat next to the Ef Keería.

"I have been honored by dealing directly with Dypónia Asélla and Tye Ćlaviath years ago," said Amani. "It is a wondrous thing to meet you, Eno, and especially you, Glasśigh."

"Thank you," said Jee.

"Commander Eno, Glasśigh, guests," began Vothíos. "I am not sure why you have come here. I certainly welcome you, and you may stay as long as we both agree is proper. However, I am somewhat confused. You have joined the forces against the Tażath? He is the rightfully elected leader of the people of Tar Asélla, according to your own laws. Taking up arms against him is a serious offense."

"We are aware of that, Vothíos," remarked Eno. "Simply put, he is a criminal and a threat to the Glasśigh and all of us here."

"Ef Keería," said Jee, interrupting. "As I understand, you and my parents saw eye to eye, as we say on Earth, when it came to the injustices happening in Tar Asélla, specifically social class treatment. Isn't that correct?"

Vothíos looked to Eno and smiled. "She is much like her mother. To the point!"

"And like her father, stubborn and at times reckless," added Eno.

"And like you, Ef Keería, a lover of individual freedom," continued Jee, somewhat annoyed at her uncle. "Where I come from, on Earth, we believe in the right to life, liberty, and the pursuit of happiness for all people."

"Yes, I have poured over the transcripts of the radio and now video transmission we capture from Earth," Vothíos told them. "It is a hobby of mine. The America? That is where you lived? The freest of the nations on the planet."

"Free? For some," Jee stated. "At least the downtrodden of America have a legal path to equality, as difficult as it is. That is not so in Tar Asélla."

"I am sure you also know, Glasśigh," said Vothíos, "that I was supportive of your parents' quest for an abolishment of the caste system in Tar Asélla. Amani worked persistently with them to achieve some solution. In the end, our failure caused the cessation of trading between the tars and restriction on our relations."

"That is a fact not expressed in the schools and media of Tar Aséllo, Ef Keería," said Reģeena.

"There has been a complete suppression of truth in Tar Aséllo," added Orgo. "In the Taźath's quest to hold power, there has been a coordinated and forceful manipulation of all people. The Front is the only resistance to his dictatorship. We are the only ones who fight against him."

"I know this to be true," agreed Vothíos. "I know of the subjugation of the Graćenta. It is sad to know that nothing has changed."

"That is why we came here," said Jee. "I have joined the Enária so I can bring justice to Tar Aséllo—"

"And exact revenge for your parent's murder?" interrupted Amani.

"Amani, please," warned Vothíos.

Undaunted, Jee answered, "Yes, I won't deny that. But when I see the atrocities, the lying, the murder, and the abuse of people, I can't sit still. These are obvious crimes, but there is also suppression by law, disguised as support. It is all a way to keep things unfair and unbalanced, to keep the Taźath and the Kośeefa in riches at the expense of the poor. You know this."

"I do," admitted Vothíos.

"As an Aséllian and an *Aséllo,* I can't just hide or ignore this," Jee said.

"So, what do you propose to do, Glasśigh?" inquired Amani. "Take up an outdated projectile gun and lead the army of the hungry few alongside Commander Talhínsa?"

"That is what many would think," replied Jee. "And possibly, someday, I will be a combatant. For now, I will best serve the resistance by swelling the ranks of the Enária with Graćenta."

Vothíos and Amani glanced at each other. Jee detected a slight nodding of heads. She and her friends were being tested.

"I know of your influence, Glasśigh," said Vothíos. "I know of your power over the Kośeefa. I watched you at the arena when you arrived. We saw you sing on the media show. There is more to your influence than just a new nose and the curiosity of your, shall I say, Earthy-ness?"

What he did not say was that since her arrival, his operatives had reported on her almost absolute popularity, especially with the Merćenta and the Graćenta. Though the official records never said anything about her visit to Éhpiloh after the air attack, the citizens of that poor city had spoken quietly. Some were able to relay the story of her kindness to the agents of the Ef Keería. The Glasśigh had something they all loved—compassion—and she could certainly use it to the advantage of everyone. *If* she knew how.

"Then let me ask another question," Vothíos requested, directing his attention to Alíthe. "Commander Afiéro, what will happen when this becomes public? What will the Tażath and his overwhelming forces do? Surely he will not just sit back and allow Glasśigh Aséllo to change his rule."

"Are you asking what the security force personnel will do?" asked Alíthe. "I have to assume some will join us, some will not. The Glasśigh has the love of many. Much of this success rests on her shoulders."

"That is a heavy burden," said Amani, now staring at the Glasśigh.

"I agree, but I have friends," Jee remarked, smiling at her companions, "and a few tricks that I will not mention. But I need your support."

The Ef Keería laughed. "You need more than my blessings, that is for certain. I know what you want of me. You want arms."

They were all silent. Yes, that was exactly why they came.

The Ef Keería asked his guest to allow him time to study the video file and confer with a few additional advisors. He would give them an answer at the break of the new day. In the meantime, they were asked to stay at his home in the Capitol Complex.

▲▲▲

The group sat inside the main room at the Ef Keería's home, nervous and unsettled. They had barely rested, each contemplating what may befall them. Though food was provided, they barely touched it, too anxious to eat.

"What will he do, Minister Commander Eno?" asked Breegan. "You know the Ef Keería best."

"I am not sure," Eno said, biting into a piece of a bread-like roll. "He must weigh many things, not the least being the idea that he could be accused of waging war on Tar Aséllo."

"I am sure he will not send personnel," said Jee. "I only need him to supply us with weapons. Gunships, transports, ammunitions."

"Even that would be a declaration of war," admitted Alíthe with a sigh. "He will not give us weapons or assistance. What were we thinking?"

"You sound like Eno," complained Jee.

"I am sorry," Alíthe said. "I am only being realistic. I do hope we can work out something here. I just don't think—"

A knock came to the door of their chambers. Reǵeena, out of habit, ran to answer. It was Amani Plagósia. She showed him into the main room.

"Please, sit here at the table with us," suggested Eno.

"Something to eat?" offered Jee.

"No, no, thank you. I must return quickly to my post. But I have news." Plagósia studied each of them in turn. "The Ef Keería commends you on your bravery and dedication to the cause of freedom for the oppressed. He is with you in belief and in spirit. However…"

The air seemed to be sucked out of the room as they waited for the verdict.

"The Ef Keería of Tar Éstargon cannot grant your request for military arms; to do so would be an act of war against Tar Asello." Plagósia shook his head gently. "He is sorry he can do no more than continue with the cessation of trading."

Reǵeena began to weep.

"Please extend our thanks for his hospitality and his confidence," said Eno.

Jee was visibly crushed, as were Alíthe and Breegan. They looked at each other with saddened eyes.

"I must be going," Plagósia said. "But first, Commander Eno, have you ever told your niece the story of Tar Éstargon's war with Tar Fortus?"

"Not in any detail," answered Eno, surprised. "Why do you ask?"

"Allow me a moment," he said. "In the years before the current administration, the two Tars of Éstargon and Fortus were at war. It was much like a war on Earth, as we have heard of them. Both nations were highly advanced technologically, meaning weapons were similar, the size of the armies were approximately the same. Though much was fought in the subterranean seas and channels below the surface, there was fighting above the fálouse, on the surface of Áhtha itself."

Eno nodded, remembering. "I believe the war was about the right to resources above on the surface and below in the hidden sea."

"Yes," confirmed Plagósia. "Eventually, after almost an Áhthan year of struggle, the war was settled by treaty."

"If you are suggesting we try to work out a treaty with a murderous dictator," said Jee, "I will share an old Earth saying: 'Power tends to corrupt and absolute power corrupts absolutely. Great men are almost always bad men'. The Taźath has absolute power over Tar Asello. He will not negotiate away a single ounce of it. But thank you for the history lesson."

"You are welcome, Glasśigh," said Plagósia. "However, please allow me to continue?"

"Of course," conceded Jee somewhat tersely. She wondered where he was going.

"Toward the end of the conflict, the technology of war machines and matériel had advanced. Greatly. The new weapons we created were never used in the conflict—they came too late; though, we do keep them for our defense, just in case."

Now Jee saw the reason for the story, or so she hoped.

"Minister," she asked politely. "The old, obsolete weapons that were used in the war? What became of them?"

Alíthe and Orgo became visibly attentive as they also connected the dots. Breegan sensed that something was breathing life back into the room.

"The old machines of war," he said, pausing for effect, "are of no use to us. We left them where they were last used. On the surface."

Jee realized what was happening. "Minister Plagósia, I am very interested in all history. And if you would indulge *me,* I also have a bit of history for you."

"I would love to hear," said the Minister.

"On Earth, there was a war, not surprisingly, between the largest force on the planet, the British Empire and a runaway colony, America. Early in this war, a fort had been captured by the Americans, and in it were hundreds of powerful guns called cannon. But as freezing weather arrived, the cannon became frozen in ice and had to be abandoned. The war escalated, and months later, the British were invading a major American city. With no large guns, the Americans were sure to suffer a horrible defeat. An American soldier suggested to his general that the frozen weapons could be retrieved. With a few hundred men and pack animals, this soldier traveled three hundred miles through a frozen landscape and mountainous terrain. They freed the weapons from the ice with their bare hands and muscle power and returned the guns to their general. That act greatly preserved the American Army from annihilation and tipped the scale of the war."

"Henry Knox," said Eno. "I remember the story. He was hung."

"No, he was captured, then escaped," corrected Jee.

Amani smiled. "Fascinating! And much like our story, except that the items frozen in *our* ice are still there."

"Would there be any documentation I could read on this subject?" asked Jee cautiously. "I am not sure if you have heard that I am a minister-level historian in Tar Asèllo."

"I would like to read as well," said Alíthe, seeing the opportunity.

"As would I," Orgo added.

Amani grinned. "Yes, in fact, I believe I may even have a map or two showing many things about the war and, most importantly, its aftermath. I will send you the information immediately, as a gesture of *historical sharing* between our two tars. As I understand our laws, that is not restricted by the official trade disruption. Feel free to make your own notes."

"Of course," said Jee.

"I must be going," stated Plagósia. "Glasśigh? Would you walk me to the door?"

The minister said his goodbyes, wished all good fortune, and walked with Jee down the long, thin hallway to the exit.

"I thank you for the time, Glasśigh. I hope to speak with you again someday. Oh! What is this?" Plagósia asked, pointing to a small lighted alcove by the doorway.

Jee saw he referred to a device about half the size of a closed fist sitting on the bottom of the alcove. It was black and had a strangely-shaped metal square sticking out of the center. Two silver prongs protruded from the square.

"It is interesting that you should have *found* this," he said, handing her the device.

Jee looked at the object, then back to Plagósia, a questioning look on her face. Returning her gaze to the gadget, she saw that the black handle had characters carved into its surface by some type of machine: the symbols *LV-487.*

"What is it?" she asked.

"Oh! I am not sure," answered Plagósia with a chuckle. "But I am certain that someone will need it. You will have to figure out what it is for, but I have a feeling you will, with little effort."

Jee nodded. "Alright then. Please relay to the Ef Keería my heartfelt thanks."

"For what?" Plagósia asked, grinning. "He officially refused your request."

"Then tell him I am his friend for life," she said with a smile and a bow.

"That I can do," agreed Amani Plagósia, returning the gesture.

Jee set the device back in the alcove as Plagósia walked away.

▲▲▲

"I can't believe this," breathed Orgo as he looked up from the material delivered by Plagósia.

On the table of the main room of the ambassador's quarters lay piles of physical paper-bound books and several ancient electronic devices that predated current PDTs. The stacks and tablets included information on the many battles fought in the Éstargon-Fortus war. It told where weapons had been stockpiled at the war's end, what types of weapons were used and how effective they were. Best of all, after hours of investigation, the Front team finally discovered the precise location of Plagósia's weapons stockpile with an inventory of what had been abandoned on the surface.

"There is enough weaponry for a land force of two to three thousand!" Orgo beamed. "Pulse rifles, particle cannons, even charging batteries for pulse-styled weapons! There are portable mines, a few older-model Klaymac rockets, VEDs and other field optics, head and helmet communication nodes, network scramblers, portable mobile aid stations and medical supplies. We could stand a chance, I can tell you that!"

"There are also over a hundred skycraft to equip a complete air wing," Alíthe pointed out. "And though they are frozen in the ice, I saw an inventory of portable heat torches! We can free them! There's a mixture of PT personnel transports, large tanker supply ships, and fifty or so *Vożeeth 4E fighters!"*

"Éstargonian Vożeeths?" questioned Breegan. "I heard they were like the AMF experimental High Altitude *Kákors."*

"Somewhat," said Alíthe. "But the Éstargonian Vożeeths have a distinct advantage over our Kákors: they can operate below—and above—the fálouse. Only select Éstargonian ships have that technology."

"Amazing," said Breegan excitedly. "A few Vożeeths could easily chew up a whole flight of Kákors in a few passes. They'd probably take out a couple of Aréus fighters as well!"

"Great," said Jee excitedly. "We have our first tactical advantage. But how do we retrieve these ships and materiel?"

"First, we must get to the surface," answered Eno. "It is an inhospitable place, to say the least. Whoever goes up will need thermal suits to keep them alive in the extreme cold. Luckily for us, I happen to know where to acquire at least one: Targan Base."

"Yes!" said Alíthe excitedly. "In the memorial to you! I saw an older surface suit on display in the museum commemorating your early years spent studying on the surface."

"A horrible time," said Eno, "but a fortunate training for me.

"At this point in our plan," Jee began, "we are all, save Orgo, captives of the Front. Someone besides us will have to steal the suit."

"I can arrange that," Orgo assured them. "We have *plants*, Front people working at Targan Base. They are maintenance staff mostly. We have never used them, but it is time to test their ability."

"Excellent!" said Eno with a smile. "Once one of us reaches the stockpile, we must quickly enter one of the larger container ships and start its life support systems. It would be preferable to start with the ship that has the thermal suits inside."

"Which one is that? There are over 30 large container ships! And how to get inside?" posed Alíthe. "I am sure they didn't leave the doors open. One can't just twist a knob. I read that the Éstargonian ships have automatic magnetically sealed heat lock doors."

They poured over the information again, looking for some clue or hint as to which ship may have the suits and how they could get in. Orgo and Alíthe searched the manifests and vehicle lists. Jee, Breegan, and Reǵeena read the other documentation, looking for clues. Eno sat deep in thought, staring out the window to the garden. He murmured to himself at times, using his tablet to look something up or complete calculations. When asked what he was doing, he ignored everyone and dove deeper into his work.

After a few hours, they had grown increasingly frustrated, especially Jee. They were so close, only to lose all hope yet again.

"Can't we just, you know, blast the doors open with some explosives?" suggested Reǵeena, "or a big gun?"

"Not if you ever want to use the ship again," answered Eno. "That would wreck the ship's heat and air lock capability, rendering it useless."

"Damn it!" screamed Jee, unable to contain her frustration any longer. "Let's just guess what ship the suits are in! I'll just run my finger down the list," Jee said. "Eno, you say 'stop' when you feel lucky!"

"Jee," said Alíthe, trying to calm her.

"The List! Give me the list!" Jee demanded.

Orgo picked up an old PDT from the pile before him and held it up. "The list is on screen—"

"Here we go!" she responded, still upset. She closed her eyes and ran her finger down the page.

"This is childish!" scolded Eno. "Stop it."

"You said stop!" cried Jee, now opening her eyes. "Here! I was on—" she looked to the list. "LV-433. Start there—"

Orgo stood up, trying to calm the situation. "We will think of something! Please relax, everyone."

Jee froze for a moment. She looked closely at the list. "LV? These container ships all begin with LV?" she asked.

"LV is short for *Large Volume*," Alíthe stated. "It is the designation of the Éstargonian container ships."

"LV? LV? Wait a moment!" Jee cried aloud. She excitedly ran back to the front door.

The other looked at each other in confusion.

Jee immediately returned with the black device Amani Plagósia had *obviously* placed in the alcove. She looked at the number etched into the side of the device. Then, taking up the PDT, Jee nervously read through the listing as she ran her finger down the screen once again. "LV-411, LV-321! LV-487! 47! Oh! Here it is! The suits are in container ship LV-487! And here is the way in!"

She tossed the black device to Eno. He studied it as Jee excitedly jumped up and down.

"It is the key! Literally!" she declared.

"It does have the symbols *LV-487* inscribed on it," confirmed Eno.

"Let me see," said Orgo, snatching the key from Eno. Alíthe, Breegan and Reǵeena rushed to have a look.

"Here is 487 on the list, as sure as Ofeetis glows!" said Alíthe as he glanced at the PDT.

"It must have the suits, or at least a manifest telling their location," reasoned Eno. "Jee, this is no coincidence that you found this key. Where *did* you find it?"

"A little birdie gave it to me!" Jee answered, still dancing with happiness.

"A bird?" asked Alíthe, confused. "You speak to birds?"

"It is an Earth phrase," explained Eno, "meaning she can't tell us who gave her the key."

"But we can guess," said Orgo as he handed the key back to Eno.

"So it *was* the Ef Keería!" cried Reǵeena. "He is helping us after all!"

They now felt hope rise inside each of them, the feeling that much sweeter as it came from a place of despair where they had dwelled only seconds ago.

"According to the information I found," said Orgo, "these LVs are fuel cell-driven. Whoever goes up will need to know how to re-activate the cells, charge them if needed—a complicated task."

"Oh, it's not that complicated," boasted Eno. "I completed fuel cell engineering every day on the surface and again on Earth to recharge the crew module in *Explorer Eleven*. But, then again, I *am* an engineer…"

"Thanks for volunteering, Uncle!" exclaimed Jee.

"For what?" he asked.

"To go to the surface and get our materiel!"

"W-wait! Wait!" objected Eno. "I-I didn't volunteer for this, this *surface walk!*"

"You are the only one who could complete the engineering, Uncle!" Jee pointed out. "And you have been to the surface! And you are a pilot!"

Eno shook his head. Logic! It can be one's friend, and also, as in this case, it can be a death warrant. But in his heart and mind, he knew Jee was right. He wasn't the best choice; he was the only choice.

"Alright, alright! But it will still be difficult," warned Eno. "Even for one as talented and experienced as me."

Jee rushed to her uncle and gave him a hug and a kiss.

"See?" remarked Alíthe to Reǵeena. "She kisses him, too."

"This is how it should work," Eno said, now putting all the pieces together. "Once I locate LV-487, I will power it up, start life support, and locate the other suits. Then, I will attempt to free it from the ice by myself. If I am unable to do so, I will search for another ship to use as a transport for the teams. I fly it back into the tar, get the team, and fly them back, right into the hangar of the LV-487. It will be our surface base—it is surely large enough to house a hundred people. We can start freeing ships as soon as possible."

"A sound plan, Uncle," said Jee with a smile.

"But we still need a ship to get you to the surface," Breegan reminded them.

"I have been working on that," said Eno. "But before I bother to calculate my solution's viability, let us address one other issue: how are we going to fly all those skycraft? How many pilots do you have, Orgo?"

"None," he admitted.

"Then we have only three pilots," concluded Breegan. "And they are all here in this room."

They had hit yet another snag. After pacing about the balcony, muttering to themselves and testing theories with each other, it was Alíthe who had the answer.

"Once we free the Voźeeths from the ice, we can move them into the other LVs hangars and use them as our *Voźeeth Wing Base*. There is no need to fly them back into the tar. We only need to bring back Orgo's ground troop supplies!"

"But there are over a fifty Voźeeths!" groaned Eno. "They are no good if you don't have fifty pilots to fly them! Where are you going to get the pilots?"

Alíthe smiled and looked to Breegan. "Easy! One goes to where the pilots go."

"Slagger's!" Breegan responded with a wide grin.

"Correct, Second Officer Arkéta!" concurred Alíthe with a smile and a nod. "Breegan, I have a mission for you. Time for a little persuasion!"

▲▲▲

Captain Josáy deposited them on the beach at the Pools of Amée Allin. Firstsun had just broken in the tar, though in this far western corner, it was as dark as Eclipse, cloudy and lightly raining. It was still warm, as it had always been here, and a light mist hung in the air.

Several Front soldiers greeted them and began to prepare the Type-G and the fastboats used to transport the teams from the base to the pools.

Jee and Alíthe removed themselves from the others, walking several yards away and finding a nearby rock outcropping that shielded them from the rain and mist of the roaring falls. Broad fronds from a covering tree arched over them. The ground was soft, and mossy grass grew from the rock wall of the outcropping to the edge of a small pond fed by a slim fall of trickling water. The pond was crystal clear, its surface dappled by the rain.

Jee reflected on how green the plants were and how colorful the fish—or whatever they were that swam in the cool water. There was a small patch of flowers growing amidst the moss, with the tiniest and most delicate yellow flowers, like daisies on Earth, but glowing the familiar way as everything seemed to do on Áhtha.

They moved to the edge of the pond, still protected from the rain, and sat on an exposed root from a great tree that grew hundreds of feet into the air. Again, they held hands, kissed, then stared into each other's eyes.

"I do not want to be separated from you, Jee," Alíthe whispered.

"I feel the same," she said. "But we have to go through with this. And we have so few to help us. People are counting on our success, Alíthe."

"I know. But it is such a frail plan; it could break at any part of the chain. Any single event…" His voice trailed off.

"I have to believe we will succeed," Jee whispered.

They sat in silence for a few moments, listening to the waterfall, the pattering of rain off the fronds and pond surface, their steady breath, and their hearts beating.

"Alíthe, you are the first real person I met here on Áhtha. And, you really have never left my side the whole time."

"It *was* my job," he admitted, adding a smile.

"No matter what happens to us," Jee continued, still serious, "if we don't live through this, or if we lose each other in the rush of the war that will come, please don't forget me."

He kissed her. "I will never forget you. Even during the days of Fullglow, I will dream of you."

She smiled and laughed softly.

"What did I say?" asked Alíthe. "Was that humor I did?"

"No, but it was poetic," Jee said.

"Poetic?" he asked.

"You reminded me of a song from Earth, a song of two lovers who are separated."

Jee began to sing softly:

Stars shining bright above you,
Night breezes seem to whisper "I love you."
Birds singing in the sycamore tree,
Dream a little dream of me.

Say nighty-night and kiss me,
Just hold me tight and tell me you'll miss me.
While I'm alone and blue as can be,
Dream a little dream of me.

Sweet dreams 'til sunbeams find you
Sweet dreams that leave all worries behind you.
But in your dreams, whatever they be,
Dream a little dream of me.

19
A Plan in Motion

The rogue media boxes of Tar Asélllo could not be shut down. Radio wave signals were usually easy enough to trace—unless they were mobile and changed frequency regularly to avoid jamming or detection. In that case, finding them was never easy.

The boxes were used to even greater effect in the days and weeks after the Enária Front made their demands. A video had been delivered to certain people that operated illegal stations in Etáin City. The video contained never-before-seen images of the Glasśigh in the hands of the Enária Front. The cubes were activated, and the broadcasts began. The citizenry, of course, watched these rogue stations as regularly as they viewed the Taźath-controlled media. They were appalled—not just the Kořeefa but everyone at every level of society.

The Graćenta, who looked on the Glasśigh as a goddess, were especially disgusted. How could anyone, even the Enária Front, harm the Glasśigh?

Also released on legal station broadcasts from the government media stations (and rogue stations that played the video repeatedly) was an address by Madam Khileetéra.

The Taźath watched with rising wrath at her statements.

"It is apparent that Pronómio Tok's policies toward the Graćenta have angered them so greatly, the oppression so complete, that their support for the Enária Front has risen. Tok's handling of the structure of our society has driven them to desperate ends. This kidnapping of the Glasśigh, our beloved and cherished child, is due to the Taźath's extremism and greed. He is responsible. I call for a vote of confidence immediately!"

The Taźath was beside himself with anger. Pronómio Tok could take anything, he believed. Still, when outmaneuvered by an opponent—especially a weak, spineless sympathizer like Khileetéra—he could do nothing but scream in rage.

The next vote of confidence would tell many things.

On a cloudy Fullglow, news arrived. The entire tar, including the Taźath and Kalífus, were shocked at the sudden appearance of the Glasśigh on the streets of Induláy Point, an industrial city on the shores of Amendis Bay, east of Etáin City. The Enária Front had kept their word and freed Jee along with Reǵeena and Breegan as well. This act made many wonder what, exactly, was the Enária Front after? When it was later rogue-broadcasted that the 'ransom' was food, medical supplies, and other items for the poor, many questioned the events even more.

Commander Kalífus dispatched a team to retrieve the women from Induláy. Within the hour, Jee, Reǵeena, and Second Officer Breegan Arkéta were in the protection of the TSP. En route to the Palace in the Taźath's skyliner, they were escorted by three formations from the Wings of Glasśigh, flying above, behind, and below the silver craft.

The Taźath met them on the palace landing pad. Immediately upon touch down, he rushed to the skyliner. Even before the engines were shut down, he was opening the door from the outside.

The media drones caught the entire event.

"Are you all right? Are you well?" he cried, hugging each of the ladies in turn.

"We are fine, but it was…" Jee began to cry.

"Come inside! Let us go to medical first, then Palace Place?" he suggested. "Commander Kalífus is there, ready to debrief you. The sooner we know what happened, from your point, the better and faster we can act!"

As the Taźath turned away, Jee gave Breegan and Reǵeena a quick smile and wink, then resumed her sad expression.

Once in Palace Place, the women tried to relax. As planned, Commander Kalífus was inside, standing by the huge window of the main room. He turned to meet them, a look of concern and determination on his grim face.

Breegan immediately paused and saluted him. Her commander strode to her, stopped within a few feet, and snapped a formal salute. He held the pose for effect—and for the ever-present drones hovering on the other side of the wall of glass. This would be on the nightly broadcast, he knew.

Jee noticed his professional stance, muscular arms, and half-hidden tattoo emblazoned across his right forearm—not a TSP, but a YSP tattoo. What a goat, she thought. He is part of the problem. Jee also observed that his tattoo had something different about it. It looked like there was a red mark across the dagger image.

"Well done, Second Officer Arkéta," commended Kalífus. "You survived."

"Yes, sir," she said as Kalífus completed the salute.

Food was brought in. As they ate, Breegan began to recount what had happened: how the passengers of the Type-G, now taken by the Enária Front, had witnessed the destruction of the three Aréus escorts. Under threat of missile attack, they were forced into the caves and split up.

"How did you get inside their caves?" asked Kalífus, testing her; comparing her answers to his findings.

"There was a doorway, made of stone. It was behind a waterfall to the eastern edge," said Breegan.

Kalífus nodded.

"We were separated, blindfolded, and moved around often," Breegan continued. "They were horrible people, all of them. I was kept awake and threatened constantly."

Jee just stared blankly ahead. It seemed to Kalífus that she was traumatized.

"We knew they were making videos of us," continued Breegan. "We could only hope that they were trying to trade us for something."

"They did. Food and the like," grumbled Kalífus with disdain. "This matches what I have seen. Second Officer, you performed well. I assure you all that we will find them and crush them—for good this time. I am tired of—"

"Eno and Alíthe are still in captivity!" exclaimed Jee, awakening from her trance. "Please wait! They must be released first!"

Jee was beside herself. She rushed to Kalífus, grabbed him, and fell to her knees. "Please! Don't hurt Uncle Eno or Alíthe! They will kill them. I just know it! They are evil!"

"We will be cautious," Kalífus assured her. "Nothing will be executed until we can ensure the safety of the commanders."

"Thank you," whispered Jee, now standing. She immediately gave Kalífus an emotional hug.

This shocked everyone in the room.

"Please help return my uncle and Commander Alíthe to me," she pleaded, still embracing him.

With a surprised look, he wrapped his arms around her and returned the embrace. Again, the drones buzzed away, capturing the moment. But as Kalífus moved his arm, his right sleeve inched upward, exposing his forearm. Jee was in a perfect position to study his tattoo. It looked like the ones in Eno's video of the *Explorer Eleven* launch attack; however, she could now identify the mark she noticed earlier. Shooting across the oppressive-looking dagger symbol was the red arc of a shooting star.

▲▲▲

In the dim light of Fullglow, Salǵeea Calćoa waited on the steps of an abandoned worker's cabin, this one still displaying a hand-carved wooden sign on the lowest step: Number 63. The surrounding land had once been fertile fields that stretched along the northern tar from Dirga's Arch in the west to Jaydí's Arch in the east and south to the shores of the Síndian Sea.

He felt safe here. Even the local security forces ignored the area. Who cared what happened to the old, abandoned buildings or the old people living in the hills beyond?

Salǵeea was born and raised here, and though his childhood was difficult, he remembered the love his parents showed him and his much younger sister. Salǵeea loved the girl; her deep green eyes and wavy, silver mane were the most beautiful things he had ever seen. He remembered a particular day with her, laughing as they ran past the tall stalks of tobafruit plants. That day, the light from Ofeétis seemed unusually intense. Burned into his memory was her image, the orange glow of the giant above them rushing through the clouds, lighting the fields and his sister's mane.

Life was beautiful and wonderful—until the trip to see the big city of Éhpiloh. His father was arrested, suspected of being a member of the Zakéema. The rest of the family waited in the city in a dingy boarding house, hoping for news. During the hours that passed, their small room was raided and his sister taken. He and his mother could only assume the worst. After searching for weeks in the brothels and industrial factories, they were forced to leave and returned to Cabin 63.

Salǵeea never saw his father or his sister again. His mother, heartbroken and weak from lack of appetite, was never the same. She was unable to work in the fields, so he, at the age of one Áhthan year, took her place. He attempted to care for her when he was home and did so until his time in Gaoule Prison separated them. Kind neighbors moved his mother into the caves to be cared for by the poor souls already there, and receiving that news while in prison almost crushed his heart. News of her death a year later did. He grieved, but he persisted. As long as he could breathe, he plotted and waited. This was the birth of his purpose.

After his escape, Salǵeea began walking down the road to his future as the leader of the fifth iteration of the Front, renamed after his sister, Enária.

But that was old news. Today, the air was warm; the sun's

reflection off Ofeétis lit the northern tar in a deep orange glow. He had good friends, all of whom would die for him. Many had. He took comfort in the fact that his cause was just, and now he had the Glasśigh on his side.

Today, Salǵeea was waiting for Orgo to return from Tar Éstargon. Salǵeea's mission during that visit was to preserve the Front, and that meant all people and supplies. Matériel was spread out across Oso-Gúrith in over twenty stockpiles. The soldiers went back into the general population of the Graćenta, waiting near the fields or in the factories until they were called upon. Only a few dozen had moved to the Front's new base.

Looking south, he saw a vehicle approaching on a dusty road. It was an old and beaten single-seat farm truck, and it made a lot of noise. That axel-bearing module is shredded, Salǵeea thought.

The clattering car eventually pulled up in front of Cabin 63. Who would have such a pile of junk? Salǵeea knew of only one man.

"Orgo, I see you have stepped up in the world," Salǵeea commented, standing.

Orgo slid out of the farm truck, stretched a bit, and then slammed the door. "Not yet." He walked to the back of the vehicle and opened the rear gate. He extended his hand to Eno and Alíthe.

"Still hauling garbage?" joked Salǵeea.

Alíthe hopped out of the truck. "That must be sarcasm."

"I learned from the Glasśigh," said Salǵeea. "Did I do it right?"

Eno now crawled out of the vehicle and dusted himself off. "It stung, so yes."

"Where is the Type-G?" asked Salǵeea.

Orgo stretched his back and rubbed his neck. "It is in the old cave depot. I didn't think it would be best to land it here—too easy to spot."

"And certainly out of place," added Eno as he looked at the dilapidated cabin.

Once inside, the men ate a meager meal, then returned to the front porch to sit and talk. Salǵeea was told of the more-or-less successful trip to Tar Éstargon and the good news about the stockpile. Eno detailed the plan for obtaining the ships and the multiple trips to the surface needed to get the workers there, free the vessels from the ice and fly them into the tar.

"If I understand you, Minister Commander," Salǵeea said, "we must complete this plan by the Festival of Jaydí. That is in eight weeks."

"Yes, it will be close," Eno replied.

"Have you come up with a way to get to the stockpile?" continued

Salǵeea. "No one can scale the tar wall. We have no craft that can survive above the fálouse, and I do not believe the Taźath does either."

"He does not, or I would know about it," answered Alíthe. "We have a solution. Risky, yes, but Commander Ćlaviath is certain it will work."

"I never said I was *certain*," Eno clarified. "I said we have no other choice. The Type-G will make the trip. It is sealed well enough to keep in the air we need for the short trip."

"But the cold!" protested Salǵeea. "The instruments and systems will stop functioning almost immediately! You will not be able to maneuver, much less land, and load up cold suits! And then return!"

"All true," agreed Eno, "except we will not maneuver or land."

Salǵeea shook his head in disbelief. "Then you will rely on what? Luck? Magic?"

Eno nodded his head at the sarcasm. "No, Salǵeea Calćoa. We will rely on the laws of physics…and impeccable timing."

▲▲▲

In Palace Place, though the eclipse shrouded the tar, Jee couldn't sleep. Lying in bed, she could hear Reǵeena breathing beside her in blissful slumber. Breegan, wanting to stay with them, was sleeping on the lounge on the other side of the room. Jee could see shadows of patrolling guards outside through the sheer curtains covering the wall of glass; probably as much to keep us inside as to keep anyone out, she thought.

At least the drones were gone.

Jee decided to get up, realizing that it was no use trying to sleep until her mind stopped racing. She sat upright, slowly moved out from the sheets that covered her, and silently walked to the closet. She entered, gently closed the door, and sat on the floor surrounded by her wardrobe.

She activated her armband. It would be a risk, but possibly, if she was careful, she could mask her actual purposes.

"Vací?" she asked.

"Here," said the soft, emotionless voice.

"Can you show me images of the official Ultos Wing tattoo?"

"The Ultos Wing did not have an official tattoo, nor does the new Wings of Glasśigh."

"Vací, I need inspiration for my speech at the Festival of Jaydí. Does any other service have tattoos or symbols?"

"Many have emblems. Only TSP officers have tattoos."

"TSP tattoos? Great! What do they look like?"

"Displaying all forty-two TSP tattoo images, including variants and precursors."

The women had stayed together for just over two weeks when Breegan asked to return to her post at G-Wing. Of course, her wish was granted and reported and celebrated in the controlled media, praising her amazing resilience. She was interviewed, there was a documentary made, as well as dolls made in her likeness, and they sold quite well, as did the posters and artwork showing her with the Glasśigh.

It was time for Breegan to execute her part of the plan.

Reǵeena and Jee began to move their piece of the plan ahead as well. They summoned Veegill, the artist, to help them with a 'special project'. Over the next two weeks, they created a presentation for the Taźath. It included particular artwork, music from Earth, and much research using Vací. They rehearsed and practiced and prepared for every possible outcome or question.

As the Eclipse began, Jee had twenty-eight hours to get a good rest before presenting her plan to Pronómio Tok. But the image of Kalífus's tattoo weighed heavily on her, and she knew sleep would be difficult unless she found an answer.

Before they dismissed Veegill, Jee summoned him and Reǵeena to her room.

"Veegill, I need a favor," she asked in a whisper.

"Anything, my Glasśigh."

"Are we friends?" she asked him.

"I-I would hope we are!" he stuttered. "I-I mean, I would be honored to call you a friend!"

"Then we are friends," said Jee with a smile. "And friends can keep a secret, right?"

"Of course," agreed Veegill.

"Reǵeena, do you have Eno's portable file?" asked Jee.

Reǵeena reached into a pocket to produce the device.

"Wait. They could be watching," Jee whispered. Then louder, she continued. "Both of you follow me into the closet. I need help picking out an outfit."

Once inside the closet, Jee closed the door and activated Eno's jamming chip. The purple light on its side blinked twice.

"Glasśigh?" whispered Veegill. "Is that a jamming chip?"

"Yes," she replied as she plugged Eno's portable drive containing the video files into her now Vací-free tablet.

"Veegill, can you use this software? The imaging scanning-thing?"

Veegill looked at the flickering image on the tablet.

"Yes, Karhu's Image Warp. I know the program very well. A master of it actually. I was an early tester back in—"

"Great," interrupted Jee. "Sit here next to me."

Veegill took a place on the floor, watching a bit of the video. He recognized the subject. "I-is this what I think it is?"

"Yes, and a bag of chips," said Jee. "Can you move it ahead for me? Until I say stop?"

"Bag of chips?" he asked as the images flickered past. Veegill had never seen the last part of the video from the *Explorer Eleven* cameras. He seemed shocked, even at the increased playback speed.

"I-is that you? The child in the pod?" he asked, but he knew the answer.

"Stop!" Jee said. "Go ahead just a bit and freeze the image. Yes, there. Good."

Displayed was the somewhat fuzzy image of the arm of one of the soldiers.

"Advance a few seconds," Jee instructed.

As Veegill complied, the image showed the sleeve moving upward as the soldier strained with the gun. In another frame, the image revealed part of the YSP symbol.

"A...a YSP officer symbol?" asked Veegill. "Underneath the sleeve...but..."

"Now you know," said Jee. She waited for his response as he reasoned and absorbed what he had seen.

"By the will of Aséllo!" he whispered, his brown mane flashing orange, then slowly to gray.

"Veegill, listen to me. I believe the Tażath had my parents murdered. And they tried to kill me. I-I need you on my side."

He was silent for a moment. He kept shaking his head.

"It is real. Commander Eno discovered this," said Reǵeena.

"Eno?" the artist asked.

"Can you copy this image?"

Veegill was shaking with trepidation. Somehow he managed to nod.

"Good. Now strip away all colors but gold and black. Then add back in the original red. Can you do that?"

Veegill tapped the screen, and soon the red began to reappear. After several seconds, the image became sharper. Before them was the same YSP tattoo they had seen, but this time, a clear and sharp red curved arc was evident.

"What is that?" asked Reǵeena.

"You recognize it, don't you, Veegill?" asked Jee, already knowing the answer. Her face was turning red, and she clenched her fists. She stood and began pacing in the small area.

"It is a YSP Superior Officer's tattoo," said Veegill. "All YSP, and now all TSP division leaders, get one when they are promoted. Though the emblem is the same, each has an added component unique to the officer. I worked with many of them personally."

"Do you remember this one? You created it, right?" asked Jee, again knowing the answer. Vací had told her about the unique images as well as who created this particular design.

"Yes," confirmed Veegill with a whisper. "I remember. This one…it was well over two years ago. But, no…this makes no sense!"

"Who wears this tattoo?" asked Reǵeena.

Veegill quickly leaned away from the image as if it would reach out and sting him. He began to tremble.

"Who?" asked Reǵeena again.

"Minister Commander Gákoh Kalífus," he said.

20
On the Surface

The Type-G Luxury Skyliner streaked across the edge of the northern tar wall heading west, a mile below the dark blue fálouse. It was almost pitch black, being the first hour of Eclipse, a bit cloudy, and it was raining on and off. A warming event from the thermal shafts had heated things up. That was good news, as the clouds caused by the increase in temperature and mist from the falls hid their passage from prying eyes and scanners.

Alíthe flew as close to the wall as possible and slow enough to remain unseen by movement-sensing tracking systems. He made his way from the central Sindian Fields, past Dirga's Arch, over the Sea of Kryménos and the Aséllian Sea, then past Asállo's Spire, past the Falls of Jovia, and entered the Caymana Strait.

The adjustments to the Type-G had been completed in the makeshift hangar hidden in the cave system of the northern tar wall behind Cabin 63. Improved heaters were installed—no easy task. They needed to warm the flight deck, main cabin, and internal systems well enough to protect the occupants and the critical equipment from extreme temperatures. It could not get too warm, or things would melt—essential components such as wiring, lubricated joints, and hydraulic pump gaskets. Not warm enough? Wiring would freeze and crack. Ice could form on control surfaces making the ship un-maneuverable once they re-entered the tar. They could die of exposure to the subzero temperature.

Of course, another wrinkle was the added complication of having to launch Eno out of the Type-G and into space.

At over six feet long, the escape tube they 'found' in the museum exhibit was just large enough to fit Eno and his gear inside. They had thought of attaching the tube to the outside of the Type-G and releasing it somehow, maybe with an automated explosive latch. However, the structure was not built to 'bolt on' anything, heavy or lightweight, explosive or not. The Type-G was not meant to go into outer space. The structural integrity of the craft would be tested enough without punching holes into it.

The best they could do was build a heated track in the lower cargo area, right in front of the ventral door and connect the escape tube to it.

"So the only reason I am on this flight," asked Orgo from the cargo bay, "is to open the door? And shove the Commander out?"

"Yes," confirmed Alíthe from the flight deck. "I can't fly this thing *and* push him out!"

"I can't jump out myself," Eno reasoned as he added essential items into his pack: a bit of dried food, a small tool kit, patches to repair the thermal suit if needed, and his ABC. He placed the pack in the slightly modified escape tube. It looked like a coffin to Eno and probably less comfortable.

"At least the heater in here is more than sufficient," he remarked as he climbed inside.

Orgo didn't like his part of the plan. Sure, he could press the button that operated the door's opening, disengage the track's locking mechanism that held the tube in place, and shove the tube, with Eno inside, right out the back of the Type-G. But the ensuing blast of icy air coming back at him from the cold and merciless surface atmosphere would be more than uncomfortable; it could kill him.

"I know what you are thinking," said Eno. "However, you won't freeze to death. The door will be open for less than fifteen seconds, we will pre-heat the cabin as hot as it can take, and you can wear a thermal helmet. And some layers."

"Layers?" Orgo asked.

"Theoretically," Eno stated, "it should be well within the limits of safety."

Orgo scratched his head. "But has anyone ever tried this?"

"Once," answered Eno as he put additional supplies into the tube.

"When was that?" challenged Orgo.

"In about fifteen minutes," said Eno. "Are you sure you can push me out?"

"I may push you out right now," grumbled Orgo. But there was no use arguing. They had no choice.

"Fifteen minutes!" called Alíthe from the flight deck. "Heaters on full!"

Eno checked his cold gear, then Orgo assisted him into the escape tube but left the lid open.

After disengaging the track lock, Orgo practiced sliding the container back and forth to get an idea of the force required to manually jettison it from the Type-G. The whole loaded tube probably weighed three times as much as Orgo, though he was able to slide it easily.

"Ten minutes! Accelerating!" called Alíthe.

Orgo re-engaged the tube's track lock.

All could feel the surge of power as the Type-G's dual thrusters ignited the fuel cell rocket modules and accelerated to full speed of four hundred and fifty miles per hour. The cabin was getting warm.

Orgo, now finished with Eno, began adding his 'layers' of clothing, donning gloves, and putting on a thermal helmet, and activating his hel-com.

"Five minutes!" announced Alíthe, this time over the com. *"The falls of Caymana are dead ahead. Approaching fast."*

"It's time," announced Eno. "Lock me in, Orgo."

"Are you sure?" asked the burly man. "We can call this off. Last chance."

"I'm good. Insane, but good. Clamp this shut, my friend," instructed Eno.

It was hot inside the Type-G. Orgo looked at the temperature gauge on the wall above the door. It was twice the temperature of the tar's floor. He was already sweating, and the number was increasing quickly. He tightened all three latches on the escape tube. Through the thick glass window, Orgo saw Eno smiling.

"Correcting to horizontal course 270," said Alíthe through his hel-com.

Good, thought Orgo, at least the radio still works.

The Type-G was heading straight to the edge of the Falls of Caymana, one mile beneath the fálouse.

Orgo took his position. Sitting on the deck, he faced the outer door and strapped himself to the metal framing between two bulkheads using restraining belts. He then placed his feet on the edge of the pod and extended his right hand to the door control panel. He lifted the safety cover.

"Ready!" he shouted.

"Going vertical!" replied Alíthe. *"On track! We are a mile from the falls! Rolling to forty-five degrees!"*

As the ship rotated, Orgo now had his back to the sky, straps straining but holding him in place. He could see condensation on the walls of the cargo bay. Moisture was dripping off the escape tube.

"Entering the fálouse! Fifteen seconds until apogee," said Alíthe, tension apparent in his voice. *"Adjusting to one degree past vertical!*

It was *hot*. Orgo could see that the edges of the door were glowing red.

"We are past the fálouse!" announced the pilot. *"Open on my mark! One..."*

Orgo could feel the craft slowing as the Type-G hit the cold of the Áhthan atmosphere with a shudder, his back pressing against the bulkhead. The temperature gauge immediately began to fall.

"Two!"

The engines sputtered and coughed, then stopped. Orgo could swear he could hear the crackling of ice as it formed on the outside of the craft. The temperature gauge had dropped to almost normal. The entire compartment was becoming covered in a mist from the condensation. It was practically impossible to see.

"Open!"

Orgo pressed the door control button. With a pop and a hiss, the door opened, warm air rushing out and cold rushing in. A buzzer sounded. The door was opened completely. Sirens blared as systems went offline.

"Multiple heat element failures!" called Alíthe through the com. *"Naviga—propulsion—om panel—can you—"*

The com system was down. Warning lights ignited for a brief second, then went out. The buzzing stopped. It was too cold for the wiring to handle.

Orgo was facing downward, looking out the open door. He could just make out the surface of Áhtha, gray and hilled with ice, the blue fálouse roiling at the tar's edge. He could feel the chill hit his legs, his chest, and his arms. Mist swirled as it turned into ice particles. The faceplate on his helmet frosted over. Suddenly, all was in darkness.

Completely blind, Orgo gave the tube a shove.

It didn't move.

Again, he shoved, he kicked. It remained in position.

"The escape tube! It's stuck! There's ice! The heater on the track must have failed!" he called, but Alíthe could not hear, and even if he could, there was nothing he could do to help.

Orgo began kicking the tube repeatedly. With a scream, he pushed again. If he couldn't get it out, the entire mission was a failure. Somewhere, there had to be enough strength! he thought. Every second that passed would push Eno farther off course from the stockpile and LV-487. He tried one last time.

"By the Light of Áhtha, get out!" he yelled as he slammed his feet into the tube, his back arching and legs thrusting with all his might and will.

He heard a cracking sound. Was it the ice breaking on the track? Or the tube rupturing?

Once more, he kicked.

The escape tube came free, sliding down the rail and out into nothingness.

The Type-G reached apogee and paused, now weightless. Orgo felt himself lifting off the bulkhead, momentarily floating. He moved his gloved hand across the faceplate of the helmet. The ice, all in one piece, cracked off just enough so he could see again. It was deathly cold; the gauge was not functioning, reading dead zero. That was as far as the system could measure. His legs, arms, and lower abdomen began to freeze. He pressed the door control. Nothing. It was frozen. He knew that would happen but had to try.

The Type-G must have completed a wing-over, as his view changed from the scarred gray surface below to completely blue as they fell sideways through the fálouse. His entire body was shaking from the temperature loss. He was entirely numb, almost completely unable to breathe.

In an instant, the hum of the heaters was audible. A crackling sound was heard. It was his hel-com.

".. repeat! Can you hear me? Orgo? Orgo!" It was Alíthe.

He could not respond, still frozen. He heard a thud and felt a slight vibration throughout his whole body.

The door had closed.

"Orgo! Orgo!"

Then he felt the first wave of warmth. The ice particles began to melt. Clear vision soon returned. He was able to breathe.

Gasping for more air, he struggled to free his arms from his sides. They felt sore as if he had been lifting crates of stone blocks for ages. With great effort, Orgo removed his helmet, warm air rushing over his face.

"Orgo! Answer! Are you all right?" called Alíthe, projecting his voice to the rear cabin.

Orgo could hear the engines wheeze to life. The Type-G was alive again. The noise of the twin M44 rockets kicked in. The inertia pushed Orgo back against the bulkhead again. Within seconds, Alíthe had the craft righted. Orgo felt his normal weight again and soon was sitting on the floor of the cargo bay.

'Orgo! Did you—"

"Y-yes," he finally managed.

"Eno?" asked Alíthe.

"Inform the Glasśigh that he is launched," said Orgo, "and utterly insane."

▲▲▲

Eno felt the release from the Type-G. After so much banging, he could only guess what had happened. The track Salǵeea had installed probably iced up. Orgo had been kicking the escape tube loose. They had anticipated that moisture from their breathing and the trapped atmosphere in the cargo bay would freeze. However, the track heaters must have failed.

As he drifted down, Eno thought about the delay in his exit from the Type-G. His well-calculated plan called for him to be released due west of the ship at one thousand feet. The westerly wind coming from the heat front caused by rising air near the Falls of Caymana was to take the escape chamber five miles west, toward Tar Éstargon. It was supposed to land him in the open area of the main ice field, within two miles of the stockpile. A leisurely one-hour walk at most. But the delay of his release had meant he was higher up. The wind would have more time to affect the distance. It would push him farther off course. How high up was he?

He glanced at the rows of readouts on his sleeve display. The altimeter showed three thousand feet above the surface—three times higher than planned.

I could land in the fálouse of Tar Éstargon! he thought. It may not mean certain death, but it might. And it certainly would be embarrassing!

The more time he spent falling, the more off course he would be. Eno reasoned it would be best to wait until he was as low as possible, about 500 feet before he deployed the chute. Also, he might get a sudden change in his reading. If he saw his altimeter suddenly move from three thousand feet to *twenty-five thousand*, then he would indeed have drifted over Tar Éstargon.

He watched the gauge, hand on the chute release. It read just over two thousand.

Fifteen hundred.

One thousand.

Five hundred.

Eno engaged the manual chute release lever. A sudden jerk signaled his slowing descent, which meant the parachute had deployed, the rate falling to less than five feet per second.

Looking out the viewport, all was dark and black. Then a gray haze appeared as the atmosphere thickened. Suddenly, he saw a tall white spire of ice. A frozen geyser. Not good. If he was near any of the ice towers, he was off course, way far north.

The altimeter read fifty feet. He felt a bump, then harsh scraping. He must have glanced off a geyser. Then, a big *bang* and a jolt, and the escape tube began spinning. Looking through the viewport, he saw the black of space and the white-gray of the icy surface flashing before him, over and over again. He was tumbling down a hill. And he felt sick.

After what seemed an eternity, the rolling ceased, and he slid a few more yards to stop with a crunch.

The tube cracked open near its bottom by his feet.

After a moment, his senses recovered. Eno took a long, deep breath and then began to wrestle with the latch releases. Two of the three latches opened. The third, by the crack at the bottom of the tube, did not. A few well-placed kicks, and it broke free, the lid flying off. He sat up.

Eno had landed in a thick forest of ice towers: soaring white and pale green skyscrapers made of frozen water from Áhtha's subterranean ocean. He almost fell over as he leaned back to see all the way to the top of the nearest one. At the base, each colossal structure was at least fifty yards wide. It was like being in New York City, except the buildings were made of solid ice, each the size of the Empire State, and no one had thought to leave room for organized streets. He would have to zig-zag his way through dozens of them, maybe more, and that would take extra time. The batteries in the suit would keep the heaters running for only about four hours.

He carefully stood, stepped out of the tube, and began inspecting himself. No bones were broken. He found no rips in the suit.

Eno checked his armband readout and tapped each of its gauges. He activated the display screen at one end of the device. It was low resolution but sufficient for determining his present location. He loaded a simple map image onto the screen. He would have to determine his position using visual sightings.

Peering between the towers eastward, he saw nothing but more of them. He began sweeping his gaze to the south. He saw nothing, just white spires reaching into the blackness until his gaze fell almost directly south. There, he saw a faint blue glow of a fálouse peeking through the whiteness. Looking further south, he saw another faint light. Yes, that would be Tar Éstargon. The first glow had to be Aséllo. Checking his map, Eno calculated that he was off course approximately four miles north-by-northwest but only three and a quarter miles from the stockpile. He had eight miles worth of comfort in this suit. At a conservative pace of two miles per hour, it would be easy!

"Might as well get going," he said to no one. "Standing here just eats up heat."

He shouldered his pack, took a deep breath, and began weaving his way south between the frozen, lifeless white city.

After an hour of walking, he had made it through the towers and paused a moment to marvel at the sheer enormity of these frozen giants. One, in particular, was significantly taller than the others, although impossible to tell by how much. It also had a deeper green color, and the ice caps and hanging daggers seemed darker as well. It also leaned at a greater angle to the southwest.

"The Jolly Green Giant," he said aloud, remembering the Earth food in a can. "I bet the Earthlings would like this big green bean!"

To his right, the ice spires marched south until they disappeared into the glow of the fálouse of Éstargon, stirring in the distance. Ahead and to his left, he could see the expanse of the ice plate all the way to the edge of the Tar Aséllo fálouse. He also could make out a large surface river that could be the main feeder to the Falls of Caymana. Using that as his triangulation point, he confirmed his position. He was just three miles north of the stockpile. With three more hours of heat, he would have time to reach his goal and find the light container ship. He adjusted his pack and began the southern trek.

Though there was an atmosphere on the surface of Áhtha, the darkness of space seemed to be surrounding him, the stars floating near and clearly visible. Adding to the spectacular sight was the fading eclipse of Ofeétis, so crystal clear and near, it took his breath away. The sun created a crescent of gold that outlined the gas giant's shape. Eerie, he thought, and a sight unable to be witnessed from inside the tar.

"My camera!" Eno realized and began fumbling with his pack. He took out his ABC and snapped a few pictures.

Soon, Ofeétis would be in quarter, and the surface would take on an orange glow. The thought of more light comforted him.

After a few minutes of walking across the ice plain, he found himself coming down a slight rise caused by a shift in the ice plate. Ahead, he could see dark shapes on the surface approximately three miles before him. Rocks? More like boulders. And a lot of them. But they seemed uniformly placed. They could be the stockpile. What he thought were boulders might be the container ships. His heart lifted, and he changed to a brisk pace.

As he progressed, he could feel an odd sensation: a vibration of sorts, coming through his feet. Could the heaters be failing? Was that vibration really the first signs of the coldness coming through his suit? Eno stopped running. He rechecked his readout. No, the heaters were working. No rips or holes were detected. Then what was causing the vibration in his feet?

Within a few seconds, the vibrations increased. He noticed small ice particles lifting off the ground. Snow? he wondered. But coming upward from the ground? A quake?

Then the sound came, like a rocket blasting off from somewhere behind. It was getting louder by the second as if it were bearing down on him. The ground was not only vibrating; *it was moving.*

The ice below seemed to be sinking slowly, causing him to spread his arms to steady himself. He turned to look behind. A half-mile away, water was spraying hundreds of feet into thin air but shooting outwards more than upwards: an ice geyser was being born. Unfortunately, there already was an ice tower in the way: the big green one. And it had begun to fall.

Eno ran wildly at first, not knowing where the tower would strike. He was only a few hundred yards past the forest. And the Jolly Green Giant was considerably taller than that. As he watched, it seemed to be falling directly toward him. If he continued running straight ahead, he would be crushed. Running to the east, his left, would mean running away from his goal.

"To the right!" he yelled to no one and ran southwest.

The ice before him shook and began to fracture, huge crevasses appearing to either side of him. Material from the few rocks that were carried upwards by ancient geysers slid this way and that. Though his spiked boots helped move him across the slick surface, they were no help when the sheet on which he ran dropped several feet or rose several more.

Forcing himself to look over his shoulder, he saw the looming tower falling, crushing other smaller ice geysers as it roared downward, toppling them like dominos in that game he had played on Earth. The tower was clearly falling toward him, still. He changed direction again, this time moving northwest.

He ran on, afraid to look behind.

In an explosive *boom*, the green tower slammed into the main plate an eighth of a mile behind him. A smaller tower in the giant's path was hit and cracked in half, each massive piece skidding ahead, sending debris of all sizes in every direction as it shattered. The ice section beneath him splintered from the shock of the green tower's impact, immediately fracturing into smaller platforms, rising fifty feet or more into thin air, carrying debris—and Eno—upward.

Everything paused for a moment, weightless, then fell at an angle, the ice cracking in half. Eno remained on one piece that slid forward while the other ice chunk fell into a newly created ravine. Massive rock-boulders rained down about him. Ice chunks collided, shattering into shards that flew past Eno, coming from hundreds of yards away, like daggers fired from cannons. The section beneath his feet slid noisily into another that had risen upward before him. The impact threw Eno ahead. He fell to the surface, slid, then stood, running as fast as he could to a newly deposited hunk of ice the size of a small building. He hunkered down on its far side. The screeching sound of ice shards flying past made him cover his head. He heard muted explosive sounds, then loud popping as the pieces slammed into the ice shield that was protecting him. Other shards whizzed past to shatter on the ice plate, scattering in crystal splinters as they skated across the slick surface.

Soon, the rumbling, cracking, and booming stopped, though errant shards of ice still fell from above. Eno remained down for a full three minutes, then, feeling safe, came out from behind the ice hunk. He turned to where the green giant once stood.

Blocked by the base of the green giant, the newborn geyser was unable to develop into a tower. Water must have sprayed in all directions, forming into a twisted mess of ice, like the arms of an octopus reaching out from a hole in the frozen white plain. The original green tower lay broken in several pieces. Eno could hear deep rumbles and sharp cracking as the main plate continued fracturing. Ice particles still lingered in the air, snowing down.

"Besides scaring me to near death, another privileged sight," Eno panted, finally taking a deep breath. His hands were still shaking, and his legs felt wobbly. At least he was alive.

But he faced new problems. He was certainly no closer to his goal. Eno guessed he probably lost a couple hundred yards or more. And the green giant and his domino friends now lay directly in his path to the stockpile. More delay, he thought. He checked his battery supply: two and three-quarter hours of heat. That's sufficient to travel over five miles. He only had a bit over three to go.

A new ridge lay directly ahead. Taking the few steps to the edge, Eno saw a crevasse about three feet wide and three feet deep. On the other side was a section of ice more or less in one piece, sloping downward from where he stood, all the way to the green tower. Debris from the event slid down the sheet: chunks and splinters of ice, medium-sized boulders, and smaller rocks. He could wait a while and then start walking, or he could sled. Like the kids did in Idaho.

That is a dumb idea! he admitted to himself.

As he watched, an ice chunk the size of a couch slowly slid past, a boulder resting upon it.

"A sign," he said.

Eno chose a nearby chunk of ice the size of a seat cushion and maneuvered it to the edge of the slope. He climbed aboard. He could see a way through a crack between the pieces of the fallen tower. It looked wide enough to walk through. Using his boots as breaks and to steer, he made his way quickly along, making up valuable time.

In fifteen minutes, he reached the fallen tower. Eno left his sled. To his right was the opening he had seen between two pieces of the great beast. He walked through, trying to ignore the odd sounds coming from the one-hundred-foot walls of the dead spire. At any second, a sliver the size of *Explorer Eleven* could break off one of the immense pieces on either side of him and come crashing down. He quickened his pace.

Checking his sleeve readout as he moved on, he could see that the batteries charging the suit heaters held enough power for just under two and a half more hours of heat. The tower had delayed him, the sledding helped, but he had lost time overall. He had only a tad less than three miles to go.

As he emerged from the passage between the broken green hunks of the tower, he saw before him another incline, just like the one he previously descended. There was still debris sledding downward, but by now, only small pieces. He strained up the incline as quickly as possible, dodging the larger ice chunks skittering toward him, but the going was slow. What should have taken him thirty minutes to walk took an hour.

He had ninety minutes of heat left as he crested the slope. His goal appeared about two miles ahead. He had just enough heat to cover the distance, but he would only have thirty minutes to locate LV-487 and get inside before he froze to death.

That's cutting it a bit close, he thought to himself.

A warning tone blared inside his helmet. He quickly looked at his armband readout. "Battery low," the screen read, flashing the words in dull orange. He expected that. The suit was programmed to let the wearer know when there was less than ninety minutes of battery left.

To his horror, the warning script changed and revealed the remaining minutes: sixty.

"What?"

How could this be? he asked himself. What had happened? Did I lose track of time? No, the band shows that I've been on the surface for only two and a half hours. How could this happen?

A hole in the suit? No, if that was true, he would feel the cold against his skin. He felt along the front of the suit for damage. Nothing. He pressed on the sides, just above his waist. Wait. What was that? Something sticking out that shouldn't be. He grabbed it and pulled. Holding the object up to his helmet, he saw that he was gripping a thin dagger of ice about six inches long. Throwing it down, he felt along the area where he had removed the shard. He realized the problem: the dagger had missed his suit but punctured one of the battery packs.

His legs were beginning to feel cold. The damaged power pack must have been for the heater mounted near his lower extremities.

On land, he could cover four miles in an hour, easily. On this slick ice, half that. He had more than two miles to cover and an hour of heat before he froze to death. He began to run.

After a twenty-minute dash, his feet became numb, and his lower abdomen began to feel the cold. He walked for a bit to catch his breath, then started running again. Ahead he could clearly make out the rows of larger ships, and he ran in that direction. After another twenty minutes, the buzzer went off in his helmet. He checked his armband, though he knew the news would be bad. A red light flashed for a few seconds, followed by the readout: fifteen minutes.

Cold and exhausted, he stumbled to the first row of ships in the stockpile. He checked the battery. His quickened pace worked, gaining precious time to locate the ship. There were five minutes of heat remaining.

Eno could see numerals on the sides of some craft peeking through the ice or just above it. He ran down the aisle: LV-258, LV-211, and LV-290—they were parked in no numerical order whatsoever!

How many were there? He tried to remember. Thirty?

"I have no time for this!" he called out loud, now in a panic.

Feet and legs almost completely numb, he contorted his torso to keep himself moving forward. He trembled as he limped along, falling every few strides. Within another minute, he was unable to feel his fingers, and his arms were tingling. Each step taken was in agony, the biting bitterness like a thousand needles piercing his skin.

Frantic, he threw himself onward; he crawled from dark hulk to dark hulk, reading the numbers on the side of the ships. His mask began to ice up, the condensation freezing inside the helmet. He would soon be blind. A final tone from his readout let him know the truth: the batteries were dead. The whine of the warning tone itself faded to a weak screech, then a hiss, then nothing, as if the sound itself had frozen to death.

Eno stumbled; his only thought was that he had failed them all. He failed the new friends of the rebellion, he failed the poor Graćenta, and he failed Jee. Why? Why didn't he just stay on Earth? They were fine there. Instead, he and his stupid ideas of society and how everything needed a place and a position—it had caused his death and, more than likely, Jee's.

Shaking uncontrollably, he had only seconds before he became immobile. One more check, he thought, and crawled toward one last dark shape. A door on this ship was accessible from a snowdrift that rose five or six feet. He kneeled at the bottom and saw numbers above the door, but they were covered in ice. He glanced upward. Ofeétis had reached half-light, the wave of its glow coming over him, lighting his surroundings. A beam cut between two hulks to one side of him and fell on the door ahead. Through the ice, he saw the numbers: LV-487.

The discovery gave him a last bit of renewed energy. He clawed his way up the drift, slithering, scraping, pulling himself closer.

Once to the door, he reached in his pack and searched for the key. Where was it? Finally, he dumped the contents on the snow and snatched the black key as it tried to roll away.

With numb fingers and trembling hands, he lifted the key, inserted the metal prongs into the panel on the edge of the door. He twisted the device one way, then the other. A click. A light glowed red on the panel. Almost immediately, water began running down the door. The key had activated powerful heaters. The ice surrounding the door and on the lock was melting quickly. A humming noise was heard, followed by a whirring sound.

Eno watched as the entrance struggled to open, then finally, with a groan and a grumble, double doors separated with a *BANG!* Shards of the remaining ice flew in all directions.

Before him was a small room with another door just a few feet beyond. It must be a heat-lock, he thought. Of course! Opening the door activated an air-lock area that also prevented heat loss! The room was heating up!

Eno, with a last bit of effort, rolled himself inside and lay on the floor. The outer door slowly closed behind him with a thud. All light was extinguished, except the dull red glow from the heaters mounted on the ceiling.

In a moment, he could feel the warmth returning to his body, and he was able to clumsily remove his helmet. He then tapped a message into his spectrogram-capable ABC: 'Alive in LV-487'. He sent it to Alíthe, who would relay it to the others.

"I could really use a hot cup of coffee," he said to himself.

21
Slagger's

Slagger's was a crusty watering hole located in the small seaside town of Point Rey, just east of the Ultos Wing base. The small, grungy town existed for two purposes: it had a fishing fleet of twenty or so gorphus boats, and it was close to Ultos Base—and the pilots and their money.

Breegan Arkéta had arrived early to the club and sat alone at a table in the back. After the message she received on her now spectrogram-capable ABC, she knew Eno successfully made the trip to the surface, and she was to continue her mission. Breegan reminded herself to watch what she said, not *tell* anyone what to do, what to decide, or even what to think. They would need to come to their own conclusions based on the video—if she even decided to show them the video. If she couldn't convince them, she would probably be arrested and executed.

The staff of Slagger's knew Breegan well. After a short welcome and some polite questions about her ordeal at the hands of the Enária, they left her alone with her order, a double *Topkick* on chunked ice.

Looking out the large window behind the bar, Breegan saw that the Firstsun was as dark as usual. However, the glow from the surrounding plants and trees and the bay beyond lit the scene well—for now. It was starting to cloud over, and a few raindrops struck the window, leaving slender finger-like trails slowly flowing to the bottom. Under a tarp-like overhang, a group of older pilots sat outside at a large table on the deck: the able-bodied *Ancients,* as they were called.

Now all-but dismissed from the AMF, these were the retired-reserve pilots of the Ultos Wing. They had served their time and now were mostly ignored by the administration and on one-third pay. Proud, yet bitter at times, they mixed with the younger crowd, offering advice and accepting a free round whenever offered. The younger pilots and crews looked up to the Ancients, and many helped the old heroes however they could.

Breegan recognized one of the Ancients immediately. Though they had never met, First Officer Pédaltee was known to all the pilots in the AMF. An unmistakable figure, Pédaltee was tall and thin with dark piercing eyes, a long dark mane, and wore a black air troop jacket, black flight suit, and black boots. She was famous, mainly due to her actions in her A2 Gunship Number 006 during the Tar Fortus war. She had the highest kill total in the history of the entire AMF Air Division. Due to her surgically accurate flying and gunning, along with her knowledge of flawless air-to-air tactics, she had earned her nickname: "The Knife."

As reliable as Pédaltee's flying, so was her appearance every night at Slagger's.

The two women nodded to each other in recognition.

It was almost time for her second target to arrive: the Wings of Glasśigh First Fighter group, to which she had been previously assigned. They would take a wheeled transport across the rickety bridge from Ultos base and Shay Point, park, and walk noisily through the door in a few seconds, as they did most nights. She watched the time click away and then heard a vehicle pull into the lot. They were here.

"It's true!" bellowed a tall, lanky man in uniform after he busted through the doorway. "Pilot Breegan Arkéta lives!"

"Hey, Kamário," she said calmly.

As the others poured in, they surrounded her, playfully shaking, hugging, touching foreheads, and laughing. A hundred questions were being thrown all at once. She tried to remain her usual, quiet, unassuming self. Yet Breegan could not help but feel the joyous connection with these twenty, her brothers and sisters. Though they were not at war and had never been in her lifetime, they had survived training together, flight school, and spent endless hours in their A4 Fighters and Katíga Rocker Bombers chatting, flying, and loving every minute of it. Most of them came from similar backgrounds—their families were Mercénta. They had enough money to enjoy life and attend decent schools where they had progressed to the secondary levels. They could then make the choice of working with their family or family friends in various businesses, or, if that sounded uninteresting, they could join the AMF, have parents call in some favors, and end up in an air wing.

"Give her a minute!" yelled Kamário. He was the oldest member of the group and bossed them around as if he owned the entire wing. He was only a Second Officer but a fantastic pilot who looked after his people. Everyone, including Breegan, naturally followed his lead.

"Pilot Zinno," commanded Kamário. "Get Second Officer Breegan another of those Topkicks. In fact, Topkicks for everyone! I'm buying!"

"Yes, sir!" answered Zinno. "Expo Force! To the spigot!" He and several other pilots swarmed the bar and began collecting drinks.

Kamário plopped down next to Breegan, pushing a few other pilots out of the way to take a seat immediately next to her. The questions for her kept coming, and soon Kamário stood up to take control once again.

"Hey! Stop gabbing on the poor woman! Instead of attacking her like a swarm of *ango bugs*, let's wait until we are all seated, and she can tell us together."

The expo group had returned with the first order of drinks as the pilots pulled up chairs and whatever else they could find to sit on. They arranging themselves around Breegan.

Officer Pédaltee had come in from the outside deck. Though still standing at the bar, she eyed the gathering with all her attention.

"It is great to see you all," Breegan said as she turned her gaze back to her friends. "I want to—"

"A toast!" yelled Kamário. They stood and held glasses straight out in front, pointed at the toastee, as was the custom. "To Second Pilot Breegan Arkéta! Best pilot in the entire wing. Luckiest pilot as well. The chosen one to fly *the Glasśigh*—"

Cheers and hoots.

"—around the tar in a Type-G, no less—"

More cheers and smiles of admiration.

"—and stay at expensive Kořeefa-only resorts while she plies the *Wing Commander* for favors—"

Out-and-out howling.

"—and one tough lady!"

"*Haaaar-nick!*" they called in unison and drained their glasses.

Zinno and his team were sent for a second round. Soon, all twenty pilots were re-seated, attentive, and eager to hear the tale.

Breegan recounted the events of the morning they visited the Kryménos Falls, the destruction of the three Aréus A3 Gunships from the TSP air group, and the communication with the leader of the Enária, and his sneaky move of attaching a tracking device on the side of the Type-G. She told of maneuvering into the secret door under the falls and then their first impression of the cave.

"Did they hurt you?" asked one of the pilots. "What did you tell them?"

"The Enária weren't after information. They wanted to use us to get supplies from the Taźath. I was mostly kept alone and then released. No big issues. Really."

"But were you afraid?" asked another.

"No," she replied. "But I learned a lot about them and what they want."

"They're a bunch of lazy, dirty—"

"No," interrupted Breegan, "not really. I have to tell you, they work hard, just as hard as we do. They gave a lot of food to needy people, or that is what I overheard. They were fair to us."

"Then when will they release Commander Afiéro? And Eno Ćlaviath?" asked another.

"I don't know," she said. "Soon, I hope. I believe they will come to no harm."

Suddenly it all seemed a bit boring. No torture, no nastiness, no exciting escapes. Just a sleepover. That was it. They knew that the Taźath had met the demands of the Enária, claiming it was for the safe return of his citizens. All agreed in principle.

The pilots scattered about the club, returning to their normal modes of relaxation. Pédaltee lingered at the bar. Only Kamário remained with Breegan.

"So that's it?" he asked.

"Yes, pretty much."

Kamário took a long pull from his drink. "I don't believe you."

"Why not?" asked Breegan. She kept her eyes glued to his, not only looking for a sign of his willingness to consider her still unexpressed proposition but to let him know that she indeed had more to tell. If he were to pry a bit, he might get at it.

"Well, firstly, their demands were just stupid. Food? They raid transports all the time to get food."

"I don't know," said Breegan. She took a sip of her Topkick. "You going to buy *me* some food? Gorphus on toasted sweed?"

"And how come they let the prize possession go first?"

"Me?" she asked, batting the lashes of her beautiful golden eyes.

"The Glasśigh," he clarified, smiling. "Something is up. Tell me. What really happened?"

"It's above your grade, Second Officer," she warned. "How about that gorphus?"

"I outrank *you*," he countered.

"Not anymore. See this medal?" Breegan pointed to the new gold-winged piece pinned on the chest of her uniform. "I am, as of yesterday, a First Officer, as per Minister Commander Kalífus. So you can take your puny little silver wings and—"

"Hey, all right!" he relented, slightly wounded. "Congratulations."

Breegan realized she may have pushed it a bit hard. It was time to relax. They sat in silence for a minute before she tried again.

"That's Pédaltee at the bar, staring at us, right?" she continued.

"The Knife? Yes, that's her."

"How well do you know her?"

"I know all the Ancients," Kamário said. "We play Gorb's Bug Mash in the park every other Lastsun. We bring them extra stuff. Those pensions they get don't cover a third of what they need."

"Do you trust her? I mean, with your life?" asked Breegan. "I assume she is a staunch supporter of the Tażath?"

Kamário let out a sigh. "She has no love for Pronómio Tok. They used her then forgot her. All the Ancients are a bit bitter. And yes, I trust her. Why?"

Breegan motioned for Pédaltee to join them. Surprised, Pédaltee grabbed another *Topkick* from the bar, walked to Breegan's table, and sat down.

"I need to speak with you both," said Breegan

"And why is that?" asked Pédaltee, coldly.

"Because…not everything is exactly as it's made out to be," stated Breegan, sipping her drink.

"Go on," Pédaltee said.

"What if I told you that we are being lied to?"

Kamário scrunched up his face. "By whom?"

"By some people pretty high up," Breegan answered. "About the Enária and what is going on in Éhpiloh."

"I try to stay out of that," said Kamário, becoming quiet.

"Fine then," continued Breegan. "But I saw things that I can't just ignore. If you want to live in a fantasy, go ahead. I just hope you don't have any love for the Glasśigh."

"What is that supposed to mean?" he probed, now interested.

"What if I showed you proof that the events at Targan Base, the story we were told, is a complete lie?"

"The *Explorer Eleven* stuff?" asked Pédaltee.

"Yes. And it is way wilder than you can even imagine," she said. "And I know because I saw the evidence. Commander Eno Ćlaviath was there—'

"Really?" Kamário asked sarcastically. "We know that."

"There's a lot you don't know," Breegan went on, returning to silence for a moment.

Kamário looked around the club. He knew Breegan wasn't one to make up things or believe what others told her. She wouldn't even play tricks on the other pilots for fun. She was always the smart one, the thinker. If she was upset about something, it was something worth being upset about.

"You know, Breegan," Kamário began, "if you have something to say, then just say it and quit playing me. I know you. You don't get upset over anything unless it's really important. What do you and

Commander Eno know?"

Breegan moved in close to them. Her mane was tinged gray at the edges: fear.

"If I show you something," Breegan whispered slowly and deliberately, "I could be killed. Alíthe Afiéro and Commander Ćlaviath could be killed. *The Glasśigh* could be killed, do you understand? I am taking a big chance here. What I will show you—it will change your world. Are you sure you want to go there?"

Kamário looked at Pédaltee for a sign. She seemed hesitant yet interested. After a moment, she nodded in affirmation.

"If the Glasśigh is in danger—" Kamário replied, "if *you* are in danger—I want to help."

"Let's see what you have," said The Knife.

"Then follow me," ordered Breegan.

Kamário and Pédaltee stood and followed Breegan out the door. Outside, clouds gathered, dark ones that promised rain. They jumped into the troop carrier the group had taken from the base and sat in the front seat. Breegan activated her armband, took a portable mini drive out of her pocket, and activated its local network connection. The video that Eno had compiled played in 2D.

"This is the original video file of the attack on *Explorer Eleven*. It was taken by the Targan Base tower security cameras."

"I've seen this a hundred times," Kamário said.

Breegan stared at them both. "What you haven't seen—is this—the images taken from *Explorer Eleven's* capture system."

They watched intently as the video showed the scene from *Explorer*. Both took a quick breath when they saw the YSP tattoos revealed from under the sleeves of the gunmen.

When it was over, Kamário was silent. Pédaltee stared out the windshield as the rain began to fall.

Breegan allowed them a moment to process this new information. She knew they understood what they had just seen and what it meant. Did they believe it? How did they feel about it?

"Did you test this for alteration?" Pédaltee asked.

"Yes, as soon as I got back to my room at the base. I ran the seventeen algorithms. Twice. It's real. A YSP team carried out the attack that killed Tye Ćlaviath and Dypónia Aséllo. They killed the Éstargonian explorers and almost killed Commander Eno and the Glasśigh."

"I've no love for the Tażath," admitted Pédaltee with a growl. "I've seen things in the war. Things I never could explain. I was with the YSP in Oso-Gúrith when Kalífus, the *góhmar-faced chib-nob*, ran it.

Bombing tests were carried out on Graćenta, living in the cave cities. I couldn't prove it…"

"So would it be too much of a stretch for you to believe this little tidbit? All those attacks supposedly carried out by the Enária Front? They were really instigated by the Taźath and the TSP."

Kamário took in a deep breath and released it slowly. "How do you know that?"

"Every response to an Enária attack happened within three days before a vote of confidence," Breegan answered. "Not every vote, but every attack. Listen to me: the Enária have never had more than old weapons, and very few. They have four, maybe five hundred soldiers at the most. They don't pick fights with the all-powerful Gákoh Kalífus! They are out-gunned twenty to one, and that's not even counting the technological disadvantage they have. The Enária's main strategy is to raid transports and warehouses for food and medical supplies. They give them to the poor who live in the northern tar. In the caves that *we* bombed!"

This made both pilots pause.

"Are you saying that the Taźath picks fights with them—to what? Make himself more...needed?" Kamário asked.

"If he thinks he will look bad on a vote, yes! And the biggest fake was the arena attack." Breegan showed them the video of the attack, narrating the essential points. "The laser, you see here, is clearly targeting *Explorer*, not the stage or the Glasśigh or Eno. The Klaymac would have done more damage than what appeared."

"But the force field!" Kamário objected. "Commander Kalífus said the force field was turned on!"

"Kamário!" blurted Pédaltee. "Use your brain! How could Eno and the Glasśigh exit the craft while the force field on? "Do you think someone turned it back on after they left the ship? And why in the name of Kryménos would anyone do—"

"All right! All right!" Kamário growled as the truth slammed him in the face.

Breegan allowed a moment for reality to sink in. "It was a flash shell."

"Makes sense," muttered Pédaltee.

"It does," said Kamário, resignation in his voice. "This goes all the way to the Taźath?"

"Yes. And the things going on in Éhpiloh are just as bad. Remember when Commander Afiéro took the Glasśigh on that little joy ride? Do you know what really happened?

"I bet you know," stated Pédaltee.

"I do," confirmed Breegan. "They went to Éhpiloh. The Enária had an unlicensed drone follow them. I saw the video. The Glasśigh was trying to stop mass executions! She stood right in front of a squad of AMF troops, with guns pointed at her! She stood in the way of pulseguns and guarded innocent people! She freed a train full of children who were being taken from their parents! She said kids are being used as slaves! Graćenta are being killed in the streets if they are suspected of being Enária. Worse, I saw mass graves in the hills by Folvos. Piles, Kamário! Piles of children by the hundreds."

"Breegan," Kamário managed to say, his voice shaking as his mane now flashed, alternating between gray with fear and gold with sadness.

"When the Enária kidnapped us? It was a cover," Breegan continued. "The Glasśigh's servant arranged a meeting. The Glasśigh wanted to speak to them."

"What?" Kamário exclaimed.

Breegan shook her head. "Make the leaps, Kamário! The Glasśigh saw this same video of Targan Base! After conversations with the Enária leaders—that I was part of firsthand—we all, all of us captives, decided to join the Enária!"

Pédaltee laughed out loud.

"This is really crazy," Kamário said. "Eno and Commander Afiéro? They are also Enária?"

"And the Glasśigh," added Breegan.

"Unbelievable," said Pédaltee, still laughing.

"If you think I am insane or a liar, then turn me in. But this whole country is built on a pack of lies. Pronómio Tok and Gákoh Kalífus are murderers. It's time for all of us to choose a side. And I am on the side of truth, and compassion, and the Glasśigh. Are you?"

"I am stunned…" Kamário mumbled.

"What do you want from us?" asked Pédaltee.

"The Ancients need to be re-activated," said Breegan. "And I need as many Wings of Glasśigh pilots as we can trust."

22
Asello's Dream

In the heat-lock of Light Container Ship LV-487, Eno's first order of business had been to thaw out. Then he entered the ship and set about finding the power grid, re-connected it, calibrated and charged the fuel cells, and started the air generators. As lights and additional heaters came online, he searched and found additional power packs, food rations, the engine room, the small flight deck, the flight manual, and a warm place to sleep. Best of all, he found not only a storage bin that contained keys to all vehicles in the stockpile but the ultimate prize: one hundred and thirty cold gear suits. These far surpassed the range and ability of the old one he had worn during his ordeal. Next to the cold suits were a few dozen high-powered portable torch heaters and thermal tents to cover the ships. All he needed to do now was return to the tar and bring pilots and support staff back to suit up and free the ice-bound craft.

Though the plan was to use LV-487 to return to Tar Asello, there was no way he, alone, could free it from the amount of ice surrounding the craft. He needed a ship that was easy to get loose and could transfer the personnel to the surface. In his exploration of the vast container ship, he discovered a one-man surface vehicle: Mobile Traktor 5. This he could use to quickly inspect the stockpile.

Over the next few days, Eno took the traktor and began to explore and evaluate the area. Most of the smaller Voźeeth Fighters were only somewhat buried; others were buried entirely. Only two LVs could easily be extricated, but it would take a significant effort involving the entire team and all the heat torches. The LVs would have to wait.

He also found Personnel Transport Ship 10. This discovery was fortuitous for three reasons. Firstly, it was a troopship and, therefore, would easily transport the Front soldiers to and from the surface to the floor of any tar and back. Secondly, and better yet, it was built to safely dock with an LV, so his new passengers needn't don thermal gear to enter! Lastly, and best of all, *PT-10* was only buried in a few inches of ice that was mainly on the rear next to the heat-generating exhaust ports.

Over the following week, Eno created a map of the stockpile and cataloged each ship by type and effort needed to de-ice. He also set a tent over the rear of PT-10 and activated two of the bulky heat torches to begin the thaw.

On his sixth day, he was ready to leave. He piloted Mobile Traktor Number 5 along the surface of Áhtha in a straight line to PT-10. As he drove the clunky vehicle, Eno happily sang to himself, mostly tunes remembered from Earth: *Buttons and Bows* (doing his best Dina Shore), *It's Magic* (he felt his and Doris Day's voice were identical—he was wrong), and *Four Leaf Clover* (actually, he was good with this one, it being a bar-room, drunken romp good for those with little tone, or those who were tone-deaf). As his niece told him years ago he wasn't half-bad as a singer, he was *all the way bad.*

Eno checked the time—he was right on schedule. He moved the traktor to the other side of the path and made his way to the flight deck of PT-10.

"Here goes nothing!" he said aloud.

He ignited the engines. The ship jostled and shook as Eno applied more power. He then engaged the hoverjets. Though the remaining ice was melting from the ship's exhaust, the jet turbines barely moved.

"More juice," he said and applied additional power.

The ship groaned. The engine's whine rose in tone. The shaking increased. A stress alarm sounded. Eno checked the readout: 'approaching hull integrity limit.'

"*Approaching,* not exceeding," Eno clarified and applied a bit more fuel. More ice cracked as the ship struggled to break free. The left side of the craft suddenly shook loose in an explosion of ice and vapor. The vessel listed to the right. The alarm sounded again. Eno checked the readout: "exceeding stress limit."

"Come on!" he growled, increasing the power just a smidge more.

The ship shook violently.

Finally, the hoverjets began to spin faster.

"That's it!" Eno cried as he set the jets to fifty percent. "Just a bit more!"

In an explosive bang, the ship broke free of the ice, lifting away from the surface. Eno quickly reduced power to three percent, but not before PT-10 flew at an angle, smashing its right side into the antenna tower of a nearby LV, clipping it in half.

"Oops!" Eno said, but to his pleasure, the alarms ceased.

He checked the panel before him. Engines reported normal, doors sealed, hull integrity just slightly below normal. Good enough. The ship stabilized and hovered at ten feet. He increased thrust to seventy, and PT-10 rose quickly, straight upward to one hundred feet.

"Walk in the park! Oh, I do love those Earth maxims!" He adjusted the engines to horizontal. PT-10 started forward slowly but soon was streaking through the thin atmosphere above the ice shelf.

As he sped toward the fálouse, Eno noticed a dark swirling maelstrom in the far distance: an *Ágviost Blizzard*. Most storms on the surface formed in the same manner—quickly cooling moisture vented up from within the tars and froze almost immediately, turning to snow. But when excessive evaporation was forced to the surface, enormous clouds many times the typical size gathered quickly, and super-events like Ágviost Blizzards occurred. Eno remembered one from his earlier study on the surface. Though these storms traveled across the moon's surface slowly, dangerous, unpredictable winds inside the storm could reach almost two hundred miles an hour. 'Flakes' of snow the size of one's hand fell down, and temperatures dropped. All one could do was wait until they passed, then dig their way out.

The storm would not interfere with his flight today; however, it would reach the stockpile in a day or two at most.

Not good, he thought.

In less than an hour, Eno had flown PT-10 through the fálouse, just to the southwest corner of the Falls of Caymana. Streaking down to the bottom of the tar, he headed east, hugging the wave tops of the sea. It was stormy today, and the drafts rocked the ship in all directions. Though Eno was an experienced pilot, he was new to this craft and needed to concentrate. He entered the towers of Pégra Pygréez, in the far western edge of the Caymana Straight. There were over a thousand of the quarter-mile-high stone giants peppered throughout the sea, hindering his way. However, the deeper he advanced into the field of towers, the less wind draft he experienced. Soon he was effortlessly maneuvering the ship through the pervasive pillars of stone. A steady rain continued to fall.

"Surface ship! Identify yourself."

The crackling of the AM radio surprised Eno, causing him to almost leap out of his seat. After avoiding a collision with one of the towers and calming himself, he responded, using the spectrogram system.

"Eno."

"It's about time," came Orgo's familiar tone. *"I was starting to think you sort of liked it up there, all alone."*

Eno smiled. "It's nice to hear another voice. Besides the ones in my head."

Orgo chuckled. *"Land on the second tower to your left, if you please. Salǵeea awaits. Welcome to the hidden stronghold of the Enária Front—once again."*

Eno landed the PT on top of a specific tower in the center of the channel, as instructed. There was Salǵeea, scanning the horizon to the east, along with several Front soldiers performing the same task.

"Greetings, Salǵeea Calćoa!" called Eno as he stepped off the PT.

Salǵeea set down his VED and walked to Eno. "How was your holiday?" he asked with a laugh as they touched foreheads. Both manes turned red at the edges.

"The weather was a bit chilly, but all in all, not too bad," Eno said. "The issue is the *upcoming* weather. I saw storms forming on the surface. An Ágviost Blizzard, surely. The storm will cause delays, I am sure of it. And communication will be impossible. No one can fly through the rough weather from the surface to the tar."

"That is unfortunate," commented Salǵeea dejectedly.

"Have the pilots arrived?" asked Eno.

"Not yet," said Salǵeea. "We still have time. But we have not been idle. We have trained almost fifty aircraft maintenance workers for duty at the stockpile. They are excited to be part of this plan, even though they are conscious of the dangerous work."

"Up there, well, it is no vacation to Aséllo's Garden Resort, I can tell you that," Eno added.

"I thank you, my friend," Salǵeea said soberly. "It was a stroke of luck having you join our side."

Eno smiled, nodding his head slightly. "I had no choice, really…"

"The Taźath pushed you into it, then? With his threats?"

"Somewhat," replied Eno. "It was her. The Glasśigh. She can be quite persuasive. And she is the only family I have left. As you know."

"She has an effect on people," agreed Salǵeea. "I'm counting on it."

They both gazed east toward the opening between the Pégra Pygréez and further to the Caymana Strait.

"Salǵeea, what is that gray cloud there?" Eno asked.

"Where?"

Eno pointed ahead and down toward the surface of the water. "Just emerging from the main channel."

Salǵeea grabbed his VED and looked toward the opening of the channel below. "Oh no!"

"Hmmm," muttered Eno. "This is either good news, or the end of the Front."

There was a formation: a full flight of twenty Aréus in attack formation. Behind them, another five rocket-bombers and two large support ships.

Salǵeea dropped his VED and brought his armband upwards.

"Base, this is tower three! Incoming unidentified craft! Repeat: unidentified craft approaching. Do not fire upon unless they engage. It looks like a flight of Aréus A3s plus support and landing craft! Issue scatter command and activate sirens."

Immediately, the wail of the eerie warning sirens echoed through the passages and off the stone towers.

"We need to get off this tower," Eno said. "Quick! Board the PT-10?"

They ran to the craft. Eno fired up the engines as the newcomers buckled in.

"Lifting off."

A stream of plasma from a pulse weapon struck the ground near the transport. The radio crackled.

"Ugly transport craft! Stand down or be destroyed!" came the voice of a female pilot. Then a laugh.

Aréus Fighters streaked toward the PT at incredible speed but quickly slowed and switched to hover as if lining up to land.

Eno quickly noticed the emblem on the wings.

"I knew it," said Eno with a smile. "Second Officer Breegan Arkéta!"

"Yes, however, it is First Officer *Arkéta now,"* she informed them. *"Kalífus promoted me. He thinks the wing is on a sweep of the area, looking for the Enária Front. Did I find it?"*

Salǵeea came forward to the flight deck from the cargo hold, smiling broadly. Laughing, he called, "Yes, we surrender!

"I'll drop off these cranky old doad-faced pilots I have in my transport, and then we take off immediately. We have a total of forty-one."

"Are the Ancients still capable?" asked Salǵeea.

"Of course," said Breegan. *"They are retired, not dead! They will fly those old Éstargonian junk clusters for you."*

"And your active wing?" asked Eno.

"We got who we trusted," Breegan continued. *"More will join us, I am sure. But for now, to be safe, we have fifty-seven. Salǵeea, you now have an air force."*

"You are a wonder," called out Salǵeea, almost breaking into tears.

"Then let us land and drop off the Ancients so we can get back before Kalífus thinks I did something stupid like join your pitiful party."

"Which you did," said Salǵeea.

"Which I did," agreed Breegan.

On a clear Firstsun, Pronómio Tok and Gákoh Kalífus stood on a landing pad attached to the main auditorium of the Hall of Ministers Building in central Etáin. They smiled and nodded to the crowd of ministers and other voting dignitaries as they filed out of the chamber and headed toward their private cars and skyliners. Pronómio held his emotions in check. He could hear the murmurs of both elation and discontent coming after the twentieth vote of confidence held during his reign.

Once alone, they walked swiftly and purposefully toward the Tażath's waiting luxury skyliner. Only now did both manes flash deep blue in anger.

"That was a close one, Pronómio," reflected Kalífus as they entered the liner. "You remained in office by only twenty percent of the confidence vote. I would have thought that the successful release of the Glasśigh would have helped you."

"It probably did!" exploded Pronómio in a burst of anger. "It would have been closer if it wasn't for her arrival in Induláy! Zola said that his information shows many Kořeefa fear more violence by the Enária, and more kidnappings. They also are afraid for Commander Ćlaviath and the pilot!"

If it were up to Kalífus, he would be done with the Enária Front, hunt them all down, kill them, and let the political future be what it will. He was tired of it. And the Glasśigh? A problem since she returned to Áhtha. Kalífus believed that things were better when everyone thought she and Eno were dead. Now, he and Pronómio were being criticized for allowing her to be kidnapped. And though the Glasśigh was recovered, Eno was still in captivity.

Back at the Palace Leadership Center, Pronómio and Kalífus returned to the main conference room to strategize. But before they began, there was a buzz at Pronómio's ABC. He pressed the answer space on his screen.

"The Glasśigh and the artist Veegill are here, Tażath," announced an aide.

He had forgotten. "Show them to the main conference room," he said with a sigh.

"The Glasśigh?" asked Kalífus. "Now?"

"And the artist. She requested a meeting last week. She has some ideas, whatever that may mean."

Upon entering the conference room, Kalífus and Pronómio were stunned at the Glasśigh's appearance. She wore a blue dress that came in at her waist to then drape straight down off her hips and fell just past her knees. The fabric was light, silk-like, and transparent at the ends of the hemline. The dress moved like a breeze as she walked.

Pronómio stood and moved quickly to her side, almost knocking Veegill over in his rush to greet the woman. "Our Glasśigh! Always a pleasure! And that outfit—truly stunning! You look as if you are about to address the Ministers at the Yearly Summit of Warrenites!"

"Oh, that sounds too scary for me, but thank you," replied Jee modestly. She bowed slightly.

The Taźath could see that her eyes were red, her face flush. She seemed a bit nervous. His mane flashed a sincere and full gold, expressing his sadness and concern. When she appeared vulnerable like this, how could anyone not want to assist her? Pronómio wondered. And when her eyes filled with tears, and she opened them wide, the Glasśigh looked even more beautiful than ever.

Pronómio had a problem now. He desired her, and it took all his will to restrain the showing of purple in his mane. His mind was filled with thoughts of passion, but to show his feelings would be a mistake, at least at this juncture. As was his practice, he thought of another emotion. In this case, confusion would work.

But as his mane turned from gold to orange, a slight flash of purple appeared. The Taźath was unaware. However, Jee noticed and kept the observation to herself.

"Are you…are you well, my dear?" he asked.

Jee looked down in embarrassment.

"If I may, my Taźath?" asked Veegill. He paused from unpacking his boxes. "The Glasśigh is distraught. She worries for her uncle and her friend, Commander Alíthe."

That broke her. The crying began.

"Kalífus!" ordered Pronómio forcefully, "please be useful and get some water for the Glasśigh!"

Shocked at the command, as if he were some kind of waiter or servant, Kalífus was prodded into action.

The Taźath held her close and tried to comfort her, but the tears continued to fall. She shook uncontrollably, and even when trying to drink the water Kalífus offered, she had trouble holding the glass steady. It was a full minute before she could speak.

"I am sorry, Taźath. I am such a bother."

"Not at all, not at all," he responded. "I understand. We are doing everything we can to ensure the safe return of your uncle and Commander Afiéro. You have my word."

She smiled, her eyes still watery.

"So, what is this you have brought?" asked Pronómio in a lively tone.

"It is a project, my Taźath," she answered, rallying.

Together, Jee and Veegill placed an ABC on the large stone council table. Jee then stood at attention, cleared her throat, then turned to face the Taźath.

Veegill started the presentation. A holographic image was projected on the table: Madam Khileetéra.

"A problem," said Jee flatly.

Another image appeared: Salǵeea Calćoa.

"The tool of the problem," Jee said.

A third image now appeared: the Glasśigh at the Arena of Aséllo, upon her arrival. She stood before the throng of adoring Kośeefa.

"The solution," she continued with a smile. "How do you stay in power and get rid of the Enária and the opposition?"

"Tell us," murmured Kalífus.

"That last vote of confidence is a warning," she posed. "Something has to change, my Taźath. Madam Khileetéra is *gaining* support, not losing it. And she is using the Graćenta and the unrest caused by the Enária to seed her victory. Unless we take away her cause."

"And how do we do that?" asked Pronómio.

"We have a saying on Earth. One gets more flies with sweets than with salt."

"What is a fly?" asked Kalífus.

"A pesky insect, but in this case, votes of confidence. With all respect, Taźath, you are handing this government over to Madam Khileetéra. We must take away her cause."

"I am listening," said Pronómio, now slightly intrigued.

"Veegill?" prompted Jee.

The image on the hologram changed to various pictures of Graćenta working in the dusty fields, dim-lit factories, toiling in shops and kitchens. Other images were of laborers returning home to dingy apartments, completing their household chores in run-down buildings with small, dirt-field yards.

"Not much of a life," she said.

"That is what they are for. It is their role," retorted Kalífus tersely.

"True, and it will forever be," Jee acknowledged. "Until Madam Khileetéra wins and frees them. But what if you, Pronómio Tok, gave Graćenta what the Enária Front is giving them: food, medicine, and hope? Give them choice and a vote."

"Preposterous!" thundered Kalífus.

"Is it?" asked Jee. "If you were their savior, Pronómio, and you gave a little, that would end the Front. And it would end Madam

Khileetéra's cause. It would also open up trade with Tar Éstargon. And the riches would roll in. Just by giving a little sweetness instead of salt."

Pronómio took a breath. This was getting interesting. "How do you propose we turn me into the savior of the wretched?" he asked.

"You give them a dream!" Jee said excitedly. "Through the careful use of propaganda!"

"Propa-ganda?" asked Pronómio.

"An Earth term," she explained. "It is the use of communications, like short phrases, posters, artwork, videos, broadcasts, to influence people to support your agenda—"

"We do that," interrupted Kalífus. "The 'Know Your Place' banners."

"These?" asked Jee.

Veegill changed the image on the hologram to show one of the banners.

"Honestly, my Taźath," Jee said, fixing her gaze on the man, "this will inspire no one to think of you as a savior. It is oppressive and ugly, to say it nicely. We need to present information and facts selectively, through clear and simple language and images that are *easy to understand and repeat!* We want to produce a *positive emotional response* rather than a rational one. We want to move people to action! Veegill, show them!"

The image changed to a banner being unfurled, displaying a stylized farm field, with a man and a woman holding baskets filled with fruit. They were looking up at the full glow of Ofeétis, proud and happy. They both appeared to be fit and strong. Their children were at their side, holding hands. Above the image were the words 'Asélło's Dream'. Another banner appeared on the hologram, this time of a light brown-colored arm raised toward the sky, forefinger extended. The exact same 'Know Your Place' from Pronómio's poster appeared at the top, but below were the words 'Backbone of Tar Asélło!'

Pronómio and Kalífus were silent. They watched as more images appeared with the same type of message: a proud man working by some large machinery as his co-workers smiled, a woman happily tending to kitchen duties in a restaurant, children in a school learning to read a book. All looked happy. All looked proud. All knew their place.

"The study of propaganda teaches us that we can never make people believe something they do not already believe," Jee instructed. "We must use what they already believe—to get them on our side. Remind them, let them know that we, the Kořeefa, see them as proud, hard-working, and valuable members of the society. The backbone. Because they believe that already."

"Interesting concept," said Pronómio.

"This costs nothing, really," Jee went on. "But to make it effective, you have to give them something else."

"Money?" asked Kalífus. "I knew it!"

"You already give them money—they get paid for working. And the fortune lost to the thieving Enária? The expense to track them down? Police them? It would be less expensive to hand the Enária the money! But they need something else. Something they can look forward to. In reality, simple things: a place to live and call their own. A better place in society—"

"No, that is not going to happen—" interrupted Kalífus.

"Let her finish," Pronómio scolded.

"I call it 'Aséllo Dream.'" Jee said, pausing. "Give them the ability to hope and dream of achieving something better for themselves, if it is reality or not! If they think they can move up in the world, own their home, achieve a dream, *an Aséllo Dream,* that is a powerful thing!"

Now on display was another stylized, simple video of ten or so people in a neat yard near a house or apartment building—it was purposely hard to tell which—maybe in a suburb of Éhpiloh. There was a small garden, and children played in a grassy area. Adults were at an outdoor table, eating with friends. A woman was exiting the home and taking off her work gloves as she came down a short flight of stairs as if she was returning from work to join the happy event. Below were the words 'Aséllo Dream – for all!'

"Give them just a little," added Jee. "You could let them 'own' their apartment, but there would be fees, of course. Let them join the military! Start a business without Kośeefa sponsors."

Pronómio was interested, but Kalífus saw something slipping away. She would watch him closely.

"The Kośeefa will not support that," said Kalífus. "They make too much money off the advisor role they play."

"More than they made off Tar Éstargon? If this opens relations with Tar Éstargon—" she paused again for effect.

"Then the increased trade will make them all rich once again," said Pronómio. "And there are many functions of the military that we are paying Merćenta to do, that we could have Graćenta do for less pay."

"They do not have the education," objected Kalífus.

"Then train them," suggested Jee. "Have them pay to be educated from the wages they will earn! Start a school for them! Take only the best!"

The Tażath smiled and nodded.

Jee knew she had him.

Time for the big sell.

"This next point will seem odd at first," Jee conceded, "but please hear me out. It was used so effectively after a great rebellion on Earth, in America, that the results were mind-blowing."

"Mind-blowing?" asked Pronómio.

"It worked very well," she explained. "Sorry. The point is—give them a representative voice in the government."

The Tażath was stunned. Kalífus exhaled loudly as if to say, 'and there it is! I knew it!'

"Listen to me," insisted Jee with authority. "Let them decide the things you don't really care about. Let them pick who the teachers will be in their schools. Let them choose between local magistrates that you have approved. Let them be part of it. Allow a few who will follow your instructions to rise higher, maybe a Merćenta level, to use as an example, to give hope."

"But not really," said Pronómio, understanding. He seemed deep in thought. After a while, he stood. "I am their enemy now, but I can become their savior."

"Their perceived savior," corrected Kalífus.

"Exactly right, Commander," said Jee with a smile. "On Earth, there was a phrase: perception is reality."

Jee let that sink in for a moment.

"Announce 'Aséllo's Dream' on the opening day of the Festival of Jaydí," she continued.

Images changed on the projector: the Tażath giving a speech, crowds cheering in Etáin and Éhpiloh, citizens happily cleaning up their yards, enjoying a dinner with friends, raising glasses in a salute, working joyfully in farm fields, factories, and public works facilities.

"First," announced Jee, "Veegill and I will create new video and imagery to be used all over the tar, like the ones you have just seen. Then, at the opening of the Festival of Jaydí, you announce Aséllo's Dream! I can help you write the speech! We will have you mention that the only way to progress as a society is to have new freedoms for all, even the Graćenta, and that you *need their help* to make these things happen! Tell them that if they work together, end strikes and raids, then these things can become a reality."

"Just one thing," said Kalífus. "It sounds so wonderful, but why would they believe us? Do you think the Graćenta, in their simple minds, comprehend what this means? It is too complicated for them. How do we ensure they agree and accept?"

Now she served up the final piece. "They will agree—if the Glasśigh tells them they should."

After another moment of silence, the Taźath let out a long hardy laugh.

Jee smiled. *Gotcha!* she thought.

"Propaganda!" Pronómio said between chuckles. "I love it!"

"Wait until I explain taxes!" she exclaimed with a laugh.

The conversation continued, not to persuade but to set the plan in motion. The timing would have to be perfect. Preparations for media of all types had to be designed and produced. Veegill and Jee were given access to Zola Názma and his resources.

At Jee's request, the plan would be kept secret. If word got out, they would not be ready. Rumors would spread. The Enária might also react unexpectedly. And Eno and Alíthe's life could be endangered further.

"I need to get Eno and Alíthe back, Taźath," Jee said as she packed up her things.

"We will," assured Pronómio. "This will ensure it!"

"We must work together, my Taźath," Jee said with a smile. "It will be long hours, but we can do this thing!"

Pronómio smiled at the thought of working closely with the Glasśigh.

23
The Festival of Jaydí

In the days of the clan kings and queens, the people of Tar Asėllo were not restricted by the plethora of laws created by an unjust and segregated society. Though separate groups grew and prospered in those ancient times, they all considered themselves a single people. They also shared willingly with each other.

Jaydí Ćlaviath, as an aging queen of the Asėllo clan, desired to celebrate this peaceful existence, and in doing so, created the longest and most anticipated tradition in Tar Asėllo, the Festival of Jaydí. Beginning at the final week of the Áhthan new year, towns and villages from all over the tar would gather wherever they could find space enough for all. Here they rejoiced in each other's company, sharing food, drink, and wares. Soon, the festival grew to include gift-giving, story-telling, contests of strength and skill, and exhibitions of artful crafts.

Of course, under the rule of the Taźaths, referred to as the 'modern age', the three classes never attended the festival *physically together in the same location*. That would be preposterous! Unthinkable! Laws were created to prohibit such a 'mixing' of the classes. And, the differences between the Kořeefa-attended festivals and, for example, the Graćenta festivals, were stark.

Now, in the Áhthan year of 1023, if Jaydí Ćlaviath could see what had become of her festival, she would not recognize it nor the people. Though food and drink were sold instead of given away, admission was charged, and the best of entertainment reserved for the Kořeefa only, it would be the radical divisions that existed between the Asėllians that would break her heart. Today's festival was not what she intended.

Regardless of its perversion, for over a thousand Áhthan years, the tradition continued. And though most had forgotten the initial purpose, all in the tar, from every walk of life, looked forward to the week-long celebration.

Leading up to the festival, several short videos were shown between all media broadcasts. Just like the images Jee had presented to the Taźath, each piece contained the stylized animation of the 'Backbone of Asėllo,' the Graćenta, looking proud and happy. The videos announced that the Taźath was granting freedoms, the Glasśigh would speak and sing, and 'Asėllo's Dream' was available for everyone. Jee insisted on these 'messages' being shown frequently.

Veegill's workers in Etáin and Éhpiloh had done an excellent job in preparation. His team completed the construction of over a thousand immense banners and frames to be placed around the more populated areas of the tar. Posters were also placed on the sides of buildings, windows of stores, schools, and almost any flat surface where they could be seen in public. All were colorful and displayed the new images of the Graćenta: noble, hardworking, and enjoying life.

The Arena of Asėllo was arranged much like it had been the night of the Glasśigh's arrival, except for the new banners hung on the stadium's outer walls. They stretched from the highest points down to street level. More were hung inside, next to the gigantic display screens.

To hold the Graćenta, a series of naturally formed steppes in the hilly areas north of Éhpiloh were chosen. The Terraces, it was called, being several flat, naturally formed fields, each almost a quarter-mile wide and half as deep. They were located northwest of the city against the northern tar wall. Together, their grass-filled plateaus covered over five square miles.

On the highest terrace was a stage similar in space to the one in the arena. The only difference was the distinctive bright, red rock of the northern tar wall being clearly visible behind the stage. Veegill had lit the rock with white light to accentuate the bold color. In front of it were sturdy frames for banners, display screens, and lighting equipment. The crowd could watch the proceedings from the area in front of the stage and via large screens placed on all terraces. They would enjoy games, drum performances, and reasonably priced food, all supplied by the Taźath.

In both locations, the center of the stage had the backdrop of the well-known, ubiquitous black banner of the Taźath, displaying his symbol and the phrase 'Know Your Place.'

The Glasśigh's presentation was to take less than thirty minutes. Still, since there would be a holographic broadcast in the Terraces alongside the live broadcast in the Arena of Asėllo, coordination had to be perfect. Crews were hired to assist in both cities. It was a massive effort, rehearsed at least a dozen times.

Best of all, the Taźath had approved and paid for the entire event. He particularly loved the speech that Jee was to make and even approved of her use of his image as a benevolent father holding out his hands to the entire tar. He even agreed to her singing a song.

Pronómio's greatest enjoyment, however, came not from the work, from the time he spent with her, the several long evenings, the friendly chatter, her intoxicating presence. It was all he could do to hide the seething feelings, the purple in his mane. He hoped the Glasśigh enjoyed these times as well, but he really didn't know. Her inability to have a mane that changed color, well, he never knew what she was thinking. And that made it all so exciting.

Though she occasionally brought up the name of Commander Afiéro, Pronómio knew that no matter what, he would make sure Alíthe never returned. If the Front didn't kill him, maybe Pronómio would abandon his idea of sending Alíthe to Degas Point, have Kalífus kill the pilot hero, and instruct Minister Názma to say the Front was responsible. He, of course, would be there to console the bereft Glasśigh.

It took two weeks before preparations and rehearsals were complete, and exhausted, Jee returned to Palace Place. There was one remaining part of the plan that was still missing. As she walked through the door to Palace Place, the last piece greeted her warmly.

"Eno!" she cried.

"Yes," her uncle responded, standing from a lounge chair and putting down his tablet, "it is I."

Jee ran and embraced him warmly. "I can't tell you how happy I am to see you!"

"Are you just saying that?" Eno whispered in her ear. "To put on a show? I see the drones are hovering everywhere outside the window."

"I am happy to see you, not because of your release," she whispered into his ear, "but because that means the plan is still progressing."

"Well, I would think that the fact I am alive after my treacherous time on the surface of this inhospitable world would be a relief. However, I will take your hollow compassion if that is all I can get."

Louder, he informed her of the details of his release, making sure the drones could hear.

"I was set free as a show of goodwill by the Enária," he said. "They are pleased by the announcement of Asello's dream, though not entirely convinced—yet. They will hold Alíthe until they are satisfied."

Later, as the end-of-the-year eclipse began, they retired to their rooms. With no media to capture, the drones returned to their owners. Once alone, Jee and Eno met again in Jee's closet. Using Eno's jammer, they discussed the plan's progress here in the Palace, in the

Arena of Aséllo and Terraces, at the stockpile, and in the new Enária stronghold. With few glitches, they were close to being on schedule. The only issue was the Ancients and if they would be ready in time.

"The Ancients are at the stockpile now, over forty of them, and are excellent workers! Rather fun to be around, actually," said Eno. "However, blizzard conditions on the surface worsen. Jee, the ships may not be available for the Festival. It could take several more weeks before they arrive."

"Then we will have to do with half of the Wings of Glasśigh."

"If I know my niece's powers of persuasion, more will come," Eno assured her. "Breegan was smart to only take those she could trust."

"And what of Alíthe? Really?" Jee inquired. "Have you seen him?"

Eno grinned widely. "I have seen him, yes. He is fine and said to tell you that he is *dreaming a little dream.*"

The evening before the opening of festivities, after the workers had vacated the arena in Etáin and the Terraces, a specially created maintenance crew completed a final inspection of all systems. Wearing Minister of Media badges and uniforms, they worked feverishly, attending to critical power cables, video feeds, cameras, and the like. Most importantly, the team set up a secondary control booth—just in case something were to go wrong during the Glasśigh's broadcast. This would not be allowed, as far as they were concerned.

▲▲▲

Pronómio Tok was in a wonderful mood. He decided to go out of the palace for his first meal of the day to *The Precipice*, his favorite restaurant, located in the center of Palace City. Though not as private as he usually enjoyed, today, he felt like mixing with the public, even with the Gracenta workers who waited on the patrons. He ordered *siffia loaf* with *placcos* and *sweet himya*—runny and just slightly congealed at the edges. They were his favorites. To drink: *dank sgonk*, a delicacy that came from the milk of a góhmar goat and distilled marsh water.

From what he could tell, his speech, given just one day ago and broadcast live from the Hall of Ministers, had a stirringly positive effect. The news media already reported on 'As éllo's Dream' and the freedoms it would grant to Gracenta as part of the 'Boundless Society' as Pronómio called it. The news commentary, expectedly, was very positive and overflowing with praise and support. Even an interview with Minister Khileetéra had her basically speechless and, in the end, supportive.

Ha! thought Pronómio. What could she complain about?

As he strolled from his residence to the café, accompanied by a small security team, Pronómio reveled in the smiles of the workers he passed and the congratulations from the Merćenta and a few Kořeefa. They mirrored the news broadcasts: 'Asėllo's Dream' was truly a stunning and masterful accomplishment.

Pronómio laughed inside. Being a savior was as enjoyable as being the Tażath and much easier! He knew he had done nothing and that nothing would really change, nothing of consequence, anyway. He would remain in power and riches, possibly with the Glasśigh at his side, in one capacity or another.

He ordered a side dish of spicy *dóilio fantoes* in celebration. Why not?

Commander Kalífus entered the café, nodded to the security detail, and sat across from Pronómio.

"You seem pleased. No doubt the news of your 'Dream' deal is the source of this mood?"

"Yes, yes, it is. I have come to see that giving something to someone…and not really doing just that, is the same. I think that wanting and waiting is a greater thing than having."

Kalífus smiled. "I am not sure what that means, but I am pleased that at least you are pleased."

"And you are not?" asked Pronómio.

"I have seen too much of the violence and treachery of the Enária and their Graćenta supporters. The way they live, stealing from each other, destroying their neighborhoods, leaving things in complete disarray. I do not believe, as you do, that the granting of even the mildest of freedoms or the passing of a few coins will change them. And the Glasśigh will soon learn this as well."

"What you forget is that I am not giving them anything," corrected Pronómio, "just an illusion, one that I control."

Kalífus grunted. "You put your trust in that girl, Pronómio. Anything can happen. If the Glasśigh does something unexpected at the festival…at least we can cut the feeds and the lights and sound—everything—in both Etáin and Éhpiloh."

"I would hope you have checked it all," said Pronómio as he took a bite of his *dóilio fantos*, dripping a bit of the gooeyness on his chin.

"I have, as has the Minister of Media," Kalífus responded. "We have control over the power grids within both locations. A simple shut down, literally throwing a switch, and it all goes dark."

"Good," said Pronómio as he wiped his face. "Then, we can relax and enjoy the show."

▲▲▲

As the eclipse ended and the light of Firstsun sparkled above the rim of Ofeétis, cheers arose from the multitude of voices and the opening ceremonies of the first day of the Festival of Jaydí began. The crowds were huge in both the Arena of Aséllo and at the Terraces of Éhpiloh. As was tradition, millions of people walked outside their homes and looked to the sky. There were fireworks, parades, special meals for sale—and of course, drums. Colorful outfits were worn by the wealthy that resembled the many animals of the tar. Private and semi-public parties and sporting events were held. This year, many held photographs, dolls, and even signs displaying images of the Glasśigh.

Eno Ćlaviath stood in the wings next to the stage of the Arena of Aséllo. He was dressed in a stunning dark blue full-length formal coat, glowing threads woven throughout the fabric. It was open from the collar to the floor, revealing a white jumpsuit underneath.

His hands shook with nervousness, something to which Eno Ćlaviath was not accustomed.

"Are you well, Minister Commander?" asked a TSP officer who stood at his side.

"Oh! M-me?" stuttered Eno. "Yes, only a little nervous. I mean, this is the Festival of Jaydí! Seventy million people are watching from Tar Aséllo alone, not counting the many more millions watching in Tar Éstargon! And it was only yesterday that I was released!"

"You are a national hero, Minister Commander," stated the trooper with a reverential nod. "And if I may ask, where is the Glasśigh?"

"The Glasśigh? She is in position."

"Where?" asked the trooper.

This agitated Eno, but he tried to control his frustration. He was trying to concentrate, and this gorphus-faced *goat shyver* was breaking his train of thought.

"The Glasśigh has a *special entrance* if you must know," he replied. "And she is under the stage, actually. The timing must be perfect, and I must be in the proper position at the precise moment, or the whole production will fail."

"That sounds difficult," said the trooper.

"Yes, and thus the need for concentration."

The trooper nodded, and still looking at Eno, asked, "What do you have to do?"

"I have to concentrate!"

The TSP officer finally got the hint. He sheepishly retreated back to the rear of the hallway to stand with his team.

The hum of the crowd could be heard easily from Eno's position. He peeked around a stage barrier. Yes, it was as packed as the night he returned to Tar Asévllo with Jee almost a full Earth-year ago.

The music began—a low orchestral chord that built in complexity and volume. Eno assumed that in Éhpiloh, the same was occurring.

Lights slowly came up, increasing gradually in intensity. A dozen huge spotlights positioned around the stage projected beams straight up into the humid air. Other lights focused on the Taźath's massive 'Know Your Place' banner hung at the rear of the stage, lit ominously from below.

A voice boomed throughout the stadium in Etáin, in the Éhpiloh Terraces, and all over the tar, wherever people watched.

"Fellow Asévllians! Fellow Áhthans! The Taźath of Tar Asévllo welcomes you to the event of events at the Festival of Jaydí! And now, please welcome, back from captivity, High-Minister Commander Eno Ćlaviath!"

"Here we go," muttered Eno to himself. He fidgeted again with his armband, took a deep breath, and walked onto the stage.

The stadium crowd broke into thunderous applause and cheers. Eno smiled, waved, and worked each side of the stage as the drums continued to roll and their volume increased.

In Éhpiloh, Eno's hologram appeared. A high-resolution three-dimensional hologram projector had been positioned on stage, hidden in a small alcove in the front edge. Capable of the most precise projection, it looked to everyone watching that Eno Ćlaviath was there in the flesh, walking about the platform. Even the drones could not tell that he was actually over ten miles away.

Finally, Eno moved front and center. He could see his image projected onto the giant screens around the arena and on each side of the stage. He walked to the microphone and cleared his throat. The cheering slowly lessened, though the crowd never became completely silent.

Eno Ćlaviath spoke carefully, his tone gentle and contemplative. "Captivity…has taught me…one thing. I love Tar Asévllo, and I love being home."

Cheers.

"I also sorely missed someone," he said in a softer voice.

The cheers began to rise.

"I present to you…the great-great-granddaughter of Ásue Aséllo and Jaydí Ćlaviath…the Glasśigh!"

Bedlam.

The stadium shook to its foundations. Almost blocking out the view of the stage, media drones appeared, buzzing and clicking, trying to get an angle on the Glasśigh when she appeared. Smartly, Jee had ordered that no drones could fly directly above the stage or to its sides. She explained she was tired of them being in the way.

Eno moved a few feet to his right. In the front and center of the stage, a spotlight lit a small circle just to his left. From a large alcove in the stage floor, the Glasśigh arose, wearing a long, shimmering white evening gown, sleek and stunning—her hair, perfect as usual.

A deep musical chord reached a crescendo and ended just as she reached the microphone. The roaring of the crowd continued. The lights in the arena dimmed, as they did in the terraces.

Alone, the Glasśigh stood bathed in white light; even the lights projected on the Taźath's banner was extinguished. Her gown glowed, her hair falling in black contrast to it all.

Eno stood to the side, fidgeting with his armband, then slowly walked just out of the spotlight, giving Jee her moment.

The Glasśigh took a step closer to the microphone; the cheers continued.

In Éhpiloh, in the streets and in the parks, the crowds wept, and many called her name aloud. In the fields of the Terraces, the applause was deafening. Near the front of the stage was Reǵeena, proud and smiling as she watched. She knew her part and was ready.

Jee bowed her head and waited for silence—or as close to it as was possible. After a long moment, she began.

"A better day is coming," Jee said in a firm voice.

Cheering and applause rolled over both locations, though Jee did not wait for silence. She took control of the crowd by raising her hands high, and music started, sweet violins and flutes in a sad but hopeful tone. Images of Earth appeared on screens behind her, images of colorful birds and rainbows. She began to sing.

Somewhere over the rainbow, way up high,
There's a land that I've heard of once in a lullaby.
Somewhere over the rainbow, skies are blue,
And the dreams that you dare to dream,
Really do come true.

Someday I'll wish upon a star,
And wake up where the clouds are far behind me.
Where troubles melt like lemon drops,
Away above the chimney tops,
That's where you'll find me.

Somewhere over the rainbow, blue birds fly.
Birds fly over the rainbow,
Why then, oh why can't I?

"I love you," Jee said as the music ended and the cheers arose. For several minutes, the adoration and love for the Glasśigh poured out from every person in the tar. Once the roar died down, Jee continued.

"All of Aséllo made me welcome that day I arrived, and you accepted me as one of your own. For that, I am grateful."

Again, the adulation was consistent and boisterous.

"Life, for me, has been difficult."

A new music began with a more serious tone, strings moving slowly higher and lower in chords, only slightly dissonant. The display screens showed images of her arrival, the attack on *Explorer Eleven*, and her release from captivity at Induláy.

"For all the beauty in this world, I found it hard to understand Tar Aséllo and my place in it."

Here, the displays showed random scenes from Tar Aséllo, the beautiful areas of the western tar, the flourishing fields of Yamillian Province, the glowing seas, the towering falls, the people in the cities, the balcony at Palace Place.

"Each one of us must first know our place for our boundless society to become reality. But you know that. I ask you all, especially my dear Graćenta, to think about your place in this world. For it is you that belong to the city of Éhpiloh, the city that was originally called Jaydí. What is your place? What manner of people are you?"

As the music progressed, it changed in tone, now livelier and more prominent. A stylized and straightforward animation was shown on the large screens throughout the tar: a worker in a field, strong, clear of face and muscular, walking through the ripening stalks of a waist-high crop. He smiled, looked upward to the full glow of Ofeétis. Next appeared a woman, also stylized in the same simple manner. She walked in a field, carrying a bushel of fruit. She also was fair of face, smiling, healthy and happy. She carried the basket proudly. Soon, she joined the man, and together they walked straight ahead, right toward the center of the screen. The angle of the view rotated, and there they stood, amid dozens just like them, proud. Underneath the scene were the words 'Graćenta: The Backbone of Tar Aséllo'.

The screens changed from those working proudly in fields to workers in factories and shops, and smiling people returning home to handsome families and neat modest houses. The music changed tone again, this time uplifting and proud.

"You are family," Jee narrated. "You are dedicated to your loved ones, and you are faithful to them. You are humble, and you are hardworking. What I have learned in my short time here is that you, the Graćenta, are the backbone of Tar Aséllo."

The image changed to the first family again, working in a field. Bright-eyed children stood next to their parents, also holding the fruits of their labor.

"The food on our tables? Picked by you," continued Jee. "The medicine for our sick? Made by you in factories. The comforts we enjoy are born from your labor. You are the backbone of the boundless society of Tar Aséllo. And you deserve Aséllo's Dream, a dream of a better life."

The crowds began to cheer modestly, but all eyes remained glued to the images.

"But you know this. And Pronómio Tok, our Tażath, also knows this. He also knows…that many of you support the Enária Front. And he understands your reasons for doing so. That is why he has announced expanded rights for all Graćenta! Voting, additional schooling, higher wages, and new opportunities are promised to you. But you know this."

So far, Pronómio was pleased. The Glasśigh looked beautiful; she seemed to have control and remained faithful to the script at this early stage. And that song! The people were moved—moved into accepting the promises of Asello's Dream, as hollow as it was in truth.

At this moment, Pronómio Tok felt that she had finally come to accept her role—and what a role he could make for her! Kalífus didn't understand the complexities of politics. He was a tool. Yes, a great friend and loyal supporter, but it was Glasśigh Asello who would extend his dynasty into the future, and who could disagree? Who would not choose to follow the direct descendant of Ásue? When the time to retire came, she would be Tażath, and he would direct the nation through her. Yes, she would be his choice for his successor—and he would make her his mate.

"The Taźath," she continued, "in his wisdom, asks that you end your support for the lawless Enária Front because…he says that he can provide for you. He can provide rights, medicine, food, higher income, the owning of your own home. In short—he can help you achieve Asévllo's Dream."

The crowd in the stadium cheered loudly.

The multitudes in Éhpiloh also applauded but seemed less than enthusiastic. They had seen and suffered the horrors committed by Pronómio Tok's regime.

"All he asks is that you first…" she paused for a moment before continuing, "…know your place."

A clear stream of high brass voices announced the new day, and on cue, the banners containing the symbol of the Taźath fell to the floor. New banners were unfurled, showing the black rectangle as before, but in this image, the center did not have the symbol of the Taźath, but a light olive-brown arm with forefinger pointing to the sky.

"I know my place now," Jee said as the proud music stopped.

The video images changed, and new music was added, sad, mourning, inharmonious chords that struck the audiences in a way that evoked concern and fear. There was the Glasśigh, walking through Tepótah, entering a dark building. Another angle showed her talking to sick children, and the most shocking, her holding and comforting a dying child as she *sang*. The broadcasts and displays showed the entire song, with dissonant chords played behind it, uninterrupted.

When she was done, the people of Tar Asévllo, if not crying their eyes out, cheered. They held their hearts. They sobbed as the images faded.

From his personal suite at the Palace of the Taźath, Pronómio watched. He was affected deeply, a mixture of sadness and anger raged within him. "What was that?" he asked aloud, wiping tears away. "What in the name of Asévllo's rotting carcass was that?"

"I know my place, thanks to Pronómio Tok," she continued in a voice strong and clear. "For he has given me vision and purpose. Not through his words, *but through his actions!*"

The images changed again, the music also. It was angry, it was discordant, and though filled with pounding drums, it made all who heard anxious. Jee knew it as Holtz's *Mars, Bringer of War*. Selected video of the *Explorer Eleven* attack appeared on screens.

"Our Taźath," Jee said, her tone now dripping with reproach, "…is a liar and a murderer!"

The Glasśigh's voice thundered across Tar Asello, everywhere, for anyone who was listening. Her words rang loud and echoed through the Terraces, off the walls of the Northern Tar, between the great towers of Etáin, and within the Arena of Asello.

The crowds in the Etáin and Éhpiloh ceased cheering. They were confused. What was happening? What did she say?

"This is not in the script!" yelled Pronómio into his ABC. "Názma! Stop this! Immediately!"

"Yes, Taźath!" he replied.

"Kalífus!" barked Pronómio as he raised his armband to his face. "Arrest her!"

The image of Kalífus appeared before Pronómio. His face was red with anger. *"Do you still believe she can be useful? Do you still think she can be your ally?"*

"Kalífus!" growled Pronómio. "Remember to whom you are speaking!"

"I do remember," Kalífus hissed. *"I am speaking to the love-sick fool who created her!"*

"The *Explorer Eleven* attack on the day of my return—" Jee roared as the images changed, "—was ordered by Pronómio Tok! Notice the red laser targeting the craft. The rocket used was a class-7 with a flash shell, not a dangerous Klaymac! The Taźath wanted not to kill me—but to blame the Enária Front! This ensured he could pass the vote of confidence three days after the attack! In fact, every attack carried out against the Enária has been for this benefit!"

Salǵeea and his team, still wearing their stolen Minister of Media badges and uniforms, sat in the secret secondary control booth in the Éhpiloh Terraces, which they had set up the previous night according to plan.

"I sure hope this works…" Salǵeea said nervously.

In the control booths in Etáin City and in Éhpiloh, the Media Minister's directors received the Taźath's message in seconds: Stop the broadcast.

They had been instructed to literally pull the main power switches for every set of lights, all audio, video, and broadcast equipment. Only safety lights were to remain on.

The crews pulled the switches.

Every light in the arena and in the Terraces suddenly went out. The sound stopped; the screens went black.

The crowds murmured in confusion, thinking that the interruption might be part of the show; it had been terrific so far!

Then a flicker, and the stage lights, and those illuminating the surrounding areas on both stages, came back to life. The sound also was returned. The screens themselves were unaffected.

"Why hasn't this stopped?" yelled the Taźath from his private viewing suite in the arena. "Minister!"

In the secondary control booth in Éhpiloh, a few simple screens flickered on and displayed the well-lit stage.

"We have sound and video," said a technician as he checked the panel in front of him. "We are still broadcasting!"

Salǵeea smiled.

His crew congratulated each other.

"We are up and in control here at Éhpiloh," Salǵeea said into his simple and outdated ABC. "Units moving to defend and control power and camera positions. Orgo?"

"I hear you. The arena is ours," Orgo responded. *"Defending stage and secondary control booth."*

"We have literally pulled all plugs, Taźath!" Zola Názma cried as his hologram fluttered on Pronómio's ABC. *"We cut the power to the control booth. B-but it came back on! There is a new broadcast feed as well!"*

"Minister! Kill all power!"

"We have! All of the power to the stadium and the Terraces has been cut, but power is still on! It must be coming from somewhere else!"

"Then find out where!" screamed the Taźath.

"The attack on Targan Base that killed my parents was also his doing," continued Jee. "And as you can see, his 'tools' wore sleeves to cover their true identities! You were never shown this, the footage from the cameras on the *Explorer!* The sleeves of the assailants had moved, and below? This!"

A close-up image of an arm appeared, its rolled-up sleeve showing much of what was underneath. The picture was enhanced. The color was adjusted. All could clearly see the shape of the distinctive YSP tattoo with a red arc across the center. A second image appeared to the right of the original. It was a clear photograph of the same symbol. However, as the image zoomed out, it revealed the face of the owner.

The crowd gasped.

"There is only one of these special symbols in the world. It is on the arm of Security Police Minister Commander Gákoh Kalífus!"

Now the crowds in Etáin City were silent. They were stunned.

The crowds in Éhpiloh were shocked—and that soon turned to outrage.

"I am not the only one wronged!" cried Jee. "You have been as well!"

The screens showed a grainy video of the Glasśigh walking through a dark and misty wood, entering an underground bunker, walking along a shadowy pathway lit by headlamps. Then, the angle changed, and there were the bodies at Folvos.

"Here is what became of your children, the *fortunate* ones not sold into slavery! All by the hands of Pronómio Tok and Gákoh Kalífus, liars and murderers and perverts and slave-masters!" shouted Jee, her voice full of power and purpose. "He lied to me, and his promises of new freedom…are lies to you! But you know this—now. And you should also know your place! *This*…is your place," she said, pointing to the sky. "Not beneath the oppressive regime of Pronómio Tok and the rest of the slave-masters, child abductors, and killers! But at the top of Tar Asello!"

The crowds in Éhpiloh began to cheer.

Within the arena in Etáin, mostly filled with Koŕeefa, opinions began to change. The support for the Taźath wavered in these minds, while others began to feel resentment toward the Glasśigh.

Arguments broke out in the audience; some became physical.

"Rise up, Graćenta! Rise up, Merćenta!" Jee continued with strength and purpose. "I ask you to not believe the lies of Pronómio Tok, but to join us! Join us under this, this new Banner of Freedom!"

The old banners fell in both stadiums and in the streets of Éhpiloh. Gone was the stark black and white emblem, and in its place, in a ray of bright sunshine over a fading field of black, was the now-familiar olive-colored arm, finger to the sky. But across the top were words in blood-red, reading 'New Asello Front', and below, prominently bold, was a single command: 'Resist!'

The crowd in Éhpiloh went wild.

Kalífus led a team to the stage at the Arena of Asello. They swiftly walked past Eno, who moved aside. He waited a moment, then drifted back into the wings, hurried down a long hallway, and ran.

Rushing to the Glasśigh, a trooper snatched the microphone and pulled it aside. Kalífus stood in front of Jee, who, for some reason, ignored him and continued her speech.

"Join us! The Enária Front is reborn as the *New Asébllo Front!* Along with Salǵeea Calćoa, I will lead you to true freedom!"

"You will do nothing of the sort," snarled Kalífus. "You are under arrest!"

He grabbed her, but his hands passed through her presence.

In Éhpiloh, Jee stood proudly. The image of Eno Ćlaviath was moving backward on the stage. Then, his presence flickered and vanished. Salǵeea and a large team of armed Enária, dressed as media team workers and holding projectile guns, took positions about the stage.

In the arena, Kalífus tried again to grab the Glasśigh, but it was soon evident that she was not physically there.

A hologram! he realized. *But it was so real!*

"Commander! Look!" called a TSP officer, pointing to the other side of the stage.

There on the ground was Eno's 12TM ABC hologram projector, made in Tar Éstargon, the most advanced ABC on Áhtha.

Kalífus took the device and switched it off. The image of the Glasśigh now extinguished next to him with a static pop.

The screens about the arena flickered but then displayed a new feed from Éhpiloh: the Glasśigh, standing on the Terrace stage, the distinctive red northern tar wall clearly visible behind her. The crowd gasped.

"You cannot stop the revolution," the Glasśigh said slowly and purposefully, her face filling the entire screen with only the glow of the red wall behind her. *"Resist!"* her voice boomed.

The image changed to the crowd in the Terraces, hundreds of thousands of people calling out: "Resist!"

Kalífus looked on in horror. He had known the Glasśigh was dangerous from the time of her birth, and now he was proven right. It was little consolation, however. The entire event had endangered his position, that of Pronómio Tok and the entire construct of their political power.

At least, he thought, we have armed forces!

"This is Commander Kalífus!" he called frantically into his

armband. "The Glasśigh is in Éhpiloh! Her hologram was here in Etáin! Arrest her! And find Eno Ćlaviath!"

"Resist the Taźath!" Jee continued, her voice and image being broadcast over all frequencies from rogue stations throughout the tar. "Rise up against his dictatorship! Strike! Bring his world to a screeching halt! My brothers and sisters of the Graćenta, join us, fight with us…and we will emerge victors! But you know that!"

The people in the Terraces roared in approval.

A Secret Police team in Éhpiloh rushed through tents and temporary buildings that led to the stage. As they approached, Salǵeea and his men met them. A firefight erupted. Drones from the New Aséllo Front captured it all and sent files to the Front's main control. There the video was fed into broadcasts. Rogue cube-fed stations showed that the Taźath's Special Police had been overwhelmed within minutes. The remaining troops surrendered.

"And to the troops in the AMF and TSP, I have a special request of you!" Jee continued. "Join us! Do not support the Taźath and his criminal policies! You have been misled! Now is the time to right the thousand year wrong! Join us!"

The crowd roared, and the Glasśigh raised her hand for quiet. After a moment, the noise abated.

But before she could speak, a voice called out. "How? How will we defeat an army so powerful with just our hands and will?"

"How, you ask?" said Jee, her eyes glittering.

In the cockpit of Aréus 501, Alíthe listened to the broadcast. The fifty craft of G-Wing defectors circled at three thousand feet, between two prominent arms of the northern tar wall. They were less than two miles to the west of the Terraces.

"This is Commander Afiéro," he called into his hel-com. "That is our signal. Let us show them the goods."

"We hear you," came Breegan's voice, *"Flight one forming up. No word from Pédaltee?"*

"None," said Alíthe. "But we are to make an impression." He thought for a minute. "Traffic pattern, standard circle. Keep flying over the Terraces until I call us off."

"Sir?" asked Breegan.

"We will appear as a larger force," he explained slowly.

"Yes, commander," said Breegan.

"I will tell you how I will defeat Pronómio Tok, my dear friends!"

Jee continued from the stage. "A million miles away, across the stars, the Earth has been practiced in the art of war, and I have that knowledge! Earth is a world that prides itself on conquest. I have studied thousands of years of war…and I know their methods!"

"But we have no machines of war!" came a voice, again the voice of Reǵeena Ahdelfía.

"Ah," said the Glasśigh, "No machines of war, you say? You forget! *I have my own air wing!"*

The music reached a crescendo, and the lights on the stage were dimmed to almost nothing. Roaring overhead, the ships of the Wings of Glasśigh came, the 'G' emblem illuminated under each gunship's wing and upon each tail.

The cameras, now operated by Salǵeea's crews, broadcasted the rows and rows of ships in formation, flying low and slow over the crowds in the Éhpiloh Terraces. The sky appeared full of the powerful craft, and the people cheered. The lights on the stage returned to full illumination. There stood the Glasśigh, arm in the air, clenched fist, finger pointing to the sky.

"I promise you nothing," continued the Glasśigh as she spoke to the crowds. "I promise you nothing but toil, tears, pain, and blood. But in the victorious end, you will have *earned* your freedom, and the reign of Pronómio Tok and the Koŕeefa will end! Resist! Resist!"

The cheering rose again.

As planned, Reǵeena rushed the stage, ran next to the Glasśigh, hugged her, and then turned to the crowd. She thrust her hand skyward as well, and soon, in a roar of support and dedication, the peoples of the northern tar thrust their hands skyward in solidarity. They chanted, "Resist! Resist! Resist!"

People locked arms, and in groups of all sizes, marched about the Terraces. Others jumped up and down or danced to the still-playing music. Many cried and called out, "Glasśigh! Light of Áhtha" and "Resist!" Arms with raised forefingers were repeatedly thrust in the air in what was now referred to as the New Aséllo Salute. Many called out, swearing allegiance to the New Aséllo Front. Stacks upon stacks of pamphlets, placed at the exits by Salǵeea's people, offered instructions about how to strike as well as steal from matériel transports. They told the people to wait for further instructions on how to join the cause. Each pamphlet carried a stylized image of the Glasśigh, arm raised to the sky.

The images continued playing, not only in the Arena and the Terraces, but broadcasted via rogue cubes to all of Tar Aséllo and beyond.

In the city of Envemíro, the capital of Tar Éstargon, the Ef Keería and Minister Amani Plagósia watched the event on a large display as they sat in the Capitol Complex, smiling.

"Glasśigh!" called Salǵeea as he ran onto the Terrace stage. "Alíthe has sent a message. Kalífus has ordered the Raltos Air Wing from Norǵana to attack the Terraces. He and the G-wing are moving to engage them. We must go! Now!"

The images on all screens now displayed the banner of the New Asèllo Front, slowly fading to black as the crowd chanted "Resist!"

Jee, Reǵeena, and Veegill, escorted by Salǵeea and a handful of Front soldiers, sprinted past the temporary structures surrounding the stage at Éhpiloh. Avoiding the frantic crowds, they made it to and boarded a small transport that had been taken from the surface. They waited a few tense moments as dozens of armed Front fighters retreated from the Terrace stage and surrounding areas to join them. Then they boarded the transport and blasted out of the area, heading to the far western tar.

Orgo and his small team saw a different reaction from the crowd at the Arena of Asèllo: confusion. Many were frightened by the gunfire they heard and rushed the exits in panic. A small percentage of the attendees were outraged, yelling for Pronómio Tok to be arrested. At times, these dissenters clashed with more loyal subjects. Violence broke out. Others considered the possibility of the accusations being true, and if so, what was to be done? Indeed, the murdering of Tye Ćlaviath and Dypónia Asèllo could not be tolerated. And the attempt on the Glasśigh's life, even if not successful, even if staged, was more than disturbing.

As commanded by Orgo, the Front soldiers restrained the AMF and TSP personnel captured, binding them with hand and ankle cuffs to a stairwell railing. The troops of the Taźath were stripped of all technology and weapons.

Orgo and his team rushed outside the stadium. Stealthily moving through the streets, they arrived in a small, tree-filled park between buildings. A transport had been hidden there earlier. They ignited the engines and hovered for a second to check the skies. Avoiding the airborne skyliners fleeing the conflict, they accelerated at top speed to the western tar.

In their escape, they looked to the south. They could see the Wings of Glasśigh in battle. The war had now begun.

"Good luck, Alíthe," Orgo said under his breath.

Eno was to take a different path. Though he could have left the arena with Orgo, his assignment was to return to the Front's new stronghold in the Type-G. Its superior speed would be useful, and if fitted with bombs or rockets, or both, it could be used to devastating effect. As he ran from the stage, he made his way to the building's lower level docking area. He could hear footsteps behind. It had to be Special Police. Ahead, he could see the Type-G waiting next to rows upon rows of other skyliners belonging to the elite.

Once inside the Type-G, Eno started the engines. Pulsegun rounds began to strike the walls of the dock nearby. Eno wasted no time. He applied full power and blasted out of the dock.

Immediately, he began weaving his way through the crowded airspace. Once somewhat clear, he pushed to full throttle. He was slammed into the back of his command chair as he accelerated, leaving the traffic behind. Soon, he cut throttle to half, leveled off, and set a course to the Western Tar—Aséllo's Well, to be exact.

Immediately a warning tone sounded. Then a voice came from the ship's navigation and tracking system: *"Three craft in pursuit. Two Aréus A3 Gunships at your current altitude and an unknown craft at twenty-six thousand feet."*

Eno wondered if the unknown craft could be one of the secret TSP HA *Kákor* Fighters that Alíthe had mentioned. If this one had started at that height, it was diving from the fálouse and would have incredible speed. Still, the A3s were the immediate threat, and he could easily outrun them. At full throttle, the Type-G pulled quickly away.

"Unidentified craft descending. Closing distance."

"Closing?" asked Eno. "That is definitely a Kákor!"

Eno had one last option. He took the Type-G vertical, pushing the throttle to full. The power climb almost caused him to blackout. Dizzy, he could see the blue fálouse coming closer. But the course change had affected the dive of the Kákor, who overshot from its energy-rich dive and needed to recover, change direction and then give chase again. By then, Eno would be long gone. He had out-maneuvered his foe.

"Second unknown craft in pursuit, gaining. Distance one mile."

"Not—for—long," he grunted, straining against the g-forces as the Type-G roared to the fálouse.

The second Kákor had speed from its dive and was not fooled by Eno's change of direction and climb. It used its energy wisely, moving ever closer. Pulse rounds streaked past the Type-G; others grazed its sides.

"Missed!" Eno laughed, and in an instant, the modified Type-G entered the thick fálouse, heading into space.

"Ha! Pull that trick! You can't follow me here!" Eno continued upward, flicking on the heaters of the command deck.

"Unknown craft has fired a Torchette air-to-air missile. Two hundred yards behind."

"What?" screamed Eno. "There are no air-to-air Torchettes!"

"Warning: Torchette Missile has acquired."

Eno had no countermeasures. He could not outrun a Torchette, but he did have a two hundred-yard lead on it. Maybe he could get past the thin atmosphere above the fálouse and into the void before being struck. The Torchette should freeze in the extreme cold of space.

"Torchette impact eminent."

Eno angled the Type-G ten degrees past vertical, grabbing the last bit of thin atmosphere to perform the maneuver. The trick would situate the Type-G as to fall through the fálouse in a different position than where it had entered. It would allow him a chance to escape—if he didn't get blasted to pieces first.

The fálouse thinned, and the stars leaped into view above him. The Type-G sputtered as it entered near space. Eno held his breath. He looked from side to side, trying to locate the Torchette.

"Trac—ng sys— fai—ing," sputtered the navigation and tracking system.

"Where the hell is it?" called Eno.

Then to his left, he saw something slightly behind: a long metallic tube, fifteen feet in length. It was gaining on him.

"This can't be! It can't maneuver in space!" Eno braced for impact.

After a moment—nothing. Then, just out the side viewshield, less than three feet away, he saw the Torchette, with a sputtering engine on one end and an evil-looking warhead on the other. He could see the Taźath's logo on the side and even the serial number of the missile.

Eno was shocked into silence, mouth wide open.

The weapon's engine flared on and off for a few seconds, then died as ice formed on its small wings. Both craft hung in weightlessness for a moment.

The Torchette fell first, tilting toward the skyliner as gravity pulled it back to the fálouse. It passed close to the Type-G, the side of the weapon actually scraping against the skyliner's short left wing with a grating screech, then fell downward.

Eno released a long breath, relief washing over him. "That was too close!"

The Type-G began to fall toward the fálouse. At his new angle, Eno could no longer see the missile, and that was reassuring. Soon he was falling through blue clouds, then into the warm air.

The skyliner slowly sprang back to life. Eno quickly ascertained that his last-second adjustment put him about fifty miles west of where he had entered the fálouse. He adjusted course slightly and kept this nose down, speed ever increasing. As the engines came back online, he accelerated to full power. Within a few moments, he glanced at the airspeed indicator. The Type-G had achieved over four hundred miles per hour and was almost one hundred miles west of Etáin City. The Kákor was nowhere to be found.

"There you have it!" he happily called. "I am a *pilot!* I truly am! I still have it!"

"A second Torchette missile has acquired," came a voice.

"That can't be right!" cried Eno.

His ancient flight training and pure instinct proved fruitless. Within a few seconds, a loud *BANG* reverberated through the ship.

I should be obliterated! Atomized! he thought.

Eno peered over his shoulder. Both M44 engines of the Type-G were physically gone, as was part of the tail. It could have been worse, but his extreme speed and spasmodic juking motions probably caused the missile to deliver only a glancing blow. The warhead never exploded, but fatal damage was done.

Eno had little control. As he fell through fifteen thousand feet, he struggled to level out. He activated the nose hoverjets. Possibly they could allow him some control over his pitch. At ten thousand feet above the tar floor, he attempted to glide and began searching frantically for a soft place to crash land. To the west, he spotted the beach at Chanteeda Shores. Unfortunately, obstacles were blocking his way: several towers of stone rose from the water, each about a hundred feet tall.

Coming through five thousand feet, he could see his chances were slim. Not only was the surface of the tar rushing toward him, but the tracking system tone blared again.

"Five Aréus A3 Gunships vectoring on your position."

"This is Eno!" he called into his hel-com. "Commander Afiéro, do you hear me?"

A stream of static, then a response came, faded but recognizable.

"This is Afiéro! I hear you! We are engaging the enemy!"

Eno could hear the din of combat through the com.

"I am going down," grunted Eno as he struggled to pull the nose of the Type-G upward. "I repeat, damage taken by enemy fire, I have no control. I am going down near the beaches along Chanteeda Shores!"

"We are heading to assist," said Alíthe.

"No!" snapped Eno.

His ship screamed, falling lower and lower, his angle too steep to avoid the towers ahead. "It is too late! Defend the Glasśigh! Stick to the plan!"

"We will be there in a few moments!" repeated Alíthe.

"I said no! Listen to me, Alíthe! I brought this nightmare upon her! I should have left Jee on Earth! Now I am asking you to care for her!"

The Type-G was a few hundred feet from the stone towers, blocking his entry to the soft beach beyond. Eno continued to pull as hard as he could, adjusting the hoverjets, trying in vain to raise the nose of his craft.

"Alíthe! Promise me you will protect her! You are all she has in this world!"

Aboard Aréus 501, Alíthe fired on a passing Raltos Wing craft, hitting it squarely. As it exploded, he left his formation and set a course to Chanteeda, engines on full.

"Commander Eno! I'm coming—"

"Alíthe! Promise me!" pleaded Eno, then, static.

"Aréus 501 calling Commander Ćlaviath! This is Aréus 501 calling for Commander Ćlaviath! Please respond!"

Alíthe repeated the message, but there was no answer.

▲▲▲

The air battle was over. Alíthe gave the order to return to base. Once safely in the cave system, he found Orgo and recounted the call from Eno and the crash of the Type-G.

"I flew over the water, low, straight to Chanteeda," Alíthe said. "I saw the ship, down between two towers. It was on fire. It exploded. There was no way anyone could have survived that. He is gone."

Stunned, the big man had to sit down on a nearby stone bench. After a moment, he looked to Alíthe. "Are you going to tell her?"

"Yes," said Alíthe. "Where is she?"

Orgo bowed his head to his chest. "At the kitchen and dining hall, second basement."

Alíthe took leave of him and walked to the basement. There was Jee, alone, looking at her armband. She noticed him and smiled.

"Alíthe!" she called. "You're all right!"

"Yes," he said, coming to her. He tried to hide his expression, but how could he? The thought of her in anguish broke him.

"Wait until Eno hears about the crowds in Éhpiloh!" she said, standing and running to him. "They are with us! Eno will be so proud!"

"Jee? I have..." Alíthe couldn't go on. He held her close and put his forehead to hers. He looked into her eyes.

Suddenly aware of his expression, Jee pulled back slightly.

"Alíthe? What's the matter? Your mane is...gold! W-what happened?"

"Jee. Eno...didn't make it out of Etáin."

Jee was shocked. Not fully comprehending, she frowned. "So, where is he? When will he get here?"

"Jee, he...he won't be coming. H-he crashed. Shot down as he was flying away."

Alíthe watched as she slowly came to realize what had happened.

"H-he's dead?" Jee asked. The tears began to fall.

Holding her tightly, Alíthe could only nod his head as they cried together.

▲▲▲

For the next week, Jee remained in her room at the base, not wishing to see anyone. Alíthe tried to comfort her, but she kept to her room, sobbing softly. He stayed outside the door to her chamber for days, sitting on the floor at first, then on a chair that Salǵeea had brought.

"How is she?" Salǵeea asked as he brought food and drink.

"I can only hear her sobbing from time to time," said Alíthe as he accepted the nourishment. "She will only allow Reǵeena inside. I have asked her to stay with Jee, even if she wants to be alone. That has caused a few arguments to put it lightly."

"We are saddened. This is a blow to us all."

"It is war, Salǵeea, and there will be much more of this."

"I know," said Salǵeea. "But this is a critical time, Alíthe. We must plan our strategy and develop tactics to defeat the Taźath. Without her, many things may go astray—in particular, the recruitment effort."

Alíthe nodded. "We must begin, then. We should gather the team leaders and start to organize. I am not privy to the Glasśigh's strategy, but I agree, we must move ahead."

Alíthe stood as if to walk away with Salǵeea, but the Front leader held up a hand.

"I will gather the needed people," Salǵeea said. "Stay here, Alíthe.

She will need you."

As previously planned, Salǵeea produced an announcement that declared war on the regime of Pronómio Tok. He also accused Pronómio of the murder of Eno Ćlaviath. This media file was broadcast from rogue cubes and watched by those in Éhpiloh and Etáin.

In response, Pronómio ordered Kalífus to crack down on the northern region of Oso-Gúrith. The cities, towns, and settlements, including Éhpiloh, quickly changed from depressing slums and camps to depressingly occupied cities. The AMF was called to assist the Special Police in patrolling the streets. They deployed light guncars and bot copters. Strict curfews were enforced. If not on the way to work or to a work-transport station, anyone caught outside was arrested. At times, executions of suspected Front members were carried out by TSP squads in the city's streets. Any child found was taken, even with parents present.

Of course, this action by the Taźath only strengthened the resolve of Graćenta citizens to resist and turned the cities and towns into breeding grounds for recruits for the New Aséllo Front. Additionally, rogue-cube commercials that featured scenes from the Glasśigh's speech at the Éhpiloh Terraces bombarded the populace, encouraging them to join the Front. Many responded.

Orgo and Salǵeea predicted that the size of the Front had grown from barely five hundred total members to just over one four thousand volunteers, though mostly untrained. This was well shy of the estimated four thousand battle-ready TSP and AMF troops and the over thirteen-thousand support staff.

However, the New Aséllo Front was just beginning.

New members proved themselves by completing simple, non-critical assignments, such as applying *'Resist!'* posters on buildings everywhere, including Etáin City. One could then graduate to stealing a few items from a truck bound for an AMF depot, driving a nail into a tire, or loosening a traktor track to cause a vehicle to break down. Some recruits were asked to literally throw wrenches into the machinery of arms manufacturing plants.

The reprisals were severe. If a person was caught, others in the facility were made to stop work and witness the physical beatings of the transgressor. Punishment was carried out by armed TSP officers and squads, who then kept a visible presence in the workplace.

This, of course, did nothing to stop the infractions; even more workers undertook even greater acts of sabotage. Many were opportunistic. Each aided the Front in some way or another.

Encouraged by agents of the Glasśigh to remain at their posts. Those Merćenta who sided with the Front were instructed to remain at their positions in factories, transportation companies, farming concerns, and banking institutions. There, they could siphon money, food, and matériel from their businesses to the cause. Others arranged raids on their own transportation systems, so required items could be obtained for the Front with the least risk.

Still, many remained who were loyal to the Taźath. These were those Merćenta who lived in Etáin City and the surrounding areas, those who had become rich and powerful, owners of businesses and financial institutions, arms manufacturers, and those who benefited from the businesses of pleasure. Likewise, all the Kořeefa except the most anti-Pronómio factions remained loyal to the current regime. Those who did not, such as Minister Khileetéra, were placed under house arrest.

A whole week had now passed. Jee spent long hours in her room at the base, mostly sitting on a balcony, watching the workers below. They prepared for a fight, whenever it may come.

Reǵeena approached and noticed that Jee seemed more awake and aware of her surroundings. She sat next to the Glasśigh and held her hand. "The time for grieving has passed, my friend. It is time to be back at work. The Taźath needs to pay for what he has done to Eno and thousands of others. We need you, Jee."

"Time for revenge then?" Jee asked, somewhat coming out of her stupor.

"Yes," said Reǵeena. "The Front must continue planning, and that is where you are needed."

In an improvised conference room—really just a portion of the dining hall in a deep area of the caves—sat Salǵeea, Alíthe, Orgo, and Breegan around a table, looking at a large hologram map of Tar Asédllo. They had been searching for a place to attack for days, though nothing seemed suitable. They had all but given up when the Glasśigh walked in.

"Jee!" cried Alíthe.

She smiled and went to him. "What are you doing?"

"Becoming frustrated," answered Orgo, giving Jee a warm smile. "But we are glad to see you."

The entire group agreed but remained cautious, hoping that Jee was ready to work.

"What is the strategy?" Jee asked.

"That is the problem," Salǵeea confessed. "We don't have a strategy. Kill the Taźath and take over?"

"That is a *goal*," she corrected, "not a strategy. What do we have going for us?"

"You," said Reǵeena simply.

They all agreed.

"Might as well surrender then," Jee joked as she looked over the map.

"That—is sarcasm," Alíthe pointed out.

They laughed.

"I know strategy and some key tactics," she admitted as she looked over the map. "But I am not a leader of troops in the field."

"Lucky for you," said Salǵeea, "we have Orgo and others who have planned and led hundreds of raids, acquisition missions, and trained our soldiers for combat."

"I can lead the troops," Orgo agreed as he motioned to a pair of Front officers standing nearby to join the meeting. "Officers Féelikas and Kindýn. Our best. They will lead teams well."

Jee smiled. "Very good. Then let's start with the basics. Armed Troop strength?"

"Since the festival," said Orgo, "we have grown to one thousand, but more are ready to join." He tapped the holographic map. Where Front had soldiers, their locations appeared as green dots.

"Your call for AMF and TSP troops to defect was effective," said Salǵeea. "A hundred so far. That means the ones who didn't defect will deserve what they get."

"That doesn't make me feel much better, but it is good news," said Jee softly.

"We now have an air force," added Alíthe. "After the Festival, we added ten more pilots and their craft from Ultos, bringing our total to sixty-seven of the best pilots in Áhtha." He tapped the map, and green triangles appeared representing aircraft. "And each comes with one A4, the most advanced tactical gunship in the tar." He tapped again, and four blue-green triangles appeared. "We also have four advanced C7 Katíga bombers. The remaining G-Wing is under lockdown. Kalífus doesn't trust them, and rightly so. I assume, eventually, we will have them all."

"But, the AMF wings still outnumber us six-to-one," said Breegan. An overwhelming number of black triangles appeared as she tapped the map, displaying the strength of the enemy air force. "Kalífus has called up pilots from training. They also have an unknown number of

Kákors; I figure at least forty, bringing their air numbers to well over six hundred."

"If the Ancients can make it off the surface with those Vożeeths," Alíthe stated, tapping the map to display a group of forty blue shapes, "our odds would be a bit better."

"The ground is a more difficult situation," began Orgo. "We need those arms from the surface, badly. With just the arms we have stolen, we can outfit three hundred and fifty." He tapped the map, and blue dots appeared, representing the ground strength. "Committing all our soldiers against the Tażath's over four thousand ground troops, and twice that in support, would be suicide."

"That is why," said Jee, "we will only commit what we need, what the terrain and time allow. What else?"

"The raids have been very effective, as have work stoppages and sabotage missions," Salǵeea told them. "We have matériel to support limited engagements."

Jee walked around the table, thinking, glancing at the hologram from time to time. "So, we are out-gunned, out-supplied, and greatly out-numbered."

The group paused, slowing seeing the futility of their position.

"So, our strategy is a simple one," Jee said confidently.

"It is?" asked Alíthe.

"Our goal is to dethrone Pronómio Tok," she continued. "Not wipe out his forces. Our *strategy* is to outlast him militarily until the odds are in *our* favor and society is on our side. An old Earth saying: one doesn't need to win all the battles to win the war, just the last one." She paused and looked at the group. "We want to win hearts and support in the meantime. This will be a long process, and survival over the long term will be our best chance of victory."

They nodded as they all understood.

"Live to fight another day," Jee instructed. "That is our creed."

"But if we do nothing? And wait for something to magically happen?" asked Orgo.

"I never suggested we do nothing," Jee said. "To boost the ranks and win over support from the people, we need to show everyone we are serious and dedicated. We'll pull a few old Earth tricks on my friend Kalífus. The question is, when? What is Pronómio doing now?"

"Not much but harassing people," said Orgo, shrugging his massive shoulders. "He doesn't know where we are, but he is looking."

Jee smiled. "Then…we will give him a surprise before he finds us."

Jee explained her plan.

Over the next few weeks, matériel was prepared, and training began. Jee and Orgo poured over maps of the entire tar, looking for a place to most effectively utilize their ground strengths. They needed to bait Kalífus into sending his forces to the Front's chosen location.

"I believe," said Orgo, pointing to a spot on the southern corner of the holographic map, "that Treágor Delta is most appropriate."

Jee looked at the map as Orgo enlarged the area. After a moment, she smiled. "Caves within the tar wall? Rivers, thick jungle, natural barriers—yes, I like it."

Alíthe and Breagan planned the tactics of the air battle. Their pilots were well trained, and they had a minimal but talented support group. The Wings of Glasśigh, at least the half that had defected, knew the tar well. They both agreed that Jee's plan might be complex, but the risk was well worth the reward if they could execute their part successfully.

In-between planning sessions, Orgo took Reǵeena and Jee to a remote area to train with pulseguns. Though Jee protested, Orgo was stubborn and reminded her that he was tactical and procedural. She was strategy.

"All Front members get basic training on some type of weapon," Orgo informed them firmly. "No one gets within ten miles of a battlefield without it."

He handed Jee a standard-issue AMF medium-weight auto-pulse gun. It was almost three feet long.

"Couldn't I just get a small pistol?" Jee asked, jokingly. "A knife?"

"No," was his reply.

Within a week's time, Jee and Reǵeena were proficient, maybe even a little better than proficient, at firing their weapon.

"Just remember," Orgo repeated over and over: "Aim, short burst, aim, short burst, aim—"

24
Tora! Tora! Tora!

Five weeks after the Festival of Jaydí, probing flights of HA Kákors were getting nearer, diving in from above the fálouse at incredible speeds, scanning, then using the energy from the dive to run away. Kalífus and his scanning teams were closing in. Based on the search pattern, Orgo and Alíthe calculated that the AMF would locate the ground troop base in less than a week. The New Asévllo Front was forced to spring their trap.

Still, there was no word from the forces on the surface and no ability to check the status of the Ágviost Blizzard. Hopefully, the storm had passed, and the Ancients and other support personnel on the surface were on the verge of making an appearance. But, as Jee reminded them, hope was not a strategy. The Front would have to make do with the half of G-Wing and the few hundred trained soldiers they had at hand.

Before separating, Jee called Alíthe aside.

"Please be careful?" she asked.

"I will," he said. "You know, many say that I am the best pilot in all of the AMF."

Jee smiled. "Good then. I will try not to worry." Reaching in her pocket, she produced the pin Mr. Gallotta had given her. "Would you pin this on me?"

"Of course." Alíthe studied the object. "What does it say?"

"Always Out Front," she said. "It was my Earth father's. He got it for his service in a great war."

Alíthe struggled a bit but soon had the pin attached to Jee's jacket.

"I am certain his bravery and knowledge come with it," said Alíthe.

From the surface of the Sea of Jovia, Asévllo's Well appeared to be a hole in the ocean, with water streaming in, pouring over the edges. This created a tubular waterfall, hollow in the middle, almost four hundred feet across, and one thousand feet deep. At the bottom was a two thousand-acre lake fed by the fall. In the center of that lake sat an island. It was more of a small mountain, made of granite and veins of gold. The water thundered into the lake, creating a curtain of water and permanent mist and rain that engulfed the island and the newly constructed airbase of the New Asévllo Front.

Orgo and a team of technicians had created a new com device for all ships and soldiers: a spectrogram plug-in. As pilots and ground personnel spoke into their hel-coms, the plug-in would convert their voices into multiple pictures of the waveform created. When a spectrogram receiver in another ship obtained the message, it would locate the waveforms' spectrogram images and play them back. Of course, this hid all communications from the AMF and TSP, who had no concept of spectrogram technology.

Forty-eight pilots of the Wings of the Glasśigh stood to the side of the landing pad under a strung tarp, trying to stay dry. The hissing of the falling water should have calmed them; however, they were more than nervous. Some actually felt ill. Manes were gray, green, or a mixture of both. Though they had trained for countless hours, it was never for a mission like this against other trained pilots, a mission that would start a long, drawn-out war against their former country.

"Let us review," began Alíthe. "Hornet One and Two are the bait, as the Glasśigh has explained. Kamário will lead Hornet Two. I'll take One. Zinno, you have Hornet Three and your individual missions."

"Yes, sir," Zinno replied. "Each flight will split into teams of two, search for our targets and take them out."

"I have Katíga Team," said Breegan. "Túnno and I are fully loaded."

"Stay hidden and high, Breegan," offered Alíthe. "You are the surprise."

"Have we heard from Pédaltee?" asked Zinno. "Will the surface ships arrive?"

"They have had their struggles, and the blizzard has kept us out of communication," said Alíthe.

"They will make it," assured Kamário. "I know them."

"We may have hope," Alíthe said, "but we did not include them in the mission design. So be ready for anything – we are just part of the day. Remember, the ground forces may need us before we are through."

"Yes, Commander," came the chorus.

"Commander, I have one question," asked Zinno. "What is a *Hornet?*"

"Hornet? The Glasśigh said it was an Earth bug, very mean, with wings and a huge stinger that inflicts excruciating pain. They are angry all the time. Nasty black things that fly and swarm."

"Wow! I guess that's us!" laughed Zinno.

"H-how big are these hor-nets?" asked Second Officer Vayrick.

"I am not sure," answered Alíthe, "but from the look on the

Glasśigh's face as she explained them, I would assume…maybe six feet long?"

There was a collective gasp.

"I am glad I don't live on Earth!" said Zinno.

"Pilots," continued Alíthe. "The tactical mission is secondary. I would rather us fail and have you all return. This will be a long war. Understand?"

"Yes, sir," replied Kamário. "No heroics. We know that's *your* job."

"Does that count as a funny?" asked Alíthe with a chuckle. "Earth sarcasm is catching."

The forty-six Aréus A4 Fighters and two Katíga C7 Rocket Bombers boarded their machines and initiated their hover sequences. Jets rotated, noses turned upward, and the ships began their ascent. Within seconds, main engines kicked in, and teams neared top speed, streaking past the walls of water that surrounded them. The dull gray circle that was the sky grew larger and larger until they emerged into the air like a swarm of angry hornets. Engines on full, the Wings of Glasśigh headed east at various altitudes toward battle.

▲▲▲

Gákoh Kalífus had been woken by a call from the TSP Control Center's on-duty commander. He was informed that emergency Special Police reports were being received within minutes of each other, and was now rushing to the Dark Room in one of the Taźath's private cars. On the way, he watched the rogue cubes broadcasts that were filled with new audio and video of the Glasśigh and Alíthe Afiéro. They were pleading for AMF and TSP forces to defect—or stay out of all conflicts. They asked them to not fire on their "brothers and sisters", who only wanted freedom for the oppressed.

Kalífus was not surprised that Afiéro had joined the front. He would do whatever the Glasśigh asked, and that was going to be a major issue: how many others in the AMF would follow? Half of the Wings of Glasśigh had already joined the resistance—and taken their ships with them!

Within minutes, Kalífus was at his post overlooking the Dark Room's wall of screens, each showing live feeds of one disaster or another. An entire convoy was hijacked as it left the Yamillian Fields, its containers packed with food destined for Etáin City and the surrounding areas. Theft of transports filled with medical supplies were rampant. Machinery in several defense industry factories was sabotaged, rendering the production lines useless. Reports were coming in announcing work stoppages. The entire public transportation system servicing Éhpiloh, Induláy, and much of Etáin City was down, preventing people from commuting to work. Screens also showed fires breaking out in the factories of Éhpiloh, Induláy, Arimía, and other locations. A government building was ablaze in Farvis. An attack on local police in a southern port town left seven police officers dead.

"Put the Artos and Eptos Wings on alert," he said. "I want transports prepped. Get First Ground Company at Degas Point ready to move on my command."

His aides acted quickly and efficiently, focusing on their panel displays and contacting section commanders to execute the order.

So, what will you do now, little girl? Kalífus wondered. You started this. Let's see how smart—or stupid—you really are.

▲▲▲

Katíga and Hornet teams flew eastward, some less than one hundred feet above the tar floor, others, depending on mission, up to twenty thousand. The pilots flew through dark clouds in the dull morning light (a blessing), and the intermittent rain was no issue as it fell lightly with little wind. They had waited for this weather and used it to hide their paths in the thick rain clouds and fog.

They adjusted course east by southeast along the northern tar wall at roughly two hundred and fifty miles per hour. All kept eyes right, watching Etáin City, as most AMF tracking systems lay near the capital. When safely passed, they continued onward toward the elongated Sea of Geeves, which glowed a dull blue this overcast day.

Upon reaching the first waypoint at the Central Passage marking the beginning of the Óhzásó Sea, Katíga team split from the larger group and hugged the southern tar wall, continuing east.

"First waypoint reached," Breegan announced. "Time to say goodbye."

"I hear you," acknowledged Alíthe from his Aréus Fighter.

"Hornet Three changing course, back west to Etáin City," said Second Officer Zinno. *"Good luck...and resist!"*

"I will," Breegan responded. "But I will not resist the temptation to punch Commander Kalífus right in the *nork-nuggs.*"

There was a muted chuckle from the pilots as they went their separate ways.

Hornet Three split into formations of two, heading to their assigned targets.

Alíthe's Hornet One formation and Kamário's Hornet Two flight continued onward at high altitude for over an hour. They passed above the murky Óhzásó and then the tumultuous Girth Seas until they reached the Thermal Desert. Miles and miles of undulating sand dunes covered this area. At times, the heat from massive and numerous thermal vents would create a front with winds in excess of two hundred miles an hour. That could reshape the terrain and create dunes almost a mile high, making low altitude flight difficult and dangerous.

Once past the dunes, Alíthe's Hornet One formation of four Aréus A4s descended to low altitude and kept their original course. They would continue east over the low plains of the eastern desert, then head straight to Targan Base and the Artos and Eptos Wings. They would rise to five thousand when close, and hopefully, be seen.

Kamário and his *double* flight hid in a cloud bank and maintained an altitude of twenty thousand feet. They began a circling pattern over the eastern desert, just out of range of Targan Base scanners.

Further to the south, Katíga team continued, undetected.

"You with me, Túnno?" Breegan asked over her hel-com.

"I hear you. Set and able," Túnno responded from his loaded C7. Second Officer Túnno was the best rocket bomber pilot in the wing. He was quiet, unassuming, and had a second sense Breegan called a proximity compass: he knew where he was, where the target was, and exactly how his ordinance would travel at his speed, altitude, and vector. He rarely missed a target, and if he did, it was by inches.

The two Rocket Bombers headed southeast, remaining low, fast approaching the Girth Sea.

▲▲▲

"Commander Kalífus!" came a call from First Officer Gilfor. "Sector twelve, sub-sector two. I have contact. It looks like four unidentified Aréus A4 gunships at five thousand feet. Heading northeast."

"Right at Targan Base?" asked Kalífus. He looked at a display in the center of the far wall. The map of the Thermal Desert was outlined. Four flashing yellow dots moved steadily across the desert.

Only four? he thought. They must be scouts. Alíthe Afiéro is an intelligent commander. He wouldn't send just a single formation to attack Targan Base, with its two full wings with over two hundred aircraft. No matter how skillful and experienced the pilots of G-Wing,

Afiéro would know those were impossible odds.

"Mark them red," Kalífus ordered, and the dots on display changed in color. "Get a full flight of A3s from Artos up and have them engage. Put the remainder of the wing on alert. Fuel them and have the pilots in their craft. Keep them in the hangar."

"Yes, commander!" replied Gilfor.

Kalífus was cautious but confident. This probably was a scouting mission. Sending twenty AMF A3 gunships to intercept was more than enough. The other sixty A3s and twenty C6 Rocket Bombers on standby would probably not be required; however, if this was more than a team of scouts, they might be needed.

▲▲▲

Hornet Three dropped out of the clouds north of Etáin City. Zinno and Vayrick immediately spotted two flights of A3 Gunships belonging to the Taźath's Lantos Wing flying in loose formation. Lantos was the least experienced wing of the AMF, comprised primarily of newly graduated pilots. The other wings called Lantos Wing 'the hair-heads' as an insult, referring to the fact that only helpless Áhthan infants had hair—not manes—as did adults. Unfortunately, the reference was not completely inaccurate. Lantos formations were neither tight nor orderly; accidents occurred on a regular basis, pilots became lost in bad weather, and during any action, their radio chatter was constant and confusing.

"That is a good deal of traffic, sir," commented Vayrick. "It will be difficult to hit the tower with all those eyes."

"Yes," said Zinno as he accessed the situation. "Look at that mess! By the eyes of the Glasśigh, they are a sloppy embarrassment!" Zinno thought for a moment. "Let's form up with them."

"Sir?" asked Vayrick. "I'm not following you."

"See the formation directly west? At about three thousand? Moving toward toward our target?"

Vayrick looked to his right. There was their assigned target: a massive communication tower adorned with cameras, directional radar, and radio transmitters. It was positioned to report on activities to the west and near north, as far as the Asèllian Farms. Only its bottom half was visible, its purple warning lights blinking dimly against the eerie, green-muted fog. The top half of the tower was shrouded in low clouds. Glancing upward, Vayrick spotted the formation.

"I see them," he reported.

"That's our formation. Don't fly so tight, Vayrick. Slop it up a bit, and turn off all lights except wingtips. Keep the big 'G' hidden."

"I hear you," confirmed Vayrick as he turned off the exterior wing and tail lights. "Going dark."

After a half-mile of sloppily trailing the Lantos formation, the enemy ships turned north. Their formation was still loose. Hornet Three fell back, remaining on course due west toward the target.

"Lined up perfectly," Zinno said.

"Would *you* like to hit this one first?" asked Vayrick.

"Yes, I would," replied Zinno. "But don't stay too far back. I will hit this at full speed. Clean up if I miss, but no returning for a second pass. Hit and run. Got it?"

"Yes, sir. Dropping back."

In a moment, Zinno began his descent. He activated guns. "I'm hot."

"Sir, I have a Lantos on your tail," announced Vayrick. "He's…he's forming up!"

"What?"

"He is forming up on your right wing!"

Zinno looked over his right shoulder. Indeed, a gunship was flying in proper formation, just a few yards off his wing, the Lantos emblem clearly visible.

The pilot actually saluted.

Zinno returned the greeting. "What in the great glowing world…" Zinno muttered through his hel-com. "He must be lost! Let's see what he does. Vayrick, get him in your sights but don't fire if you don't have to. Continuing on!"

Zinno increased speed and dropped his nose to the tower's base.

"He's following you, sir," said Vayrick.

"Unbelievable! I'm firing!" called Zinno.

The three nose pulse cannon on Zinno's Aréus Gunship opened up. Two under-wing rockets were also released. Within seconds, sparks on the tower's base structure confirmed multiple hits. The rockets then slammed into the main support beams. The plasma warheads detonated, literally melting the metal assemblies.

Suddenly, another set of rockets and pulse rounds struck the tower.

"Commander!" called Vayrick. "The Lantos is *firing!"*

The shots from the Lantos hit their mark—more or less—and the tower structure began to fail.

"Is he on our side? Or just an idiot?" Vayrick asked.

"I don't trust anyone not vetted," determined Zinno. "I say he's an idiot. Vayrick—wound him, but don't kill him. Slap him and get clear! Full throttle!"

Vayrick sent a short pulse burst into the rear of the Lantos gunship. After a puff of flame and a stream of smoke, the enemy flipped over and slipped down.

"I see an ejection," said Vayrick as he added full power and tucked in behind his commander.

"If he survives," murmured Zinno, "he will have a lot of explaining to do."

"He can always defect!" suggested Vayrick with a laugh. "He would probably be decorated by the Glasśigh!"

As Hornet Three roared past, the tower slowly fell through the clouds. Within seconds, amid a shower of sparks and flame, it crashed to the ground.

"One com tower down, two more to go!" said Zinno.

▲▲▲

As Kalífus looked at the wall of displays, several on the far left went black.

"What happened to the western city view screens?" Kalífus barked. "I have no visual west of the city!"

"I am trying…I don't know, Commander," said Officer Gilfor. "It looks as if…wait! I'm getting something! Lantos Wing is reporting…the main communication tower at Farvis is down!"

"What? How?"

Gilfor continued to listen to reports over his head-com. "Um…a formation of A4s took it out, sir. There were three of them…wait…one was shot down! That's good news, commander!"

Kalífus was not happy.

"Sir," called another technician. "I have just picked up additional craft approaching Targan Base! They are following the original four! They are on-screen, Commander!"

"Type?" asked Kalífus.

"More Front A4s," confirmed Gilfor.

"Another formation? thought Kalífus. Most likely, they aim to hit Targan Base. How many more could be coming?

"Color them," Kalífus ordered.

On the screen, the newly arrived threats were marked distinctly in purple.

Kalífus frowned. "He will have more coming in behind him. Get the rest of Artos Wing out on the field and ready if we need them."

Breegan and Second Officer Túnno were outside of their parked C7 Katígas, standing atop a natural stone tower near the southern tar wall. Both were at the edge of the flat-topped pillar, helmets off, peering through the rainy gloom with their VEDs. Fourteen miles ahead and four miles below sat Targan Base.

Breegan scanned the area north toward Targan Base. There! A full flight was departing and heading directly North East. As she adjusted her view, she could make out Commander Alíthe and his A4 formation. "So far, so good. It looks like they saw Hornet One."

"It also seems that Kalífus has picked up Hornet Two," said Túnno. "Look back at the field. The remainder of the wing is moving onto the old runway."

"Excellent," said Breegan. "Lined up nice and pretty! Just like the Glasśigh predicted. We could really change the balance here. How about we drop in for a visit? Deliver a few presents?"

"I've never seen it before," confessed Túnno. "Targan Base, that is."

"Then let us hope this is your first and last chance," Breegan added.

They returned to their ships and soon were hovering above the stone tower.

"Heating up ordinance," Breegan called into her hel-com as she flicked the switches that activated each pod under the wings of her craft. The noise was deafening as the engines roared, and the bombs and rockets whined as they were armed. "Heading zero-point-zero at fifteen. You set?"

"Yes," responded Túnno through his hel-com. *"I am one hundred percent hot."*

Engines on full, the C7s fell through the thin clouds, vapor trails forming off wingtips. They flew on a direct course to Targan Base and the field of unsuspecting enemy craft.

▲▲▲

To the north, Alíthe and Hornet One headed straight at the approaching targets. "I have twenty Artos Gunships straight ahead," called Alíthe. "Do you hear, Hornet Two?"

High above, Officer Kamário and his thirty-two A4 Fighters circled, awaiting their order to attack.

"I see them," said Kamário. "And the rest of the Artos Wing moving on to the field. It worked, Commander!"

"Wait until we engage," reminded Alíthe. "Then call in your whole flight."

Within seconds, Hornet One engaged the oncoming Artos flight, firing controlled bursts of plasma rounds straight ahead. Once past and through, they broke formation, spreading out in pairs, and turned back toward the west, leading the Artos flight directly to Kamário's formation. Seconds later, the Hornet Two's double flight force joined the battle. Now, Artos was not only outclassed but outnumbered. Many believed that the Wings of Glasśigh were the best of the best, and as the ballet of mayhem began—ships firing, diving and climbing, turning as they searched for targets or avoided the enemy—that belief became a reality.

▲▲▲

"Commander!" called Gilfor from the Dark Room floor.

Screens around the room began displaying gun camera views of a frantic air battle.

Kalífus could hear voices screaming and calling out, though it was impossible to understand what was happening.

"Our pilots are reporting in," said Gilfor breathlessly. "The second enemy formation…is actually…a double flight of thirty or more! They are diving on our flight from above. Three Artos down! Now four—no five!"

Kalífus stood abruptly, then rushed closer to the communication officer. He could see the odds were slipping out of his favor. Four from the G-Wing against twenty from his first Artos seemed doable at first, but these were G-Wing pilots, and now there were thirty-six of them! His formation needed help and fast.

"Launch second, third, and fourth flights from Targan to assist! And get the rest of the Eptos ships out of the hangar and up!"

▲▲▲

As the battle raged, Hornet One and Two tracked targets and attacked. Their expertise showed. Within minutes, only ten of the original twenty Artos ships were still up. The third and fourth flights from Targan Base were just now taking off.

"Kamário!" called Alíthe, "The next wave is coming up from Targan. Take half your flight and go get them."

"Yes, sir. Heading over," replied Kamário.

The C7s of Katíga team were within a mile of Targan Base, still diving at a sixty-five-degree angle. Both pilots adjusted their positions. Breegan was to cover the left side of the field, Túnno the right. They were line abreast, twenty yards apart. Their heading would take them on a path over the entire length of the old runway, now lined with over sixty unsuspecting enemy craft, organized in neat rows, and all facing the opposite way. Some were just starting to take off.

"Do you see this?" Breegan called. "The hangar door is open and…it looks like they are getting the Eptos Wing out!"

"That's more than we expected," added Túnno. "Maybe a slight adjustment is needed?"

"You are the attack commander," responded Breegan. "What do you think on release? Can we hit a few more?"

"I'm increasing my release delays by an eighth of a second. That will extend the demolition field."

"Smart. Doing same," said Breegan. "Call the release, Túnno."

▲▲▲

The door to the Leadership Center's main conference room opened, and in walked the Taźath. He marched quickly to the edge of the railing and looked down into the frantic activity of the Dark Room.

"Kalífus? Is this real?" called Pronómio.

"It is real. We are engaging them near Targan Base."

"Losses on their side?" asked Pronómio.

"Unknown. The Front's first wave is soon to be wiped out."

Kalífus knew this was a lie. But Pronómio didn't need to know the details; he was only interested in the end result. Yes, the Front and the traitorous Wings of Glasśigh had gotten the jump on him. But once the rest of the Artos Wing got off the ground, that would be the end of it.

▲▲▲

As Breegan adjusted her course, rounds from Targan Base ground defenses fire began streaking into the sky in their direction. Some concussive rounds exploded near enough to rock the C7s.

"They see us," she reported.

"Let us adjust altitude randomly, but keep the same line," suggested Túnno.

"Concur," Breegan replied. "Twenty seconds, and we will be on them! I'm sending the call to command."

Still staring at the field below, the bomb release just moments away, Breegan flipped the switch on her hel-com to activate the spectrogram transmitter. "This is Katíga Flight! Do you hear us? This is C7 Flight!"

"Salǵeea here. I hear you," said the Front leader.

"Go ahead, Katíga!" came the anxious voice of the Glasśigh.

"Tora! Tora! Tora!" Breegan yelled over her screaming engines as she descended the last few yards to the bombing altitude of fifty feet. "Whatever that means!"

▲▲▲

"So all is well, it seems?" inquired Pronómio. He had moved down a metal staircase from the conference room to the floor of the Dark Room. He approached the wall of screens.

"Yes, yes," answered Kalífus. "They are just probing us—"

"Probing?" questioned Pronómio as he motioned to the Dark Room screens showing the battle. "That seems more than just—"

"Commander!" called Gilfor. "We have a live video feed from Targan Base Tower! On screen!"

The large center display showed a landing field filled with aircraft, rows upon rows of Aréus A3 and A2 Gunships on the field. Some were hovering; others were being fueled and prepped, though the vast majority appeared dormant. In the distance, two slightly larger craft were airborne, moving fast toward the camera, descending from a low cloud bank into a light rain. Gilfor had just 'colored' them in yellow transparent circles that appeared on screens.

"Enlarge!" ordered Kalífus.

A flicker, then, on the screen: two C7 Katíga Rocket Bombers, approaching fast.

"C7s!" Gilfor cried. "Loaded to three eighty-five!"

"W-what does that mean?" demanded the Taźath.

Kalífus was speechless. *'Loaded to three eighty-five'* meant the C7 Bombers carried the maximum ordinance load possible.

▲▲▲

Side by side, the C7 Katíga Rocket Bombers roared at over three hundred and fifty miles an hour across the Targan Base runway.

"Prepare to deliver! Túnno called. "Bombs loose! Bombs loose!"

"Bombs loose!" called Breegan. "Rockets loose! Rockets loose!"

"Rockets loose!" repeated Túnno.

The nose of each C7 dipped slightly. Bombs fell, tumbling through the parked fighter craft with metallic clanking sounds, then ignited seconds later. Rockets exploded off pods as if on a rail, streaking forward, leaving a hundred trails of yellow-hot smoke behind. They sliced the humid air, speeding toward the parked rows of Artos Gunships, C5 Rocket Bombers, and the entrance to the Eptos hangar.

▲▲▲

Kalífus and the Taźath watched in horror as the two C7 Katígas held course at less than one hundred feet above the field. The attack run lasted less than six seconds. In that time, the enemy craft released 770 individual packages of destruction. Explosions began at the far end of the field, striking the most distant fighter craft, and grew in intensity as the enemy roared toward the tower.

It seemed as if the two attacking craft were pulling a nightmarish blanket of fire and destruction behind them, covering the entire field in a catastrophic inferno. On the ground, explosions erupted everywhere, and fragments flew in all directions as the gears of the Taźath's Artos Wing war machine ignited in orange clouds of fire and black smoke.

All bombs released, the C7s launched rockets that hit the first several Eptos gunships nearest the door of the hangar and many inside.

Dumbfounded, Kalífus and Pronómio watched the annihilation, a rolling wall of death growing more extensive and denser as the enemy continued.

As an added insult, the pulse cannon on the front of each Katíga fired directly at the tower. The camera caught the amazing and horrifying view of the attackers, now dangerously close, as if they were about to crash into the Targan Base tower. At the last instant, the Katígas pulled up amid the barrage of cannon fire. The image flickered and froze on screen.

Kalífus and Pronómio clearly saw the underwing of a C7, pods empty, and the unmistakable emblem of the Wings of Glasśigh.

After a long moment, the image flickered again and went black.

The room fell into a devastating silence.

"Maybe giving her an Air Wing was a mistake," said Kalífus, sarcastically.

▲▲▲

"Wooo!" screamed Breegan as she pulled up, looking over her shoulder at the destruction left behind.

"Dear Asëllo!" Túnno screamed. "If we didn't get them all, we got all but one!"

"We are burning out of here, Tunno!" Breegan pushed her throttle to full and toggled her hel-com again. "This is Katíga Formation! Do you hear us?"

"Salǵeea here!"

"This is Jee! I hear you!"

"Attack run completed! Reporting massive success!" announced Breegan excitedly. "At least fifty ground units destroyed, most likely more! Control tower is also down! No losses on our side, heading home."

"Great job, Katígas!" declared Orgo.

"Wow! Oh my god!" added Jee.

Breegan took a well-earned breath. "We hit those nork-nuggs right in the…in the nork-nuggs!"

▲▲▲

"W-what just happened?" asked Pronómio, horrified. "Kalífus?"

In the Dark Room, the screens presented new images from the remaining cameras around Targan Base: ships on fire, burning with no attempt to put them out, pilots running from planes as their war machines exploded, the control tower falling over.

"How could this happen?" Pronómio demanded.

"I warned you!" Kalífus shot back, his anger now flaring. "And now, it is apparent that your pet Spearbill Blood Bird has begun to suck blood!"

25
The Pillar at Mángee River

The Treágor Delta was a cloud-covered, rainy area covering over one hundred square miles southwest of Aséllo's Spire, stretching north from the deep jungle at the southern tar wall to the Aséllian Sea. What appeared to be green fields at the shoreline were mostly swamps covered with a floating type of grass that grew on the bay's usually calm surface. Rivers and streams fed from nearby Treágor Falls formed fingers of lazy water, some running over seven miles long as they twisted their way through the soft soil north to the sea.

Navigating the Treágor Jungle that lay between the tar wall and the bogs was difficult and treacherous. There were few maps, and none were accurate for more than a few weeks at a time. The jungle grew rapidly upwards and outwards and within itself. It was ever-changing, and it changed daily. Monstrous green and yellow ribbed vines over a mile long and up to seventy feet thick wound across the soft jungle floor, creating living, growing, ever-shifting highways for hordes of insects, crawling creatures, and larger, more dangerous predators. Flowers of every conceivable color and shape grew from glowing blue-green plants that sprouted in open spaces. Many clung to giant boulders that had been shaken off the tar walls thousands of years before, deposited randomly as they tumbled down into the delta.

The canopy above the floor was dense, with various layers created by the leaves of thick brown-trunked *gorbi trees* that reached over three hundred feet high. Each stretched its blue and purple-gray branches outward, allowing the twelve-foot-long, green bioluminescent leaves to create an umbrella that equaled the tree's height. There were streams of light that seemingly came through openings in the canopy, but this was an illusion. Tall *pilgon vines* grew upward, using existing trees to reach into the rich, green canopy. There they sprouted sixty-foot wide orange and yellow flowers, each blazingly glowing from the underside. These illuminated the jungle with a thousand miniature suns, their rays streaking through the foliage on the way to the ground.

The animals that lived there existed in no other place in the tar: snake-like things with rear legs, hives of red and black larculls, and other carnivorous insects. Bizarre lizard-predators roamed the treetops. Hair-covered little ball-like things with nasty teeth and sharp claws scurried along the soft, moist ground looking for something to bite.

There were fist-sized Spearbill Blood Birds—colorful, fragile, and delightfully beautiful—until they begin swarming and using their needle-like beaks to suck blood from any creature larger than themselves.

If there was a Garden of Eden on Tar Aséllo, this place was the Devil's version.

In the waning hours of Eclipse, as the Wings of Glasśigh began their mission, a cool rain began to fall across the western tar. The Front's chosen ground forces readied for deployment, flying toward Treagor in two old carrier transport ships.

There would be a total of five teams on the ground. One was led by Frist Officer Féelikas, who would have Jee and Reǵeena by his side. The other teams were each led by Salǵeea, Orgo, and First Officer Kindýn. The last was the rocket team.

One transport ship landed near the *Pillar at Mángee River*, a massive brown and black rock formation almost a quarter of a mile in height and the same in diameter. Moss and gnarled, woody vines covered its lower quarter; the upper portion was bare rock that jutted far above the jungle canopy. The Pillar greatly dwarfed the surrounding stones that had fallen from the tar wall ages ago and now littered the waterway, causing the river to twist and turn, digging a path to the sea.

It was here that Ground Officer Féelikas and his team would be positioned. Designated *Cave Base*, they remained just south of the pillar and set up an observation position in the mouth of one of a dozen caves in the tar wall, facing north into the jungle. With him were the Glasśigh and Reǵeena Ahdelfía. Though they desired a more engaging role in the battle plan, Salǵeea and Orgo forbade it. Jee and Reǵeena were to command the Cave Base communication link for all operations. Using the best VEDs the Front had acquired, the best adjustable AM radio transmitters, and one of the newly-created Spectrogram Data Broadcaster/Receivers, their role was to communicate enemy troop movements and send critical messages on appropriate frequencies. Hopefully, they would not fire a shot.

The second troop carrier held the teams led by Salǵeea, Orgo, and Kindýn. These eighty-odd mostly experienced Front soldiers disembarked the ship with a variety of weapons, the appropriate ammunition, along with food and medical supplies. They proceeded to a position designated Point X, at the most northern edge of Treagor, where the jungle met the bogs, along the *Edǵeeha Stream*.

Team Orgo, consisting of twenty soldiers, departed from the main group and continued westward. They had a three hundred-yard trek through wet river and sticky mud-filled sinkholes that lined the Edǵeeha Stream. The murky water was filled with no-one-knew-what that could bite, suck, sting, or just chew on any interlopers.

Salǵeea and Kindýn led sixty soldiers south into the dark tangle of trees, around twisting vines and soft, dark, green-covered ground that was the Treágor Jungle. The going was difficult, moving through the thick brush, over fallen trunks of Gorbi trees, and avoiding some of the more curious, larger lizards that hunted in the canopy. The smaller nasties were a common and consistent irritant.

After a few minutes, Salǵeea stopped at a fallen Gorbi tree, its trunk over four feet in diameter. Here, Ground Officer Kindýn would set up the twenty soldiers assigned to her team and five other '*tree scouts*' into the jungle's canopy. At strategic points, they were to climb trees and report the enemy's movements back to the Glasśigh at Cave Base. The remainder of *Team Kindýn* continued south, deeper into the jungle. Thirty minutes later, they took position and waited.

Team Salǵeea with the remaining twenty soldiers turned due east. His assignment was to cross the *River Rabin* that ran from the southern tar wall, more or less in a straight line north to the bogs. There was a rocky area where the river narrowed, the current swift. But a crossing could be made using the stones as a bridge. It would be slippery and difficult but would get his team on the opposite side of the river.

There was one other group of Front members that were not soldiers—not in the fighting sense, anyway. *Team Rocket* had deployed via fastboats from a remote Front base near the Treágor Delta's northwest point. From there, they rushed to the area designated *the Pocket,* a medium-sized cave in the Tar Wall, overlooking the upper Mángee River. Inside, they positioned three class-7 rockets in the cave's shallow recess. Each rocket was capable of carrying a variety of warheads, the Klaymac being the most dangerous. But the Front had none. And that was fine with Jee.

The object of the rocket attack was to lure Kalífus and his troops into a trap, not kill innocent people. Thus, the rockets had to only *appear* dangerous. Instead of just launching a rocket with no warhead, Orgo suggested mounting a 'shell' of a Klaymac to each missile. He would fabricate them from spare parts, and, if scanned by the AMF defense systems, the enemy would assume the warheads were real.

Once set and activated, the rockets faced east, immediately overlooking the murky water of the river and the bog fields beyond, waiting for the launch command. The team left the Pocket, taking fastboats upriver a few hundred yards to hide in the tall reed-beds that grew at the mouth to the bay. From this position, they awaited orders.

At the western edge of the Treágor Jungle, overlooking the green bogs to the north, Orgo and his team arrived and took their positions in the murky-brown water of Edǵeeha Stream, a thousand feet southeast of the Pocket. The stream was shallow—four feet deep at the most. Standing in the cool water and leaning against its northern bank allowed the Front's soldiers a line of sight through the short grass, across the bogs.

Armed with pulseguns, repeating guns, and older projectile weapons, all silently waited as the light rain fell, and the low, dark clouds drifted overhead. A few hoots from some lonesome bird of the jungle carried eerily across the bog.

Soon, Orgo's head-com crackled.

"Ahdelfía here. Can you hear me?" came a soft voice. It was Reǵeena.

"Ah!" said Orgo. "I hear you, Reǵeena."

"Kindýn reports his teams are in position. Salǵeea Team advancing according to plan," she said.

"As is Rocket Team," he confirmed. "My team is set. Time to start the game."

"I hear you," said Reǵeena.

"One more thing," added Orgo.

"Yes?" replied Reǵeena.

"Take care of yourself, Twiggy. Live to fight another day."

"Twiggy?"

"You are thin," Orgo explained clumsily, slightly embarrassed. "T-that's all I could think of."

"All right. This is Twiggy...signing out."

He heard a slight laugh from her as the link ended. He sure hoped she would make it. Reǵeena was extremely cute, he thought. Probably too cute for a góhmar goat like me.

He toggled his head-com and sent a message. "This is Orgo. Everything's in place."

After a moment, he received a reply.

"This is Team Rocket Commander. We are at the boat, awaiting your command."

"Press the button. Let them fly," Orgo ordered without hesitation. "Repeat: Let them fly."

From the dark gray mist covering the rolling hills, white light emitted from the cave at the Pocket, growing in intensity. Within a second, the first rocket burst out of the cave and into the sky at a thirty-degree angle, roaring into the low clouds as it headed east. The glow of the rocket's flame illuminated the surrounding clouds in flashing white and red, like a wailing specter, burning in anger as it flew its course.

Orgo watched as the remaining two rockets leaped into the sky, rushing into the dark clouds.

"Three Class 7s in flight," came the message.

"Confirmed," Orgo answered. "Hit the boats. I'll see you back at base."

Team Rocket headed north from the mouth of the Mángee River and disappeared into West Treágor Bay.

"We are set, Glasśigh," said Ground Officer Féelikas as he approached the mouth of Cave Base. "The old gun barrels are in place at the mouth of the cave, as you directed."

They heard a deep rumble. From their position, Jee's team had a clear view north above the Mángee River, where the winding waterway had cut a path through the jungle, allowing a glimpse of the dark sky above. They could see the three rockets begin their flight.

"He better take the bait," Jee whispered.

"Kalífus?" asked Féelikas. "He's wanted to get at us for years, and at last, he's been let loose. He will jump at the chance."

Jee had based her assumptions about the AMF and TSP forces on what she knew of Kalífus. He was trained and confident and had abundant resources. On the other hand, he was *over*confident and had never fought a real battle. Kalífus and his black-uniformed thugs had only picked fights with the almost defenseless Enária foot soldiers who were untrained and ill-equipped. He knew bullying, not strategy, let alone complicated battle tactics.

Jee had learned well from her time with Mr. Gallotta, from his books, maps, and stories, and the endless hours of sitting with him deep into the night discussing the history of war. She had no practical experience and could not invent it. However, the knowledge she had—her enemy did not.

So much rested on her overall strategy for what would be a long war. If she failed, could she live with that? If she did fail, she realized she wouldn't have to *live* with anything. She, like many others, would die fighting.

▲▲▲

In the Dark Room of the TSP Command Center, a tracking

technician called out above the din. "I have two, no—three class-7 rockets inbound over the Sea of Kryménos!"

Kalífus jumped up from his command chair. "Class-7? You mean Torchettes?"

"No, sir," said the tracking officer. "Older Type 2 class-7s with Klaymacs! Second stages just ignited!"

"How did they acquire Klaymacs?" asked the Tażath, still monitoring activity but now from the balcony overlooking the Dark Room.

"What is their destination?" demanded Kalífus, ignoring Pronómio's question.

"Current trajectory indicates…" Officer Gilfor checked his screen. "The Palace of the Tażath!"

"My palace?" bellowed Pronómio.

"Activate the X-gemma Defense Rail system over Etáin," Kalífus ordered. "Knock them all down."

"Locked on, sir," said Gilfor.

"Fire," said Kalífus. "Calculate where they came from."

Above Etáin City, sirens blared. Those outside looked up into the sky. Others ran to windows to try and see. Shocked, they watched as hundreds of silver-hot, ten-foot-long X-gemma rails leaped into the sky from the surrounding hilltops, some from the roofs of tall buildings and others from concealed positions on the beaches. Contrails of vapor appeared behind each rail, like thin, painted white lines in the darkened sky. Other citizens pointed at ghostly white flashes to the far west, three of them, moving among the clouds.

As the X-gemma rails entered the clouds like a swarm of angry insects, they disappeared from view. Then, tremendous flashes of orange and red flame appeared as they struck the incoming rockets.

"Did we get them all?" asked Kalífus, watching the main screen.

"Yes, sir," verified the tracking officer. "All three destroyed!"

"And where did they come from?" he asked.

"We have plotted the course," said Gilfor. "The cave systems near Treágor Delta. I have precise coordinates. Sir, the Wings of Gla—I-I mean *Ultos Wing,* sir. They are closest."

"Ultos is compromised," said Kalífus. "Half of the wing has joined the traitors, the rest are in lockdown. Get me Raltos Command and Degas Point First Company Commander."

"Yes, sir! They are…now plugged into your com."

Kalífus tapped his head-com switch. "Raltos Command? I need a

C6 rocket-bomber formation sent to the incoming coordinates immediately. Knock out suspected Front launch site at Treagor Delta. Put two Aréus gunship flights in the air as cover. Deploy two personnel transport ships to Degas Point. Degas Command?"

"Yes, sir," came the reply over the com system. *"Commander Mánsil here."*

"Mánsil, Deploy First Ground Company," Kalífus ordered. "Begin ground operations immediately. Find those Front *hognoffs*—they are most likely in the caves or in the jungle. Wipe them out."

"Understood, sir!"

▲▲▲

Four Raltos C6 Rocket Bombers in trail formation descended from the clouds over the bogs of Treágor Delta. Skimming low over the jungle canopy, they quickly acquired a visual on their target: a cave located in the low hills against the tar wall, near the mouth of the Mángee River. Each ship's targeting system locked on the cave's opening as the pilots continued onward to the most effective range: two hundred yards.

"Target locked," called the flight leader. "Firing."

The flight leader launched four *Exrizi* thermal vapor rockets at the mouth of the cave, then pulled strait upward out of the trailing ship's line of fire. Once the second ship fired, that pilot also pulled up allowing the third, and finally the fourth ship to unload ordinance. The rockets raced toward the cave opening. Once inside, they slammed against the rear rock wall. Sixteen separate warheads detonated on impact, creating a series of fireballs and explosive forces that splintered much of the surrounding rock and sent flames through the depths of the cave. The attack run took all of ten seconds, but the results were devastating. Nothing could have survived the attack.

"Raltos Bombers breaking off," called the flight leader. "Ordinance unloaded on target."

▲▲▲

On the edge of the jungle, Orgo and his men waited. Seeing the Raltos Rocket Bomber formations turning south, the Front team members held their breath and sunk down under the water. After the thundering sounds of aircraft faded, they emerged.

"Keep your eyes on the field," Orgo commanded. "Gun teams, get those old AFPs set up along the edge of the bank. We only have a few minutes. Hurry up!"

As rehearsed, the large-gun teams rushed across the water to the south side of the river, quickly assembled the Auto-Fire Projectile guns, and faced them north toward the open bog. These guns fired a basic projectile bullet at five hundred rounds per minute from a single clip-canister. The AMF considered them obsolete since the development of the pulsegun; however, the Front had been collecting the old AFP guns for years. Now, thanks to the many raids on factories and transports, the Front had the ammunition needed.

As expected, Orgo saw two personnel transports enter the space over the bogs in front of the Pocket. He watched the landing craft touch down lightly on the swamp, keeping their hover blades operating—a good call. If the landing craft's total weight was placed on the marsh, it would sink into the mud, stuck forever.

The double ventral doors opened up, and out they came: a full AMF company. Over two hundred and twenty-five troops and support personnel of the AMF charged from their ships and sprinted across the bogs to the western hills and the Pocket.

"I have contacts," Orgo said to his men over his head-com. "Wait until I get back, then open up on them when they get close. Really close, got it?"

They replied in the affirmative.

Orgo had a single hand-carried power launcher, capable of firing several fist-sized bomblets, one at a time, through the air, then exploding on impact. With a range of a hundred yards, it wouldn't do much damage, but the enemy would know he was there, and that was what mattered.

He jumped up from the water, and as he ran, he chambered seven bomblets into the auto-feeder.

Running past some low scrub, he could easily make out the ground troops, even without his VED. But they had not seen him, not yet. Another ten seconds and he was to the edge of a small copse surrounded by knee-high ground plants. He slid in behind the spot and armed the power launcher.

"Try knocking this down, you swarm of *helmateen skavos!*"

Holding the launcher in his lap, Orgo aimed high into the air and set the first round off. With a *thoomp* sound, the first bomblet was airborne. He watched it sail through the air in a high arc and then fall to the side of the lead squad of AMF troops.

As the explosion's dull thud rolled across the bogs, three AMF troops fell in a flash of yellow flame. The rest of their squad hit the ground, as did the trailing troops. Orgo let another fist-sized surprise loose. Again, it sailed through the air, this time falling on a support team towing supplies of some kind, probably ammo—the explosion was bigger than he expected.

Orgo stood, making sure he was seen, and fired the launcher rapidly, sending the remaining five rounds in the enemy's general direction. The AMF squads saw him, and though disoriented, their commanders rallied them, and they began to return fire and give chase.

Orgo ran as fast as he could back to the stream, pulse rounds hitting the wet bog around him. When he was within twenty feet of the water, he called out. "Now! Let them have it! Open up!" He leaped into the air, and not-so-gracefully, flopped into the stream.

Immediately, the team began firing from their hidden positions, steadily spreading fire on the approaching AMF ground troops via the few individual pulseguns, the old projectile arms, and the ancient but still effective AFPs. Though a great show, the Front forces were hitting targets less frequently than desired. But they were successful as per their mission objective: get the AMF to chase you into the jungle.

"Time to run!" Orgo called.

His squad ceased firing, abandoned the larger AFPs, and ran along the edge of the trees to point X. They paused for a few moments, returning fire, then ran into the dark of the jungle.

▲▲▲

"This is Commander Mánsil reporting."

Kalífus looked to the Dark Room wall screen displaying the video image. Yes, there was Mánsil, in full gear. Over his shoulder, it was clearly visible that his troops were moving, readying to advance into the jungle.

"We have located them, sir," reported the commander. *"My team reports a group of approximately twenty moving quickly along the edge of the jungle. They are retreating into the brush. We are pursuing."*

"Excellent Commander Mánsil," Kalífus acknowledged. "Proceed. Clean them up! Report back as soon as you have news."

"Yes, sir," said Mánsil. *"Proceeding with First Ground Unit."*

Commander Mánsil of the AMF First Ground Company ordered his troops to assemble on the edge of the river, take up defensive positions and set up communication systems. He then called the first unit's commanding officer to his side.

"Unit Officer Lormin," said Mánsil addressing the unit leader, "status?"

"I have one hundred troops ready to fight, sir."

"Good. Take two full squads. Go get those Front *squalibons* and wipe them out. No prisoners."

"Yes, Commander!" agreed Lormin. "First and second squads! Let's go!"

Unit Officer Lormin and his two squads, totaling forty members, spread out in a line abreast at the edge of the tree line. On command, they ran into the jungle. Lormin checked his VED as he watched his team rush ahead. Yes, maybe fifty yards south, he could see the Front's soldiers rushing away into the brush.

"Pulseguns ready!" Lormin called into his hel-com. "They are just ahead. Move quickly."

Picking up the pace and focusing straight ahead, Lormin's first and second squads gained on their prey with each step. Soon they had closed the gap by half. Checking his VED, Lormin could see the fleeing Front soldiers leaping over a fallen gorbi tree and continuing onward.

"They just went over the tree," he called. "We almost have them!"

Orgo and his team members looked over their shoulders as they cleared the fallen gorbi tree. Orgo could just make out the distinctive flat-topped helmet of several AMF troops as they followed. He ran another twenty yards just to make sure the AMF continued the chase.

"Down, down, down!" Orgo ordered in a harsh whisper. He and his fleeing team threw themselves onto the ground. Landing on his side, Orgo rolled over quickly to his belly and spun around to face the approaching enemy—they were just twenty yards from the tree, approaching fast.

Then an odd clicking sound. A signal.

Right before him, thirty heads cloaked in leaves and moss rose upward from his side of the fallen gorbi tree and set weapons across the log, aimed at the oncoming enemy. It was Kindýn's team.

"Fire!" Kindýn cried.

Orgo watched as the entire width of the Front's line laid down a devastating torrent of death from behind the safety of the log. The AMF troops could not even bring weapons to bear. As their bodies fell, they seemed to melt into the soft ground, almost disappearing into the vines and plants that covered the jungle's floor.

The barrage only lasted several seconds.

"Hold fire!" called Kindýn. The shooting stopped. "Both teams! Retreat!"

"Get a move on!" yelled Orgo, his deep voice booming as he stood.

"Kindýn! Lead them out! I'll take the rear!"

With that command, the Front soldiers of both Kindýn and Orgo teams stood, turned, and fled south. "Retreat!" they called as they ran. "Retreat!"

At the edge of the jungle, Commander Mánsil could hear the firing from within the tangle of brush and trees. After several seconds, it stopped.

"Lormin, report," he said into his hel-com.

A moment passed, then a response.

"This is Squad Officer Aggar," came a voice. "Lormin is dead."

"What?" asked Mánsil, shocked. "What are your losses?"

"Just me and Karlgon are left, sir! We were several yards behind them. They were right in front of us, twenty of them at the most, running in retreat! Then, then twice that number popped up from behind a Gorbi! They opened fire! I-I don't know..."

Mánsil thought on this. How could his well-trained troops lose a gunfight with a bunch of untrained *foobs* with old weapons? Maybe his team was too anxious, but he knew the fog of battle. The initial reports of twenty enemy troops must have been incorrect.

"Where are they now?" he asked.

"We can see them running into the jungle in retreat! Still moving south!"

"Aggar, report back to the aid station," Mánsil instructed via his hel-com. "Unit Officer Vortrag! Proceed into the jungle with Second Unit."

Mánsil took direct command of First Unit, now down to sixty troops. Considering the arrival of Second Unit and their one hundred members, he entered the jungle with a formidable force. He immediately dispatched one team of advance scouts ahead of his main force and two other teams to the far left and right. They were to watch for enemy maneuvers and maintain constant communication. With their assignments, they disappeared silently into the trees, vines, and gloom.

After passing the site of the first encounter, Mánsil left a small squad back to move the dead and dying. He continued forward with the main element.

In another one hundred yards, Mánsil was called forward by the team of scouts in the central position. They had arrived at the bottom of a knoll made of loose stone and dirt that rose at a steep angle to a ridge, fifteen feet above the floor of the jungle. The knoll seemed to run for a hundred yards or more to the left and right.

"We saw Front soldiers moving as we approached," said the lead scout. "They were shouting for a retreat."

"Then they can't be that far ahead," said Mánsil. "Take your scouts up the knoll and check. Stay low and out of sight. Scan ahead for weapons. Report back quickly. We don't want to lose them!"

The scouts made their way slowly up the incline. Not many plants grew on the coarse ground of the knoll, but a few vines supplied a handhold to the troops. Like ropes, they used the vines to reach the top of the knoll. Peering over, it looked clear.

"Commander, we see them moving away, about fifty yards ahead. Hard to see through the overgrowth."

"Third and fourth squads!" Mánsil called out. "Get up there and chase them down!"

The third and fourth squads made their way quickly up the knoll. When they reached the top, the squad leader called back to his commander. *"Clear here. No one ahead, just a few visible running away. We are moving in pursuit."*

Mánsil waited at the bottom of the knoll as those at the top moved onward. After a moment: gunfire—a lot of it.

"Taking heavy fire!" came a voice over the hel-coms.

"They are to the left and right of us!" came another voice.

"I'm taking fire from behind!"

"Find some cover!"

"There is no cover—ahhh!"

"What is happening?" Mánsil called frantically into his com. Of course, no one could hear him above the popping of the Front's old projectile weapons and the less frequent bark of AMF pulse guns. The attack continued for a full thirty seconds. Then, all firing stopped.

Mánsil slowly began to climb up the knoll. A gunner followed him. They tried to move as slowly and quietly as possible. The troops at the bottom of the knoll had weapons trained on the edge of the ridge, just in case someone decided to fire down upon them.

At the top, Mánsil peered cautiously over the edge. There lay the bodies of possibly forty troops.

"Again?" he uttered in complete disbelief as he took in the grotesque scene. There were undoubtedly more than twenty Front soldiers in this jungle. They must have positioned a full company in here during the middle of Eclipse. They had baited him! And he had fallen for the trick twice! Almost eighty AMF troops were now gone, killed by running into a line of fire and being mowed down like weeds in a field. The commander thought about his options, about the risks. He needed to be smart here—no more blundering into the jungle.

▲▲▲

"This is Orgo," came the call over Jee's head-com. *"Engagements at the tree and the knoll were successful. Four casualties on our side."*

"And the AMF?" asked Jee.

"Four squads—about eighty or so troops—are down."

Jee realized that she was responsible for actual deaths. Soldiers, Áhthans, were dead because of her actions. How could she…

"Think of the children in the tunnel," said Orgo, sensing her concern.

He was right, Jee knew. Time to grow up.

"Now the bad news. Our tree scouts reported that the AMF has brought in a second unit," added Orgo. *"That's over one hundred additional AMF troops. That's twice what we expected."*

Jee had not believed that Kalífus would deploy a second unit. At this point in the plan, they were to lure the remaining AMF from the first unit toward Cave Base, capture or destroy the last twenty of them, and call it a day. With this second unit, the Front was vastly outnumbered, and her troops were still split in half: Salǵeea on the eastern flank and Orgo and Kindýn coming up the middle.

The contingency plan for this was to cut the mission short and leave. They had already inflicted severe damage on the first unit of the AMF. She could call the whole thing off now if she desired.

"*Glasśigh*," said Orgo. "*Salǵeea is protecting the eastern flank and the path to the transports. I say we end this.*"

She remembered a quote from Attila: 'see what your enemy brings you, and then see what you may take.' Kalífus had just given her something. But how could she take advantage of it?

Jee considered what she had: two split forces and a superior enemy. If Kalífus saw her forces like this, literally with their backs against the wall, she could lose both her teams and possibly the entire war, all in the first battle.

"Fate favors the bold," she said. "If Kalífus has sent more troops, then I thank him for the gift."

"The AMF commander will spread out to search the jungle," Orgo stated. *"He will eventually see Salǵeea. They have the numbers to pursue his team and mine. We can't contain them!"*

"We can if I show them the bait!" she said. "I will make sure that all his units converge on the pillar."

"Glasśigh, we already showed them the bait," objected Féelikas. "The rockets!"

"Oh, I have something juicier than that!" Jee said, smiling. "Orgo, proceed as planned. Reǵeena, bring up the AM transmitter."

"The AM? The enemy will hear us," Reǵeena pointed out. "Should we use the spectrogram system instead?"

"No," Jee replied. "It's a special broadcast. AM is best."

▲▲▲

"Commander Mánsil! I have an enemy communication!"

A junior officer approached with a mid-sized portable transmitter. "We picked it up in a routine frequency scan. It came from the southern tar wall, just ahead of our position."

"What is it?" asked Mánsil.

"More like *who* is it, sir," clarified the trooper.

"Who?"

"Sir, it's the Glasśigh! She is here! We tracked her position from the broadcast."

Mánsil was amazed. What was she doing here, in a war zone? On second thought, that wasn't too much of a stretch; she *had been* in Éhpiloh during the raid.

"Can you replay it?" he asked.

"Yes, sir, Commander!"

It took a moment, but the junior officer set a dial on the front of the transmitter and handed his commander a lightweight headpiece. Mánsil replaced his hel-com with the new device.

"This is the Glasśigh! We have seen an additional company enter the jungle at point X! Repeat, an additional company of AMF has entered the jungle. We will be overrun! Return to the Pillar for extraction!"

"Extraordinary," Commander Mánsil said. "Are you sure of the location?"

"Yes, sir. I have the coordinates. The Pillar at Mángee River."

Mánsil replaced the lightweight headset with his battle hel-com. The entire Front force was moving to the caves at the southern tar wall? And waiting for extraction? If he could move in quickly, with thermal rockets at the ready…

"Officer Vortrag! I need all of Second Unit on me!" he called into his hel-com. Within a minute, Second Unit Commander Vortrag appeared, followed by her second officer, Jovús.

"Officer Jovús! You are now leading what is left of First Unit. Bring light racks of thermal rockets with you. All of them! Vortrag!" he said as he pulled up a holographic map of the area using his ABC and turning his attention to his officers. "We have intercepted a communication. The Glasśigh is here near the Pillar," he pointed out. "She Probably has set up a base camp ahead, against the tar wall."

"The Glasśigh?" exclaimed Vortrag. "Wow!"

"Will she sing, do you think?" asked Jovús hopefully.

"Shut up!" yelled Mánsil. "This is not a game! She is a traitor! A terrorist!"

"Sorry, sir. We are ready to fight," Jovús said, embarrassed. "Your orders, sir?"

"I can tell you what we will NOT do!" Mánsil barked. "We will not run into an ambush! Vortrag, I want you to split your unit. Take half to the left and have them move beyond this knoll and fan out as far as the River Rabin. Follow it south to the wall. If the Front is anywhere between the center line and the river, you will see them. I will take your remaining troops."

"Yes, sir. We will cover the left flank to the river."

"Jovús, take the rest of First Unit and go right, past the pillar on the far west side and circle around to the river. Protect that flank. I will take the majority of our force up the middle. If we do this right, we can pinch them against the river and the wall. Watch for ambushes. Send small recon teams ahead."

"Yes, sir!" the officers responded.

"Go!" commanded Mánsil.

Though he had received two deadly blows, Mánsil was motivated to continue. Now, there could be a fantastic prize: The Glasśigh! He could only imagine the feeling of placing her bounded and gagged at the feet of the Taźath.

"This is Orgo," he spoke into his hel-com as he ran. "Pick it up a bit."

Orgo's and Kindýn's merged team of fifty moved in a single column, more or less, heading south. Additional reports confirmed the AMF was still behind, but closing the gap. The Front soldiers continued ahead for another two hundred yards, then the massive pillar came into view. Now close to the river, they could see the Cave Base against the tar wall.

Orgo's hel-com crackled.

"Orgo? Nice to see you again," Jee said.

"So far, so good," he replied. "We have a column of AMF troopers behind us. Scouts say they split into two other columns on each flank. Not sure of their positions."

"They will come to the pillar, don't worry. We are moving out of

the caves, to the upper ridges."

As Orgo signaled for the Front soldiers to move past him and around to the pillar's west side, Kindýn approached from behind, out of breath.

"They are on us, Orgo! They came up faster than expected!"

Pulse rounds began to fall about them, hitting the ground, trees, and the side of the pillar.

"Hurry up, people!" Orgo hollered. "Get around the pillar to the west, and by the heart of Dirga, get into defensive position! They are behind us!"

"Bring up the thermals," called Mánsil into his hel-com. He halted his group and had them hide in the thick brush. Peering forward through his VED, he could see a dozen or so gun barrels facing down on his position from small caves in the tar wall. It had to be their base, he thought. Either way, the thermal rockets would do the job. Anyone inside, within a hundred feet of the cave entrance, would be killed.

Turning his VED right, he could see several Front soldiers peeking around the corner of the pillar, watching him. He would deal with them in a moment.

The rocket team had set up the mobile racking. Within a moment, twenty laser-guided rockets would be ready to be unleashed. Mánsil could see the faint red lasers lighting the mist before him, dots appearing on the guns he saw in the mouth of a dozen caves.

"Thermals are set, commander," came a voice over his hel-com.

"Fire!"

The rockets fired. Twelve deadly spears flew to the cave. Upon impact, the warheads sprayed a liquid and gas flammable propellant from a compressed container in each rocket's body. Within a second, flame appeared, and hot balls of fire were racing inward, licking every space, pocket, and crack of the cavity. The blaze lasted five full seconds. Then, a poisonous fume lingered, slowly moving back to the entrance where it exited, rising in a cloud of grayish-orange smoke.

"Nice shot!" came a voice through Mánsil's hel-com. *"But you missed me!"*

Mánsil was confused. Was that the voice of the Glasśigh?

"Identify yourself!" he demanded, shouting into his hel-com.

"This is Glasśigh Asèllo. To whom am I speaking?"

How could this be? wondered Commander Mánsil. No one could have lived through that rocket attack. He looked around, searching for where the Glasśigh might possibly be.

To the east, he saw that Vortrag had arrived in time, her forty-three troops taking positions on the far side of the river on a sandy beach about fifty feet away. She had the cover of some medium-sized boulders. Once Jovús arrived on the west side of the pillar and moved forward, the AMF force would have the Front soldiers in a crossfire.

"This is First Ground Company Commander Mánsil," he said calmly into his hel-com. "I would suggest, Glasśigh, that you surrender. We have your people on the side of the pillar in our sights. We outnumber you. I am sure you can see my team straight ahead and—"

"Yes, I do," she interrupted. *"And I also see your team to the east on the beach."*

"Then you know this is over, young lady. You are effectively surrounded. I will accept your surrender immediately. If you do not comply, we will wipe you out."

"Commander Mánsil, you are quite the tactician! I'm impressed. But I have a better idea: why don't you *surrender? Maybe join us?"*

Mánsil laughed. "Why would I do that?"

"Because, if you do, I will introduce you to Salǵeea Calćoa! The leader of the New Aséllo Front! Think of that!"

"I will get to him sooner or later," retorted Mánsil smugly, "if he ever comes out of his hiding place!"

"Oh, I can assure you he is out. In fact, look beyond your beach team at the river. There is Salǵeea now! With the bulk of our force!"

Mánsil looked to his left. Focusing his VED, he saw them. It looked to be almost twenty soldiers of the Front with repeating guns lined up across the shallow river, aimed at the backs of Vortrag's team.

"Unconditional surrender, how is that?"

Considering the new Front team at the pillar, it was Mánsil who was surrounded—for now. But Jovús had called in. He was only minutes away from flanking around the pillar, completing his mission. He needed time.

Consulting a map on his ABC, Mánsil confirmed the position of Salǵeea's force. They were on the edge of the jungle, right at the river's edge.

Idiots, he thought.

He raised his ABC to his face. "This is First AMF Company Commander calling Kalífus! I have a request. Urgent! I repeat, urgent!"

▲▲▲

Salǵeea and his team kept the AMF troops in their sights, waiting for the order to fire. They knew the Glasśigh would try to obtain surrender—no one wanted to kill needlessly. The Front had been lucky in only getting a scratch from this fight so far.

A sound was heard to the north, a low rumble. Salǵeea turned his VED. At first, it looked like a swarm of birds, barely visible through the small openings in the canopy. But as the shapes appeared over the river, it was obvious that they were not birds.

"Approaching gunships! Due north! They are opening fire! Take cover!"

The Front soldiers by the river looked up to see a full flight of twenty AMF A3 gunships approaching low and fast.

▲▲▲

"Do you have a visual on the targets on the east side of the river?" asked Mánsil. He had called in a strike on Salǵeea's position. Though the canopy was thick and offered some protection from aerial attack, it was considerably thinner by the river's edge. Pulse rounds and rockets could easily penetrate to hit targets on the ground.

"That is affirmative," crackled a voice over his hel-com. *"This is flight leader. We have visual."*

▲▲▲

The enemy gunships closed in. Rapid pulse beams were noisily walking their way to Salǵeea's team.

"Get down!" Salǵeea cried. "Behind the rocks!"

▲▲▲

Jee also saw the incoming enemy gunships. But all she could do was watch. How could I have missed this? she thought. A modern battlefield is three-dimensional! This is my fault!

In the confusion, Mánsil had his teams open up. With Salǵeea under attack from the air, the AMF ground troops sprayed pulse rounds at the hillside, seeing several Front soldiers there. They also engaged Orgo's team by the pillar. Soon both sides were exchanging fire.

Salǵeea took cover as his team was hammered from above. He could hear their cries and saw three soldiers go down. A second wave was now diving. Salǵeea knew it was over—this second wave was Katíga Rocket Bombers, and they wouldn't need to be so precise as the A3s. Their ordinance would cover the entire east side of the river in a thirty-yard swath. He had nowhere to run.

As the Katígas approached, Salǵeea saw the third wave behind them. More Aréus Fighters from the looks of them. As his heart sank, a message cracked over his hel-com.

"Stay down, Salǵeea! You are in our way!"

"Alíthe?" he called in surprise.

Salǵeea watched as the third wave, now identified as the Wings of Glasśigh, dove into the Katígas. Within seconds, the air was filled with exploding enemy ships. Some flashed into pieces in midair; others fell from the sky in burning wrecks, crashing into the jungle canopy. A few managed to scramble, though they were chased by the G-Wing in a desperate dance that only led to the Katígas' slaughter.

"Back to you positions!" commanded Salǵeea. "Fire away!"

"It's Alíthe!" Jee called out, pointing.

Jee, Reǵeena, and Féelikas watched the battle from the west side hill near Cave Base. They had moved to this high ground, fifty feet above the river's water level, and were well-hidden behind scrub and vines. They could easily see the air battle unfold as well as the firefight at the pillar. It was relentless.

The AMF forces were unable to get shots off effectively, as they were now being hit from all sides.

The Front was receiving minor casualties, and their fire proved more effective.

Watching through her VED, it was evident that thanks to Alíthe's quick thinking, her new plan had worked. The AMF would soon either surrender or perish.

Jee grabbed the AM transmitter and called Mánsil. "This is pointless, Mánsil! Surrender! We will not harm you!"

"You can go over a rainbow!" he shouted.

"That's…that's not what that means," said Jee, but he was gone.

Why would he keep fighting? She wondered. His force was undoubtedly down to half! It made no sense.

Unless she had missed something else.

In the air, Alíthe and his Hornets had an easy time taking out the Katíga flight and most of the Aréus A3s.

"Nice shooting, Hornets!" commended Alíthe. "Form on me."

"We have quite the sting, huh?" said Zinno.

"Let's move to give the Glasśigh and the ground teams some air cover," Alíthe ordered.

"I still have rounds left," said Vayrick. *"What else are we going to—"*

A BOOM was heard, and out of the corner of his eye, Alíthe saw Vayrick's A4 burst into flame. Diving through the smoke and debris came a TSP High Altitude Kákor.

Another A4 exploded to Alíthe's left.

"Kákors above! Scramble!" he ordered.

The A4s immediately spread out, each pilot looking upwards. The enemy was easy to see—forty or more Kákor High Altitude Fighters diving on their position in waves. As one wave would pass, they used their energy to climb again. Then the next wave continued the attack.

"Zinno! You can't dive away!" Alíthe called. "They will get you! Keep altitude and juke left or right!"

It was clear the Kákors had them at a considerable disadvantage. It was only a matter of time, but even as the G-Wing spread out, the Kákors were still able to deliver a horrible amount of damage. Many were already hit, limping along until they were seen by the returning Raltos A3s.

It couldn't get any worse, thought Alíthe.

"Where in the shafts of Aséllo's Well are you guys going? Scared of a few Kákors? Kamário, you dripping gorpus pustule! Get out of my way! You're blocking my shot!"

"Pédaltee!" cried Kamário.

"The Knife!" called Breegan.

"Ancients engaging," Pédaltee confirmed. *"We got forty ships now diving on those HAs."*

"I see you!" said Alíthe. "Hornets! Re-engage!"

▲▲▲

"We are being fired upon!" called the Kákor flight leader.

"From above! Repeat, from above!" said another Kákor pilot. *"Vożeeths!"*

"Vożeeths? From Tar Éstargon? They are in this?" asked the flight leader.

In brilliant flashes of white and orange flame, three Kákors exploded in succession. Others scattered, trying to get away from the diving foes.

"Pull up!" yelled the flight leader. "Use your speed to climb!"

The TSP pilots were too busy evading, rolling, and banking to climb. The instinctive evasion tactics they employed spent energy—the energy they needed for their escape.

"Those aren't Éstargonians pilots in there!" called another Kákor pilot. *"I just saw one up close! There's a huge 'G' on the wing!"*

The Kákors were outnumbered. The more powerful Voźeeths dove on them with a precise rotation that gave the TSP craft no opportunity to go on the offensive. From below, the more nimble Aréus A4s promptly re-engaged, chewing on the now slow-moving, clumsy Kákors. Within minutes, they were all but wiped out.

The remaining A3 gunships of the AMF's Raltos Wing, seeing the Wings of Glasśigh had now focused on them, escaped while they still could, heading east at full speed.

▲▲▲

"Glasśigh!" called Féelikas. "West of the pillar!"

Turning her VED, Jee peered through the jungle. Shapes were moving. It was an entire squad of AMF troops.

"They must have broken off from the main column!" she exclaimed. "How did they get around the pillar so fast?"

"They must have been sent there before we engaged!" replied Féelikas.

"They will be behind Orgo!" cried Reǵeena.

"I will take a squad down the hillside and come at them from behind!" said Féelikas. "Inform Commander Orgo!"

Jee watched as Féelikas gathered his squad, rushed down the hill, and ran across the shallows of the river. What he didn't see was the two-man team at the AF-pulsegun that was set up just to his right behind a small bolder, protecting the late-arriving AMF squad's flank.

"Keep running!" Féelikas called to his team as they rushed across the ankle-high water over the sandbar of the river. "We will be on them in no time!" By the time he saw the AF-pulsegun, it was too late. It opened fire.

Jee watched in horror as Féelikas' squad was mowed down in the river's shallows. When the firing ceased, the enemy team disassembled their gun, then ran to catch up to their squad. Soon, they would be at Team Orgo's rear.

Instinctively, Jee grabbed a pulsegun.

"Jee! No!" called Reǵeena.

But it was too late. Down the rocky hill the Glasśigh ran. Reaching the bottom of the slope, she splashed through the shallow river and was soon across. Now the enemy was ahead, just fifty feet away, rushing full speed toward Orgo's rear flank. But Jee's long legs and light load made her faster.

The AF-pulsegun team was now set up, and with the others, began firing. A few Front soldiers hastily turned to protect the rear, but Jee knew their old weapons were no match for the AF-pulsegun.

She was now thirty feet away.

Close enough, she thought.

"Gayaaaaa!" the Glasśigh roared above the din of battle. "At your back!"

The AMF squad turned and looked behind. Shocked and oddly excited, they watched the Glasśigh running full speed toward them, hair billowing outward in a black wave, then stopping at twenty feet.

Jee followed the procedure that Orgo had taught her: short burst, aim, short burst.

The enemy team was down in a matter of seconds.

▲▲▲

When the firing at the Pillar at Mángee River had ceased, the bodies of almost one hundred AMF ground troops lay dead by the edge of the river. Maybe a handful escaped or were hiding in the brush. Orgo sent teams through the surrounding area to secure their position and their path to the waiting transports. Weapons and communication devices were taken from the fallen. Salǵeea moved his team in an arc to the near south, just to make sure the base was safe and to cover their short trek to the transport ships waiting upriver.

All the death shocked Jee.

Yes, it was her plan. Yes, she had copied the tactics of George Washington, altered slightly.

Still, this part, the reality of violent death, was never fully understood until now. In a daze, Jee moved from behind the pillar to the ground by the sandy river. Wading across, she came upon the bodies of the dead. Dumbfounded, she looked at the destruction she had waged.

"Glasśigh!" called Orgo, and he rushed through the water of the river.

Of the many bodies before her, one stood out: an officer of some sort, his chest a pool of red blood. One arm was pinned under another AMF trooper. His other arm was exposed, and on it was an active ABC. There was a two-dimensional flickering image of someone. The sound was crackling. A voice was calling out.

"Report! Mánsil, Report!"

The message repeated again and again.

Jee knelt down to the communicator and stared at the projected image. It was Kalífus.

"Mánsil! This is Command! Report!"

Jee grabbed the armband and ripped it from the officer's arm. Staggering, she spun the ABC about, aiming it at the scene before her: at the piles of bodies lying in the dirt, the bloody sand, and the water of the river. Jee then turned the ABC's camera to her face.

"You!" seethed Kalífus, realizing what had happened.

Orgo immediately reached Jee and forcibly attempted to take the communicator away. "Glasśigh! Stop!"

Jee would have none of it. She squirmed away easily.

Pointing the ABC in all directions as she ran through the shallows of the river, Jee showed her enemy more of her destruction. She then turned the camera back on her face.

"You're next, you bastard! And I'm going to kill you myself!"

Orgo grabbed her violently, took the communicator away, and threw it into the river.

"He knows you are here! They will be back. Glasśigh, we need to leave for the surface—*immediately!* It's the only place they can't attack."

Still stunned, Jee tried to shake him off, but this time, Orgo would not let go.

"To the extraction point!" he called into his armband. "All teams!"

The command was repeated. Quickly, the soldiers of the New Aséllo Front moved east along the shores of the Mángee River until it curved south. After a short trek, they had reached the two transports waiting by the river's edge, boarded them, and left the jungle and its death behind.

26
The Crown of Asélło

After landing his gunship in Asélło's Well, Alíthe had taken a transport to the surface of Áhtha, hoping to find Jee. He now stood on the landing deck of LV-487, looking out a viewport at the dark gray moonscape that faced directly toward the blue fálouse of Tar Asélło's western edge.

Alíthe couldn't stop pacing. He was anxious. The stupidity of allowing Jee to be in the field! If anything happened to her, not only would the resistance crumble, but he would as well. Next time, he would be more firm with her—no more battle duty. She must stay on the surface of Áhtha.

Out toward the fálouse he stared. As before, he had seen the small black dots approach—the PTs, transporting soldiers. Eventually, one more appeared.

It has to be her, he thought. There are no other PTs remaining.

"PT-09 on approach, Commander," came the message over the LV communication system.

Alíthe ran to the massive inner airlock and watched the outer LV door open. He held his breath as the transport appeared, slowed, hovered for a moment, and gently set down inside the LV. The exterior door of the LV automatically closed, and flooding the airlock with heated air. The transport's door opened, and within seconds soldiers began exiting.

Alíthe ran to the ship, looking, searching for Jee. He saw Orgo with his arm around Reǵeena as they approached.

"What is this?" asked Alíthe in surprise.

"This?" asked Orgo, noticing his arm being around the young woman. "Oh! Um…it was pretty ugly down there. Jee and Reǵeena—they saw the worst of it."

"You should have seen her," said Reǵeena, still in a daze brought on by what she had witnessed.

"Amazing," agreed Orgo. "The AMF was on our rear! She took out an AF-pulse team—got the whole squad all by herself."

"But is she all right?"

"She is fine," Orgo replied. "Just a bit shook. She was just…incredible. She's more than a leader. She is an inspiration."

"Is she aboard?" Alíthe asked.

"Yes, yes!" answered Reǵeena.

Alíthe made his way up the ramp, past excited and smiling soldiers. As the hold emptied, he could see Jee sitting in a transport seat, Salǵeea sitting quietly by her side. She was staring straight ahead, not moving, not smiling.

Alíthe approached cautiously. "Jee?

"She's still a bit shook," said Salǵeea. "I think she will be fine. Just needs to process it all."

"Jee? Are you hurt?"

There was no response. She blankly looked at Alíthe.

Salǵeea stood slowly. "She has a few scratches and bruises but no missing appendages. Except for her fingers, but that was Eno's doing. Take your time. We are safe here. Just sit with her."

As Salǵeea left the ship, Alíthe sat next to Jee and took her hand. He could hear her breathing, and at times she would blink. After a few minutes, he placed an arm around her shoulders.

Jee turned her face to his.

"Alíthe?" she asked softly, coming a little more out of her daze.

"Yes, Jee?"

"Good," was all she said.

An hour later, Jee had recovered, and though still a bit reserved, she was talking. Now and again, a smile appeared. At one point, in front of a group of technicians, she suddenly grabbed Alíthe, kissed him passionately, then smiled.

The technicians also smiled. Some even clapped.

"That—that was a nice kiss," stuttered Alíthe, a bit stunned.

"I missed you," she said.

"I missed you as well."

Soon they joined the commanders of the ground and air wings in the corner of the LV's hangar where supply crates and boxes had been set up as a makeshift command center. After congratulations and some discussion of activities during the battle, Pédaltee explained her delay from the surface. The blizzard had pounded the area around the stockpile for weeks. All the team could do was wait it out. But not being the kind that sits and waits, the Ancients developed new procedures. They fashioned additional heaters and tents that, together, acted like small ovens. Once the tents were placed over several Voźeeths at a time, they fired up the heaters. This made up some lost time.

"I am sorry we missed the festival, Commander Afiéro," said Pédaltee.

"I believe your delay made the Kákors overconfident. It worked well."

Reǵeena joined them and handed Salǵeea a tablet. It displayed the confirmed results of the Battle of Treágor Delta.

"Is this the final tally, Orgo?" Salǵeea asked.

Orgo nodded. "The Aréus, Voźeeth, and Katíga totals came from wing camera files. The ground numbers are less reliable, but we feel they're close."

Salǵeea read the statistics to an eager team. Zinno and Vayrick had destroyed half of the Taźath's communication towers. Other flights had also knocked out enough communication towers and scanning relays to effectively blind Kalífus and the AMF to all activities west of Chanteeda Shores.

Alíthe and Hornet One and Kamário's Hornet Two wiped out thirty of the Artos Wing in his mission near the Thermal Desert.

Breegan and Túnno singlehandedly had wiped out over sixty Artos gunships and bombers and at least ten support craft on the ground. A dozen Eptos ships burned as well. They had effectively rendered Targan Base useless for months to come.

Over Treágor Delta, the combined Hornet teams added twenty-one more kills—all to the Raltos Wing. Pédaltee and the Ancients had used the Voźeeths to great effect on the TSP Kákors. They were credited with thirty Kákor kills.

The Wings of Glasśigh had lost only three pilots.

"And now the ground battle," announced Salǵeea solemnly.

All looked at the Glasśigh. She had seen much of the destruction and death, but not in its entirety. None of them had. Each had only seen their own small part.

"In our *retreat* through the jungle to Cave Base, and in the final battle there…we lost twelve Front soldiers."

There was a long moment of silence.

"The AMF First Ground Company lost," Salǵeea paused for a moment and looked up. "Over one hundred and eighty. Almost three-quarters of the whole company."

A mixture of disbelief came over the entire room. Even the most hardened soldiers were shocked at the huge loss of life, yet, after a few moments, the cheers erupted again.

"Jee," said Alíthe, shocked. "I-I do not know what to say. This is an astounding victory."

"We did lose one other aircraft," Reǵeena reminded them, sobering the room.

"The Type-G," said Jee. "And my Eno."

The room again fell into silence. After a moment, Jee stood and addressed the team.

"I will not allow my sorrow to spoil this for you. What you accomplished today…would be talked about on Earth for hundreds of years. Technically, it was a loss of ground, yes. I am reminded of a famous Earth war. An ancient Earth king named Pyrrhus of Epirus came to a battle against the Roman Republic. Pyrrhus outnumbered the Romans greatly. He attacked relentlessly for months, and in the end, Pyrrhus won the field, but his army suffered irreplaceable casualties. It is said that an aide congratulated him on the hard-won victory, to which Pyrrhus responded: 'If we are victorious in one more battle with the Romans, we shall be utterly ruined.'"

The Front soldiers laughed.

"Our strategy is not to win the ground or even the air," she continued. "The war will be fought on many fronts—the most important of which is winning the hearts of the citizens of Tar Aséllo. Our goal is to survive."

The teams nodded their heads.

"And—" added Jee, "to inflict as much damage as possible on the AMF with every retreat we make!"

They cheered and thrust their arms to the air in the New Aséllo Salute.

The word *Resist!* echoed through the ship.

▲▲▲

Two days after the battle at Treágor Delta, the AMF moved in and took the entire jungle area without a fight. Literally. There was no attempt by the Front to hold the useless land; there was nothing in the jungle or the rivers of any value, nor was it particularly strategic.

The AMF Ground Forces and its remaining air wings had almost complete control over the central and eastern tar. However, the New Asello Front held on to the far western tar, from Asello's Spire to the Falls of Caymana. This area was easily defended from ground attack due to the rough seas about the Pégra Pygréez. The proximity of the Voźeeth Fighting Wing added protection: The Ancients could launch quickly, and, diving like hawks from above the fálouse, they could attack any unwanted air traffic that ventured into the area. At this point, the damage done to the AMF and TSP air wings during the previous battle was so extensive, Kalífus was unable to mount any significant attacks. He was on defense for the time being.

The Special Police watched Éhpiloh closely, looking for any sign of the Front. Though wracked with strikes and minor sabotage of machinery, there was little action there.

Not to lose face, Pronómio Tok had taken to the media outlets, telling of the glorious victory against the New Terrorist Front, as he called it, which was "…led by the ungrateful and polluted mind of the Glasśigh." He promised a swift and complete return to normalcy.

There was tension, of course, between the Ef Keería of Tar Éstargon and Pronómio Tok. In a private conversation, the Ef Keería told the truth: he did not give any arms to the New Aséllo Front. He knew nothing about it and only learned of the theft of his stockpile on the surface when the Taźath had mentioned it.

Accusations flew.

In the end, the Ef Keería said that there was nothing he or the Taźath could do about it. Did Pronómio want to declare war on Tar Éstargon? Pronómio, disbelieving the excuses but unable to press the Ef Kéeria further, had to return to his thoughts. At this point, he could not even imagine a conflict with a power as strong and technically advanced as the nation of Éstargon.

After the battle, the New Aséllo Front had escaped to the surface, using carrier transports and larger LV ships to move personnel and matériel away from the AMF. Some supplies and the lower altitude gunships and rocket bombers remained hidden in the western tar, namely in Aséllo's Well and within the valleys that made up the Pégra Pygréez.

Over the days following the battle at Treagor, the G-Wing would randomly sneak in over Éhpiloh and roar through the city, just to let the populace know that they were there and not giving up the fight.

▲▲▲

On the eleventh day after the Battle of Treagor Delta, a ceremony took place at Asélło's Spire. It would be captured by media drones now under the control of the Front, and its content broadcast across Tar Asélło via rogue cubes and sent to Tar Éstargon via submarine. All non-duty members of the New Asélło Front had been invited to attend. Over a thousand had come on the clear Lastsun—so clear, and with an almost invisible fálouse, that some said they could actually see stars surrounding the blackness of Ofeétis as if he wore a crown. The multitudes climbed the thousand steps to the Prominence of Asélło. There they stood, looking up at the tower room, fifty feet above. Many had taken positions as early as the previous day.

The entirety of the Front's air force was on patrol as a layer of protection during the ceremony. The only pilots not in the air were

Commander Alíthe Afiéro and Second Commander Breegan Arkéta. They, along with Reǵeena, had been requested to escort Jee up the final steps of Aséllo's Spire to the Crown Room.

Jee wore what she had at her arrival to Áhtha: the replica of the ceremonial gown of the House of Aséllo, the garment of gold strands that sparkled with each step.

"What is that above your eye?" asked Alíthe upon seeing her, a concerned look on his face. On closer inspection, he saw a *krísi*—specifically, a circle with the two parallel lines above it that identified Jee as a Graćenta.

"Veegill gave it to me earlier."

"I want one too," said Breegan.

Reǵeena also saw the mark and ran to Jee, weeping tears of joy.

"Now, we are truly sisters," said Jee to her friend.

Once they arrived in the hallowed hall, they were greeted by Salǵeea, Orgo, and others who had participated in the battle two days ago. Veegill was also there, photographing and sketching. Reǵeena checked on him from time to time, making sure the sketches were appropriate.

On a small stool, unceremoniously placed, was the Crown of Aséllo. Though they could not see her, the crowd outside began to cheer. How they knew she had arrived, no one could tell, but it brought a smile to everyone's faces, even to the Glasśigh's.

"Have you decided who will crown you?" asked Reǵeena. "Or shall you crown yourself?"

Jee laughed. "I remember the last time I was here. It was with Eno. He told me about the history of the crown. I was also told that Jaydí Ćlaviath crowned Ásue Aséllo. I would have loved having Eno Ćlaviath crown—" Jee stopped short.

Reǵeena held her in comfort as Jee steadied herself.

After a few moments, she had regained her composure. "Eno told me that 'to claim the crown would be to claim the whole of Tar Aséllo, and that is for the Taźath." Jee paused, remembering that day. "If I did crown myself, it would be very Taźath-ish, yes?"

They all laughed.

"Salǵeea?" Jee called.

Salǵeea walked to her and bowed his head ever-so-slightly.

"I see there is a power in you, Glasśigh," he said. "And it comes from your heart. It has put us in a position to free an enslaved people. That is your doing, and I am proud and honored to have you as my friend."

Jee smiled and lifted his chin with her slender hand.

"Then, as my friend, I ask you: please help me continue this work, and place the crown on my head."

As Jee walked out onto the balcony, the crowd roared. Looking down to the prominence, she could see the thousand people who had gathered: soldiers, pilots, support mechanics, communications people—all of them cheering, manes flashing every shade of red. She smiled widely. Newly acquired Front Media drones hovered, though not too many, and caught the proceedings for broadcast.

Looking upwards, she could see Ofeétis beginning to eclipse and a multitude of stars surrounding it. The sea below sent a powerful blue-green glow upward, lighting the spire. A feeling of strangeness came over her. This was surreal. Just a few days shy of an Earth year, she had come to this place, afraid and confused. And today, at least ceremoniously, she was the leader of a nation, a nation filled with people she loved. They needed her, and she needed desperately to belong.

Salǵeea stood to her side and raised the Crown of Aséllo high for all to see. The crowd erupted in applause and shouts of joy. It seemed the tower and the heavens shook.

Salǵeea turned to her and smiled. "Are you sure you want this?"

"I am sure," she said, "that I do not. But it is bigger than me."

Gladys Gallotta…Jee…the Glasśigh, the young woman called by all these names bowed her head.

The crown was placed upon her.

She then stood tall—but not proud.

"It fits," she said softly to Salǵeea, though there was no need to whisper. The crowd's roar made sure of that.

After the ceremony, Jee sat and spoke with as many of the people that had attended as she could. It seemed like she was a queen at a royal reception—greeting guests, shaking hands, and thinking of something kind to say to each and every one.

The drones present captured images to be sent to the rogue broadcast cubes. Within hours, all of Tar Aséllo knew of the ascension of the Glasśigh. Ceremonial or not, the crown stated, 'I am here to stay.'

As wonderful as it all was, Jee found it exhausting. Eventually, as Eclipse was now well underway, Alíthe escorted the last visitor from the Crown Room. Tired but grateful, Jee thanked each of her friends in turn: Reǵeena, Orgo, Salǵeea, Breegan, and Veegill.

They returned to the resort at the base of the spire, where many of the Front soldiers were now stationed. Jee was assigned the same room she occupied when they had taken their 'vacation' here weeks ago. One-by-one, the team retired for a long sleep. Only the occasional dull roar of an Aréus A4 on patrol would interrupt their slumber. The sound reminded them of their recent deeds and ever-present protection.

Alíthe walked Jee to her room and bowed his head slightly. "I do not know if it makes me appear any better or worse in your opinion; however, Salǵeea has just moments ago promoted me to the First Commander of the *Air Force of the Glasśigh*."

"And what does that mean?" Jee asked, looking into his eyes.

"It means, um, that I am, ah, in charge of the Air Force." He paused. "All of it."

"I thought you were already," Jee said, feigning seriousness. My, he's so gorgeous, she thought, especially when he's trying to impress me.

"No, I was the Commander of the G-Wing," he said. "Technically, only half of the G-Wing. Actually."

"What else is there? I mean, who else do you command?"

Responding eagerly, Alíthe continued. "The Voźeeth Wing! And there will be more as we swell our ranks. I have on good authority that the Eptos Wing has many that wish to join us! We are vetting the remainder of the—"

Jee laughed. "I am teasing you, Alíthe."

"Teasing?" he asked. "Is that like sarcasm. I do not understand the manner of—"

Closing the distance, Jee kissed him passionately.

Once they separated, Alíthe's mane turned a shade of purple, then red, then purple again.

"I have always meant to ask," said Jee, pointing to Alíthe's mane, "though I think I know the answer, but…what does purple mean?"

"Oh, w-well…" stuttered Alíthe. "Um, it is t-the color of…passion. Yes."

"Oh!" squeaked Jee. She tried not to smile.

"I am at a loss," Alíthe said. "What happens at this point?"

"Well," whispered Jee leaning into him, "if I had feathers instead of hair, they would be flashing all sorts of purple."

"Oh," exclaimed Alíthe in surprise. "I, um…I see."

Smiling, Jee took him by the hand and led him into her room.

In the middle of the night, Jee awoke with a start. Something was buzzing.

Alíthe lay to her side, asleep. Jee rose, grabbed a blanket from the bed, and draped it over herself. She walked to the archway that overlooked the northwestern tar and the Falls of Jovia. By the opening sat a stone table. The buzzing came from there. It took her a moment to locate its source: her armband communicator, glowing with a pulsing green light.

Odd, she thought. Who would be calling at this hour? And who had her number other than Reǵeena?

Curiosity had her, and she picked up the band.

"No way," she breathed.

She walked out to the balcony with the armband. The Eclipse was waning, the glow of the sun just peeking through the right side of Ofeétis. There were so many stars out; the fálouse was barely visible. It happened sometimes. She remembered Eno explaining it to her, though she couldn't remember why.

The band buzzed again.

She finally answered the call. An image appeared in a ghostly 2D form.

"Pronómio Tok," she muttered. "What a pleasant surprise."

"Sarcasm," he said. "I like it." He stared at her for a long, uncomfortable moment, then took a deep breath and exhaled. "The Crown of Aséllo? Really? That decaying relic? It has no real power. It means nothing."

Jee grimaced. "To you and your selfish followers, yes," she replied, "but I am not concerned with them. The real heart of this tar, the Graćenta, and—if you must know, an ever-increasing number of Merćenta—believe in the power and right of the crown and in true freedom and equality. So, I couldn't care less what you and your vain, self-centered minions believe. You are nothing to me."

The Taźath laughed. "I outnumber you still, little girl, and—"

"Shut up," Jee barked. Her tone changed. She was not even feigning pleasantry. Suddenly, her manner was superior and threatening. "If you want to challenge me, then, as we say on Earth: *come on snake, let's rattle!*"

"What does that even mean—"

"You created me, Pronómio Tok, you and your oppression. What happened in Treágor Delta is just a taste of my capability," she snapped. "I will take you down from all sides, in all places, in all ways, and every way you can think of. Then, I will start taking you down in ways you *can't* imagine. And after I kill your sidekick, I will come for you. I am no *little girl.* I am a woman. I am an alien from a planet steeped in war—and one who knows how to deal death expertly. I am sure you have seen the pictures from Treágor? From the

Pillar at Mángee? Tell your gullible Kośeefa what lies you will. Our total victory will be achieved by your demise, and it will be by my bare hands!"

"You do not scare me, you spoiled little—"

"Keep your hard-won jungle, Pronómio!" she interrupted. "You will need the soft ground to bury your dead!"

The Glasśigh ended the transmission. She was not interested in his thoughts or comments. Instead, she turned and went back to bed.

Pronómio Tok sighed heavily. He knew a war was coming, and there would be no surrender from either side. It would be him or her.

The end of book one.

Visit www.lightofganymede.com for maps, movies and more stuff…about Jee, Áhtha and Tar Aséllo…

Other Books by Peter Greene

Have you read *The Adventures of Jonathan Moore* series?

Winner of the Chanticleer Young Adult Series Award!

Warship Poseidon

1800: Homeless and alone on the streets of London in 1800, twelve year-old Jonathan Moore survives a harsh and dangerous world using courage, intelligence and determination. His dismal fate changes dramatically one day after he is abducted by a gang and pressed into service aboard HMS *Poseidon*, a forty-four gun fighting warship of the British Royal Navy. However, there is more to the event than just a change of address.

How is it that some members of the crew, including the Captain, already know his name? Why do the officers seem to favor him above the other new crew members?

As Jonathan endeavors to solve these mysteries, he is thrust into a daring mission to recover a hidden treasure on a remote Caribbean isle.

Unfortunately, the crew and officers of the *Poseidon* are not the only ones searching for the prize. In a desperate race across the Atlantic, Jonathan is pitted against sword-wielding spies, engages in terrifying ship-to-ship battles and in the end, must match his wits and courage against a ruthless and cunning French Captain and his infamous 74-gun battleship.

Castle of Fire

The once-orphaned Jonathan Moore is now reunited with his father, though he soon leaves the comfort of family and London on what is considered by all to be a "peach" of a mission. However, with the arrival of another midshipman holding a severe but unexplained grudge, life aboard HMS *Danielle* is anything but pleasant. Why are the new midshipmen his enemies? Who is stealing food from the ship's stores, and why must Jonathan and Sean sneak into a heavily guarded Spanish fort in the middle of the night to do some burglary of their own?

Jonathan must capture a stolen British ship from bloodthirsty pirates, solve the mystery of the surprising stowaway, and defend his honor and his life during a fierce duel to the death with a murderous adversary. Alone and vastly outnumbered, the crew of the *Danielle* engages in a violent battle on the wild seas south of the farthest tip of Africa. Only Jonathan, Sean, and an unexpected guest can turn the tide of the struggle by unlocking the secrets of a mysterious castle and reigniting the ferocious power of the *Castle of Fire*!

Paladin's War

1802. Midshipman Jonathan Moore, Marine Private Sean Flagon and adventurer Delain Dowdeswell enjoy the company of family and friends during a delicate peace between France and England. However, mysterious spy networks now freely roam Europe's great cities, and the ships and armies of all nations remain on the edge of war.

Now aboard the eighteen-gun HMS *Paladin*, Jonathan and Lieutenant Thomas Harrison execute their mission: to deliver an important treaty to a clandestine location.

In London, Delain encounters a shadowy black rider sneaking about the mansions of London's elite. She soon enters a web of secret meetings, spies, coded messages and kidnapping. The investigation turns deadly as she finds that all clues lead to the *Paladin's* mission and her friends, now thousands of miles away and in grave danger.

At sea, the boys are pursued by HMS *Echo*, though she avoids all contact. A sabotaged gun, a mistrusted crew, and a vicious assault on their ship have the crew and officers of the *Paladin* anxious. Led to waters far from home, the boys now fight for their ship and their lives against a rogue naval commodore with a war plan of his own.

To return home, Jonathan must defeat his powerful enemies in the Black Sea and survive the final conflict of the *Paladin's War*.

Made in the USA
Monee, IL
28 April 2022

95556057R10239